CLASS REUNION

CLASS
REUNION

Rona Jaffe

A DELL BOOK

For Zeke

Published by
Dell Publishing Co., Inc.
1 Dag Hammarskjold Plaza
New York, New York 10017

Dell ® TM 681510, Dell Publishing Co., Inc.

ISBN: 0-440-11408-X

Reprinted by arrangement with Delacorte Press
Printed in the United States of America

First Dell printing—May 1980

Prologue

1977:
Going Back

They had come by the thousands on that sunny June day, drawn by the mystique of their own past, or for some, the celebration of the future. Harvard Yard, usually a tranquil enclave in the middle of the bustling city of Cambridge, was filled on this special morning with a mass of people that stretched from the wide stone steps of the Widener Library across to the Chapel, and pressed out to the black wrought-iron gates that bordered the Yard. The buildings and the huge leafy trees were very old; the people were of all ages.

They had come for the Radcliffe Reunion, and for the recently combined Harvard-Radcliffe Commencement, which was the first event of the three-day festivities. Alumnae were here from the Fifth Reunion Class to one woman from the Seventy-fifth. There were also husbands, some grown children, the parents of the graduating class, and the graduating class itself, in cap and gown. Every folding chair in Cambridge that could be rented had been set up on the lawn and the walks, but it was already clear that there would not be enough.

The alumnae were to line up at the Johnson Gate, at the edge of this chaos, find their own class, and then the classes would march in separately, announced by the Harvard Marshal. Eventually it would be spectacular and moving, but right now it was noisy and in confusion.

For Annabel Jones it was her twentieth reunion. She had never been to a class reunion before and hadn't expected so many people. She had found the place where her class was lining up and now she eyed the other women warily, remembering the past. Had they changed, or were they still such prigs? She remembered those glances of hatred and curiosity that had followed her so long ago. Would they welcome her now, everything forgotten, or would they still be the same?

At college people had always said Annabel looked just like Suzy Parker, and she did. Everything about her looks was extraordinary. Her hair was copper with gold tints, wavy soft, thick, worn shoulder-length when almost everyone else was cutting theirs short. Her eyes were cool green, innocent and amused. She had high cheekbones that made her look sophisticated, and a sprinkling of freckles that made her look like a child. She was tall and slender, and her voice was a southern drawl filled with laughter. She was happy and smart and popular and rich, qualities that would have made her admired, but at the end all the girls hated her.

There had been a questionnaire sent out this past winter for the Anniversary Album. One of the questions was: "Have you fulfilled the expectations you had after you graduated from Radcliffe?" Two of the women had answered: "I had no expectations." One of them was Annabel. She wondered what the other one had meant by that. Her own answer was both hopeful and bitter. After she graduated she had expected life would come to her with surprises because it always had, and she was open to it. But she had also been hurt. No expectations . . . what a strange attitude for a twenty-one-year-old!

She wondered how many of the thousands of people here today looked back affectionately at the past and called it a simpler time. Annabel knew better. There had been nothing simple about the past; people just remembered it that way because there had been rules. "It was the best of times, it was the worst of times." She was generous and absentminded, and she had assumed that other people were the same. But they weren't; they were stingy and they remembered everything, the lies as well as the truth.

She wished that Max could have been here. She hoped nobody was dumb enough to ask: What ever happened to that friend of yours? But at least Chris was here somewhere. She kept looking around for Chris, but she couldn't find her. Once Chris showed up the two of them could stick together and laugh and make bitchy remarks about everybody, and then it would be fun.

Nobody had made her come. She had been unable to resist the challenge, and the curiosity. She wanted to see what had happened to all those people she had lived with so closely for four years, what had happened to their lives and their dreams. It was as if the past was waiting in the closet to jump out and hurt her, and she wanted to face it head on, teeth and claws and all, and laugh in its face.

Christine Spark English left the huge, impersonal complex of Currier House, where three hundred alumnae (counting husbands) were staying, and walked through the crowded Radcliffe Quad to take a look at her old room in Briggs Hall where she had lived twenty years ago. In those days the Radcliffe Quad had been small, but now it was built up so much that she could hardly recognize it. There was a security desk in Currier House, and enough locks for a prison. There were cars parked where the girls used to keep their bicycles. She hoped they were alumnae cars.

Annabel had thought she was crazy to stay in a dorm for the reunion instead of with her at the Ritz-Carlton Hotel in Boston. But staying in a dorm and coming here on the train instead of on the air shuttle from New York was the beginning of the journey into herself. She wanted to go back to her college years to find out where it had all started. College and Alexander . . . they were inextricable. The mystery and fascination had started here, more than twenty years ago, and pursued her for the rest of her life.

Her old dorm, Briggs Hall, looked reassuringly familiar from the outside. Small, made of red brick, with the stone terrace in front where couples used to neck, and the same rows of windows where some girls used to look out of their rooms to watch. She didn't stop to tour the dorm because she didn't want to be late for the commencement, and she rushed upstairs. There was a lock on every door here too, but since the students were gone and their rooms stripped bare she could go in. Her old room was nothing more than a cubicle, the walls painted dingy yellowish-white, a few pieces of battered furniture that belonged to the college. She had liked her room—it had suited her monastic spirit. When she thought of the innocence and ignorance of herself at Radcliffe she almost couldn't believe it. She had been a terrified little girl who wanted to be invisible.

She saw herself again, the old Chris, with her straight brown hair parted in the middle, sometimes tucked behind her ears with two bobby pins, and her horn-rimmed reading glasses that she almost never took off. The college clothes she chose at Peck & Peck looked like austere prep school uniforms: plain dark shetland cardigans, white cotton blouses, subdued plaid skirts, worn with knee socks and loafers. She had rejoiced because Radcliffe meant she could live away from home. No one would know anything about her home life and she would be free.

But at the last moment, on the day of her liberation, her albatross had followed her. Her mother, that bitch, had shown up at the train station to see her off, dead drunk as usual, loudly sentimental, telling everybody this was her little baby going off to college. There had been two other girls getting on the train to Boston, going to Radcliffe too, standing there with their dignified parents, and they had looked at Chris and her mother with something that seemed like horror. She thought she would die of embarrassment. Then it turned out that one of the girls who'd seen her mother making a fool of herself at the station was not only in Chris's dorm but had the room right next to hers! Emily Applebaum, the pretty Jewish girl. Chris had been so afraid Emily would say something, but she'd never even mentioned it, and had never said a word to anyone else. Her apprehension about Emily had turned into gratitude. Emily wasn't going to tell. She could take such things as a drunken mother in her stride. It never occurred to her until years later that Emily probably had problems of her own and couldn't care less about some stranger's mother. She wondered if Emily was coming. She'd heard a rumor that Emily was in terrible trouble, but that was a long time ago.

Now she was in trouble. She left the room and walked down the bleak hall. This was only the beginning: there were places to visit, memories she had to bring back, all the little bits and pieces of the girl who had fallen in love with Alexander. Things could not stay the same. Maybe coming back for the reunion and reliving the past would give her the insights she needed so she could see how to go ahead. It was a decision she couldn't put off any longer. She hurried out of Briggs Hall for the long walk to Harvard Yard.

Emily Applebaum Buchman checked her appearance nervously in her compact mirror as the taxi lurched through the crowded streets. She was going to see all those girls she hadn't seen in twenty years, all the girls she had been afraid of and awed by, and she wanted them to think she looked young and attractive. Or at least, please God, not worse than they did! She had been pretty at college, small and delicate with dark hair and gray eyes and porcelain skin. She'd had more cashmere sweaters than any girl in the whole dorm, and so many clothes that she had to buy a cardboard closet to set up in her room. But it hadn't helped to give her confidence. She wanted to be like the others, and they knew things she could never know because they had lived different lives.

She still remembered what it had been like to be Jewish at Radcliffe in the Fifties, accepted under a quota system; a minority, a strange animal whom some of the girls had never seen in their entire lives. She'd been such an oddity to them that some of them hadn't even known she was Jewish and had said hurtful things. It was all so long ago, but now she was nervous again. They had made her feel ashamed to be Jewish. She had wanted to belong.

The one who had scared her the most had been Daphne Leeds. That supergoy debutante with hot potatoes in her mouth, who managed to be both athletic and feminine at the same time, and who was the most beautiful girl in the dorm. A lot of people said Annabel Jones was the most beautiful, but Emily always thought Daphne was. Daphne had straight blonde hair that turned under at the bottom, and slanted cornflower-blue eyes. Her eyes were so blue that they were the first thing you saw in her face when she came toward you, the incredible color of them. And she was tall. Emily hated being "petite," which was a euphemism for getting stuck with all the short boys on blind dates.

Nobody cared about men's height very much anymore, just like it was wonderful to be Jewish now and she couldn't imagine being anything else, but in the Fifties . . . and she had been nouveau riche and

Daphne and Annabel were old money. It was a gap
her parents couldn't understand, but Emily could. It
was Daphne's camel's hair coat. How desperately
Emily had longed for a camel's hair coat like Daphne's
—understated, sophisticated, collegiate. But Emily's
mother wouldn't let her have a cloth coat. It was
too cold in Cambridge, her mother said, so she got
Emily a gray muskrat coat and told her she was lucky
to have it. Emily didn't like boys staring at her fur
coat in class and girls asking what kind of fur it was.
She wanted a camel's hair coat that swung jauntily
behind her when she ran, and straight blonde hair
that swung too. She wanted to be Daphne.

She wondered if Daphne would be at the reunion.
Would she still be beautiful? Would her hair be
blonde or gray? Would she still talk with hot potatoes in her mouth? Talking like that was a joke now;
Wasps were suddenly the minority. All the minori-
ties were turning into majorities in the Seventies.
Would Daphne remember her? Or recognize her?
Emily knew she would recognize Daphne. She could
never forget the Golden Girl, the one everyone in the
dorm admired, part of the golden couple in senior
year. Oh . . . It was dumb to be scared. They were
grown women now. But Emily couldn't help it.

The cab stopped in Harvard Square. How tacky
it looked, with all those new stores and restaurants
and the mobs of people milling around. It looked
like Broadway and 42nd Street, not the sweet college
town she remembered. All it lacked was a porno shop.

"I can't get any closer," the driver said. "You'll
have to walk."

Emily paid her fare and got out. There was the
gate, the black wrought-iron entrance to her past,
and she had never seen so many people in her life.
How could she find her class? How could she find
anybody? What a noise! She clenched her fists. Her
heart was pounding. This trip to her twentieth re-

union was the first time she had ever gone anywhere
alone in her life, and she was going to enjoy it if
it killed her.

Daphne Leeds Caldwell, lining up with her class,
lit a cigarette and looked around for people she knew.
It was amazing to see so many people all gathered
here to celebrate Radcliffe; it gave you a sense of con-
tinuity that was overwhelming. Look at those little
old ladies who had graduated long before she was
born! It must have taken a lot of guts to go to college
then. She felt moved and her eyes filled with tears
for a moment. It had taken *her* a lot of courage to
get through Radcliffe with her lonely secret, and for
four years she had lived with the fear of being found
out. She had been so proud at her own graduation,
but now she felt even prouder, for she was a part
of an immense tradition. She was special. No one
understood the way in which she was special—they
had always looked at her in superficial ways, and she
had fooled them.

They had all thought she was perfect at Radcliffe,
the Golden Girl. They even called her that; they were
so romantic in those days. Golden Girl. Bullshit. And
she, with her need to seem that way, had encouraged
them to think so. In the Fifties everyone had wanted
to be perfect. Life was a genetic auction; catch the
best man, have bright healthy children as quickly as
possible, train them to follow in your footsteps. There
was no room for the flawed. They could too easily
become the weird—pariahs. People were afraid of
things they couldn't understand.

The husbands were off somewhere in the middle of
the Yard, trying to get seats to watch the ceremony,
except for Richard who had gone off on a sentimental journey of his own and said he would meet her
at the picnic later. Daphne wondered how she would
ever find him in this mob. She thought how different
her life could have been if she had trusted him enough

to tell him about herself years ago. But soon everything would be all right. She had come to Radcliffe with her secret and left with it, and now she had come back twenty years later to give it up at last.

Over there by the tree she saw a familiar head of auburn hair. Annabel Jones . . . she'd recognize her anywhere. She didn't go over to say hello to Annabel. The past had suddenly returned too vividly. She wondered why Annabel would want to come back.

A small, dark-haired woman came rushing over to her. "You're Daphne! I'm Emily! Emily Applebaum, remember? You look exactly the same. I knew you right away."

"Well, thank you," Daphne said. She smiled. "You haven't changed either." Which was a lie of sorts, because she could hardly remember Emily Applebaum at all.

Part 1

The Fifties:
Rules

Chapter 1

That year all the nonfiction best-sellers were religious books, except for three. They were the Kinsey Report on female sexuality, Polly Adler's story of her life as a madam, and a book on golf. It was a time of furtive guilty sex. People talked about love all the time and married strangers.

Emily Applebaum's parents came with her on the train to college to help her get settled. It was the first day of Freshman Orientation Week, a clear, sunny fall day, the leaves turning. The red brick buildings under the blue sky gave the campus the look of a New England picture postcard. Emily had been assigned to her permanent room in Briggs Hall, a single as she had requested. Her mother had wanted her to ask for a roommate so she could be assured of one good friend from the start, but Emily had been uncomfortable about having to share a room with someone she didn't know, and when she saw the tiny cell she knew she had made the right decision. It was a narrow rectangle, at one end a door opening onto the long hall lined with similar rooms, on the other end a big window looking out at the grassy area they called the Quadrangle.

Briggs Hall was one of seven dorms set around the

Quad, and each dorm had a reputation for having
its own character. Briggs was supposed to be the social dorm, with the prettiest, most popular girls. Emily
was delighted she had been assigned there. College
was going to be such an adventure—on her own for
the first time, and all those Harvard men to date!
There were not only the Harvard undergraduates,
but all the graduate schools full of men: the medical
school, the law school, even a school of architecture.
And there was M.I.T. down the Charles River, a
school for big brains.

"You'll certainly find a husband here, if you want
one," her mother said, helping her unpack. "I hope
you'll remember to study, so you won't flunk out."

"You can flunk out after you're engaged," her father said, and laughed. He knew Emily was too smart
ever to flunk out. He was so proud of her. Her father's
father had come to New York from Europe, lived in
a tenement on Hester Street, worked in a factory, and
spoke with a heavy accent until the day he died. Her
father, who never went to college, had become the
shoe king, owning a chain of shoe stores all over the
East. They lived in a nice Colonial house in the suburbs and belonged to the country club, and now Emily
was the first girl in her family to go to college—and
it was Radcliffe!

So here she was, about to be independent for the
first time in her life, in a strange city, in a huge university; and she was scared to death. Her father was
setting up the cardboard closet her parents had bought
her because there was only one closet in her room. Her
parents had given her a small checking account in
the bank in Harvard Square—another first—so she
could buy her school books and furnish her room.
She looked around in dismay. A narrow single bed
with a striped mattress, a battered desk and chair,
a matching clunky dresser, all chipped, and a bookcase. A dark metal lamp sat on the desk. Emily felt

a lump in her throat and knew she was homesick already.

She was an only child, and the only trips she'd ever taken were with her parents. On her school vacations they took her to resort hotels, in Florida, Bermuda, Hawaii, Vermont, New Hampshire, where she could meet nice Jewish boys. She'd even had years of tennis lessons although she hated sports. You could always meet boys on the tennis court.

"Remember, Emily," her mother said, "I don't want you to waste your time doing laundry. Don't be afraid to send it home."

"All right, Mom."

Her mother looked around the appalling little box where her daughter would spend the next year. "You'll buy a bedspread and a little rug and you'll see how nice you can make this room," she said encouragingly.

The coarse white muslin sheets from the college linen supply service were folded neatly at the foot of Emily's bed. She was sorry now that she hadn't asked to bring her own sheets, but there had been so much to bring. She felt more homesick than ever. She took her memory candle out of her suitcase and set it on top of the bookcase and felt a little better.

"Oh, Emily, you didn't bring that disgusting thing!" her mother said.

Emily was an inveterate collector of memories. The memory candle, which she had made herself, was a memento of her graduation from Scarsdale High. It was a glass filled with colored water, and placecards, matchbooks, a pencil stub a boy had used to write down her address at college, the ribbon from her corsage, even the butt from the cigarette her date had smoked at the dance. On top of these treasures she had melted a thick layer of wax, to preserve them. The experiment had been rather a disaster, with everything losing its color and shape and floating dispiritedly in the viscous blue fluid. Still, her memory candle was all she had left of her big graduation prom, and she meant to keep it. She had bought a large scrapbook for college, and she intended to save every souvenir that came her way from the social life she was going to have. She was looking forward to that social life because she knew it would be her last chance to have fun and play the field, because when she graduated she would get married and settle down.

A good college was as much a planned part of Emily's path to a good marriage as the years of tennis lessons and the resort hotels had been. But college meant something else, and although she didn't say anything to her family for fear they would laugh at her, she sometimes dreamed of an alternate life. She wouldn't marry until she was twenty-five. That was really old; maybe she'd make it twenty-four. Before she got married she would go to medical school. The dream stopped there. She didn't know if she would have the guts to go all the way: intern, resident, actually practice medicine. But she had gotten into one of the best colleges in the United States, and she could study anything she wanted to, under the best professors. She'd always been interested in medicine, and she liked helping people. Perhaps she could be a pediatrician and work with little kids. It was an image that was both intellectual and feminine. And maybe she could marry a doctor and they could work together. He would work with grown-ups and she with children, and then at the end of their workday they would eat dinner together (prepared by their cook), and they would compare their experiences.

"Is that the *only* bathroom, the one down the hall?" Her mother's voice brought her out of her daydream.

"I don't know," Emily said.

"Well, don't leave your towels there. Someone will use them and you'll get who knows what. And put paper on the toilet seat."

"Yes, Mom."

"And don't use that awful bathtub. Take a shower. I don't care how much you try to clean that bathtub, it's not the same as home."

"Okay."

Her father was looking at his watch. "We'd better get going. She's a college girl now, she can take care of herself."

"Don't forget to eat the fruit I left you," her mother said. "Bartlett pears, apples, and those seedless grapes you love. They're all washed. Share them with the other girls, you'll make friends fast."

Emily watched from her window as her parents got into the taxi they had called. It moved away, and suddenly she wasn't homesick anymore; she was filled with excitement. The adventure was beginning.

She inspected the dorm. Girls were still arriving, struggling with their luggage up the four double-flights of steep stairs. Freshmen had to live on the top floor because they were the least important. Downstairs, on the main floor, there was a huge living room with a fireplace at either end and dark, gloomy-looking furniture. There was a large entrance hall with a desk and switchboard at one side, next to the front door, and a little mailroom on the other side of the front door, with a cubbyhole for each girl, where she would receive mail and phone messages. Off the large main entrance hall there were two card rooms where bridge tables and chairs had been set up, and further on there was a cheerful dining room with a lot of windows in it, a fireplace, and doors leading to the dormitory kitchen. There was a phone booth on the first floor, and some more rooms down a long hall to the side.

That afternoon there was a meeting in the living room and all the rules were explained to the new freshmen.

Curfew was at ten o'clock. Freshmen were allowed two one o'clocks a week. On Sunday night you could stay out until eleven, so it was obvious that Friday

and Saturday nights were the ones to use your late
privileges. You were given a key. In the front hall
of the dorm, next to the door, there was a sign-out
book. You had to write down where you were going,
what time you left, and most important, what time
you came back. You were not to lie. If you came back
after one o'clock—and you would be caught one way
or another—you would have to go before the House
Committee, an elected group of girls from your dorm
who would mete out your punishment. The punishment was Social Pro, which meant you had to be
upstairs at eight o'clock for however many nights they
decided, and you could have no dates. Naturally you
could not have visitors, since men were never allowed
upstairs in the dorm under any circumstances.

The work program, which they all had to partici-
pate in to keep school costs down, consisted of waiting on tables in the dorm dining room, scraping
dishes, and answering calls on the switchboard, a job
known as Bells. Upperclassmen usually got Bells, because it was much more desirable than working as a
waitress. You had to work for two hours two days a
week. When on Bells you would buzz the girl who
had a phone call or a caller—each room had a buzzer
and a light over the door for calls, and there was a
phone in the laundry room on each floor. If the girl
wasn't there you were to leave her a note in her mailbox. Since men never asked to be called back and it
was unthinkably pushy to return a phone call, Bells
wasn't as hard as it might have been because you
didn't have to write down numbers. Emily decided
that if possible she would never get stuck waiting on
tables at breakfast because she hated to get up so
early.

In the evenings after dinner the House Mother
would serve demitasse in the living room, a ritual
known as "gracious living." It was important for a
Radcliffe girl to know how to live graciously and to
be a lady. Blue jeans were never to be worn to class,

nor in Harvard Square, nor to dinner in the dorm. Since Emily didn't own any, that question was academic. Nor could you wear slacks or any other sort of pants to class, even in the snow.

Smoking in your room was forbidden. There was a smoker on each floor.

Everyone was handed a mimeographed schedule of the week's events. In the morning they would register for classes, and there wold be conferences with their college advisors about their possible choice of majors. Some courses were mandatory, like Freshman English, which was composition. They had to take that one at Radcliffe, but they could take all their other courses at Harvard if they wished. Emily definitely planned to.

They were not to go into the men's dorms with a man unless there was a third person in the room to act as chaperone, or, of course, if it was a party. This was a rule of the Harvard houses, and they could get the men into trouble if they broke it, not to mention getting into trouble themselves. They laughed at that, because they all knew what it meant.

This week they would also take the fire rope-test, to show them how to get out of the dorm in case of fire, and the swimming test. You couldn't graduate unless you could both swim and float, so you might as well get it over with as soon as possible. Emily wondered if knowing how to swim and float were also necessary attributes of being a lady.

She looked around the room at the other girls. At high school the girls had tried to make themselves look exactly alike, but these girls all looked different. She had heard regional accents for the first time in her life, and she thought what a miracle it was to be living in a dorm with girls from all over the country, people she might never have met if she hadn't come to college. There were so many strangers here she didn't even know their names yet, and she wondered which ones were Jewish.

After the meeting was over the girls milled around casually, getting to know each other. Emily felt shy and went upstairs to her room to get her cigarettes. She had brought her own little ashtray from home, and because she felt too timid to go into the smoker she sat on the floor outside her room and lit a cigarette. Just this one, she told herself, and the next time I'll go into the smoker and meet some people. She was sure the other girls felt as shy and strange as she did, but still she wished someone would come up to her and start a conversation.

Two tall, beautiful girls came up the stairs chatting. One had long red hair, the other blonde. They were unmistakably *not* Jewish, she could tell that at a glance. They stopped in front of Emily.

"Well, I guess we're next-door neighbors," the red-haired one said. She had a southern accent. "I'm Annabel Jones."

"I'm Emily Applebaum."

"I'm Daphne Leeds," said the beautiful blonde one. She spoke as if she had a mouthful of hot potatoes and Emily could tell she was some kind of supergoy socialite. "What a pretty name . . ." Daphne said. "Applebaum. I never heard that before. What kind of name is that, German?"

"Um, I think so," Emily said. If she knew it was Jewish she probably wouldn't talk to me anymore, she thought. "Are you two roommates?"

"No, Daphne's two doors down. Neither of us have roommates. Do you?"

"No."

"Oh, you brought an ashtray!" Annabel said. "How smart of you. Well, I'll just share it." She fished a cigarette from a pack in her skirt pocket and sat on the floor beside Emily. "Did you ever hear so many silly rules in your life?"

Daphne sat on the floor beside them and blew a perfect smoke ring. "I thought they had rules at

Chapin," she said, "but this is ridiculous. After all, it's college. What a bore."

"We're allowed to smoke in the hall," Emily said quickly.

"I know," Annabel said. "I mean all those dating rules. If we're going to do anything we can do it *before* ten o'clock just as well as after." She laughed. "What incredible hypocrites."

"I'm not looking forward to that fire rope-test," Emily said. "Do you think we have to jump out the window?"

"It can't be too bad," Daphne said. "It's in the gym."

"As far as I'm concerned, anything that's in the gym is bad," Annabel said.

Emily giggled in relief. "Oh, do you hate gym too?"

"I loathe it. I like to ride horses, but mainly because I like the drinking that comes afterward."

Emily looked at Annabel in amazement. She had never met anyone so sophisticated and worldly in her life. She could just picture her in riding clothes, like someone in a movie, being escorted into a hunt breakfast by two tall, handsome young men. Did she drink mint juleps? Champagne?

Annabel finished her cigarette and stubbed it out in Emily's ashtray. "I happen to have a little care package in my room," she said. "If you two wish to join me. If dinner is anything like lunch I think we should fortify ourselves first."

What did she mean, Emily thought, *liquor?* Certainly *her* mother didn't make her pack fruit.

The three of them went into Annabel's room. It was an identical cell to Emily's, but there the resemblance stopped. The room looked as if she had lived in it for a year. Cashmere sweaters and tweed skirts were tossed on the chair, across the bed, dropped on the floor. A few things hung in the closet. Shoes, unpaired, were scattered on the closet floor, and there was a jumble of makeup and toilet articles on the dresser. All the drawers were open. The only thing that was neat was the bookcase. Annabel had obviously brought her most treasured books from home, and had put them in order on the shelves. There was a complete collection of the Oz books, all the Winnie the Pooh, the complete works of F. Scott Fitzgerald, Emily Dickinson, Sarah Teasdale, Edna St. Vincent Millay, Yeats, and T.S. Eliot. There was a portable phonograph on the floor, and next to it a pile of old 78 rpm Noel Coward records. Annabel put on "Someday I'll Find You," and pulled a box out from under the bed. It contained water biscuits, caviar, a tin of smoked oysters, cheese, and two splits of champagne.

"You didn't," Daphne said.

"I did."

"We'll get expelled our first day," Emily said in delight and terror.

"Go get your toothbrush glasses and we'll lock the door," Annabel said.

The champagne made Emily slightly tipsy. She could tell that Daphne and Annabel were used to such things because they didn't look high at all. She didn't feel so shy now, and she thought how incredible it was to be here with these two from such a totally different world and to be getting along with them. In many ways Daphne and Annabel were different from one another—their accents for one thing—but in other ways they seemed the same. Both had gone to fancy schools. Both were Wasps. Both were rich, and had a careless self-confidence Emily knew she would spend years trying to attain. But Annabel was warm and friendly, while Daphne seemed aloof. She was pleasant enough, but it was hard to tell whether she was just being polite and well-bred or if she really liked you at all.

"Are you coming out in Atlanta or New York?" Daphne asked Annabel.

"Atlanta," Annabel said. "But I might go to the Grosvenor Ball."

"Oh, do," Daphne said. "Then you can come to my party before. I'm having a supper at the Maisonette."

Emily had never met anyone who came out. She'd read about it in the newspapers, skimmed over it really, because it was of no interest to her and had nothing to do with her life.

"Are you coming out?" Annabel asked Emily. She shook her head, feeling a little embarrassed. "Oh, that's all right," Annabel said quickly. "You can meet all the same Harvard men right here at the great high point of Orientation Week, the Freshman Mixer."

"Freshmen," Daphne said. "I don't want to meet freshmen."

"Upperclassmen will crash, you wait and see," Annabel said. "They're all here right in their dorms, waiting to see the new crop. That's us."

New crop, Emily thought. They were like flowers, opening, waiting to be discovered and picked. It was all so romantic, frenzied and short-lived, their wonderful college days. She tried to imagine the men in their dorms, waiting to meet her, waiting to fall in love. How great to be eighteen with a whole world of men out there, hoping to find her, hoping to be found. Somewhere was the right one, the one with whom she would fall in love. She had four whole years of parties and mixers and Jolly-Ups and football games and dates to find him. *Someday I'll find you, moonlight behind you* . . . It was just like in that record Annabel liked so much.

The next day Emily had a meeting with her freshman advisor. It was a fair-sized walk to the Radcliffe campus where her meeting was scheduled, and a long walk to the Harvard campus where most of her classes were, and Emily could see she was going to get a lot of exercise. Many of the girls were getting bicycles, but she was afraid of bikes ever since she had fallen

off one as a child. Besides, your skirt kept getting in
the way. She didn't mind walking. There were so
many new things to look at, and Cambridge was really
pretty, with its cobblestone streets and all those his-
toric little old houses tucked away behind fences and
gardens. Even the Radcliffe Yard—she had to remember to call them "Yards" not "campuses"—had a sense
of history. She could picture the first brave women
who'd gone there years ago, in their hats and long
skirts, arms full of books, seeking higher education
and all the things that were forbidden to women,
walking down these same paths beside the same mani-
cured lawns, entering the same venerable red brick
buildings, even fingering the same books in the library. In those days women didn't have much choice:
if you went to college you hardly ever got married—
you just became an intellectual, a bluestocking. But
now of course you were *expected* to go to college, if
you could get in. Life certainly was better for women
now in the Fifties.

Her advisor was an attractive middle-aged woman
named Mrs. Tweedy. "Sit down, Emily," she said
pleasantly, looking through a folder she had on her
desk. "I see you came to us with an excellent academic record. Have you thought what you'd like to
major in?"

Emily took a deep breath. "I'd like to take premed."

"Premed?" Mrs. Tweedy looked surprised.

"I thought I'd go to medical school. I've always
been interested in medicine."

"Well, now, let's see . . ." More exasperatingly slow
looking through the folder. "You want to be a doctor?"

"Well, yes." She didn't know why she was starting
to feel so silly. Why couldn't she have an exciting
career? She was eighteen and the world was ahead of
her.

"You had four years of math in high school, four

years of biology, but no chemistry. *You didn't have any chemistry,* Emily, you're way behind."

"Nobody told me you were supposed to." Now she was really feeling embarrassed, as if she had suddenly been revealed as a pretentious fool. "I could take it now and make it up, couldn't it?"

"Well, I suppose that would be possible," Mrs. Tweedy said with no enthusiasm. "People who want to be doctors plan their careers, Emily. You haven't had any advice, haven't made any plans. You can't decide to be a doctor just like that."

"I know . . ."

"Let's be realistic. You should major in Social Relations. You can take lab psychology, you'd like that. And you'll find the related courses very interesting. Then if you want to you can go on to graduate school, and then do social work. That way you can have a normal life and a part-time career if you want it."

Emily had heard the girls talking about Social Relations. It was supposed to be a gut major. A social worker wasn't glamorous or exciting. That was only a step removed from what her mother did with her free time—volunteer work. Her mother had never gone beyond three years of high school.

"I think you'll enjoy Social Relations, Emily." Mrs. Tweedy closed the folder and patted it, as if she'd just tidied up Emily's life. She smiled, and her face took on that confidential look older people put on their faces when they were going to let you know how much they knew and how little you did. "If you're so interested in medicine, Emily, you marry a doctor. You'll meet a lot of very nice young men here who are going to be doctors. The Harvard Medical School is one of the best in the country."

She stood up and held out her hand. Emily shook hands with her and left. She walked slowly back to the dorm through the cobblestone streets and she no longer felt like a part of the great history of intellectual women; she felt like a dimwit. Life was out there, and she was on the outside looking in.

Marry a Doctor; good-bye Emily. Her parents would be delighted, and Mrs. Tweedy would feel that in five minutes she had solved all Emily's problems. She could be The Doctor's Wife. She could run a nice home so that he could do his important work in peace. She could bring up his bright children. And if she got bored she could do part-time social work. What was so terrible about that? Marrying a doctor had always been half of her daydream.

Emily felt confused and miserable. She would never be anybody on her own. She would only be important because of her relationship with somebody else. That was what marriage was; you made a good catch. What was wrong with that? She didn't want to be a doctor. Chemistry was boring. She hadn't really tried, so why did she have this dull, let-down feeling that she had failed? She had exposed too much of herself, she had revealed that she was a silly person. She decided that she would never talk about her dopey ambitions again.

At lunch in the dorm dining room Emily sat with Annabel and Daphne. They introduced her to a new girl, Christine Spark, who was called Chris, and who it turned out had the room on the other side of Emily's. Chris, Emily was relieved to note, wasn't frighteningly pretty or sophisticated. She had a neat, quiet plainness that was reassuring, and her clothes looked like a school uniform, as if she wanted to pass through life unnoticed. Emily remembered seeing her at the train station on her way to college. Chris's mother had been obviously drunk. At the time it hadn't made much of an impression on Emily because she had been concerned with her luggage, and besides everyone knew that the goyim drank like fish.

Over a buffet lunch of asparagus on top of soggy cornbread covered with a gloppy white sauce, a meal none of them could eat, they talked about what they were going to major in. Annabel was going to major in English. Daphne was going to major in Fine Arts. Chris was going to major in Medieval History. When Emily told them she was going to major in Social Relations none of them seemed to think there was anything wrong with that. Social Relations and English were the two most popular majors.

"Isn't it nice that we all know what we're going to major in already?" Daphne said. "It saves so much time. Now we can concentrate on important things, like men." She smiled to show that she was kidding. They all knew Radcliffe was going to be very difficult and they would have to work hard.

"Let's go downtown to the doughnut shop," Annabel said, pushing her untouched plate aside. "I'm starving."

"I have some fruit in my room," Emily offered.

"Oh, good," Chris said. "That's not so fattening."

"*You* don't have to diet," Emily said in surprise. "You're so thin."

"Yes I do," Chris said. "I'm careful."

How odd she was, Emily thought. When you looked at her straight, mousy hair tucked behind her ears, and her scrubbed face, and those horn-rimmed glasses with fingerprints on the lenses, you'd think she couldn't care less about how she looked. But she evidently cared a little. She supposed nobody was impervious to the demands of society, even Chris.

By the end of Orientation Week all the girls felt more at home, less scared. They had chosen their courses, figured out how to get to the necessary buildings without getting lost. They had bought their school books at the Harvard Coop, which was like a combination of the largest bookstore and office supply store that Emily had ever seen. It was in Harvard Square, which was to be their city, with Harvard on one side, the mysterious place of knowledge and men, the reason most of them had come here in the first place.

Harvard! Radcliffe had its own cachet as the best of the Seven Sisters, as the seven top women's colleges were called, but a lot of people had never heard of it. But when you said, "It's part of Harvard," then everyone knew.

Emily, who had never had much school spirit before, bought a crimson and white Harvard banner and put it on her wall. They had all furnished their rooms with bedspreads, lamps, cushions, rugs, and individual touches, some from home, some bought here. Daphne had taped up small museum reproductions of famous paintings and prints. Annabel's room remained in the same disarray it had appeared in the first day, and since she never once made her bed no one knew if she had bought a bedspread or not. Chris was the only freshman on the floor who hadn't bothered to fix up her room at all. Her only purchase had been a good floor lamp. Her room looked like a monk's cell, and she liked it that way.

Annabel had gotten her hands on a copy of the *Harvard Freshman Register,* which contained not only photographs of each of the boys, but their home addresses and the names of the prep schools they had graduated from. That book was the most pored over of any book in the school, with girls rushing in and out of her room to choose the ones they wanted to meet.

The girls in the dorm were mixing more with each other. Emily had met some Jewish girls, and she felt at home with them. Daphne had found some more debutantes. But because Emily, Annabel, Daphne, and Chris had met at the beginning, and because their rooms were all in a row, they had a certain closeness. They got in the habit of sitting on the floor together outside their rooms to smoke. Emily thought how amazed her mother would be to see her with such unusual friends.

The four of them sat together during the Dean's speech to the new freshman class. "Look at the girl

to the right of you," the Dean said, "and the girl to
the left of you." They all looked at each other and
smiled. "Each of those girls was the valedictorian of
her senior class," the Dean said. "The competition
will be far different here than it was in the schools
where you came from. You will be up against the
top students in the country. You will be expected to
work very hard."

Imagine, Emily thought, this big room all full of
leaders. She began to feel inferior again. Annabel's
father was a famous heart surgeon, and Chris's father
was a chemistry professor at Columbia. Daphne's father was the senior partner of the leading prestigious
Wasp law firm in New York. And her father owned
a chain of shoe stores. Her parents weren't intellectuals. All those other girls seemed to have come out
of generations of power and birthright. They'd all gone
to private school. She wondered if she could keep up.
She really wanted to do well.

"Education for education's sake," the Dean was saying. "For the enrichment that education can bring
to your lives . . ."

Not for careers, is what she's saying, Emily thought.
To be a better person, an educated person. It all
seemed simple now. You always had to try to be perfect. Your cashmere sweater sets had to match the
colors in your plaid skirts, your hair and nails had
to be perfectly done, you had to be polite, witty, sympathetic, interested. You had to be *interesting*. Getting good marks and a good education was just another part of it. She was glad that at last she understood. A good education was never wasted.

Chapter 2

Annabel Jones was putting on her makeup for the Freshman Mixer, the culmination of their Orientation Week. The ritual of preparing for a dance or a party was almost as much fun as the event itself. There was always an air of anticipation before it, the knowledge that tonight anything could happen. . . . She had washed the scratchy little bathtub and taken a bubble bath, slightly nostalgic for her great big tub at home where she could stretch her legs out. Her auburn hair, freshly washed, gleamed. She had chosen her favorite black taffeta dress with the swirly pleated skirt, and it was lying on the bed. She put on the second coat of mascara and dabbed Arpège on all her pulse points, and then into the cleavage made by her strapless bra. There was a stack of Noel Coward records on her phonograph, playing sweetly, and she hummed along with them, dancing around her room by herself, her happiness rising. College was strange and new and a bit frightening, but this ritual, at least, was familiar.

She loved parties. In a room full of men, with music playing, she felt suffused with giddiness, a mad euphoria that made everything anyone said seem funny. She was tireless, she loved to dance. She knew there would be nothing alcoholic to drink at the Freshman Mixer, but she didn't mind, she didn't need it. She would just have to walk in the door to be drunk with happiness. Parties always affected her that way, and she thought it was her destiny to be a debutante forever, a southern belle, to go to dances, to flirt, to be held in a man's arms and whirled around and passed on to another man who was waiting. She always felt the center of attention at parties. She knew she was beautiful; people had been telling her that for years. But more than that, she gave off her own excitement. She loved men.

She slipped into her dress and, holding it together with one hand, went to the room next door to be zipped up. Emily wasn't there, so she went to the next room to Chris. Chris was sitting in bed, reading, wearing her pajamas.

"My goodness," Annabel said. "Are you sick?"

Chris looked up, those huge glasses sliding down her nose. "No," she said calmly.

"Would you zip me up, please?" Chris did. "Why aren't you getting ready for the mixer?"

"I'm not going," Chris said.

"Why not?"

"I don't feel like it."

Annabel sat down on the foot of Chris's bed. "Don't be shy," she said. "Everybody's scared. Those men are more nervous than we are."

"I'm not scared," Chris said. "I hate parties, that's all."

"Hate parties?" She was astounded. "Why?"

"People saying silly things. You can't get to know somebody when you dance with him for two seconds. At a party when you talk to someone he's always looking over your shoulder for somebody better. How would he know the difference?"

"Well, you just look him straight in the eye like you would a snake." Annabel said. "That's how they charm snakes, you know."

"I thought they played the flute."

"Oh, it doesn't matter." She jumped up. "Let's pick you out a dress, and I'll help you do your makeup if you want. I love to do makeup." Poor Chris, she thought, she's probably afraid she'll be a wallflower, and I'll bet someone was really wretched to her once.

"I didn't bring a party dress," Chris said matter-of-factly.

Oh . . . so that was why. She really was poor Chris. Annabel had never before known anyone who had no money, except servants, and she felt awful. How could she lend Chris a dress without hurting her feelings? Well, she'd just offer to, that's all. People were always borrowing clothes.

"You're blushing," Chris said.

"No I'm not."

"Look, if I wanted to bring a dress for this thing I would have. I didn't buy one because I don't intend to go to parties."

"You are deranged," Annabel said. "*Absolument folle*. You have to have a social life, that's part of college. Don't you like men?"

"Oh sure, it's just that I never met one I could stand."

"You went to a girls' school, what do you expect? So did I. But in Atlanta we had the country club, and everybody gave lots of parties. How many college men have you gone out with?"

"None," Chris said. "They never asked me."

"Well, they will tonight. Come on, get out of that bed and make yourself useful."

"Oh, Annabel . . ."

Annabel grabbed Chris's wrist and pulled her out of bed. She allowed herself to be pulled quite easily and Annabel was pleased.

"Have you got a black skirt?" She was already in Chris's neat closet, poking around. "This will do fine. What goes on top?"

"That blouse," Chris said.

"No, I'll lend you a much sexier blouse. And you need a big, wide, patent-leather belt."

"I don't have one."

"I do."

"This is very sweet of you, Annabel."

"I just hate to see potential wasted," Annabel said.

They were among the last of the girls to get to the dance, but it was worth it, Annabel thought, because Chris had been transformed. Annabel had even persuaded her to leave her glasses in her room. The gym was mobbed with attractive men, and she had been right; upperclassmen had crashed. It was easy to tell who they were because they seemed not only older but much more self-assured than the Harvard freshmen. And now that the Korean War was over there were veterans, who were the most sophisticated of all. There was a live orchestra. Annabel felt the joy and giddiness begin as a handsome man asked her to dance the minute she'd walked in the door. She smiled up at him, and noticed over his shoulder that someone had already asked Chris to dance too. Good.

"What's your name?" he asked.

"Annabel Jones. What's yours?"

"Richard Caldwell."

Oh my, wasn't he the best-looking thing she'd ever seen! Tall and blond and sexy, with that classic profile, and that gorgeous jaw.

"Where are you from?" he asked.

"Atlanta, Georgia. Where are you from?"

"New York."

They didn't have time to say another thing when a short little funny-looking boy cut in on them. "My name is Charlie Bliss. Who are you?"

"Annabel Jones."

"I play ice hockey."

"Really!"

She supposed that was where he'd broken those chips off his two front teeth. It made him look like a vampire. The last thing in the world she'd ever want to do was kiss *him*. The band segued into the song from *Moulin Rouge,* and he pulled her close and tucked his head under her chin. Annabel smiled across the room at Richard Caldwell. He couldn't cut in again until someone else did, that was the rule. He winked at her and she made a funny face. Then Richard Caldwell cut in on Daphne, and the man Daphne was dancing with cut in on Annabel.

What a relief; he was beautiful. Then, just her luck, the band started playing "Don't Let the Stars Get in Your Eyes," and they had to jump around like two fools. Annabel giggled at the irony of it. But he was the best dancer she'd ever danced with, she could tell that right away.

"I'm Maxwell Harding the Third," he said. "My friends call me Max."

"I'm Annabel Jones. My friends call me Annabel."

"Have you met Miss Jones . . ." he started to sing, against the music.

"Oh, stop it," she said, and laughed. "Where are you from?"

"New York."

"Why are New York men so good-looking?" She smiled up at him and he smiled back, flattered. He wasn't only beautiful, he had such a nice, merry face, with dimples and pretty golden eyes with dark lashes, and sandy hair that she could tell would be curly if he didn't have it cut so short the way they all did. He looked like a tall, graceful faun. "What class are you in, Max?"

"Freshman."

"I never would have guessed. What are you going to major in?"

"Getting by."

"Getting by!" She laughed. "I didn't know that was a major."

"It's the gentleman's major," Max said cheerfully. "I want to work in the theater when I graduate."

"An actor?"

"No, a director or a producer. Maybe both."

"How divine. Every man I meet wants to go into business. They're all so stuffy."

"I know."

"Are you going to be a bohemian, Max? Are you going to live in Greenwich Village?"

"First I'm going to go to Paris for a year."

"*Are* you! But that's my dream!"

Someone was just about to tap Max on the shoulder to cut in when he whirled around expertly and steered Annabel to the other side of the room. He looked very pleased with himself. "Well, come with me," Max said.

"I will. When we graduate, if neither of us is married, let's go to Paris together and live in sin."

"On the Left Bank."

"What a divine idea," Annabel said. "We'll get a little garret apartment with gargoyles on the front."

"You're thinking of Notre Dame," Max said.

"Was I? Well, I'm sure we can find an apartment with gargoyles in all of Paris. Even if they're just on the bathtub."

"Okay, it's a promise."

Richard Caldwell cut in. Annabel was sorry to lose Max but happy to get Richard again. She could see college was going to be everything she had dreamed. Richard held her close and they danced cheek to cheek while the band played "Rags to Riches."

"What are you going to major in?" she whispered in his ear.

"You," he whispered back, and then he gave her the most bewitching smile so that she didn't know if he was kidding or not.

When Max cut in again almost immediately, contrary to the rules of etiquette, Annabel thought he must be in love with her.

"Let's go outside and smoke," Max said. "Would you like some punch?"

"Both," Annabel said. "It's terribly hot in here, don't you think?"

They took their cups of punch outside on the lawn and lit cigarettes. The moon was streaked with thin threads of clouds, like party streamers, and the Radcliffe buildings were silhouetted against the dark sky. "I don't think you should dance with Richard Caldwell all evening," Max said.

"Well, I danced with him only twice. You're not jealous?"

"It's just that he's married."

"*Married?*" Annabel choked on a puff of smoke and coughed. "How do you know?"

"There are a couple of old classmates of his in my house. It's no secret. His wife is going to have a baby in November."

"He looks so young," Annabel said, bewildered. How dare he say he was going to major in *her*?

"He's a freshman."

"My goodness, I bet it was a shotgun marriage. You never know who you'll meet, do you?" She was surprised he'd even had the nerve to come to the Freshman Mixer and try to take up her time when he wasn't somebody she could ever go out with. "I'm glad you told me. *He* certainly didn't mention it."

"Do you want to go to the Princeton game with me?" Max asked.

"Oh, I'd love it!"

"There will be a lot of parties afterward," Max said. "We'll go to all of them. And I'll take you for a ride in my 1928 Stutz Bearcat. It's yellow."

"You have a real Stutz Bearcat?" She had found her soul mate, it was almost too good to be true. "I adore the Twenties. I always thought I should have been eighteen in the Twenties instead of now. The Fifties are so dull."

"Me too," Max said. "I love all the songs. The music today is terrible. And people have no style. You would have made a perfect flapper."

"My mother was the right age in the Twenties," Annabel said. "But she wasn't a flapper. My grandfather was a minister. My mother never went to a speakeasy in her life and she wouldn't even bob her hair. She missed it all. I would have appreciated it. She let me try on her wedding dress once. Oh, I was born in the wrong time! I've read everything F. Scott Fitzgerald ever wrote, and I have all the Noel Coward records."

"I can play all his songs on the piano," Max said.

"How lucky that we met." She leaned closer to him and looked up at his beautiful faun's face in the moonlight. She wondered if he would try to kiss her. No, he was a perfect gentleman, he wouldn't dare. They hadn't even had a date yet. But she felt as if he were her friend.

Maybe Chris had been right about parties. Annabel hadn't ever really thought about it before, but that dance had been like a cement grinder; all those people, no time to talk. But they were there to meet people—how else could you? You had to find out as many names as possible, and ask those dumb questions about their majors and their backgrounds, quick before someone else cut in, and then if you didn't like a boy's looks or pedigree you wouldn't even go out with him and you'd never find out if he was nice or not. That was so superficial. Well, it wasn't as if she were going to marry any of them—she had four years of college ahead of her and plenty of time to think about getting serious. If she were thinking about marrying someone it would be different; she'd take the time to really know him. She wondered if she would want to marry Max.

"I guess I'd better stop monopolizing you," Max said.

They walked back into the gym. Chris was dancing with Charlie Bliss and looking bored to death, and Daphne was dancing and chattering animatedly with Richard Caldwell.

"Go cut in on him," Annabel said to Max. "So I can tell her."

As soon as Max cut in on Richard, Annabel took Daphne's arm. "Thank you, Max," she said sweetly. "Come to the ladies' room with me, Daphne, I feel faint."

Daphne was staring at her. Annabel almost dragged her to the bathroom that had been reserved for the girls and pushed her inside. "Richard Caldwell is married!" Annabel said.

"Married? But I thought he was a freshman."

"He is. And his wife is having a baby in November."

"What a nerve," Daphne said. She took her compact from her evening bag and began powdering her nose. "Can we smoke in here?"

They both lit cigarettes. "I thought I'd better tell you before you wasted your whole evening on him," Annabel said. "Max told me."

"The gall," Daphne said. "And I don't even like freshmen."

Chris came bursting through the door, heaved a sigh, and flopped down on the bench against the wall. "That boy had wet hands," she said. "Ugh."

"Christine, you must really try not to look so pained on the dance floor," Annabel said. "You'll never meet anybody nice that way."

"I don't care," Chris said. She lit a cigarette. "I'll never see Charlie Bliss again. The one with the teeth. I was just mesmerized by those teeth. He told me most hockey players don't have a tooth left after a few years. He said it was masculine. Beating each other in the face with sticks, that's masculine. Well, he invited me to the Princeton game, and I couldn't help it, it just popped out: I said, 'If it's so masculine, ask me again when they're all gone.' " She started to laugh. "Oh, my God, I couldn't help it, it just came out of my mouth."

"You should go to the Princeton game," Daphne said.

"With him? I'd rather be dead."

"Maybe he has nice friends," Annabel said. "I'm going with Maxwell Harding the Third, known as Max."

"I'm going with Billy Trueheart," Daphne said.

"I'm not going," said Chris.

"Oh, don't be silly," Daphne said. "Somebody will call and ask you."

"I don't want to go. I hate parties and I think football is boring."

"Of course it's boring," Annabel said. "That's not the point."

"It is to me."

"Good grief," Daphne said.

"Now Chris, you aren't having such a bad time, are you?" Annabel said. "You must have met other men besides Charlie Bliss."

Chris looked at her watch. "I can go home now."

"Alone?" Annabel said in dismay. "But you look so pretty, and the evening is just getting interesting."

"I'd rather be by myself than with those idiots." She walked out of the ladies' room leaving them standing looking after her.

"If she doesn't look out," Daphne said, "she's going to be by herself for the rest of her life."

"Oh, let's go back and dance," Annabel said. "I don't want to miss anything."

Chapter 3

Of all the girls, Christine Spark was the one who most fervently believed in Education for Education's Sake, and who gave the least thought to anything but the immediate future. While the other girls sat in their rooms at night having philosophical discussions about what life meant and what they would do with it, she did her homework. On Saturday nights, when the girls who hadn't been invited to the after-football-game parties were ashamed to be seen downstairs in the living room, and either hid in their rooms or went in glum little groups to the corner for a late snack, Chris curled up in front of the living room fireplace with a book. She didn't care when boys came driving up to the door looking for last-minute blind dates. She ignored them. She knew they probably wouldn't want her anyway. And if they did, she doubted if she'd want them. In the social game she had been dealt the worst possible combination: she wasn't pretty and she had good taste.

She was often quiet, and others had always taken that as a sign of dignity and maturity. She was sharp-tongued, and people thought she was confident. Nobody knew how frightened and shy she was, except Annabel, who had zeroed in on it immediately. Chris hadn't expected at first to like Annabel, who was too beautiful and too frivolous, but now she thought Annabel was the nicest girl in the dorm.

Chris came from New York, where she had been a scholarship student at Dalton, the most liberal of the private girls' schools. The high school students wore smocks over their clothes, not as a sign of exclusivity like the uniforms of other private schools, but to avoid clothes competition. Lipstick was forbidden. The liberal attitude of the school was in the mix of students and in the freedom of study. In her junior year she had been elected class president; in her senior year she had been president of the student government. Her shyness made her appear aloof, therefore a leader. She studied all the time and made straight A's. She was valedictorian at graduation. But outside of school hours she had no real friends. She never invited any of her high school classmates to her family's West Side apartment. On Saturday afternoons all the girls who didn't have dates with boys made dates with each other, to have lunch and go to the movies. The few times anyone had the courage to invite an august personage like Chris, Chris suggested they go to a restaurant. She didn't want anyone to come home with her and see her mother lying around with a hangover, or worse, up and drunk at noon, and passed out cold by dinner. It was the secret she shared with her father, a kind, quiet man who was a professor of chemistry at Columbia. Her father didn't speak about her mother's drinking, and he forbade her to criticize her mother, so she didn't.

But Chris hated her. Her father demanded so little, and seemed so devoted to her mother—Chris couldn't understand it. Her mother was an embarrassment; always making scenes, irrational. When Chris was accepted at Radcliffe she rejoiced because it meant she could live away from home. No one would know anything about her home life and she could start all new. Maybe she could have real friends.

She knew what a college education cost, and she had no intention of wasting it. She adored medieval history, and planned to spend hours in the library immersed in the sort of wonderful research books she had only dreamed about, and she would get good marks. It surprised her to find that a lot of the girls laughed at "greasy grinds." She didn't care. She didn't want to go to drunken football weekends or find a husband. She was terrified of liquor. She'd never had a drink in her life and didn't intend to. Even food prepared with wine frightened her. She wouldn't be like her mother, she'd kill herself first.

At Radcliffe no one elected her president of anything. If you were shy in an enormous school like Radcliffe people simply ignored you. They didn't fantasize you had leadership qualities you didn't possess. And that suited her just fine. She melted into the peaceful intellectual atmosphere, dreaming of the cloistered walls of medieval French abbeys . . .

And then she fell madly in love with a boy in her French class with whom she hadn't exchanged two words.

She hadn't known she was capable of such feeling. At first she didn't even know his name. It was his looks that mesmerized her. He was so different from all the other boys—she thought of them as boys, not men, although the other girls called them men—he was an individual. He was dark, aesthetic, brooding, tragic. He looked like Heathcliff should look. His hair and eyes were black, his mouth had an impatient line, and he spoke to nobody. He dressed in the same impeccable tweed jackets, gray flannel pants, oxford cloth shirts, and striped ties as the other boys who had come from snobbish prep schools, but he didn't seem to have their dilettante natures. He kept to himself. Chris couldn't stand society boys; they didn't know anything about the real world. The only colored people they had ever seen were domestics, and they weren't sure they'd ever seen a Jew, except maybe two of the three Marx Brothers. But she knew her Heathcliff was different, even though he was a preppie. He seemed capable of dark, secret passions.

The class was in advanced conversational French, so she finally got to hear his voice, because eventually they each had to get up to recite. His accent was excellent. His voice did not disappoint her. She found him incredibly sexy. But she still didn't know his name. The professor was no help; he called everybody "you." "You," he would say, pointing a bony finger, when he wanted you to recite. Supercilious creep.

She wanted to sit next to Heathcliff so she could find out his name and perhaps even talk to him, but it wasn't easy. Their class was in Sever, a cavernous, ancient, dusty building filled with classrooms, people rushing around to be on time, pushing each other on the crowded iron stairs. She and Heathcliff came to class at different moments, and she couldn't very well change her seat; it would look like she was chasing him, which she was. The only thing to do was to wait in the hall right outside the classroom door, pretending to be doing something, and then when he had sat down, to rush in and grab the seat next to him before someone else got it. She managed this on the third try. As she sat down she dropped her books, but he didn't attempt to help her pick them up. She picked them up herself, gave him an apologetic smile, which he scarcely returned, and glanced quickly at the open notebook on his lap. No name. Why would he write his name in his notebook anyway?

Chris lived for those French classes. In between she studied as hard as ever, but sometimes she would find herself daydreaming, lost. How could she talk to him? What could she say? How could she get him to notice her? She finally confided in her new friends in the dorm. They were delighted that Chris liked someone at last, and were full of suggestions.

"Bum a match," Daphne said.

"He doesn't smoke."

"Just talk to him," Annabel said. "He's probably shy."

"You haven't seen him."

"He sounds conceited," Emily said. "I wouldn't want to meet a man who didn't want to meet me."

In the end he spoke to her. She had been sitting next to him for six classes in a row, and finally one morning when they came out into the bright fall sunlight of Harvard Yard he turned to her and said, "That's a tough class."

"Yes," she gasped. Her heart was pounding. "I only took it because I thought it would help with my major, but now I'm sorry."

"What's your major?"

"Medieval History, mostly Medieval French History, and I wanted to be able to read some reference works in French so I . . ." Oh hell, she shouldn't have sounded like such an intellectual, now he would hate her. "What's yours?"

"Economics," he said.

"Are you going into banking?"

"Yes."

"Do you need French for that?" Ask him about himself, that was better. At least now he was talking.

"You can always use a foreign language."

"Yes. I'm Christine Spark—Chris. What's your name?"

"Alexander English."

Oh, what a beautiful name, she thought. He had started to walk and she trailed along beside him like his puppy. She hoped he had another class and wasn't going to his dorm or she would look like a fool. Leaves from the tall old trees that helped make the Yard so beautiful had fallen on the path, and they crunched under their feet. Alexander English walked on to University Hall and went up the stone steps and Chris went right in beside him, right into the class.

"I didn't know you took Shakespeare," he said, glancing at her.

"I hardly ever go, I hate it," she lied.

"You hate Shakespeare?" He looked incredulous.

She remembered hearing Annabel say something about it in the dorm. "It's just that the professor stops talking and gives you those looks if you cough or anything . . . I had a cold, but it's gone now."

He seemed to accept the lie, even though she hadn't coughed in all those French classes when she'd sat next to him. She realized he hadn't even noticed her enough to care. They sat down together in the Shakespeare class and opened their notebooks. She glanced around to see if she could find Annabel. It was such a big class. She thought she saw a glimpse of Annabel's red hair in the front row, but she wasn't sure. The professor started his lecture on *King Henry V*. Chris had read all Shakespeare's plays in high school. She took notes on a blank page of her French class notebook and smiled at Alexander. She wondered if he had a girl friend. Why would he want *her*? She was so plain, nobody ever looked at her. This was crazy. She had gym in twenty minutes. What was she doing here?

After the class was over it was lunchtime. Chris kept close to Alexander through the mob of exiting students and walked beside him through the Yard. He was greeted by a few boys and he gave them his frosty little half-smile. She was excited to be seen with him and pretended that he liked her and she was his girl friend. This time he stopped where the paths crossed.

"I guess I'll see you Wednesday," he said.

"Yes," she said, and gave him an enormous smile. Please like me, she thought.

"So long."

After lunch at her dorm Chris went to the administration office and cajoled her way into the Shakespeare class. It was late in the term, but she said she had been afraid of taking on a fifth course until she saw how difficult the other four were going to be. She promised to make up all the reading. Then she changed her gym class. It meant she had to take tap dancing instead of swimming, a stupid and useless pastime if she ever saw one, but she would do anything for Alexander.

She couldn't think of any way to get him to like her except to hang around him until he got to realize what a nice person she was. She was sure he didn't have a girl friend. He seemed like a loner. She had always had good instincts about people.

When she got back to the dorm and told her friends what she had done they all praised her ingenuity. It never occurred to any of them that she was carrying her crush a little far. After all, everyone knew a girl had to be crafty to get a man, and looking at Alexander English's picture in the *Harvard Freshman Register* they all agreed he was well worth it.

Chapter 4

By mid-fall of her freshman year Daphne Leeds had
already acquired the superficial reputation that set
her apart from the others: she was the Golden Girl.
It was not so much her honeyed skin and golden hair
that gave her the name, but the sheen of gilded privi-
lege that touched her like sunlight wherever she went.
She seemed to have everything: the best men, the
easiest sophistication, looks that made people turn
around, an unerring sense of style, money, background,
confidence, and intelligence. She even won regularly
at their nightly bridge games in the dorm, unless she
had a stupid partner. Nobody was jealous of Daphne
—she was too superior. You could only be jealous of
someone who wasn't really better than you were and
who seemed to be taking unfair advantage.

But Daphne had come to Radcliffe with a secret,
and she would gladly have traded at least half those
attributes the other girls admired . . . she sometimes
thought they had been given her to compensate for
the bad thing. If anyone knew about her they would
think she was a freak, they would be uncomfortable
with her, and who would want to marry her? She
would die an old maid and a virgin. Daphne was an
epileptic.

She didn't let the college know when she applied. When she took the physical examination required of all freshmen she lied on the form. *Do you have epilepsy? No.*

Her seizures had started when she was around six. No one was quite sure when they had started because she would simply lose consciousness without falling down. She would come out of these seizures aware that time had passed, feeling disoriented, but not understanding what had happened to her. A bus she had seen right in front of her would have vanished. People would be doing different things than they had been doing a moment before. Once, in the country with her parents for the summer, she was climbing the ladder to get to her tree house when she blacked out and fell down and broke her arm. Her parents thought she had been careless, as most active children were. But then she started having seizures several times a day, and her "absentmindedness" worried her mother. Daphne was taken to her family doctor, who sent her to a neurologist. She had petit mal.

She was not to go swimming alone; she might drown. She couldn't go up in the tree house anymore. She had to stop her riding lessons, just when she was getting good at them. But most important of all, her mother warned her, she was not to discuss it with her friends. Only Dr. Michaelson and the school nurse would know. It was to be a secret because other people wouldn't understand.

When she was nine Daphne had a real convulsion. She was in her ballet class, the first year she had been allowed to go *en pointe,* and she was turning, turning, feeling she could float away, when she found herself lying on the ground, frightened children around her, the teacher distraught. But there was something besides fear on their faces; there was revulsion. She didn't know what had happened.

The ballet teacher told her mother. It was horrible. She had made a spectacle of herself, writhing, grunting, stiff, her eyes open, her mind asleep. And she had wet her pants. No one had known what to do. They had thought she was dying. Daphne wished she had died.

When her mother suggested gently that perhaps she would like to stop her ballet lessons for a while Daphne knew she had to decide something more important than that. She was a bright child, and she could already see her life ahead of her: protected, fearful. She refused to quit the class. She knew she didn't want to be a real dancer, but that wasn't the point. What mattered was that she *would* be normal, she *would* do what everyone else did.

But the other students treated her oddly after that. They were afraid it might happen again. It did, when she was eleven, but she was at home. She had medicine: two kinds of little white pills. The blackouts that had happened several times a day when she was young had tapered off to only about once a month when she was twelve. No one at school ever noticed. But she was wary now, knowing how easily people could stop liking you if you were weird.

She had her last seizure at fourteen. That didn't mean it would never happen again, but it gave her some measure of peace. Dr. Michaelson tapered off her medication until she was eighteen and started college. Then she took none at all, but she had a prescription with her, just in case. She was not a cured epileptic; there was no cure. The affliction was simply lying dormant. Maybe it would come back and maybe it wouldn't.

Do you have epilepsy? No.

Her parents didn't know how she had gotten it. It could have been inherited from some forebear they hadn't known about, hidden away in fear and superstition, or it could have been a brain injury at birth. How could they not know? They knew the bloodlines of every ancestor back to William the Conqueror, for God's sake—wasn't there once a William the Epileptic? William the Idiot Savant? William locked in the attic because he threw fits and frothed at the mouth and people thought he was crazy?

No one would ever marry her. He wouldn't trust her not to pass it on. No one was ever going to find out.

The irony was that Daphne was the most popular girl in the dorm, sharing this honor with Annabel. There was a friendly rivalry between them that was not really serious because they both knew more men than they had time for. Other girls were happy to have one date, but Daphne was often called for by two men at the same time, who took her off to Boston like a treasure between them. Daphne's dates always behaved like gentlemen. She never had to fight any of them off. On the second date they would try the permitted goodnight kiss. On the third, perhaps a few more. If she really liked a man she might permit necking in his car, from the waist up, on the fourth date. There were rules for all these things. You could add a few of your own if you wished, and Daphne did. When it came time to try necking from the waist down she always removed the offending hand from her person and that was that. Her dates were willing to have her reject their hands as long as she didn't reject them.

There were several reasons why Daphne was determined to remain a virgin. For one thing, she was terrified of being made pregnant and she didn't trust condoms. Everyone knew those men carried them around in their wallets for years. For another thing, if you went all the way men talked. And once people knew you were easy it was all over, all the admiration, the love, the fun. Those men had to keep on respecting the Golden Girl and falling in love with her. She needed to be popular more than anyone else did, because the other girls were normal. Daphne really didn't care about sex, and sometimes that worried her. All she wanted was to be loved. Love was much more important than sex because love was a sign of approval, while sex was secret and . . . well, not quite nice. Sex was lust, and lust meant being out of control. To her, being out of control had only the most frightening connotations.

One Friday night Daphne arranged a double date for herself and Annabel with two Harvard juniors. They were named Doug and Binky, they had gone to Groton and belonged to the Porcellian Club, and they were tall and handsome, if slightly interchangeable.

Waiting in the upstairs hall for their room buzzers to sound, smoking, dressed elegantly for a weekend evening in Boston, Daphne thought with approval that she and Annabel were the two best-looking girls in Briggs Hall. "It's terrible," she said to Annabel, "I go out so much that sometimes I think: Did I tell *him* this story before or was it someone else?"

"Serves them right," Annabel said. "They always tell every girl the same story."

Doug had a car. He and Binky had decided that the four of them would go slumming to the Old Howard, the infamous Boston burlesque house. Daphne had been there before, but pretended enthusiasm. Men liked to take girls there, apparently hoping they would be titillated, or at least find it sophisticated. She wondered if her dates became aroused by watching strippers take their clothes off, and what they did to get over it. She wasn't sure she wanted to think about that.

The Old Howard was a small, dark theater in Scollay Square, an area that was sleazy, neon lit, and disreputable, and therefore a favorite of the college students who were on their own for the first time. The four of them found seats near the front. Daphne looked around. There were the usual college boys with dates or in a group, laughing and hooting, and the Dirty

Old Men who sat with their hats on their laps. She was repelled by the possibility that some men would come there because they took it seriously.

"Look at that old cow!" Binky said in delight. The woman on the stage had tassels attached to her nipples and her G-string, and she was managing to twirl all three simultaneously. Her naked body in the purple stage lights looked like unbaked dough.

Doug was Daphne's date, Binky was Annabel's. Doug was trying to decide whether or not he should hold Daphne's hand. She could tell what was going on behind his eyes. He finally decided it would be unsophisticated to grab her hand in this place, and she leaned back in her seat, more relaxed.

A man came down the aisle hawking dollar magazines, guaranteed to be dirty, and "surprise" packages guaranteed to contain shocking sexual gifts. The regulars already knew the merchandise was a fake. Two more strippers came out in turn to do their undistinguished acts, and then the star appeared—Lily St. Cyr. Everyone applauded wildly. Daphne was thirsty and tried to decide whether she would have a gin and tonic or a whiskey sour when they went to the Fife and Drum Room afterward. Men always took you to the Fife and Drum Room to dance after they took you to the Old Howard, as if to prove they had good taste after all.

"Wasn't that fun!" Daphne lied when they left the burlesque house and got into the car.

"I must learn how she twirled those things," Annabel said. "I would be the hit of the next party if I could do that."

"I bet you'd do it too," Binky said. "Wouldn't you?"

"I would," Annabel said.

The Fife and Drum Room was considered a chic place to go. There was red plaid fabric on the walls in the entrance, and then beyond that was the very dark room where you danced. There were little tables around the perimeter of the room, and in the center a dance floor filled with couples standing glued to one another, not moving but rubbing up against each other and occasionally moving their feet a little to give the semblance of dancing. A live combo was playing "Just One of Those Things." Daphne, Doug, Annabel, and Binky ordered drinks and went out onto the floor. Doug held Daphne very close, and immediately she could feel that hard thing prodding her stomach. God, how she hated it when they got a hard-on! They always did. She didn't want to be used as something for him to rub up on. It embarrassed her. But she didn't know how to get away without letting him know she *knew,* and she couldn't do that. They both kept standing there shuffling their feet in the same place and pretending that nothing was happening.

As soon as the set was over she went right to the table. "I'm dying for a drink," she said.

She drank her whiskey sour and looked for Annabel. It was difficult to see in the dark. There she was, attached to Binky as if they were one person, and resting her head on his shoulder. The blind date seemed to be a big success. Annabel had better watch out or she would give him ideas.

Doug took Daphne's hand. She smiled at him and removed her hand from his gently to take a cigarette from her pack. "Will you go to the Yale game with me, Daph?"

"I'd love to, but I already have a date." He was the third man who had asked her and the game was a month away.

"Well, then I guess I'll see you at the parties." He looked dejected. Daphne wondered if she should invite him to be her escort for one of the deb parties over Christmas vacation. There was plenty of time for that; she could do better.

They ordered more drinks. "I was *smashed* last weekend," he said proudly. "We had a party in our rooms, my two roommates and I—bring-your-own-bottle. We had a big bowl of grape juice and gin and ice, and everybody who came kept adding to it, a little of this, a little of that." He laughed. "You'd be surprised, if you put in enough different things you can't taste any of it. Nobody added any more grape juice. Guys were passing out, they were throwing up in the wastebasket, I don't even remember the end of the evening. I must have had a gallon all by myself. When I woke up there were six guys I'd never seen before passed out all over the living room. I had a hangover for two days." He laughed.

Daphne wondered why men always told you how drunk they had been as if that made them attractive. Drinking a lot was one thing, everyone did that, but making an ass of yourself was another. He obviously couldn't tell the difference. She smiled and pretended she thought his story was as funny as he did.

They danced again and sat down to drink again, and Annabel and Binky never left the dance floor. Now Doug was telling her how drunk Binky had gotten the previous weekend. He thought it was hilarious. Daphne laughed with him. Her feet hurt.

They had to leave at twelve fifteen in case there was Friday night traffic getting back to Cambridge. All the way home in the car Annabel and Binky necked in the back seat. Daphne could hear the rustling of Annabel's taffeta skirt and she was afraid to turn around to look. She dreaded to think where he had his hands. A blind date!

All the couples on the large stone terrace in front of the dorm were locked in frantic last-minute embraces. It was one o'clock. The House Mother, wearing her bathrobe, opened the door and looked out. The couples separated as quickly as if she had been their own mother. Doug, in the car, kissed Daphne and put his tongue in her mouth. She wondered what was the point of that, when she had to go right in anyway. Men were masochistic. Annabel and Binky finally unglued themselves and Annabel ran into the dorm, waving good-bye merrily. Daphne followed her, shocked in spite of her attempt to seem sophisticated.

They went directly to their mailboxes to see if there were any messages. Daphne had a phone slip that said Richard Caldwell had called.

"What a nerve," she said, and tore it in half. "I'm certainly not going out with any married man."

They walked up the stairs together to their rooms. When they got to Annabel's door Daphne stopped. She was still so disturbed that she had to say something about Annabel's reckless behavior. "Annabel . . . how could you?"

"How could I what?"

"How could you neck with Binky like that on a first date?"

"I thought he was cute."

"But you can't neck with a man on a first date—especially a blind date—just because you're *attracted* to him," Daphne said. "People will start saying things."

"Well," Annabel said tartly, "you like to play bridge and I like to kiss."

"Did he ask you out again?"

"He will."

"I bet he will. You'd better watch your step."

Annabel laughed. "Do you think he's going to jump on me?"

"What do *you* think?"

"I declare," Annabel said. "Men are such beasts."

It was untactful, but she just had to ask. "Annabel . . . are you a virgin?"

Annabel looked at her with wide, amused eyes. "Isn't everybody?" she said.

Daphne wondered.

Chapter 5

There wasn't a day lately that Richard Caldwell didn't think remorsefully: *How did I ever get into this mess?* In only three months his life and perspectives had changed so much he felt as if the romantic Richard Caldwell of last winter was a young and foolish stranger. He wanted to smash that stranger— he wanted to cry.

The small New England town where he had gone to prep school was divided into two social strata: the preppies and the townies. Richard was a preppie, the president of the senior class, the leader, football hero, best squash player, sophisticate and ladies' man. He was tall, blond, and handsome, with smooth manners and confident breeding. He was a Caldwell, and had been registered at St. Martin's at birth, as he had at Harvard, because his father and grandfather had gone to those schools. It was not neecssary to make straight A's; all he had to do was do presentably and his future would be assured. When he graduated from college he would go into his father's real estate business, marry a suitable New York debutante, and have several children. The boys would of course go to St. Martin's and Harvard, unless they were morons. It was not likely that a Caldwell would be a moron.

The St. Martin's boys thought about sex and girls all the time. Most of the boys were virgins. When they got really horny they would pile into the few jalopies they owned and drive to the local roadhouse, the Oaks, to get drunk and pick fights with the townies, who went to the local public high school and were as foreign to the preppies in dress and attitudes as if they lived on another continent. Richard was one of the lucky boys who had his own car, a 1947 Plymouth convertible. Six boys piled into it, vying for the honor of being his friend, and when they got to the Oaks all the preppies wanted to sit in Richard Caldwell's booth, and the younger boys, who were too shy to sit with him, copied all his gestures. Besides having a certain golden radiance, Richard was the only boy at St. Martin's who had a regular sex life with a girl, and so he was a celebrity.

The girl was Hope Loughlin; she was the daughter of the owner of the roadhouse, and she was the waitress. She was seventeen years old, sexy and curvy, with dark wavy hair and the face of a startled pussycat. Hope was the closest thing to a sex symbol anyone had seen in that town and Richard had gotten her. It seemed fitting. It never occurred to any of the boys at St. Martin's to think that Hope had gotten Richard, because of course when he graduated he would never see her again. That was the way of their world. They knew Hope was madly in love with Richard—you could tell from the way she looked at him—but they didn't know he was in love with her.

And then Hope got pregnant and Richard eloped with her.

Marriage meant using his weekend passes from prep school to spend weekends with Hope in the motel on the outskirts of town. They would bring in bags of hamburgers and bottles of Coke and spend the weekend in bed. Marriage meant being an adult, stable, with a person who always had to be on his side. Hope worshiped him. He was only eighteen, and

going to Harvard in the fall. Richard had never admitted it to anyone, but he was afraid of going to
college, of starting all over again as a new boy after
being the big man on campus at prep school. Harvard was so huge. All those strangers to win over, to
impress. Now he wouldn't have to go there alone.

Marriage also meant that for the first time in his
life Richard's father wouldn't be able to make him
feel inferior and childish. Oh, his father would take
him seriously now, all right, at last! But he was afraid
to tell his parents until after graduation, when he
drove to New York with Hope and made her wait
in the car outside his parents' huge apartment building on Fifth Avenue while he went upstairs to con-
front them with the news.

He had forgotten how beautiful his parents' apartment was. For almost all his life, since the age of ten,
he had been away at school, and then in the summers
they went to Newport. The wallpaper in the large
living room was hand-painted silk, the carpets were
thick and soft, the sofas oversized and upholstered in
pale velvet. The elevator man carried Richard's suitcases into the entrance hall. His mother kissed him
on the cheek, his father smiled and handed him an
icy martini, his acceptance as a man.

His mother: cool and ladylike. His father: cold and
exacting. In this room, so far removed from the yearn-
ings of his prep school nights, he had to tell them
that he had married a pregnant waitress. All hell
broke loose.

After an hour of recriminations his father had once
again planned Richard's life. Everything Richard had
done had been ludicrous and childish. He had no
money, no job, he was going to Harvard in September. He had thought Hope and the baby would make
him a grown-up, and his father thought they were
cheating him of the last happy days of his childhood.
College was supposed to be fun. An education was
necessary for a gentleman, but so were parties and

dating and friendships with other young men of his class that would continue on into the business world. What was he going to do: live in a squalid little apartment off campus, take a part-time job, starve, flunk out, ruin his life? It was unthinkable. No. Richard was to go to Harvard alone and live in the dorm. Hope would go home and live with her parents. No one would annul the marriage, even though they were both underage. Richard could see Hope on weekends provided his marks were good. His father would support Hope if Richard agreed to these rules. And when the baby was born, divorce proceedings would be instigated, handled by Richard's father's lawyers.

There was really nothing he could do. They had him trapped. He agreed to his father's terms, knowing in his heart it was only to gain time, and held back the angry tears. He didn't tell Hope; he told her everything would be all right as long as they loved each other.

How could he have known that college would be so different from what he had been afraid of? It was an adult world, but he was part of it, a sophisticated college man. The girls were fantastic. There were girls from his world, fresh-faced and glowing, funny, eager to charm him, to have fun and adventures. He didn't have to explain things to them as he always did with Hope; they had their own kind of mutual shorthand. He had slid into college life, fit there as perfectly as his father had always expected him to. Hope became a stranger, an outsider . . . an *inferior*. Every time he saw her she seemed a reproach. She tried to be a part of his life, and that annoyed him because it made him feel guilty. He didn't want her anymore.

His son . . . Richard Caldwell, Jr. Hope had insisted on that name, had put it on the birth certificate in the hospital. No one had told him that he would not feel like a father, would feel only panic. The infant cried and spit up, sometimes seemed to smile, and

Richard felt nothing toward it but hideous responsibility that made him want to run away. He never
went back to see Hope anymore, but when the girls
at college found out he was a husband and father
they treated him like a leper.

And Hope would not give him a divorce. "Never,"
she told his father's lawyer. They offered her money
beyond her wildest dreams and she talked of love.
Richard had never imagined that soft little compliant
Hope would turn out to be so tough-minded. She
thought something had happened to Richard at college to drive him away from her, and that if she
waited long enough he would return to his senses.
There seemed to be no way he could get rid of her.
He had deserted her, not she him, and she was blame-
less.

His father cut off Hope's money. Hope seemed perfectly content to live out her meager little life and
wait. Richard had forgotten why he'd ever loved her
at all. She had tricked him. He hated her. If she
wanted to wait, he could outwait her. The hell with
her. But in the meantime, he wanted to go out with
Radcliffe girls, but they were all looking for a man
who was single.

He knew he was ingratiating and good-looking, so
what he needed now was some explanation of his pre-
dicament that would arouse their sympathy. It came
to him quite naturally in the end, and he almost believed it himself after a while.

"My father made me marry her."

His father, in this story, was an old-fashioned moral
tyrant. Hope, in this same story, was only after the
Caldwell money. The negotiations would be long and
bitter, but some day he would be free, and meanwhile, poor Richard, didn't he deserve affection and
sympathy? The girls found his story exciting and moving. He was now a sophisticated and rather sad figure,
no longer a villain. Any one of them, if she had
gone too far, might have had to face the horror of

becoming pregnant with an illegitimate child. Who could blame Richard, so young at prep school, for fooling around with the local tramp? Wasn't that what boys did?

So finally, with the minor inconvenience of two wrecked lives behind him, Richard Caldwell began to have the social life for which he had been intended.

Chapter 6

Emily had a recurring dream. In this dream she was on her way to a class in Harvard Yard, but she couldn't find the building. She was frightened, knowing she would be late. Lost in the enormity of all these buildings and the hurrying strangers, she felt inadequate, as if she were a small child again. For some reason, in this dream, she never asked anyone for directions. Her heart pounded, and she was ready to burst into tears as it grew later and later; it seemed as if she would never be able to find her way around and would always be an outsider to whom the college world was unfamiliar and bewildering. When she finally found the building it turned out that there was an exam that day. No one had told her today was an exam day! She was unprepared! So she sat in her chair in the classroom, reading the questions, and discovered she did not know the answer to a single one of them. What had she been studying all this time? What were these questions? What was this course? She would fail and be thrown out in disgrace. Her terror gave way to numb resignation. She was unprepared. She obviously couldn't take care of herself the way everyone else seemed able to. The authorities—THEY—would find out. She would be unmasked as an impostor.

When she woke up she would lie in bed for as long as she could, trying to understand the dream and wondering if it were possible that she was even more afraid than she knew. Then she would get up and rush to get ready for her classes, the classes she loved, that weren't really so hard, in this college where she was having the most exciting time of her life.

Her favorite course was Psychology, and there were so many others she wanted to take that sometimes she thought she might go on to graduate school after all. Of course, that would depend on whom she married. In her Psych course she had learned that a dream could be either symbolic or a mishmash of things that had happened during the day, or both. She knew she felt like an outsider; she was aware of that while she was awake. She was even afraid she would always feel like a beginner. The more she learned here at Radcliffe, the more she felt herself to be a hopeless innocent. She was so popular with men that she could hardly believe it. But she felt as if she had landed in a foreign country and was dating the natives. There were all sorts of things she didn't dare tell her parents.

She had never even heard of the Social Register, and now most of the men she dated seemed to have their names in it. "He's a Biddle from Philadelphia," someone said, and she didn't know what that was, but she did know it was someone you should be glad to go out with. "The Lowells speak only to Cabots, and the Cabots speak only to God," went the well-known poem. They also, apparently, were allowed to speak to Emily Applebaum.

Her scrapbook was already filled with souvenirs: cocktail nakins, swizzle sticks, phone messages, photos, stubs of football tickets, menus, programs, matchbooks, and the little cartoons Chris used to draw and leave taped on her door for her when Emily went out. They were usually caricatures of Emily with her dates. Chris's pen was as lethal as her tongue, and everyone who was lucky enough to get one of her caricatures saved it. When Emily went home to Scarsdale for Christmas vacation she left her beloved scrapbook in her room at the dorm because she knew her parents would want to see it, to share her life, and they would never understand those cartoons at all—not the private jokes, not the way those boys looked, not the way of life the drawings represented.

Her parents asked her who all her friends were. "What was his name before?" her mother wanted to know. Then her parents saw the men who came to the house to pick up Emily for dates, and they didn't ask anymore. They knew, and they were displeased. They sniffed out the truth like a dog smelling a cat. There was No Future in those people. They would Hurt Her. She was Wasting Her Time.

But wasn't college supposed to broaden your horizons? Could she help it if those men asked her out? You met one or two and then you met their friends. Didn't her parents know that Harvard had a Jewish quota too, just like Radcliffe, and suitable husbands weren't exactly falling at her feet? But she was still so young. She intended to find somebody eventually, and get engaged in senior year, and married right after graduation, but in the meantime she had a lot of growing up to do. Didn't her parents realize that she had never in her life been to a real nightclub before this year?

"You're skating on thin ice," her mother said.

She was relieved to go back to school after Christmas vacation, even though the bad dreams started again.

It was terribly cold in Cambridge that winter. The dorm never seemed to have enough heat, especially at night. Emily slept in flannel pajamas with knitted cuffs at the wrists and ankles, wool socks, and sometimes even her bathrobe. Trudging to class over the icy paths that had been shoveled between huge snow piles, she forgot there had ever been cobblestones underneath. It seemed as if there had always been only ice. If your date didn't have a car, and few did, it was a nightmare. That long hike to Harvard Square, freezing in your nylon stockings and thin party dress under your coat, the wind whistling through the bare branches of the trees in the Common, and the seemingly even longer hike back when it was colder, made a date almost as much to be dreaded as looked forward to. A lot of the eager men who had come to Briggs Hall looking for girls disappeared during this period, and Emily could hardly blame them. They had to walk twice as far as the girls did: they had to come get you, take you out, take you home, and then go home themselves. Brr . . .

Everyone studied very hard for exams during Reading Period. Emily worried, and spent long nights going over her class notes, rereading her textbooks. When she got two A's and two B's she couldn't believe it. She had made the Dean's List! And she had been worried that she would fail. Daphne had made the Dean's List too, and of course Chris had, with all A's. Except for an A- in creative writing Annabel had all C's, and she didn't even care. Annabel didn't bother to study very much. Annabel and Daphne were the only two girls in the dorm who still went out all the time no matter how cold it was, except of course for the girls who were going steady.

Emily looked on everything about Daphne with admiration and awe. Daphne was so beautiful, and so chic, but most of all she was so nonchalant. Life wasn't full of all kinds of little perils for someone like Daphne. She really was the Golden Girl.

It was a Saturday night, and Emily had managed to get out of kitchen duty this week by trading with a junior who had been stuck with Bells on Saturday night and wanted to get out of it. She was pleased with this coup, since she had nothing better to do.

It was slow after the rush of men came and went. No man would have the nerve to call a girl on Saturday night to ask her out; even if she had no date she wouldn't go. Emily was sitting at the switchboard reading a copy of *Vogue* she had borrowed from Annabel.

The front door opened to a blast of frigid air and Richard Caldwell came in. Emily wondered who was lucky enough to have a date with him tonight. She smiled at him, trying to look efficient.

"Hello, Emily," he said. "What are you doing here on Saturday night?"

"Well, somebody has to do it," she said casually, feeling flattered. "Who did you want to see?"

He leaned gracefully against the bannister leading to the upper floor and lit a cigarette with a gold lighter. He was wearing a camel's hair polo coat—the man's version of Daphne's coat that Emily so coveted—and Emily thought he was the best-dressed and most self-possessed man she'd ever seen. "I just wanted to get in out of the cold," he said.

"Oh, sure," she said.

"It's cold as hell out there."

"I know."

"I'm trying out my new car," he said.

"Oh? You got a new car?" She couldn't believe she was really having this conversation with him. He'd danced with her once at a Jolly-Up, and she'd been thrilled for weeks. He was so sophisticated that he was really out of her league altogether.

"Yep," he said. "Look out the window."

She turned and looked out the small window behind the switchboard. She could see the front of what seemed like a long blue convertible. "What kind of car is that?"

"Jaguar," he said matter-of-factly, as if everybody had one.

"How nice," she said matter-of-factly, as if she always rode in one. The truth was she'd never even seen one. The people her parents knew drove Cadillacs because they were big and safe, and spoke disdainfully of small foreign cars.

He glanced at his watch. "Do you want to go to a party with me after you get off Bells?"

She couldn't believe it. Richard Caldwell asking her out! Even though it was the last minute on Saturday night, who cared? It might be the only chance she'd ever get.

"I don't get off till ten," she said.

"I know. It's ten of now."

"I'm not dressed," she said. She was wearing her pale gray cashmere sweater set with the plaid kilt skirt that matched, and she had makeup on, because you never knew whom you might see. If you say I'm dressed wrong and take that invitation back, she thought, I'll die.

"You look perfectly fine to me," Richard said. "That's what all the girls will be wearing. Come on, it'll be fun."

"All right," she said. She felt as if she had just successfully negotiated a top-level diplomatic maneuver. He was actually trying to talk her into it! What in the world would she say to him for three hours?

At two minutes to ten Emily turned off the switchboard and ran up the four flights of stairs to get her things. She looked at her muskrat coat with hatred. It was so dressy, so nouveau riche. She wished again for the hundredth time that she had a camel's hair coat like Daphne's. When a man came to call on Daphne unexpectedly she would yell upstairs. "Throw down my coat, someone!" and that camel's hair coat would come hurtling down through the stairwell, and Daphne, long-legged and laughing, would be off with her date. Sometimes Emily was the one who threw Daphne's coat down to her. Emily, who always carried a handbag, because how could you go out without a comb and lipstick and compact and your key and mad money? Daphne never worried about those

things. She wasn't always looking in the mirror like
Emily. And men didn't dare make passes at Daphne
to force her to use mad money to escape them. Emily
ran down the stairs in her fur coat, hoping Richard
Caldwell didn't think it looked too Jewish.

Richard smiled when he saw her. "What a pretty
coat," he said. "It suits your personality—it's so feminine."

She knew then he was not only the most sophisticated man at Harvard but in the whole world.

He helped her into his Jaguar convertible, and
they drove through the black icy streets. He had the
top up and the heater on, and Emily snuggled into
her fur coat, sneaking glances at his perfect profile,
feeling very luxurious and pampered. They drove to
Elliot House, one of the upperclassmen's houses facing the river, the dorm where the rich, chic Wasps
lived. Emily had been there before. They went upstairs to a suite where a party was in progress. The
rooms were dingy and nondescript, furnished with
the usual college furniture that looked as if it should
be given to the thrift shop. A card table had been
set up at one end of the room and it was covered with
various bottles of liquor and a glass punch bowl filled
with Purple Passion. Emily looked around at the
guests while Richard took her coat into the bedroom.
She knew right away this was a Social Register type
party. Everybody looked alike. She supposed these
people thought all Jews looked alike, but they were
wrong: *they* looked alike. The girls all looked as if
they had majored in hockey at boarding school. She
felt the familiar little rush of fear. Then she relaxed
and reminded herself that she was very popular, that
Richard Caldwell had chosen her tonight, and that
she always got along anywhere.

Richard handed her a paper cup of Purple Passion.
There was Daphne, with a date, surrounded by couples all talking and laughing. Emily smiled across
the room at Daphne but Daphne didn't see her.

Richard introduced her to everybody in sight. Everyone, the girls as well as the men, had either two last names or some icky diminutive for a first name like Topsy or Muffy or Wink or Binky. Oh well, Emily thought, they should come to my country club; they'd be hysterical.

"How's the Jag?" Wink said.

"Great," Richard said. "Wasn't it, Emily?"

"Lovely," Emily said.

"Richard is the only man I know who could afford it," Wink said.

"Oh no, don't be silly," Richard said. He smiled his dazzling, confident smile. "When you go to buy a car you just have to know how to Jew them down."

Emily looked away, embarrassed. She hoped they couldn't tell about her. They didn't seem embarrassed at all. Maybe it was just an expression and didn't mean anything. . . .

Richard took her elbow and steered her adroitly through the crowd until they came to Daphne's group. "May I interrupt?" he asked, and introduced Emily around. Daphne gave Richard a curious look.

What does that mean, Emily thought—is she wondering why he'd go out with *me*? No, he must have asked her out first and she was busy. That's what it is. Well, so what? Richard Caldwell goes out with lots of girls.

The group was talking about parties they'd been to in New York during Christmas vacation, and people they knew. Emily didn't know any of those people. It occurred to her that during Christmas vacation when she and Daphne had both been in New York they'd never seen each other. She hadn't seen Chris either. They were friends in the dorm, but when they went back to their real lives it was as if all that had never been. Maybe her parents had been right. College wasn't your real life. College was a period when you went away and learned skills and found a good husband and then went back to the serious business of living. These people at this party who had obviously known each other forever would go back and marry each other, or people just like them, maybe some of the ones they were talking about, and they would keep on doing all the things she had never done.

"We're going skiing during Easter vacation," Daphne said. "It's the last of the good snow."

"I'm going to Bermuda," someone else said.

"Oh," Emily said, "I've been to Bermuda!"

"Good parties," Richard said. "Who do you stay with?"

"We stayed at the Princess Hotel," Emily said. There, that would get them. It was the best hotel on the island.

"Oh. I never stayed at a hotel." He seemed to be dismissing her. "We stay with friends."

Friends? Who had friends in Bermuda?

"I'd rather go skiing," Daphne said. She blew one of her perfect smoke rings and watched it, amused with herself. "You get fat lying around on the beach and drinking all day."

Only Daphne could get away with that and not have it sound like sour grapes, Emily thought. Why did some people have a certain way about them that made everything they did and said seem right, while other people could do and say the same things and seem wrong?

"Where do you ski, Daphne?" someone asked, and they were off on a discussion of which places were the most fun. Emily would never dare to ski; you could get seriously hurt.

She had learned very quickly how to fake it with these people. You just kept your mouth shut and they assumed you were like them. They had never seen anyone who wasn't like them. In their own way they were just as protected as she was. At first she had thought it was so wonderful to be on the edge of a glamorous new world, but now suddenly she was tired of always being on the edge and never inside. Richard Caldwell hadn't really been interested in her, not even for a second. He had just wanted a decent-looking girl to bring in to this party, to show he could get a date at the last minute. She had just happened to be sitting there. Emily felt humiliated. She didn't like any of these people anymore; why would she want anybody who didn't want her? That had been her motto and she should have stuck to it. But how could she have known?

She was getting a headache. She looked around the room at all these snobs, listening to snatches of their conversation and hearing the same old thing. These people even all had the same accent, no matter where they came from.

"Can we borrow a bottle of gin?"

Now how did that accent get in here? It was pure New York, the kind of New York she knew and felt comfortable with. She looked toward the voice and saw a really cute man, sandy-haired, with a freckled, turned-up nose and a compact athletic build. He was in tan chinos and a blue Brooks Brothers shirt with the sleeves rolled up, and no tie.

"I'll replace it on Monday," the cute man said. "I promise."

"Oh shit, Buckman," Wink said. "All right."

Buckman? *Buchman?* He was Jewish? The cute man saw Emily looking at him and he smiled at her. She smiled back.

"Can I help it if fifty people crashed my party?" Buckman-Buchman said pleasantly. Emily had the feeling he was saying it for her benefit. "And they all drank gin."

Wink handed him a bottle of gin. He took it and made no move to leave. Emily walked nonchalantly toward the booze table, knowing that nobody in her alleged group would notice. She started to help herself to a cup of Purple Passion, and Buckman-Buchman quickly ladled out a cupful for her.

"Hi," he said. "I'm Ken Buchman, who are you?"

"Emily Applebaum."

She saw the warmth of his smile reach his eyes for the first time, and she knew he spelled his last name with an *h*. "Are you having a nice time here in the Wasp's Nest?" he asked.

She giggled. "Don't let them hear you."

"Would you like to come down the hall to my party?"

"With all the drunks who drank your gin?"

"They're not drunk. And my punch is much better than this. I'm in premed, and I mixed it with the hand of an expert. Just enough of each ingredient."

"You're going to be a doctor?" Emily asked, very pleased.

"I hope so."

"What kind of a doctor?"

"A good one."

"No, silly," she said. "I mean, what specialty?"

"I don't know yet." He winked. "I also am going to be a rich one. Now will you come to my party?"

"I might as well," she said agreeably. I'm invisible here anyway, she thought. If I leave they won't even see me. "But just for a while."

They walked together down the hall to his rooms. His party was noisy and cheery, and Emily recognized two of the Jewish girls from her dorm. She felt at home right away. There was the same old tacky Harvard furniture, but the people were different. They didn't scare her at all. Ken Buchman put the bottle of gin on the booze table next to the inevitable bowl of Purple Passion. He poured cups of punch for both of them and then took her to a corner where they sat on the windowsill, the only place that was unoccupied.

"Where do you come from?" he asked her.

"First Scarsdale, New York, then Briggs Hall, and then that boring party."

"Scarsdale! I'm from Lawrence, Long Island."

"We're practically neighbors."

"What class are you in, Emily?"

"Freshman. And you?"

"Sophomore."

She thought how if it weren't for the pure chance of everything that had happened tonight she would never have met him at all. This place was just too big.

"And what do you want to do when you graduate?" he asked.

Do? What did any girl do? Get married and have two children, she thought. He was the first man who had ever asked her what she wanted to do when she graduated.

"Well, don't look so pained," he said. "You don't have to know what you want to do."

"But I do know," Emily said. And now, suddenly she did know. "I want to take a master's and be a psychiatric social worker."

Ken looked delighted. "I knew you were smart as well as pretty."

"How could you tell that?"

"You came to my party."

She smiled at him. "What's your favorite sport?"

"Tennis. What's yours?"

"Tennis, I guess. I'm not very good though."

"I'll teach you."

"You will?"

"Sure. When it gets warmer. In the meantime maybe we'll go out to dinner. Would you like that?"

"Yes," she said. Would she *like* it? Men never took you out to dinner, it was too expensive. They took you out drinking and dancing after you had free dinner in your dorm. Dinner seemed very sophisticated.

"We'll go to Locke Ober's and we'll have lobster Savannah and the best chocolate ice cream in Boston."

"That sounds divine," Emily said. She glanced at her watch. "I have to go," she said regretfully.

Ken turned his wrist and looked at his watch, which he was wearing on the inside of his wrist. Emily had never seen anyone wear his watch that way before and she thought it was sophisticated, too. Ken had sandy hair on his wrist and she thought he was sexy. Hands and wrists were the second sexiest part of a man, after his face. "You just got here," he said.

"But I have to get back to my dorm or I'll get in trouble."

"I'll call you," he said.

"Please do. Briggs Hall."

He leaned over and gave her a light kiss on the cheek. It made the back of her neck tingle as if all the little guard hairs were standing up. Oh, he was definitely sexy. "I remember," he said.

Emily went back to the first party and nobody had even noticed she was gone. She thought about Ken Buchman all the way home in the car, and when Richard Caldwell leaned down and kissed her goodnight in front of her dorm she was so entranced by Ken she didn't even realize what he was doing. A couple of hours ago she would have practically fainted if Richard Caldwell had kissed her, but now it was nothing. All she thought, idly, was that it was typical of Richard Caldwell's arrogance not to bother to walk her to the door.

"Thank you, I had a lovely time," she said, and got out of the car and ran into the dorm.

She stayed near the phone for three days, only leaving to go to classes. She had a feeling Ken wouldn't call before Tuesday, and he didn't. He asked her out for Saturday. She liked that; he was considerate. *He* wouldn't show up at ten minutes to ten on a Saturday night looking for whatever he could get.

On Saturday night Ken showed up in a borrowed car. Emily was impressed. He had so many friends, and he could even persuade one of them to lend him a precious car on a weekend! He took her to Boston, to Locke Ober's as he had promised. It had dark wood-paneled walls and was filled with adults because it was very expensive. The lobster Savannah was rich and creamy and the best thing Emily had ever tasted. She didn't have any problem making conversation with Ken—she was so comfortable with him, and he gave her the feeling that he admired her and would take care of her. The more she looked at his cute face the more she liked it. She wanted to crawl right into his pocket. She thought she was falling in love with him. And when he kissed her goodnight, in front of her door, she loved the way he kissed: gentle, slow, sexy, and not one bit wet.

He called her the following Monday and asked her out for Friday and Saturday. Friday night they would go dancing and Saturday there was a party. Ken was rushing her: he liked her as much as she did him. Emily thought about him all week, and her heart began to pound hard at the oddest moments. She relived his goodnight kiss in her mind. She tried the name out in her fantasy, just for fun: Mrs. Kenneth Buchman . . . Dr. and Mrs. Kenneth Buchman . . . She liked it.

It was so nice to have his arms around her on the dance floor. He always made her feel protected. And when he took her to the party he never let her out of his sight for a minute. Even when they were each talking to other people he would glance over at her and wink at her so she would know he was still with her. She thought he was probably the kindest person she had ever met.

She was really in love with him. She knew it was real. The next Friday night he took her out dancing again, and afterward he parked his borrowed car in the space on the side of the dorm where people always parked to neck. He put his arms around her and kissed her, and then he said, "I love you, Emily."

Her heart turned over with joy, and yet she wasn't surprised. They had gone out together only four times but she felt as if she had known him forever. She knew he meant it and wasn't just telling her he loved her so he could get her to go further. Not Ken. He was honest and he respected her virginity, which she meant to keep until she was safely married.

All her fantasies of love opened up into an explosion, like fireworks. "Oh, I love you too," Emily whispered against his sexy mouth.

When she got back to the dorm her friends could tell from her face that something momentous had happened. "He loves me!" Emily announced breathlessly. "Ken Buchman loves me!"

And after that Ken and Emily went together, in relentless Fifties togetherness, like one person, with never a thought that was out of harmony, if only because they both tried so hard to like the same things. Being alike was their gift of love to each other.

Because his family's home was within driving distance of hers they saw each other constantly during vacations as well as at school. Emily's parents were very pleased that she was going steady with Ken, and they hoped she would marry him. He was polite and attentive to them, and sometimes when the young couple was going to be out late the Applebaums invited Ken to spend the night in their guest room. He became almost a son to them. Since his appearance in Emily's life she had become more serious and responsible, and her parents approved of that too. During the school terms Emily spent almost every evening with Ken in the library, studying. Premed was difficult, and he planned to apply to Harvard Medical School. So now not only did Emily have this good catch—a young man of fine character, attractive looks, and a family that would be compatible with theirs—

but she was also keeping up her good marks. She made the Dean's List every time.

Emily loved being with Ken. He was exciting, and she also felt so peaceful with him. She showed him her secret scrapbook from high school and explained everything in it. She didn't show him her scrapbook from her first term at Radcliffe, however, because she didn't want him to think she was trying to make him jealous. They both liked the same things. Ken liked jazz—Dave Brubeck, Erroll Garner, the Modern Jazz Quartet—so she did too. She liked Frank Sinatra and Johnny Mathis, so he did. She had a sensible career ambition, which wouldn't interfere one bit with marriage, and Ken encouraged her.

She assumed she and Ken would get married if they continued to get along as well as they did now. She couldn't imagine not getting along with him. They had never had even one fight. When he went to Harvard Med School (because of course they would have to take him) she could finish Radcliffe and then do graduate work at Harvard. He would be very busy while he was interning, so she would work. Even though Ken's parents had plenty of money, it would be good to have an income to bring into their own home. She loved these plans, but she didn't tell him too much because she didn't want to seem to be pressuring him to make a commitment. She knew when the time came he would propose.

Although Emily was terrified of breaking any college rules, she nonetheless let Ken persuade her to come to his rooms on weekend afternoons after he had sent his roommates away, and they necked on his bed. They both knew the rules of their own relationship and did not argue about how far he would be allowed to go. Emily would take off her skirt and sweater and bra and fold them neatly on the chair, putting her shoes side by side underneath the chair, and then in her slip and pants and garter belt and stockings she would lie down and they would do as much as they could without either removing the rest of her clothes or going all the way. Ken remained in shirt-sleeves and chino pants. Emily thought he was the most attractive, sexiest man she had ever known, and although she adored necking with him she didn't understand why her mother had always warned her in such dire tones about "getting carried away." She was much too scared to get carried away, even with Ken. To be carried away—or to go all the way, which was the same thing—was to ruin one's life.

Then, when his roommates returned, Ken and Emily would go out to a Chinese restaurant in Harvard Square, which was their favorite. If there was a party on the weekend they would go to it, and if not they didn't care.

It was a very secure, almost domestic life they led. It was also romantic. She carried his picture in her wallet and he carried hers. She knitted him a six-foot scarf; not striped the way she'd made for men she'd only liked, but argyle, which took forever because it was so hard to do. And he gave her silly presents, like an ashtray with the inscription: *Tant pis—my aunt has to make a telephone call.*

Emily never made a decision without consulting Ken first, just as if they were already married. She grew to depend on him completely. But except for little health tips, he didn't like telling her what to do. He wanted everything to be *their* choice, *their* preference. The more favorite things they had in common, the safer they felt.

She figured he would propose in her senior year, they could get engaged then, and they could be married right after her graduation. There wouldn't be any point in waiting anymore after she had graduated.

Chapter 7

Annabel was, more than anything else, a romantic. She had no more idea what went on inside men's heads than the other girls did, but she liked to think they were as romantic as she was. The ones she dated certainly acted that way. They seemed to be in and out of love every other week, but she was the same way. Collge was so new and exciting, and she was so popular. She necked with every man she found attractive and sexy, and if she found him so on the first date, what was the point of waiting just to play games? She loved kissing. It was romantic and sensual; the closeness, the softness of being petted and stroked, the excitement of being held in the arms of a man who held the possibility of real love. And when he touched her in places that were supposed to be off limits, she let herself glide along with the tingling feelings and just never mentioned it to the other girls. She already knew what prudes they were, or at least pretended to be, and she was no fool.

The summer before she came to Radcliffe Annabel had had her first and only affair. It was with a gorgeous twenty-year-old man from Georgia Tech who had a summer job teaching riding to the little kids back home in Atlanta. Annabel went riding every day and of course she had met him. All the girls had a crush on him, but she had gotten him. Nobody knew she wasn't a virgin anymore; it was her secret.

She had been a little surprised when he didn't write to her, but she understood about summer romances. They were beautiful, but not expected to last. And now, after an autumn of dating and football games and parties, she thought she might be really in love again.

The man she was in love with was a junior named Happy Foster. He was big and dark-haired and kind of shaggy; he wore leather elbow patches on his sports jackets and had frayed lapels on his overcoat, and he wanted to be a journalist. He was a writer on the *Harvard Lampoon*, the satirical magazine. Annabel thought everything about him was fascinating. She had met him at a party the previous weekend, and after she had talked to him for a while she knew he was much brighter than any man she'd ever met. They liked all the same poets. The day after they met he called her and asked her out for this Saturday night. All week she had looked forward excitedly to their date, feeling lightheaded and happy.

The football season was over but it wasn't too cold yet. He appeared in a station wagon, and suggested they go to Cronin's for a few beers. He looked so shaggy and marvelous in that station wagon, she could just picture him in the country. She thought they made quite a nice couple.

Cronin's was in Harvard Square and it was the place to go. It was huge, cavernous, full of dark wood booths and tables, like a beer hall, and it was always crowded on weekends. People roamed up and down the aisles between the booths and around the tables, stopping to talk to friends, sitting down for a beer and then moving on. It was like a big party. Happy steered her to a long table full of people, pulled up two chairs, and sat down and ordered. Annabel was a little disappointed, because she had wanted to have him to herself. You couldn't talk much here; it was so noisy, and everyone was saying funny things and laughing. She could see that Happy was very popular. She laughed at the jokes and flirted with him, and after a while he put his arm around the back of her chair and asked, "Are you having a good time?"

She smiled at him. "Yes, but I wish we were alone. There are so many things I want to talk to you about."

He whisked her right off to a secluded little booth for two, and sat across from her, looking into her eyes, and took her hand. "You didn't drink your beer," he said. "You don't like beer. I should have realized that. I know what you like."

And quickly there was the waiter with a split of champagne.

"Oh, Happy, how did you know?"

"You are definitely a champagne girl," he said. "Do you remember in *The Great Gatsby* when Fitzgerald says: 'Her voice was full of money'? The sound of money, you know, gold coins clinking, and the excitement of being on top of the mountain? Well, your voice is full of champagne. I can hear bubbles in it, and I see celebrations."

"That's lovely," Annabel said, moved. "Thank you."

"I wish I could always buy you champagne," he said. "But I'll probably be a starving newspaperman."

"That's all right. Tell me more about yourself. What's your real name?"

"Happy."

"No, I mean your *real* name."

He lowered his voice to a whisper. "You must promise not to tell anybody. I hate it."

"I won't tell."

"Swear."

"I swear."

"It's Horatius."

"Oh, my God. But you'll like it better later when you're very distingiushed and famous," she said quickly.

"Do you think so?"

"Yes, of course. When you win the Pulitzer prize."

"If I do win it, will you come to see me get it?"

"Oh, you'll have forgotten me by then," Annabel said lightly.

He looked intently into her face. "I'm not so sure about that. I think you are going to be very important to me. Do you believe in love at first sight?"

Her heart turned over. "Sometimes . . ." she said.

"I never did before I met you. I can't take my eyes off you. You're so beautiful. You're Scarlett O'Hara. You have so much spirit—and poetry—and you're brave. You're an optimist. You will have anything you want in this world."

"Do you really think so?"

"Absolutely. Would you mind if I fell in love with you? I promise not to stand in front of your dormitory window singing off-key."

She laughed. "You can do that if you want."

"Fall in love or sing?"

"Fall in love. Not sing."

"All right," he said, and smiled, and then she knew she was in love with him.

At eleven o'clock he said, "Hey, let's get out of here. I just want to kiss you."

"Oh, me too," she whispered.

He drove his station wagon out of Harvard Square and into the suburbs somewhere, and then through a bumpy country road into the woods. It was so dark she couldn't tell where they were. There were a lot of little secret wooded places hidden around here where people could go to neck, if they could find them. He parked under an arch of dark, softly rustling branches. It was very quiet, cozy, and romantic.

He put his arm around her. "When you're not writing poems for that poetry class of yours, would you write one for me?"

"Really?"

"Yes, really. Would you?"

"I might." It would be a love poem, she thought.

"Sometimes it's hard to tell someone how you feel about things unless you write them down. And I want to know a lot more about you."

"You're so sweet," Annabel said tenderly.

They started to neck then, and it was lovelier than it had ever been with any other man. He was so affectionate and gentle, and he kept gathering up her long hair in one hand as if it were the most sensual thing in the world.

"Look," he said reasonably, "I'm too tall for this front seat; it's very uncomfortable. I'm dying."

She had been in a lot of back seats before, but this time she was a little nervous. She loved him, and she might not want to make him stop. The back seats of the station wagon had been removed, and there was a mattress on the large space that was left. They lay on it and he put his coat over both of them and they started to kiss again.

"I do love you, Annabel," he said.

"I love you too."

Now his hands were deftly removing bits of her clothing, moving all over her, and she knew she couldn't wait much longer before making a decision. Men were so fickle . . . But he was an upperclassman and an intellectual. He loved her. He was a serious person. . . . She opened her eyes and saw the white gleam of a condom in his hand.

"Don't be afraid," he whispered. "I love you."

She kissed him. She wasn't afraid.

Then suddenly he seemed in such a rush, so frantic, as if he were the one who was frightened. They were perfectly safe here and Happy was acting as if the Yard cops were coming any minute. He had seemed so sure of himself before, but now he was just the way her riding instructor had always been. Annabel couldn't understand it. Lovemaking was so wonderful—why did men seem to want to get it over with? Maybe it's different for men, Annabel thought. Maybe this is enough for them.

As soon as it was over Happy rearranged his clothes and lit a cigarette. She did the same, and then she put her arm around him and kissed him on the cheek affectionately because she did love him so much. He cast her what she thought might have been a look of panic. Then he put his arm around her and she put her head on his shoulder and they sat there peacefully, smoking their cigarettes, looking at the thin little moon outside the rear window. Finally she looked at her watch.

"I have to be back at one o'clock. We'd better go."

"Okay," he said quickly. They got into the front seat and he drove her to Briggs Hall.

"I'll call you," he said. He kissed her goodnight.

"I'll write you that poem," she said. She went upstairs to her room singing.

She worked on the love poem for Happy very hard all week, to make it good enough to show him, waiting for his call.

But he never called her again.

She felt miserable, confused and betrayed. He'd never loved her at all; he'd used love as a weapon to get her. He probably didn't know what love was. She hoped she would never run into him again—she couldn't stand to look at him after he'd humiliated her that way. But Harvard was huge, and he seemed to be avoiding her too. She thought about Happy a lot, and about what had happened, and she resolved she would be a great deal smarter and never let another man fool her. But neither would she let this experience turn her into an unfeeling zombie. She would just be very careful.

And after a while Annabel's resilient spirit healed,

and she started to fall in love again, and to neck with any man she found irresistible. But even though she never did go all the way they still kept disappearing, after making all kinds of passionate declarations. She decided that most men were children: a hopeless combination of horny and guilty.

There was only one man she knew who was different. Max Harding had become her best friend. Ever since that night they had first met at the Freshman Mixer they saw each other at least once a week, and had long phone conversations in between. They made each other laugh, and they had so much in common they might have known each other all their lives. They went to Boston to the theater, he took her to parties, they drank beer at Cronin's and champagne at the Ritz. He let her drive his sacred Stutz Bearcat. She adored Max. Nothing was too outrageous for him to do if she suggested it. Once they went to a costume party, and Annabel had the inspiration that she go in a rented white tie and tails and top hat and he go in an evening gown and a lady's wig borrowed from the Hasty Pudding productions. They won first prize.

Max was the only man she knew who behaved like a gentleman. In a way she was relieved that he never tried to go further than their goodnight kisses. She didn't know what she would do if she ever lost Max. But she suspected that he knew about her other men —there was a Harvard grapevine about these things— and he intended to last with her after all the others were gone and forgotten.

Whenever anyone jilted her it was a great comfort to be able to call Max. Annabel was the only girl in the dorm who had the nerve to telephone a man instead of waiting for him to call her, but she was also the only girl who had a man for a best friend.

"Oh, Max, come take me for a ride."

There he would be, a long striped scarf wrapped around his neck over his silly Twenties raccoon coat that he'd bought at a thrift shop for twenty dollars, his cheeks pink from the cold, his golden eyes warm. They would hug each other hello and get into his Stutz Bearcat. Emily had knitted six-foot striped scarves for all the men she liked until she started going with Ken, and she had even made one for Max because he was so nice, even though everyone knew Max belonged to Annabel.

"Where should we go?" Max asked.

"Just anywhere. Max, why are men so crazy? You know. You know all the secrets of Harvard Yard."

"Men are not gods," Max said, and laughed.

"They want me to love them and then they don't. They get so scared. They don't seem to think they're worth liking."

"A lot of them aren't," Max said.

"You are," Annabel said. "I'd die without you, Max."

"I'm not going anywhere."

"I'm glad you and I aren't in love," Annabel said. "That would ruin it. I don't trust love anymore."

"Till next week," Max said cheerfully.

"I swear I don't understand men, Max. And they don't understand me. Do men understand each other?"

"Not really."

"We're all alone," Annabel said thoughtfully. "All of us crammed into those little rooms together in that big dorm, all strangers. The only one I really trust is Chris. She's so honest. The others are all hypocrites. They talk and talk about life, but at the same time they're pretending to be perfect. Sitting in the cars putting lipstick on before they walk into the dorm at one o'clock, so nobody will know they were necking. Who cares what they did before? I don't."

"But they do," Max said. "So don't tell them."

"I wouldn't dream of it. I am a perfect lady."

Max never minded when Annabel called him away from his classwork because Max never seemed to study. He took all the gut courses, like the Twentieth Cen-

tury American Novel, and would have been content
with C's, although he often got A's. Annabel knew he
was very smart. Max had a different date every weekend, all of them pretty. He's really just like me, Annabel thought; we are absolute soul mates. The only
difference between us is that he's too smart to get
his heart broken . . . unless he doesn't tell me?

In the spring of her freshman year Annabel began
to go out with Richard Caldwell. She thought he was
gorgeous, and she found the story about his marriage
and entrapment very sad. He was suave and charming
and had beautiful manners. They necked for hours
in his little two-seater convertible and after a few
dates it started to drive them both crazy. He wanted
to sneak her into his room. Annabel was very much
tempted. He couldn't possibly hurt her because she
would never fall in love with a married man, and so
if he left her so what? And in the back of her mind
she thought that because he was married he would
know all about sex, and it would be what she'd always
known it was supposed to be instead of what it had
been.

But when finally she agreed, and he sneaked her
into his room at his freshman house, having arranged
with his roommate to absent himself, Richard Caldwell turned out to be no better a lover than Happy
Foster. He was furtive and in a hurry. He jumped on
her as if he was terrified, and it was all over in a
minute. Since she didn't care what he thought of her,
Annabel decided to tell him she was not as thrilled
as he expected her to be.

"I'm not your wife, you know. It's different with
a date. I wanted to be courted."

"You bitch."

"Go to hell," she said cheerfully, and dressed and
left his room.

He phoned her two days later. "I think I have
something to show you that you'll like."

"You'd better show me that you're a gentleman."

"I will."

He brought her a single red rose when he picked her up. An upperclassman who had known Richard at St. Martin's had lent him his rooms in an upper-class house, a suite, which was safer and more relax-ing than where Richard lived, where the presence of any woman at all was strictly forbidden. There was a bottle of chilled champagne and a copy of the *Kama Sutra*.

"Good grief," Annabel said, "we're not going to do all those weird things, are we?"

"You said you wanted to be courted. That's the most romantic book I could find."

His technique, however, was right out of *Ideal Mar-riage,* which Annabel suspected he had bought and read during the two days she hadn't seen him. He had been furious when she told him that he wasn't a perfect lover, but he was also aware that gossip went two ways. He didn't want her telling people he wasn't as sexy as he looked. She was quite touched and flattered that he was trying.

They experimented with various positions and tried oral sex. She liked it better when he did it to her than when she had to do it to him, but she felt fair was fair. At the end of the evening Annabel had her first orgasm, two in fact, and she decided she was in love with him even though he was probably as big a rat as all the other men who had broken her heart.

They cuddled together afterward in the narrow bed. "How's your afterglow?" he asked.

"My what?"

"You're supposed to be having an afterglow."

"Oh, I am." Whatever that was.

"Let's go away next weekend. You sign out to a fictitious uncle in New York and we'll go to a motel near Boston and stay in bed all weekend."

"What a divine idea!"

It didn't bother Annabel in the least to invent a

fictitious New York uncle. She used the name of an
actual uncle who lived in Atlanta. She wondered why
none of the other men had thought of it, and decided
being married did make a man more sophisticated.

She saw quite a lot of Richard that spring, and they
both learned many new things, but in the end they
got a little bored with each other. Neither of them
wanted to go steady. A lot of attractive, eligible men
kept asking Annabel for dates, and she didn't like
having to turn them down. As for Richard, he was
afraid to get involved with one person. She understood. While she wasn't in love with him anymore,
she still had a very fond feeling for him, and she
thought he probably was one of the best things that
had ever happened to her at college.

She had no way of knowing then that he was going
to turn out to be the worst.

Sophomore year. Unlimited one o'clocks. Rooms on
the third floor instead of the fourth. For some lucky
people Bells instead of that loathsome kitchen duty.
Everything should have been wonderful, but here
was Annabel sitting outside one of the card rooms
with another criminal, waiting her turn to be tried
by the House Committee for having come in fifteen
minutes late the previous Saturday night. She had
come back at one fifteen, had been caught and reported.

The other girl sitting out here, looking frightened
and weepy, had come in ten minutes late. Her name
was Martha Fuller, and she was large and ungainly
and not pretty; the sort of girl who didn't get a
chance to date very much, and now she was afraid
her social life was going to be nipped in the bud.
It was nearly the end of the football season and the
most sociable time of year for everyone. If they got
Social Pro it would mess up all their plans. Annabel
thought how vile and arbitrary school rules were.
She'd done plenty of other illegal things, but this
time she hadn't done anything.

The door opened. "We're ready for you," the head of the House Committee said. Annabel and Martha went in.

The four members of the House Committee had been elected mainly because they looked totally forbidding, with not a shred of humor. Girls like that always got elected to positions of power by their peers, Annabel thought—the people who voted for them must have been looking for the reassurance of the mommies and governesses they'd left at home. She herself had not bothered to vote at all, not that it would have mattered.

"All right, Annabel, you were fifteen minutes late on Saturday night. What's your excuse?"

"I was at a party in some suburb—Needham, I think. There were two other couples sharing the car, and the other two girls were seniors, so they had two o'clocks. I said I had to go home, but they didn't want to leave. My date wouldn't take me back."

"You could have called a cab."

"I didn't have enough money with me, and I didn't know where I was," Annabel said. "Besides, there wouldn't have been enough time."

Take a cab? Who left a party alone and fled home? Your date took you home, that's what men were for. Men were supposed to take care of you. It had never occurred to her to call a taxi.

"Your duty is to get here on time, no matter how," the head of the House Committee said. "All right, Martha. You were ten minutes late on Saturday night. What's your excuse?"

Martha gasped and turned red. "I was running to get back to the dorm . . . running across the Quad . . . and there was a wire from the volleyball net . . . I bumped into it and had the wind knocked out of me."

"And . . . ?"

"And I lay there until I could catch my breath and then I ran to the dorm, but it was too late."

What a crock of shit, Annabel thought.

"All right, you two, you can go outside while we discuss your cases."

Annabel and Martha went back into the hall. They sat on the bench and didn't look at each other. Martha was sniffling into a wet tissue. I'll be damned if I'll cry for them, Annabel thought, but I probably should have. After a few minutes the door opened again.

"You can come back."

They sat in the card room waiting for the verdicts. "All right, Martha," the head of the House Committee said. "Since you really tried and you were hurt, we'll let you off this time. See that it doesn't happen again."

"Ah, thank you!" Martha said. She folded her wet tissue righteously and put it into her pocket.

"Now, Annabel. You didn't even try. We have decided to give you six weeks of Social Pro."

"Six weeks?"

"Six weeks. Be upstairs at eight o'clock every night. No dates, no callers."

"But I've got a date for the Yale game."

"You'll have to cancel it, won't you? You can go now."

Annabel was stunned. She looked at the four hatchet faces in front of her and they actually seemed pleased. It was totally unfair. Her punishment was entirely out of proportion to her crime, and they had let Martha with her fishy story off completely. Six weeks was practically until Christmas vacation. She wouldn't have a man left.

When Annabel got upstairs she told Chris, who was horrified. "They really must have had it in for you," Chris said.

"They did. You should have seen their faces."

"They're just jealous because you're so popular," Chris said.

"They hated me, Chris. Why do they hate me so much?"

"Because you go out and they don't."

"No," Annabel said. She thought about it. "Daphne goes out all the time too. Nobody hates her."

"She never got caught coming in late."

"People are so mean," Annabel said. "I don't understand it. What did I ever do to them? They acted like I didn't know my place and they were going to put me in it."

"They just wanted to put you in *their* place," Chris said. "A bunch of wallflowers."

"No, it's something more."

Chris looked pained and didn't answer. She knows they all detest me, Annabel thought. But why? I don't even know those people.

"Well, the hell with them," Annabel said. "I don't care what they think. I hate them too."

For six weeks she was in her room every night at eight o'clock. Soon the phone calls stopped coming. Nobody thought to call just to talk, except for Max. Annabel enticed the dorm cat to stay in her room, bribing it with goodies left over from dinner and a saucer of milk. She bought it catnip and toys. She figured she was going to turn into a regular old maid with a cat. But then the cat, being a creature of habit, fled to its old nighttime haunts and left her alone again. She forgave the cat. She even forgave her boyfriends.

No one could remember anyone getting six weeks of Social Pro before. You got a few days, a week, or if you did something dreadful you could get expelled. But this was like a prison term. Although Annabel had the freedom of the upstairs hall, she never deigned to come out and socialize in the smoker with the girls who had betrayed her. She stayed in her room like a queen. She read and ate cookies and wrote poetry for her poetry class, enough for the whole year. Max gave her his silk paisley bathrobe, and she wore

it every evening like a ceremonial robe. She gained
ten pounds. Except for visits from Chris she was totally alone.

When Annabel finally got off Social Pro everyone
seemed to think she was still on it. Nobody asked
her out but Max; it was as if they had all forgotten
her. The girls in the dorm seemed pleased. They
thought they had won. But Annabel knew better. It
took her a few months, but she finally had a whole
new collection of suitors.

Her total ostracism started suddenly. One day everyone just stopped sitting with her at meals unless
the place next to hers was the only one left, and nobody would double-date with her anymore, and no
one even spoke to her in the halls. Except, of course,
for Chris, who was her best friend, everybody in the
dorm simply shut her out. It was like a nightmare.

Annabel was too proud to admit to any of them
that she had even noticed. She couldn't decide whether
they wanted her to suffer or if they couldn't stand to
be near her. But she knew now what had happened.
It was her sex life. She's always had a bad reputation
because she necked too much, and now she was posi-
tive someone had told that she went all the way.
And those girls probably thought she slept with everybody—who knew what they imagined? She had never
dreamed they would behave as if sexuality was a com-
municable disease.

Dear, blessed Chris, who had no sex life at all but
didn't give a damn if Annabel slept with the whole
world, went out of her way to sit with Annabel at
meals and to be seen with her on other occasions as
often as possible. Annabel knew she would always be
grateful, for that and for the fact that Chris never
told her what the other girls were saying. Annabel
pretended she didn't care what they thought of her,
but she did.

"Who do you think started this?" she asked Chris
one night in Chris's room.

"I don't know," Chris said.

"Which man and which sneaky, hypocritical girl? I bet it was that Daphne. She always looks sort of guilty when she's near me."

"Maybe torture is against her principles."

"I don't care anyway," Annabel said. "The hell with all of them. They don't bother me at all."

It seemed as if she was saying that all the time lately, to Chris and to herself.

Even after everyone went away for summer vacation, when they came back Annabel was still the dorm pariah. She finally got used to it, and she kept pretending she didn't care. She had her work, she had Max and Chris, and they were worth a hundred of those other people. And she still had more boyfriends than anybody.

And then a new scandal came up to enliven their lives. It was the most infuriating thing that ever happened to them. Someone had been stealing money from wallets during fire drills in Briggs Hall. The fire drills were always in the middle of the night, and people left their wallets in their rooms when they were awakened by that loud clanging bell and had to rush downstairs to assemble on the lawn. Some of the girls, like Emily, hid their wallets under their clothes in their dresser drawers as a matter of course, but most of them simply left their wallets in their handbags. People were honorable and trusted one another. Until now . . .

The girls who had been robbed, and the one who were afraid they might be next, made such a fuss that the House Mother finally called the police, who sent a detective. He appeared in Briggs Hall, a man in his forties, dressed in a beige suit: Lieutenant Palmer. The girls were impressed. He looked like authority. They had never seen such an older man in the dorm before, except for people's fathers who came to drive them home at the end of the term. A police matter was important. They felt important, grown-up. Lieutenant Palmer went into one of the first floor card rooms and had the girls go in to see him one by one, in privacy, to confess if they wished, or to tell him whom they suspected.

Annabel was pleased that something so interesting was happening. The idea that a kleptomaniac was loose in their midst gave her a creepy feeling, as if she were about to be violated, even though she herself had not been robbed. She wondered who among them was so disturbed, and thought again how many secrets their bland, sweet faces covered.

After the detective had seen everybody the House Mother told them they could all go about their business. But as Annabel was about to go upstairs she put her hand on Annabel's arm and said softly, "Not you, dear. You stay."

Nobody looked at Annabel as they dispersed, but they never looked at her directly anymore anyway. The House Mother led her back to the card room as if she didn't know the way by herself. "He wants to talk to you alone."

Lieutenant Palmer was standing in the card room, looking out one of the tall windows at the Quad, watching some girls from Cabot Hall across the way playing volleyball, jumping around in their short little gym uniforms. Annabel went in and he turned to face her.

"Close the door," he said. She did. "Cigarette?"

"Thank you." He lit cigarettes for her and for himself, and then he indicated a chair. She sat. He remained standing, now a few paces in front of her, like an interrogator. What did he want *her* back for?

"You're Annabel Jones?" he said.

"Yes."

"I think you should know that several of the other girls mentioned you as a suspect."

"*Me?*" She was horrified. Of all people! Why would she steal anything?

"You were the only person anyone mentioned," he said.

"I don't understand that." She knew they all hated her, but this was carrying hazing too far. She found it hard to believe.

"Annabel, you won't go to jail. If you did steal the money, you can tell me. There must have been a good reason."

"I didn't steal it," she said, angry now.

"You know," he said, "stealing things you don't need is a kind of sickness. We never punish people for being sick. You could talk to a very good doctor here in the Cambridge area, and he would help you."

"I didn't steal anything."

Of course those girls had said she was the klepto-maniac. Why hadn't she realized why right away? If you slept with men you were a whore, and if you were a whore you were capable of anything, even robbery. She was just glad nobody had been murdered.

"If they said I did it," Annabel said, "did they give any reason why they suspected *me*?"

"Do you know any reason?"

She smiled, a small, bitter smile. "Yes. But I'd like to know what they said."

"Why don't you tell me the reason?"

"You first." She put out her cigarette in an ash-tray and looked at him. She could sit there all night and wait for him to answer her, and he knew it. She crossed her legs and folded her arms.

He cleared his throat. "They said . . . you had the type of character that made them suspect you."

"And what is that?"

"Annabel, they didn't know. They said it was an instinct they had."

"All of them?"

He nodded. "Were they right?"

"Who?" she snapped. "I have a right to know their names."

"What does it matter?"

"I want to know." Now I'll see who the ringleaders are, she thought. Now I'll find out which mean-spirited people are behind this thing.

He took a piece of paper out of his pocket and unfolded it. He looked at the list and then back at Annabel. "I can't tell you," he said, "but there were twenty-four."

She was stunnned. Then she burst into tears.

He handed her a clean handkerchief and patted her shoulder. She accepted the handkerchief but pulled away from his touch. She tried to stifle her sobs in case any of those bitches were listening outside in the hall, but she couldn't stop. What could one person do when faced with such a wall of solidarity? All the pain at being ostracized, the outrage at being the object of contempt and hatred, the effort her pride had cost her to keep acting nonchalant, all of it poured out in a convulsion of grief. The lieutenant of detectives paced up and down, not quite sure what to think. Finally she had no more tears. She wiped her eyes and blew her nose.

"May I have a cigarette?" she said. He handed her one and lit it. She inhaled quietly and looked at him. He was wearing a wedding ring. She wondered what he thought about girls who engaged in premarital sex. She'd bet anything he would never have married a girl who wasn't a virgin. Maybe he too thought a girl who went all the way with men would steal money from wallets.

"Why don't you tell me now?" he said kindly.

She fixed him with a calm, level gaze. "I didn't steal a thing," she said. "They're all just jealous of me."

There was nothing more he could do with her and so he let her go.

She went to her room to get some change, hoping she had been robbed. The dorm was such anathema to her now she couldn't wait to escape. She ran to the phone booth on the first floor where she called Max.

"Hey, Max," she said. "Let's go out and get drunk as coots."

"Are you all right?"

"No."

"I'll be right over," he said.

She was waiting on the front terrace when he came driving up in his yellow Stutz Bearcat. She rushed into the car before he had time to get out to open the door for her, and she hugged him and covered his face with kisses. He looked surprised.

"Oh, Max!" she said. "I can't wait to graduate and get out of this hellhole. How am I going to survive? How can I stand it? It seems like a century before they'll let me out!"

Chapter 8

Chris had been sitting next to Alexander English in
two classes for almost her entire freshman year now,
and although he was always pleasant he acted as if
she were just one of the boys. It never seemed to occur
to him to ask her to have a cup of coffee with him
after class, or even to try to get to know her at all.
He was the only man she wanted. A few others had
asked her out, but they were jerks and she said no.
Alexander was her project, and she was at her wits'
end.

He was Max Harding's roommate, and since Max
and Annabel were best friends she made Annabel find
out everything she could about Alexander. Annabel
reported triumphantly that Alexander did not have
a girl back home. Max had said, "Who would want
him? He's too grouchy." Well, Chris wanted him,
grouchy or not, and obviously Annabel had told Max,
because now Max had come up with the humiliating
idea that the four of them go out on a double date.

"I can't," Chris told Annabel.

"Don't be silly. Of course you can."

"If Alexander wanted me he could have asked me
all this time," Chris said. "I can't face him."

"But if he didn't want to go he would have said

no," Annabel said reasonably. "He knows it's you. It's not a blind date. It's your big chance."

"Did you tell Max that Alexander would be my first date since I came to Radcliffe?"

"Why would I tell him that?"

"It was my idea not to go out. I don't want him feeling sorry for me."

"Nobody's sorry for you."

"I bet you told him that I have a big crush on Alexander."

"I didn't tell him a thing," Annabel said, her green eyes innocent. "You and I are friends, and they're friends, so what would be more natural? Come on. I'll do your makeup, and I'll make you so beautiful you won't have a chance to be your usual little paranoid self. And you can wear my black dress."

"Well . . ." She would look different than she did in class, and maybe Alexander would realize she had the capacity for more than just sitting there behind her notebook. "All right," Chris said finally, although she was terrified.

The double date was set for the following Saturday night. The men would pick them up at eight thirty and they would go dancing at the Fife and Drum Room. Chris sensed the fine hand of Annabel in these plans; Annabel knew how much she wanted to be in Alexander's arms. On Friday, after their last class together, she smiled at Alexander and said, "Well, I'll see you tomorrow night." He nodded but he didn't smile back, and she knew for certain that Max had forced him into this and he didn't like her at all. She wished it were all over and this were Sunday, so she could kill herself.

On Saturday Chris washed her hair and let it hang loose, and Annabel made her up skillfully. She didn't look so bad. Her heart kept pounding and she was afraid her hands would be wet when she danced with Alexander and he would find her not only a nuisance but repulsive. She couldn't eat a thing at dinner in the dorm. I've just got to remember to keep my mouth shut, she thought; say only nice, polite, lady-like things, no nasty wisecracks like I always make when I have to talk to men.

Emily and Daphne came to her room to inspect her before they left for their own dates, and they said she looked beautiful. When the buzzer rang Chris felt sick.

Max's Stutz Bearcat had only a front seat. Chris had to sit on Alexander's lap. She was thrilled and frightened to be so near him, and worried that she was too heavy. Max and Annabel jabbered all the way into Boston while Chris and Alexander sat there mute. She felt like Charlie McCarthy perched there on his knee—she'd never be able to speak unless he did. She felt Alexander's breath on her cheek and it seemed a recklessly intimate gesture, although he had to breathe, didn't he? They were strangers and yet they weren't.

"Have you been to the Fife and Drum Room before?" Chris asked finally.

"Yes. Have you?"

"No."

They were there; checking their coats in a red-plaid entrance hall, going into a very dark main room where a band was playing one of those old songs that Annabel and Max loved. They all sat down at a tiny table where they were practically touching knees. Alexander and Max and Annabel ordered gin and tonics and Chris ordered a Coke.

"You don't drink?" Max asked.

"No." She took out a cigarette and for the first time Alexander lit it for her. He'd never done that after class. He was going to be different now, he was going to try to be nice, she could tell. Her heart be-gan to pound again when she looked at him. He was a man, not a boy; he was a thousand times better than all the rest of them. Never had there been a man so handsome, so sexy. She could imagine him as he would look when he was in his twenties and she knew he would be devastating. She wanted to be there then—she wanted to be with him for the rest of her life.

They got up to dance. Alexander was a very good dancer, much better than she was. When he put his arms around her she imagined that they were hugging, not dancing, which was easy to do because there was so little room on the crowded dance floor and nobody was moving very much. But she could feel how impersonally he held her. Her confidence evaporated. He was being polite tonight, but she had been right the first time; he didn't like her.

At the end of the set the four of them went back to their table. Annabel and Max were trying to remember the lyrics of a Cole Porter song and having a friendly argument about it. Alexander made concentric circles on the shiny tabletop with the bottom of his wet glass.

"Well, Alexander," Chris said, "tell me about yourself. What does your father do?"

"He's a banker."

"Oh, what you're going to be."

"Yes."

"And you're from New York, Annabel says. So am I."

"I know."

"Do you have sisters and brothers?"

"I have a sister. She's fourteen. Her name is Pooch."

"Pooch!" Chris said. "Do you call your dog Sis?" She stared at him aghast, feeling the flush cover her face. She'd done it again with her big mouth.

Alexander laughed. It wasn't a big laugh, but he was clearly amused. "No, we call our dog Throckmorton."

"Really?"

"He's a tiny little dog, a mutt. Half-cocker and half-Maltese."

"Half-cocker and half-Maltese!" Annabel said. "What kind of dog do you call that?"

"A cock-tease," Chris said. The minute it was out of her mouth she wanted to run out of the room. She'd really done it this time. It was one thing to be harmlessly insulting, but girls never talked dirty in front of men. It was the end. He would think she belonged in the gutter. Her eyes filled with tears.

Alexander and Max and Annabel burst into howls of laughter. "She's funny!" Alexander said.

"I told you she was funny," Max said.

"Christine is the funniest girl in the dorm," Annabel said. "She pretends to be shy, but just you watch out."

"Sometimes people get angry," Chris said.

"What do you care about them?" Alexander said. "Be yourself. The trouble with this world is that people can't be themselves. They're always trying to be just like everybody else."

"Except me," said Max proudly.

"And me!" Annabel said.

Alexander looked at Chris and smiled. It was the first time she had ever seen him give a real smile, and it made her heart rock. Oh, I love you, she thought. "Ready for another Coke?" he asked.

The rest of the evening was enchantment. They laughed at everything—even things Chris hadn't thought were funny when she said them. They were all suddenly at ease. Annabel danced with Alexander and Max danced with Chris.

"Alexander likes you," Max told her. "I can tell."

"Really? Does he really?"

"I know him better than anybody. He likes you." Max gave her a little kiss on the cheek. "Don't be so hard on yourself."

When they had to go back for their one o'clock curfew Chris leaned gently against Alexander's shoulder while she sat on his lap in the car. He had his arm loosely around her. She was happy. At the front terrace of the dorm Annabel and Max removed themselves discreetly so Chris and Alexander could be alone.

"Thank you," he said at the door. He didn't try to kiss her.

"Thank *you*. I had a lovely time."

"Maybe we'll study together one night next week. If you want to."

"Oh, I'd love that," Chris said.

He put his hands into his pockets. "It's cold. Goodnight." She watched him walk to the car and then she ran into the dorm.

"He wants to see me again!" she told Annabel, and they hugged each other and jumped up and down with the joy of their triumph.

After that, Chris and Alexander started to study together in Widener Library twice a week. She had never been in Widener before because it was the Harvard men's library. She studied at the Radcliffe Library. The enormity of this place awed her. It looked like Grand Central Station and smelled faintly like a zoo. There were rows and rows of long wooden tables, with boys hunched over them, some of the boys with dates. She spent more time looking at Alexander than she did studying, but he never seemed to notice.

After they had finished studying Alexander would take her to the cafeteria in Harvard Square, the Bick, where everyone went, and they would have coffee. It was brightly lit and antiseptic, but Chris thought it was romantic because she was with him. Then he would walk her home through the idyllic little streets of Cambridge, with the moonlight flicking the new spring leaves, and when they reached Briggs Hall he would give her a chaste goodnight kiss. She was so thrilled when he kissed her that she relived it over and over afterward. She fantasized more some day, when he fell in love with her . . .

The truth was that right now she was a little afraid of him and of sex because she knew so little. She wouldn't let him touch her unless he loved her. What if she couldn't control herself and then he didn't respect her anymore? She had heard a sad story from Annabel about being rejected by a man after she'd gone all the way, and Chris knew she couldn't stand it if that ever happened to her. Oh, but she knew she was lying to herself: If Alexander ever wanted to go further she would let him, and so she was grateful that he never did.

She worried that perhaps he thought of her only as a friend because he never asked her to go dancing again. But Annabel told her (thanks to Max, their source of information) that Alexander really didn't have much money. His parents were divorced and his father had been very stingy with the divorce settlement. Alexander and his sister lived with their mother. Chris felt sorry for him. She wondered what it was like to have divorced parents. Did he feel bad? Ashamed? He never mentioned it to her. She thought of her secret—her alcoholic mother—and it seemed as if she and Alexander each had a tragic secret of their own. She wished her parents would get divorced. Then she and Alexander would have the same thing in common. Someday, when she knew him better, she might even tell him about her mother. She knew he would understand.

Then, one night, the strangest thing happened. Alexander came to the dorm looking for her. They went into the little room on the main floor where the Coke machine was and sat on the floor sipping their Cokes. It was the first time Alexander had ever come over like that and all the girls who had seen him were very much impressed. Tactfully they left Chris and Alexander alone in the little room. Alexander looked terrible; his eyes were wild with some dark grief.

"I'm so unhappy," he said.

"What is it?"

"I'm going to commit suicide."

"Why?" Chris asked gently but urgently. She was frightened. "Why?" She wondered if he really meant it.

"I'm miserable," he said. Then he put his head down and covered his face with his hands. She wondered if he was going to cry, and she was even more frightened. If he cried in front of her he would be so embarrassed that he would hate her afterward. But a part of her felt motherly, and she wanted him to cry so that she could comfort him and show him that she would always be there in weakness as well as in strength.

"Cry if you want to," Chris whispered. She didn't touch him. Then he jumped up, cast her a look of agony, and ran out of the dorm.

Now she was terrified. She thought he might actually kill himself and she didn't know what to do. Had she said the wrong thing and humiliated him? Did he think she wanted him to be weak, so she could control him? I should have kept my big mouth shut, she thought.

Some instinct told her that it would be wrong to telephone Max, or even to tell Annabel. Whatever was going on was Alexander's secret. He had shared a part of it with her and she wouldn't betray him. She spent the night sleeplessly, and the next day she went casually to the building in Harvard Yard where she knew Alexander had his Economics class. She stayed far enough away so he wouldn't see her if he was there, and when the class was over she saw him come out of the building with all the others. She was vastly relieved. He looked perfectly normal.

They had their two classes together the next day and he acted as if nothing had happened. She didn't dare bring it up. She decided that he was even moodier than she had expected, but not suicidal. And why wouldn't he be unhappy? Poor Alexander—she knew life had hurt him. She wanted to make it up to him, to make him feel happy and loved, to make him laugh. She knew she was the only person who could make him smile and laugh. She would devote her life to making him happy, if he would only let her.

It was full spring now, everything bursting with new life. Couples went to Walden Pond to study or to neck under the trees, they drove to Revere Beach to picnic on the sand, they watched the boat races on the Charles River and got drunk. Chris and Alexander continued their chaste library courtship. Annabel told Chris that Alexander got all A's, like she did, that he was an intellectual like she was, and that they were two peas in a pod. Chris realized that people thought of her and Alexander as a couple. But he had never yet said that he cared for her, and while everybody else was enjoying spring Chris was already worrying terribly about summer.

Alexander and Max were planning to drive across country to California. It was Max's dream to see Hollywood. Chris knew that Hollywood was full of would-be starlets, beauty contest winners from all over America, and people in Hollywood didn't care who they went to bed with. It was the land of sunshine and loose morals. Alexander wouldn't be studying for his straight A's this summer. She was sure those two boys were going to have a wild time, and she prayed that Alexander wouldn't fall in love with anybody.

She had already gotten a summer job in New York. Her father, who knew everybody at Columbia, had arranged it for her. She would be filing at the Columbia summer school. It would start two days after the term at Radcliffe ended. It was the only way she could think of to get out of the apartment and away from her drunken mother. She would come home to sleep, that was all. It would be nice to have the extra money too, which would enable her to eat in restaurants and go to movies. She didn't mind eating alone, or going to movies alone. She was a loner at heart. She was the only one of her friends who was going to work this summer, and it made her feel grown-up. She hoped Alexander would write to her, even just a postcard. There was no way she could write to him because he and Max would always be on the road. They didn't know yet where they would stay in Hollywood. Chris knew she would spend the whole summer worrying, and as it happened she did.

She did not receive a single postcard from Alexander all summer. When fall finally came and they were back at college he didn't phone. She was desperate. She couldn't let him just disappear. Although she had signed up for her favorite courses in Medieval History, and one in Comparative Philology that seemed intriguing, she knew she loved him too much to be able to hide in her work and forget him. She had Annabel ask Max what courses Alexander was taking this term, and then she registered for the only one she could fit into her schedule. It was Economics, it was hard, and she hated it.

But she could sit next to Alexander again, and after class they could talk while they walked to their next classes. She told him the course was hard for her and asked him to help her. Her excuse for taking the wretched thing—did he believe her?—was that her father insisted it was good for her to get a well-rounded education. Alexander seemed more flattered than annoyed, and they again resumed their twice-weekly study dates in Widener Library, and their cup of coffee together afterward. He was so beautiful she couldn't stop looking at him. She thought it was a good thing she didn't have to study much to keep her grades, because while he was immersed in his book his nearness made her unable to concentrate at all.

Many times Chris wondered what Alexander saw in her. She wasn't a beauty, she wasn't sweet, she had never been popular. Alone in her room at the dorm she made a list of her good qualities and scrutinized it, as if to find out the answer to this mystery. *I Am*:

Smart, Funny, Well Informed, Honest, Moral, A True Friend. What a ghastly list of qualities! Who could fall in love with a girl like that? But at least she knew she and Alexander were friends. He was at ease with her and he seemed fond of her. He always seemed pleased to be with her. And she worshiped him, which had to have some impact on him.

But she wished so much that he would invite her to a football game. She knew he didn't have much money and tickets were expensive. She also knew that a man like Alexander had too much pride to invite her to the parties after a game without having taken her to the game beforehand. A lot of boys went to the parties stag. Social life was easy for them, not the way it was for girls, who had to wait in their rooms night after night until someone called. She couldn't offer to pay for her own football ticket; nobody did that. She would do anything for Alexander, but he didn't ask her for anything.

Then one Friday afternoon Chris saw Alexander coming out of the subway kiosk in Harvard Square with a small blonde. The girl was wearing a baby blue gabardine suit and carrying a baby blue overnight case to match. She had curly hair and a turned-up nose and looked so cutesy-poo that Chris wanted to smack her. The blonde and Alexander walked as if they knew where they were going, and when they stopped at the curb for a red light the girl turned to him and handed him her overnight case to carry. Chris thought with a mixture of love and jealousy that it was typical of Alexander to forget to carry his date's suitcase for her. Who was that girl? Someone from another college, or maybe from New York. Was she his new girl friend? She was important enough for him to bring her up for the weekend. He doesn't think I'm pretty enough for him, Chris thought despondently. I'm just his old pal.

She had Annabel ask Max about the girl. "She goes to Finch Junior College and Max says she's nobody to worry about," Annabel reported. "It's their first date."

"He asked her to the *game*," Chris said.

"Look, Chris," Annabel said, "why don't you stop waiting for him and start going out? He'll get jealous when he sees you at parties."

"What if I don't see him at parties?"

"The word will get out," Annabel said. "Besides, you might have a good time. Did you ever think of that?"

"I can't go out with a jerk. I'm not a human sacrifice."

"You can get somebody nice. You got Alexander, and he's the most impossible man I ever saw. Nobody ever got anywhere with him but you. If you'd try half as hard with someone else as you did with him you could get a terrific date."

It was easy for Annabel to say, Chris thought. But she knew she had to do something. The next boy who asked her out, even if he was stupid and boring, as long as he was good-looking she would go.

The next boy who asked her out was Richard Caldwell. Chris was in the Briggs Hall living room studying by the fire when Richard came in, looked around, and went over to the girl on Bells.

"Is Daphne Leeds in?"

"Sorry," the girl on Bells said after ringing Daphne's room. "Do you want to leave a message?"

Richard shrugged, put his hands into his pockets, and strolled into the living room. "Hi, Chris," he said, and smiled at her.

He was very good-looking. Not her type, too perfect and blond and conceited-looking, but certainly handsome. Alexander would have to be jealous of Richard Caldwell. "Hi," Chris said.

He stood over her as she sat there on the couch by the fireplace. "Studying hard?"

She smiled and closed her book. "Not really."

"Want to go out and have some coffee?"

She took off her glasses and looked at him. Should

she go out for coffee and look too eager, or should
she take a gamble and play hard to get? Boys like
Richard Caldwell liked girls who were hard to get.
"I don't go out during the week," she said. "I have
too much work."

"You go out with Alexander English."

"We take a course together and we study at night."

"You'd better watch out or you'll turn into a
greasy grind," he said lightly.

Chris picked up a strand of her hair and looked
at it. "I don't think so," she said, in the same ban-
tering tone.

"You do go out on weekends," he said. It seemed
almost as much a question as a statement. Did he
know she never went out?

"If I like him," Chris said.

"Is it true what I hear, that you have a secret lover
stashed away?"

"Not yet," she said.

"Aha!"

"Aha what?"

"Just aha," Richard said. He smiled at her again
and Chris decided he thought his smile was devastating and that was why he smiled so much, not because he was good-natured or because he liked her.
She didn't care; she'd just love Alexander to see Richard Caldwell smiling at her in that appealing way.
"Well," he said, "see ya around."

Chris nodded and put on her reading glasses again.
When he reached the front door he glanced back at
her, but she was already bent over her book.

Two days later Richard Caldwell phoned and asked
Chris to go to the Dartmouth game the following Saturday and the party afterward that was being held
in his house. She accepted.

Annabel was delighted, Daphne was pleased, and
Emily told her it was about time she was doing the
sensible thing. After all, she had met Ken at a party
with Richard Caldwell, and maybe the same thing

would happen to Chris. Nobody understands anything, Chris thought.

Hundreds of happy students were walking down the broad avenue towards Soldiers' Field, where the football stadium was: kicking up the fallen leaves, singing spirited school songs, holding hands, loving being young. At the edge of the avenue men were selling Harvard and Dartmouth pennants, flowers, programs, and other souvenirs. Chris plodded along next to Richard, her throat hurting, feeling unfaithful to Alexander.

They sat on a hard little bench in the stadium, surrounded by fanatics. The football game was excruciatingly boring and Chris was freezing. The people around her kept passing a little flask back and forth and taking gulps of whiskey or something out of it. She refused. She didn't know anything about football and so she had no idea when the game would be over, but it seemed endless. Those fools out on the field would run about two feet and then hurl themselves on top of one another in order to achieve as much mayhem as possible. Who cared? And then when it was over and Harvard won, all the fools in the audience rushed down to the field to tear the goalpost to shreds. They were so excited you'd think it was important. Richard had bought her a big yellow chrysanthemum which Chris pinned to her lapel, and she tried to feel festive since it was her first football game, but all she felt was relief that they could get out of the cold and into a nice warm Harvard house for the party.

The party was held in a suite of rooms in Elliot House, an enormous old building facing the river. Alexander's house! Chris thought the size of the suite palatial. She wondered if Alexander's suite looked like this, with brown doleful-looking furniture and a fireplace. There was a long table set up against one wall of the living room and it was covered with a profusion of bottles: gin, vodka, scotch, rye, bourbon, and mixers. There was also a large glass punch bowl filled with purple liquid and a lump of ice.

"Purple Passion," Richard said, handing her a paper cup full.

She shook her head. "I don't drink. I'd like a Coke, please."

"You don't drink? Why not?"

"I don't feel like it."

"But this is a party," Richard said. "Everybody drinks."

"I don't."

He raised his eyebrows and got a Coke for her. "You ought to loosen up," he said. "You're so serious all the time."

"I'm better when you get to know me," Chris said. She tried to look around the room at the other people without Richard noticing. Could Alexander possibly be here? Would he be with the same girl he had up last weekend? Another girl? Alone?

"I'd like to get to know you," Richard said. He took her arm and steered her to the sofa. The room was full of boys and their dates, everyone making a lot of noise, smoking, drinking, laughing, and apparently having a good time. Since the party had just begun, everyone was still standing up. Chris and Richard sat on the sofa side by side. He pressed her knee with his and she tried to decide if it was on purpose or an accident. She moved her knee away, pretending she had to move around to get a cigarette out of her handbag. Richard smiled and lit her cigarette with a gold lighter.

"What would you like to know about me?" she asked.

"What you're like under that hard little shell."

"I'm sort of an acid-tongued bitch, if you want to know."

"Great! Show me."

"I can't do it on command," Chris said.

He held his cup to her lips. "Have a little Purple Passion. It's just grape juice."

She turned her head away. "And gin."

"You can't taste the gin."

"Let's talk about something else," Chris said.

"Well," Richard said, "let's talk about something that isn't either taboo or boring. Sex—that's taboo for you, I can tell. Am I right?"

"Why would you want to talk about sex?" Chris said.

Richard laughed. "I'd rather do it, but it's a bit crowded here."

"Tell me what you're going to major in," Chris said.

"I don't know yet. Probably English. It's easy."

"What are you going to do when you graduate?" she asked.

"Go into my father's real estate business. This is a boring discussion, do you know that?"

"Not to me," Chris lied.

"I'd rather talk about why you don't drink."

"For the same reason you do drink," she said.

"What's that?"

"It makes me feel grown-up."

A look of anger crossed his face and then he smiled. "You were right; you *are* an acid-tongued bitch."

"I told you," she said. She wanted to leave. She hated this party, all the noise, the drunken yelps from the merrymakers, and this arrogant, handsome boy sitting here trying to manipulate her. But she couldn't just get up and go when the point was to *be* at the damn party. She'd just have to try harder to be pleasant.

Richard seemed to know everybody. Couples and boys who were stag kept coming by and saying hello and then moving on. Richard was making it clear that he wanted her to himself, and Chris couldn't understand why since he didn't seem to like her very much and she didn't like him much either. He was supposed to be one of the best dates around, despite being married, and if he was a sample of the best then she'd obviously not missed very much. She thought about Alexander and felt miserable.

"I'm getting another drink," Richard said. "Stay here and save my seat."

She put her handbag on the vacant space on the couch and sighed with relief. She looked at her watch. Didn't these people ever eat dinner? She was starved. She lit a cigarette and looked around the room. There, by the window, she saw him—Alexander—and her heart jumped. His dark, brooding beauty made her catch her breath. Then the crowd moved a little and she saw the girl. Alexander had his arm flung around the girl's shoulders in a gesture that was both casual and protective, and he was looking down at her. She had dark hair and seemed very vivacious. In one hand she was holding a drink and in the other a golden chrysanthemum, the same as the one Richard had bought Chris at the game. The girl was gesturing with the hand that held the flower, and Alexander was *smiling*.

Richard came back carrying two cups of purple punch and sat down. "Here," he said, holding out one cup. "There aren't any more Cokes. Just taste it, it won't kill you."

Numbly Chris took the cup of punch and sipped at it. It was quite good: sweet and tasting of grape juice. The first sip made her feel a little less choked up and she took another. Just leave me alone, she thought, all of you. I wish I could fly away into the sky and never have to talk to any of you again.

"That's not so bad, is it?" Richard said.

"No. Why don't they play music?"

"They *are* playing music. You just can't hear it over all this din." He put his arm across her shoulders in the same half-casual, half-protective gesture

Alexander had used with his date, and Chris emptied her cup. "Good girl," Richard said. "I'll be back in a jiff."

She sat there waiting for the refill, glad to be alone, and felt her pain growing dimmer. Liquor did help. She thought about her mother, that drunk she'd always resented, and it occurred to her that perhaps her mother had been unhappy too. Was it possible her mother drank to kill some secret pain of her own? How strange . . . Parents were just there, and you wanted them to be like all your friends' parents, but they were human beings underneath, and they had disappointments and frustrations they never talked about. Maybe she should try to be nicer to her mother.

Richard was beside her, his arm around her shoulders again. The cold paper cup was in her hand. She sipped at it. It tasted a little different this time, a little stronger. Maybe that was how the second one tasted. She was feeling relaxed. Richard was talking at her, smiling that smile, looking into her face with that sincere dip of the head he did so well, as if she were the only girl in the room, and she found it very easy to tune him out. Once in a while she smiled at him, looked into his eyes and then looked down. She decided she could get through the whole party this way, perhaps even the whole evening, if she could just stay a little high.

She didn't keep track of how many cups of punch he brought her, but she was aware that he was playing with the tips of her hair with two fingers and then he was playing with her earlobe. She supposed he was planning to try to seduce her. Boys were so stupid. What made Richard Caldwell think that if she was drunk she would want to let him put his hands all over her in some car, or maybe even go all the way—she was drunk but she wasn't unconscious.

He pulled her up to her feet. The party had thinned out quite a bit and now she could hear the music clearly. "Let's dance," he said, and pulled her into his arms, resting his cheek against hers.

Standing and moving were different from just sitting there: the room was going around. Everybody was a blur. Suddenly Chris felt a great wave of nausea rise from her stomach to her throat, and she put both hands over her mouth and rushed, staggering blindly, in the direction of the bathroom. She was bumping into couples, they were moving aside for her, and she rushed into the bathroom in time to throw up all over the sink.

She wanted to die. She fell on her knees on the bathroom floor, her hair soaked with perspiration, tears running out of her eyes, and she knew she was a disgrace and a horror and a pig and everybody knew it. The bathroom door was open in case they had missed anything.

After what seemed endless time she got up and closed it, and then she tried to clean the sink and herself. She glanced into the mirror above the sink and she had never looked uglier. She dabbed at her smeared makeup with water and a filthy-looking towel, and found some mouthwash in the cabinet, which she used. She would walk out and just go home . . . if she could walk.

Someone was knocking on the door. "Just a minute," she called in the meanest voice she could muster, and crept out, holding onto the wall.

It was Max. "Are you all right?" he asked.

She nodded. She looked around the room for Richard.

"Richard's gone," Max said.

"Gone?"

"He said if you wanted to meet him for dinner, he'd be at . . ."

Before Max could finish she started to cry. He was wiping her eyes with a big handkerchief and finding her coat, he was telling some girl he'd be right back, and then he had Chris out in the cold air under the swimming stars. He tucked her into his Stutz Bearcat and started it.

"I don't want to see Richard," Chris sobbed.

"I'm taking you home," Max said calmly. "You get a good night's sleep and you'll just have a hangover in the morning."

"I'm so embarrassed . . ."

"What for? Everybody gets drunk."

Chris wondered if it ran in her family. She'd been right never to have a drink before. Look at what had happened the first time she'd tried. She was a slob and a fool.

"They saw me get sick . . ."

Max laughed. "If you don't get sick at least once at Harvard you're not considered a true *bon vivant*."

"But I'm a *girl!*"

"Girls are always getting sick at parties."

She started to cry harder. "Alexander had another date. Why doesn't he want me?"

"He likes you the best," Max said.

"Why does he go out with those other girls then? And he never asked *me* to a football game . . ."

"Do you want him to be an old monk?"

"Yes! No . . ."

"He's nineteen," Max said. "And so are you. Life is for fun."

Chris put her head on Max's shoulder. She felt perfectly safe doing it; he wouldn't think she was being forward. He was sort of her brother-in-law. Darling Max, he was so nice. Why hadn't she fallen in love with Max instead of Alexander? Why, Chris wondered, do we never fall in love with the nice ones?

When she was safe in her bed at the dorm Chris made a resolution. She had been out with one of the best dates at Harvard and he was a dud. She had been self-destructive getting drunk like that. Obviously social life wasn't for her. She would never go out on another date, unless it was with Alexander. She would make Alexander fall in love with her, no matter how long it took, no matter what she had to do to get him. No one who wanted something as badly as she wanted Alexander could be doomed to failure.

Chapter 9

Daphne thought she had handled her life very well this year, her first at Radcliffe. She had a busy social life with many different men, she enjoyed her courses, especially Fine Arts, and was getting good marks, and most important, she hadn't had even a trace of a seizure. There were even times when she could convince herself that there was nothing wrong with her and that she would never be sick again.

Everyone was cramming like crazy now for final exams. She was sorry she had taken five courses instead of four. You needed five to go out for honors. But at times like this five seemed just too much—she'd been getting only a few hours' sleep the last three nights and she was exhausted. To make matters worse, today she had kitchen duty, which she loathed. The steamy kitchen, the maids telling you what to do, the heavy trays of dishes to be carried, the noise, the slop you had to scrape into those huge disgusting garbage pails, the hissing dishwashing machine disgorging plates too hot to touch, and the constant rush all got on her nerves. She couldn't wait until next year when she could get Bells instead.

"Hurry up, Daphne, we haven't got all day!" Couldn't they see she *was* hurrying? She ran out to the dining room, whisked people's plates away while they still had their forks in their hands, piled all the dishes on her tray and started back.

And then she was standing there with shards of broken crockery all around her on the floor, the steel tray lying under the table where it had slid, and all the girls staring at her in horror. She didn't even remember dropping the tray. She hadn't heard the crash, or the girls' screams.

The maid came out of the kitchen, large, red-faced, and angry. "Are you just going to stand there?" the maid said.

"No, no, of course not," Daphne murmured. She felt a chill of fear, and when she kneeled down to begin gathering up the broken dishes her hands were trembling. Oh God, she'd had a seizure, right in front of everybody!

Chris and Annabel, who were closest, came over to help her. "I was just so startled," Daphne said, to cover for the lost time. She wondered how long she'd been standing there. Not more than a few seconds at most.

"I don't blame you," Annabel said.

"I guess I've been studying too hard," Daphne went on, trying to sound nonchalant, hearing the fright in her voice and hoping they didn't.

"I'll come in and quiz you later, if you want," Chris said. "I don't mind."

"Would you?'

"Sure. It's easier when somebody helps you."

Daphne smiled at her. "Thanks. That would be so nice of you. But . . . make it around nine, okay?" That would give her time to get to the pharmacy on the corner, fill her prescriptions for Dilantin and Tridione, and get back. The seizures couldn't be starting again, she wouldn't let them. She fought back the tears. "I guess I'm just not meant to be a waitress," she said cheerfully.

She hid the vials of pills in the back of her closet,

in the pocket of a jacket she seldom wore. Nobody ever went in there anyway; they were honored just to be invited to her room. Chris helped her all through the rest of exam period, and Daphne thought what a really kind person she was. It wasn't just that Chris's help was saving her health; it was saving her secret. Daphne decided that if the girls at Radcliffe ever found out that she had epilepsy, she would leave. She knew that to go would break her heart, and so she tried not to think about it, but each day had a bittersweet pleasure to it, as if it might be her last.

She came back after a relaxing summer in the country with her family, feeling fine. She hadn't had another seizure all summer, and maybe things were under control again. Her sophomore year was as wonderful as her first had been. And then one winter day Richard Caldwell came back into Briggs Hall like a bad penny, and right into her life.

The girl on Bells told her she had a caller, but didn't say who it was. When Daphne saw Richard standing there in the front hall it was only her good manners that kept her from laughing right in his face.

"Are you sure you haven't made some mistake?" Daphne said to him.

He looked at her with the most innocent and admiring expression. "No. I came to see you."

"*Me?*"

"Yes, you."

She surveyed him coolly and didn't even bother to ask him to come in and sit down. He'd been out with just about everybody, and she wasn't a bit impressed. She'd give him two minutes.

"Do you have a cigarette?" she asked.

He took out a cigarette, put it between his lips, lit it, and handed it to her.

"My, aren't you the sophisticate," Daphne said, amused.

"Daphne, why do you always give me such a hard time?"

"I don't intend to. I'm going back upstairs in a minute to study."

"Could we just go in the living room and sit down?"

"Richard, what is it with you? Are you trying to work your way through the entire dorm?"

He took her by the wrist and led her to a secluded alcove in the living room beside the fireplace. She could have shaken free but she didn't bother. She didn't dislike him, it was just that he was such a child. Men were all children, and so predictable.

They sat down. There was a fire in the fireplace and he looked very golden and pretty in the firelight. She knew why he was so conceited; women must have been falling in love with him all his life.

"I'm not working my way through the entire dorm," he said, sounding wounded. "You were always the one I wanted. But you would never go out with me."

"Then why did you come over tonight?" she asked.

"Because I wanted to ask you why you don't like me."

"I don't dislike you, Richard."

"Then why won't you go out with me? I've been trying for almost two years."

Daphne smiled. "It seems pointless. I don't go out with married men."

"I won't be married much longer. You know that. Everybody knows that."

"Poor Richard—it's a very sad story, your little marriage. But I really don't hold it against you anymore. I know you'll be divorced one of these days."

He looked at her with a sincere, pleading intensity. "Will you go out with me Saturday night?"

Daphne laughed. "Lucky me—my turn at last."

"I told you, you were always the one I wanted. Just you. You're the Golden Girl. You're perfect."

"Did you tell that to Chris and Emily and Annabel too?"

"Chris is so stiff I felt sorry for her," Richard said.

"I just tried to loosen her up a little. It was nothing. I only took her out once."

"Mmm."

"Well, you can't be angry about Emily!" Richard said. "I came over looking for anybody, just to make you jealous. I wanted a pretty girl to take to that party because you were there. I mean . . . Emily! I can't even remember what we talked about. I never took her out again."

"You took Annabel out a great deal."

Richard looked at her with genuine surprise. "You're not counting Annabel as a date?"

"Well, what else?"

"Oh, for God's sake, *Annabel*," he said. "Everybody knows about Annabel. That was just for a couple of quickies."

Everything she'd suspected about Annabel was true! She looked away, not wanting him to see how embarrassed she was, trying to pretend she could take such things as casually as he evidently did. But she knew she was blushing.

"I'm only human," he said. "I mean, everybody does it with Annabel. I thought you knew."

"I don't gossip," she said.

"I know you don't." He took out his handkerchief and wiped his upper lip. He was nervous. She was making him nervous. It rather pleased her, and made up for the way he'd shocked her about Annabel. "Daphne, please go out with me Saturday night. I'll take you anywhere you want to go. Just the two of us—we'll talk and get to know each other. I'm not so bad."

She was surprised to see him so contrite and humbled, begging her to let him have a chance. She'd always thought of Richard Caldwell as conceited, immature, and spoiled. Maybe she'd been unfair. Some people thought she was conceited and spoiled too until they got to know her; her first appearances were so superficial.

"All right," she said. "You can take me to dinner."

A dazzling smile lit up his whole face. "You'll see," he said. "I'm not so bad. I'm really not."

When he left she went upstairs and got her cigarettes. But when she came outside her room to light up there was Annabel sitting on the floor outside her own room, smoking. It was something they'd both done perhaps a thousand times since they'd met, but this time Daphne couldn't meet Annabel's eyes and couldn't bring herself to sit down next to her.

"Who was your caller?" Annabel asked.

"Oh, nobody," Daphne murmured, and went down the hall to the smoker.

There was another girl in the smoker, Helen Peabody, who wasn't really a close friend of Daphne's but was someone Daphne knew was a virgin too and would understand. She had to tell somebody.

"I just heard something so awful," Daphne said, and sighed.

"What?" asked Helen, bright and alert for disaster.

"Annabel Jones is the Harvard whore."

The revelation was all over the dorm in a day. Helen told her two best friends, who told their two best friends, and suddenly no one in the dorm would go near Annabel, except for Chris. When Daphne saw what had happened she regretted it. She wasn't a spiteful person, and it had never occurred to her that people would treat Annabel so badly. But she didn't know what to do. She certainly couldn't admit she had been the first one to tell. But she couldn't bring herself to go back to being friends with Annabel either, not right now.

What really sealed their breach was when Daphne went out with Richard Caldwell and he turned out to be as nice, charming, and interesting a date as she could wish for. He told her all about himself and she realized they had so many things in common she felt as if she had come home. It was as if they had known each other all their lives. She was sorry Rich-

ard hadn't met her before he got involved with that
waitress, because maybe then he might have controlled
himself. Daphne really liked him. She was sorry she
had been mean to him, and she thought it was generous of him to forgive her. And it was on their third
date together that Daphne discovered something about
herself and Richard together that was different from
anything that had ever happened to her before.

Richard made her like sex.

On their first two dates he didn't even try to kiss
her goodnight. He always treated her as if she were
a little bit better than he was; an attitude that was
smarmy in other men, but in him seemed unexpected
and flattering. He was the only man she had ever
danced with who had the good grace to hold her away
slightly when he got an erection, instead of staying
there for a cheap thrill. He didn't do it as if he was
embarrassed, he did it to spare her embarrassment.
And because he was always such a gentleman it piqued
her curiosity. She wondered what he would be like
when he decided to make his first move.

After their third date he pulled the Jag into the
parking space on the side of her dorm instead of
taking her right to the door. It was twelve fifteen.
Daphne felt a gentle fluttering in her stomach. Forty-
five minutes was a very long time.

The car radio was playing an Elvis Presley song,
softly. "Don't be cruel, to a heart that's true. . . ."
She had never liked Elvis Presley before, but now his
deep raunchy voice seemed more sensual than vulgar.
Richard touched her hair, very lightly, and then he
touched her lips, and then her cheek.

"You're so beautiful," he said.

She didn't say anything. He put his arms around
her and kissed her without opening his mouth until
she relaxed, and then he opened his lips and she
opened hers. He put his hand on her breast, over her
coat, and then after a few moments he slipped it under her coat and under the top of her scooped-neck

dress, into her bra. She couldn't breathe. Her nipple
hardened under his fingers and she felt a strange sensation between her legs. She wanted to stop him . . .
she was afraid he would stop. She heard his breathing
quicken but he didn't pant or gasp or make any ugly
noises, and he still kept kissing her. Then he had his
hand under her dress and into her pants. She knew
she had to stop him now, but the waves of sensation
his fingers were causing her were new and strangely
irresistible. She didn't want to be this excited; she
was afraid. They were in the two bucket seats of his
little two-seater car with the gear shift in between
them, so her virtue was perfectly safe. But she suddenly wanted to be lying with him, she who never
wanted anyone to touch her at all!

He hooked his fingers around the elastic of her
pants and pulled them down. She pulled them up.
He went back to doing what he had been doing and
the second time he pulled her pants down she let
him, because what could he do in that car? The combination of his warm fingers and the cool air on her
skin was very sensual. There was something obscenely
exciting about half lying in the seat with her camel's
hair polo coat on and her skirt pulled up and her
pants off. He was trapped behind his steering wheel
and floor shift. She kept expecting him to grab her
hand and put it on himself, or open his fly, but he
didn't, and she realized that for some reason all of
this sex wasn't to get her to do something for him
but because he wanted to make her feel this pleasure.
He was very gentle and slow and persistent.

She had read everything she could find about or-
gasms but she still had difficulty figuring out what
they were like: all she knew was that they were something like a seizure, and she was terrified that if she
ever had one it would bring a seizure on. How could
you ask your doctor about a thing like that? And
while she was thinking this the sensation Richard's
fingers were giving her grew until she thought if he

stopped she would die. She felt herself melting away. Was *this* what it was all about, this feeling that was almost like pain? She began to tremble and then she heard someone groan, and she knew it was herself, but she didn't care anymore; and she was there, she was conscious, she was safe.

The news went on the radio indicating that it was five minutes before the hour. Daphne moved away from Richard, stunned, and pulled up her pants. She was all wet. Her mouth felt bruised. She was embarrassed. She had acted like an animal and she wondered if he would still respect her.

"I love you, Daphne," he said.

She sighed with relief.

He walked her to the front door, past all the couples pasted together in last-minute embraces. Richard put his arms around her and she hugged him back and put her head against his chest. It was so good to be held by him. The poor thing still had his erection. She had heard horror stories about what happened to men who went back to their houses with hard-ons. They called it Blue Balls. She hoped fervently that nothing bad would happen to Richard.

"I love you," he whispered in her ear. "Do you think you could love me?"

She nodded against his chest.

"Don't go out with anybody but me," he whispered. "Please?"

"Okay."

"I'll come over tomorrow night, all right?"

"Yes."

After that Daphne and Richard began to go together, and everyone knew they were radiantly in love. But after that first night a strange thing happened: Daphne, who had never been jealous of anyone in her life, began to really dislike Annabel. She wondered if Annabel had taught Richard all these things. Annabel had done all this and more with

Richard, and Daphne resented it. Even though she knew none of it had mattered to Richard, she could hardly bring herself to say a civil word to Annabel ever again.

Chapter 10

Richard's feelings alternated between joy at having won Daphne and fury and fear when he thought about Hope. Despite what he told everyone, Hope was as adamant in refusing the divorce as she had ever been, and now, in their junior year, Daphne wouldn't go steady with him anymore, even though she loved him, because he was still married. In English class Richard was reading Theodore Dreiser's *An American Tragedy*, and he felt it was in many ways his own story. He wished he had killed Hope, drowned her the way the hero had killed that bitch in the book. But unfortunately, Hope could swim, and perhaps more unfortunately, Richard was not capable of murder. In his heart he killed Hope a hundred times, but in real life he was as helpless as anyone else.

Daphne would see him only twice a week. It was torture. She had gradually become unafraid and even tender with him, and more eager and passionate than he had expected, but she was as strong as iron about her future. Of course she wouldn't go all the way, and he didn't pursue the issue. He wanted to marry her. He adored and respected her; she was precious, he wanted to spend his life with her and have lots of children. The three-year-old boy he'd had with Hope had no reality to him anymore except as another obstacle.

"Please," Richard begged his father, "please make Hope divorce me! You've met Daphne—how can I let a girl like her get away?"

His father smiled. "Richard, I can't *make* Hope do anything she doesn't want to. Your mother and I would be delighted if someday it works out for you and Daphne. But you know, we pay for our sins long before we go to hell . . . if there is such a place."

"There is," Richard said. "And it's here."

Chapter 11

Senior year they were all suddenly close to reality. It was their last chance to keep the promises they had made to themselves when they entered college. For some of them, the promises had changed. The Harvard men sharpened up their skills to get employment in what was called the "rat race." Most of the Radcliffe girls knew senior year was their deadline to find husbands or to cement their relationships with the men they had already chosen. The Dean of Women, in a landmark speech, said it was possible to combine a career with being a wife and mother. But everyone knew how hard it would be. Men had careers, girls had jobs. A girl worked to kill time, to have a brief adventure—or she worked if there was nothing else, if she was poor and had no man. But marriage and children was serious living, and so senior year was serious business. It was frightening out there in the world, and very few girls wanted to have to try it all alone.

After the disgraceful evening in sophomore year when Chris had gone out with Richard Caldwell and thrown up at the party, by some miracle Alexander started taking her to football games. During Christmas vacation he didn't date her in New York because he was invited to all the coming-out parties, but he continued to see her at school. He spent summers in Cuernavaca with his mother. His parents shared their vacation house at different times as a condition of their divorce, and his mother got it in the summer when it was even hotter and more unpleasant in Mexico than it was in New York. Boys never invited girls to visit their families during the summer. Alexander invited Max.

But Chris was making progress. During Easter vacation of their junior year she saw Alexander in New York for the first time. He took her out four times, to two movies, two museums, and a whole afternoon uptown exploring medieval art at the Cloisters. And he brought her home to meet his mother—the greatest triumph of all. His apartment was rather shabby, but homey, and his mother seemed delighted to meet her.

One day Alexander pointed out a five-story white marble building on a tree-lined street in the East Sixties and said, "My father lives there. I never see him."

"My God, it looks like the Frick Museum," Chris said.

"Mausoleum," he said.

Alexander had spaces in him that were secret and mysterious. Other people had spaces, but they filled them with meaningless chatter. He never did, so Chris had to fill his spaces herself with her fantasies.

She loved Alexander so much, and now it was the beginning of their senior year, their last year together, and she didn't know what would happen. She was going out for honors, and would be writing her thesis on "The Romantic Ideal in Medieval Chivalry." The idea appealed to her because it reminded her of the way Alexander treated her. He would have been a perfect medieval knight. He never did more than kiss her goodnight. It drove her crazy and she hated it.

"Annabel," she asked during one of their late night

private talks, "how am I going to get Alexander to make a real pass at me?"

"How real?" Annabel asked.

"I'd go all the way if he wanted to," Chris said calmly. "I love him."

Annabel looked surprised. "Does he love you?"

"He never said, but I think he does."

"You never discuss *love*?"

"Of course not. I don't want to scare him away."

"If you two aren't the limit," Annabel said. "You act like my grandparents. I don't understand you two at all."

"Do you think I do?" Chris said.

"Well, I'll tell you exactly what to do," Annabel said. "If he ever tries to get you up to his room, you just go. He'll take care of everything else after that."

How the hell was she ever going to get him to ask her to his room? *Alexander?* And then one Saturday night after the football season was over, with no warning, he did. They had been to see an old Humphrey Bogart movie at the University Theater in Harvard Square, and afterward had stopped for coffee at the Bick. Instead of turning to the left to walk her back to her dorm, he turned to the right.

"Come on up to the house," he said casually, as if he were inviting her to a party. But she knew there were no parties. It was a very quiet weekend. Max had gone to New York to be one of the ushers at a relative's wedding, and Alexander had the room to himself. "It's early," he said.

Her heart turned over. She wouldn't have cared if it was ten minutes to one. She would have gone, and worried about the consequences later. "I've always wanted to see your room," she said, just as casually.

"Well, now you will."

They walked quickly through the cold night. Chris was shivering, partly from the wind but mostly from fear. She'd read everything about how to do it, but reading and doing were two different things. She

would just let him take care of everything, as Annabel had advised, and pray she wasn't too awful at it.
Alexander was whistling tunelessly through his teeth
and she wondered if he was nervous too. Maybe he
wasn't planning to make a pass at all. Maybe he
thought she would back out when they got there.
Girls did that. She knew how shy he was and she
wanted to make him feel sure of her, but she didn't
know how without seeming forward. She wanted him
so much. When he finally reached out and took her
hand she breathed a sigh of relief, and gave his hand
a reassuring squeeze to tell him: *I'm coming to your
room; I won't give you a hard time, I love you.*

All the Harvard houses looked alike to her: big,
dignified, unapproachable. Rows and rows of lighted
windows, behind which men were doing all the things
girls knew nothing about. Whatever men did, whether
having conversations with each other, or alone with
their own thoughts, was a closed world. The room
Alexander and Max shared was really a suite consist-
ing of a living room, a smaller bedroom, and a bathroom. The living room had their desks in it, and
the bedroom had two single beds and two dressers.
The furniture was standard drab college issue. Alexander hung their coats in the closet and took off his
jacket and tie. He hung his jacket over the back of
one of the desk chairs and tossed his tie on the desk.
Chris pretended to be very interested in the marble
mantelpiece and the pictures hanging over it. One
was an etching of a clipper ship, and the other was
a class picture taken during Alexander's senior year
at prep school.

"Which one is you?" she asked.

He came up behind her. "See if you can guess."

How could she pick out one tiny face from a group
photo, much less think at all, with him behind her
and his breath on her neck? She finally found the
one, a younger, more vulnerable Alexander, and she
pointed at it. "There."

Alexander kissed the back of her neck, a gesture she found so sexy and romantic that she could hardly breathe. He put his arms around her. She knew he could feel her heart pounding because it was crashing so hard. He turned her around until she was facing him and then he kissed her, but this time for the first time he put his tongue into her mouth. Chris put her arms around his neck and felt herself dissolving into him as if they were one person. She opened her eyes and saw the familiar line of his cheek and his long black eyelashes, the face she had desired for all these years. Oh, I love you, I love you, please love me, she thought.

He moved out of their kiss and took her hand, and then he led her to the bedroom. She lay on one of the beds and Alexander lay on top of her, both of them still fully clothed, and they kissed some more, and she could feel that he was aroused. He moved off her and ran his hand over her breasts. She kept thinking they were too small and hoping he didn't mind. It was so wonderful to feel him touching her at last that she wished he would keep doing it for hours. She didn't know what to do next. If she took off her clothes it would be too pushy. Should she wait for him to do it? There was no way for him to pull her sweater over her head in a romantic way. She'd just have to do it herself, but when?

"You know how much I care for you," he whispered. It was the closest he had ever come to a declaration of love, and Chris began to tremble again. "I do . . ."

"Oh, I do too," she whispered.

He had his arms around her and was kissing her neck, and Chris could feel that he was trembling too. He was just as nervous as she was! She felt such a rush of love for him that she reached for the zipper of her skirt and unzipped it, wriggled out of it, and dropped it to the floor beside the bed. She would have to sit up and push him away to get her sweater off, and she'd sooner kill herself. Neither of them said a word. He buried his face in her shoulder and put his fingers between her legs for an instant and then he turned away and took off his pants. Chris yanked off her sweater and slip and bra and underpants, tangled in them, frantic not to break the mood. He rolled on top of her again with a full erection and tried to enter her.

It hurt like hell. She closed her eyes and prayed that he would be able to do it, that she wouldn't be a failure at this too and ruin her life forever. She knew then that he was inside because it hurt so much and because he was moving up and down. She opened her eyes again and looked up at that face she adored. His eyes were closed and he looked as if he were hypnotized with pleasure. She suddenly felt a great power over him. *She* could give him this much pleasure. *She!*

It was all over in less than a minute. Alexander rolled off her and continued to hold her in his arms, his head on her shoulder. She covered the top of his head with tiny kisses.

"You are wonderful," he whispered. "You are so wonderful."

She thought she would die of joy.

Alexander held her for a long time and then he got up and went into the bathroom. She heard water running. She sat up and inspected herself. They had made an icky mess on the bedspread, and she looked for something to wipe it up with so he wouldn't be annoyed. When she stood up there was more of the icky mess running down the insides of her legs. But she told herself guiltily that it was beautiful because it was Alexander's. She was glad when he came out of the bathroom and she could go in and wash up. So this was sex, the dreaded and worshiped act she and her friends had thought about and talked about ever since they were twelve years old. For this, Annabel had become the dorm pariah. For this, Richard Caldwell was trapped in a loveless marriage and unable to propose to Daphne, who adored him and was suffering. Did Emily and Ken do this in his room, even though Emily swore they didn't? Was this supposed to bind Alexander to her as a love slave, forever? It all seemed ludicrous. But on the other hand, he had been so romantic . . . the kissing, the touching, and what he had said. *You know how much I care for you. You are wonderful. You are so wonderful.* She replayed the lines in her head and she knew everything would be all right. The first time was always said to be strained.

Alexander held her hand the whole time they walked back to her dorm. When he kissed her goodnight at the front door his kiss was a real kiss. Chris could feel a different warmth in him.

"I'll call you tomorrow," he said.

When she was alone in her room, in her bed, she went over every instant of their mutual seduction again and again. She wanted to take as much responsibility as he had. It made her feel womanly to feel that she had managed to arouse him so much that he had finally gone to bed with her. She had gone past the last barrier. He had to love her now.

The next day she told Annabel, who was delighted. She didn't give Annabel any of the details because they were private, but when Annabel asked if Alexander had been prepared Chris realized she hadn't even thought about it. Annabel was horrified.

"Promise me you'll make him use something," Annabel said.

But Chris didn't have to worry, because the next time she had a real date with Alexander, not just a mid-week study date, was the following Saturday night, and he had bought some condoms. The condoms made it hurt even worse than the first time. But as the Saturday nights went on, she and Alexander grew comfortable together. It didn't hurt anymore, and she began to like it. But what she liked the best was when he held her afterward and said sweet things to her, kissed and nuzzled her, and put his head on her shoulder. It was the only time that Alexander was ever sweet. He seemed to be relieved of whatever pain gave him such an unhappy look the rest of the time, and his mouth curved in a soft and gentle smile. As for herself, she understood the legend men passed around that once a woman had sex she was hooked. This closeness was just what she had dreamed about all those years waiting for Alexander to make his move.

Chapter 12

Ken was doing very well in his first year at Harvard Medical School. He and Emily talked about "when we're married" quite often, but he had never yet proposed formally, and she wondered when he would. It was her senior year already, but still she didn't think it was her place to suggest that firm plans were in order. She guessed one day he would just take her to Tiffany's for a ring—or God forbid to some wholesale diamond place because his mother thought it was practical. Or maybe there was some heirloom diamond lying around in his family's bank vault. She thought it was venal to discuss her engagement ring with him, although she thought about it often and changed her mind even more often about what shape diamond she would like.

Ken took her home with him for the weekend for his parents' twenty-fifth anniversary party. Emily liked Ken's parents most of the time and felt at home with them. They were very much like her own. She knew his parents felt that she was a satisfactory catch, even a good catch, for their precious son, and they always treated her like an almost-member of the family.

She and Ken drove back in one of his parents' cars,

which they had lent Ken for the rest of the term. "Do you know what my mother said?" Ken asked, sounding quite pleased. "She said when we're married she's going to give us a set of dishes exactly like hers."

For the first time in all the years with Ken, Emily was dismayed. "You mean those dishes with all the gold paint on them?"

"Gold leaf," he corrected her.

"But Ken, they're so dressy! And sort of . . . middle-aged dishes. We're young. Don't you want us to pick out what *we* want?"

"You told my mother you liked those dishes," he said.

"Well, I had to be polite, didn't I?"

They rode for a while in silence. "Don't be mad," they both said, finally, in unison, and then they laughed.

"I guess I can stand them," Emily said.

"They're just for parties," Ken said. "My mother says they're very expensive, and she says since she and Dad plan to leave theirs to us when they die, they'll match ours."

Emily couldn't imagine his parents growing old and dying. She couldn't even imagine herself giving formal parties with those gold leaf dishes. When she pictured herself married to Ken they were always young. That is, if they got around to being married while they *were* still young.

"When are we getting married?" she said.

"How about right after Labor Day?" he said.

"Don't you want to get married in June?" Emily said.

"Well," Ken said, "the thing is, my parents just told me they're going to give me a trip to Europe this summer. I'm going to sail as soon as the spring term is over, and go to France and England and Scotland, and then come back the third week in August."

"You're going to *Europe?*"

"It will be my last fling before we get married," he said mildly. "Med school will be even harder next year, and then I'll be interning, and then residency, and then trying to set up a practice—I don't know when I'll ever be able to have a real vacation again."

Emily was appalled. "But we could get married right after I graduate, and then they could send us both to Europe for our honeymoon. My parents would pay for my half. What's the matter with your parents, don't they like me?"

"Of course they do. They love you."

"Then why are they sending you away to Europe?" She was trying not to cry.

"You have to make all the plans for the wedding," Ken said. "You have to decorate our apartment, and you have to buy a trousseau."

"I could buy a trousseau in Europe."

"What's the matter with you, Emily?" he asked. "What are you getting so irritable about?"

"Don't you want to decorate our apartment with me?"

"We already decided on Danish modern," Ken said. "And white walls."

"You want me to do the whole thing with my mother and then you'll just unpack and move right in."

"But that's what everybody does."

"We're not like Everybody," Emily said. "We're special."

"Of course we are," Ken said. He took his hand off the steering wheel and patted her knee. "We each always understand the other's needs. Don't I always encourage you when you say you want to work? Don't I tell you you'll get accepted at grad school? Do I insist we have children right away?"

"No . . ."

"Well, then, if I want to go to Europe and have a last fling before I settle down, you have to understand."

She thought about it. She didn't understand. What was he going to do in Europe—go to a French whorehouse to find out how to act on their wedding night? He would date other girls, she just knew it. He would meet them, and they would chase him, and he would take them out. She bit her lip. If she made a big fuss he would think she was a shrew and then he wouldn't want to marry her at all. He'd think she was going to turn out to be a henpecking wife. She'd better just keep her mouth shut.

"I guess a lifetime with just one woman must seem . . ."

"What?" he asked.

"Nothing. Never mind."

"Seem boring? Are you kidding? I *want* to spend my life with you, Emily."

"I want to spend mine with you, Ken."

"So what are we arguing about?"

"Nothing, I guess."

"Do you think I'm being unfair?" he asked.

Of course I do! she wanted to scream. Unfair and selfish, and I hate your parents and I hate you too! "No," Emily said. "Do you think I am?"

"You're never unfair," Ken said. "One of the reasons why I love you is that you're so understanding and feminine. It's as if you can read my mind. I could never be happy with anybody else. I'm very lucky that I found you, Emily."

"I'm lucky I found you too, Ken."

She put her head on his shoulder, and he turned on the car radio to play romantic music. The discussion was over. He put his arm around her. The station was playing the big hit song, "Around the World in Eighty Days." "Around the world I searched for you . . ." sang the vocalist. What an ironic song to be playing just now, Emily thought. Oh, shit, piss, hell.

She hated it when Ken drove with one hand on the

wheel; she always thought they were going to be killed. But this .time she didn't say anything. She cuddled up closer to him, being understanding and feminine, and scared to death.

Chapter 13

That fall, her last at Radcliffe, Annabel was dating a tall, rather Lincolnesque law student named Bill Wood. She had stopped going out with anyone else, and she felt it was real love at last. The other men she'd had crushes on had all been silly boys, but Bill was an older man, and brilliant, capable of doing great things. Because he was at the Harvard Law School he didn't know any of the gossip that had followed her into each romance with the Harvard undergraduates, and he seemed worldly enough to be able to handle it if he should ever find out. Bill had to work so hard at law school that he couldn't see her every night, but he always called, and she preferred waiting for his call to spending an evening with someone who didn't mean anything.

But now, just when she was so happy, the terrible thing all the girls feared seemed about to happen to her. Her periods had always been regular, but now it was thirty-five days and nothing. She kept running to the bathroom to look. She had tried many hot baths, and jumping up and down, but with no luck. She didn't even know where to get a rabbit test. At some hospital? Nobody she knew went to a gynecologist until she was about to get married. Then the doctor would give her her first examination and fit her with a small size diaphragm, to be exchanged for a larger one a month or so after the honeymoon. Annabel knew if she was pregnant she would have to get an abortion, and she didn't have the faintest idea of how to go about finding someone. She certainly wasn't going to let some back-alley butcher kill her, but on the other hand it cost a lot of money to go to Puerto Rico to have it done.

"Chris," Annabel said, "do you know the name of your mother's gynecologist in New York?"

"I don't know if she even has one. Why?" Chris suddenly looked stricken. "Annabel, you're not in trouble?"

"I think so. I'm a week late. I heard they have shots to bring on your period. I had an aunt once who had them."

"Well, why don't you go to her doctor?"

"Back home? Are you kidding? I'd be disgraced forever."

"Oh, Annabel . . . did you tell Bill?"

"No. And I don't intend to."

"But maybe he'd marry you," Chris said.

"I don't want anyone to marry me out of pity," Annabel said.

"But he loves you!"

"And I'm going to keep it that way," Annabel said grimly.

Trouble. That was what they called it, and they worried about it all the time. No one could really prove you had had sex, but if you got pregnant they could, and you were branded.

"Listen," Chris said, "if you got two doctors to swear you were going to go insane, maybe you could get a real doctor to give you an abortion."

"What should I do—slit my wrists and drink Lysol?"

"Oh, no! Annabel, you wouldn't?"

"I meant pretend," Annabel said. "I could do a great fake suicide scene."

They sat there in silence and misery, looking at each other.

"A week late isn't so much," Chris said finally.

"Not to you it isn't."

"Why don't you look up a doctor in the phone book?" Chris said. "I'll go with you. We can buy a wedding ring in the five-and-ten. And after you have your rabbit test maybe you'll find out you aren't pregnant at all."

"How am I going to know he's a gynecologist? I'll just have to ask somebody else."

"Who?"

"Well, not any evil prig in this dorm," Annabel said. "I'll ask Max. Max can find out anything. And he can lend me the money too if I need it. Max has loads of money."

"You would really tell Max?"

"Why not? Max doesn't shock easily."

"I don't know," Chris said sadly. "I just always hoped . . . I guess it's silly . . . but I wish you and Max would fall in love and get married. But if you tell him . . ."

Annabel told him. She asked Max to drive her out to the country to Walden Pond, where they could be alone and nobody could eavesdrop, and she told him.

"I think I'm pregnant."

Max picked up a stick and broke it into little neat pieces. He piled the little pieces into a neat heap. Then he looked at her.

"Will you marry me?" he said.

She was astonished. "You want to marry me?"

He looked very earnest, his golden faun's eyes catching the last rays of the sun. "We get along better than any two people I know," he said. "We really care about each other. And if it didn't work out, we could each go our own way and we'd still be best friends."

"You mean, get divorced."

"No, I mean we could . . . I mean, you could have a lover, or I might meet somebody . . ."

"Max, that's not a marriage! I don't want to ruin your life for my mess. It was really dear of you to offer, but I couldn't."

"It's Bill, isn't it. You love Bill."

"I do love him," Annabel said. "But I love you, too. I won't let anybody marry me to *save* me."

"What can I do then?"

"You could lend me some money, and you could ask some of those men who are always bragging about how sophisticated they are if they know the names of any good abortionists in Puerto Rico who won't kill me. And I will be grateful to you for the rest of my life."

"All right," Max said. "I'll lend you as much as you need. Are you going to tell Bill?"

"Of course not."

He looked annoyed. "You won't tell Bill, but you'd marry him afterward, wouldn't you?"

"I don't know. He might not want to marry me anyway."

"But you might."

"All right, I might."

"Well, what kind of a marriage do you think that would be?" Max said. "At least you and I would be honest."

"I don't know if I want to be that honest," Annabel said. "It has to be romantic too, you know."

"I just wish you were tougher, Annabel."

"Oh, I'd hate that, Max. And you would too." She hugged him and he hugged her back. "Do you know what I'm going to do just as soon as all this is over?"

"What?"

"I'm going to get a diaphragm," Annabel said. "You just can't trust men."

During the next two days, while she was waiting for either her period to begin or Max to give her what she needed to take some action, she thought a lot about her life. Bill was handsome and gentle, he spoke slowly and wisely, and he reminded her of Jimmy Stewart. He came from Indiana, but she thought she might be able to enjoy living in a place so alien since she had been able to adjust to Cambridge. He wanted to be a trial lawyer. Someday, when they were both much older, he might become a judge, and she would be a good wife for him, keeping his home life full of fun and keeping him from getting too serious or working too hard for his health. It was time for her to settle down. Bill Wood was someone who always made her feel she was capable of important things herself, just because he had chosen her. If she could get him to propose to her eventually, she would accept.

The night she made this decision she went out with Bill, and after they had finished making love in his room she looked down and saw a small stain of blood on the sheet. She began to laugh hysterically with relief, and Bill, thinking she was embarrassed, tried to reassure her it was all right. She rushed into his bathroom and found that God had rewarded her for deciding to reform. Her decision to marry Bill was blessed. She had been given a sign, and everything would be wonderful from now on.

That spring Annabel and Bill became engaged. He gave her an engagement ring with a small round diamond set in yellow gold in an antique setting. She began to use her hands a great deal when she spoke, and often sat in a pensive attitude, her fingers on her chin, so that her ring would catch the light. The girls in the dorm didn't like her any better now that she was respectable; in fact they disliked her more, and she knew it. The ones who weren't engaged yet were thinking: Why the Harvard whore and not me? It went against everything they had ever been taught. Every time she flashed her little diamond at them Annabel smiled inside.

Bill thought it was sensible when she began to use her newly acquired diaphragm. They agreed that after he was established in his practice they would have not less than two and not more than four children. Bill was crazy about children and animals. He wanted to have a house with a lot of land, where he and Annabel, and eventually their kids, could ride horses. His family was well off, but not rich, not nearly as rich as Annabel's. He would have to become a success to afford all this. He thought he would be a good trial lawyer because there was a little of the actor in him. He was not unaware of his resemblance to Jimmy Stewart. Annabel was sure that he would be wildly successful and make a lot of money, and told him so all the time.

She introduced Bill to Max, and the three of them went out drinking together and had a hilarious time. She made sure that Bill understood that Max was her best friend and not her ex-boyfriend. She didn't want any jealousy. As for Max, he was never jealous of Bill, only pleased that she was so happy.

She was happier than she had ever been in her life. Now that she had someone to lavish all her affection on she blossomed. She sent a sweet letter to Bill's parents saying how much she was looking forward to meeting them and how glad she was that she was going to be a member of their family. She said she knew she'd love them because people who had brought up such a lovely son had to be wonderful people. After she mailed the letter she worried that perhaps it had sounded too smarmy. When Bill's mother wrote back thanking her for the note and saying they too were looking forward to their meeting, Annabel felt relieved. She thought Bill's mother's note was a little formal, but perhaps midwesterners were different from southerners.

Her own parents were delighted. They were only sorry that Annabel was not going to marry an Atlanta man and stay home, but they understood. After graduation Bill would come home to visit her and there would be all sorts of parties. He would be graduating from law school this June too, and they planned to be married in September and go to some romantic place like Venice for their honeymoon.

Of course their European trip would have to include Paris, because Max was going there after graduation to spend a whole year, and he could take them around to all the places that were fun. Max would be a Parisian by September, and she and Bill would be tourists!

Her routine with Bill continued the same after their engagement as before. He had so much work to do. Annabel thought with a twinge of regret that he would always be busy, and that no matter how much you loved a man you could never be with him as much as you wanted to unless you married a playboy. But who wanted a playboy? She wanted a man she could respect and look up to, whose life made her proud. Bill was an ambitious man, but he was also a loving one. She thought he was probably perfect.

Chapter 14

In her senior year Daphne began to make decisions which only a year or two before she would have considered unthinkable. She started to go steady with Richard again, even though he was still married. She realized that she loved him too much to play games, or to pretend to herself she could find someone to replace him. She didn't know what would happen when they graduated; the one thing she was sure of was that there would be social and family pressures on her either to marry him or get rid of him. This was her last chance, and she wanted to be with him as much as she could.

Some of the girls were starting to sleep with the men they were engaged to. They didn't talk about it, but she could guess, even though there were other girls who wouldn't believe it if they *had* told. And there was wild Annabel, who had managed to become engaged to Bill Wood, who was a good catch and no dummy. A lot of things were shaking up their world this year.

For several months Daphne had been thinking seriously about going all the way with Richard. She wanted him desperately, and at night she had nightmares about The Waitress that made her wake up in angry tears. As long as Richard was stuck in this impossible trap, Daphne wanted at least to have as much of him as possible. She knew he really loved her and that he would still respect her afterward. When she told Richard that she had made up her mind he was very touched. He took care that the first time was neither frightening nor unpleasant. He was a very skilled lover, and Daphne enjoyed losing her virginity more than she had ever dreamed. After that they became very good together. She knew she had made the right decision; they were one person now.

They made love in his room as often as possible. They could never get enough of each other, and Daphne realized she would never be able to give him up, even if Hope didn't divorce him for years. But as graduation grew near, Richard started to act peculiar. He became possessive and nervous, as if she were going to fly away. She realized it was he who was afraid of being jilted. He knew when they both graduated and went back to live with their parents he would begin to look like the villain again.

One night after they had made love Daphne saw that Richard had tears in his eyelashes. She could hardly believe it. Men never cried in front of anyone. She held him in her arms and kissed his cheeks, his eyelids, tasting the salt tears.

"What, darling, what?" she whispered. "Please tell me."

"I can't give you anything," he said. "The things you want—marriage, a home, kids—I know you want that. I'm so afraid I'll lose you."

"We'll have that some day," Daphne said.

"You know how much I want to marry you."

"I know," she said.

"Your friends will get married and you'll start to hate me."

Daphne smiled. "No, I'll hate them. That's a joke; come on, smile. I'm going to be with you."

"It's different out there," Richard said miserably.

"I know," Daphne said. "And I have it all planned." She had been thinking about this too, and now she was sure she had made the right choice, even though it meant taking an extraordinary step. "You'll get an apartment in Greenwich Village, and I'll live with you."

He sat up and stared at her in astonishment. "You'd live with me?"

"Yes," she said calmly. "And I'll get a job in an art gallery and we'll have a perfectly normal life. Peope can do anything they want to in Greenwich Village."

He hugged her so hard she couldn't breathe. He was laughing now, with happiness and relief. "Oh, Daphne! You are a wonder!"

"Hey, you're smothering me, Richard."

He loosened his grip. "I'm sorry. I'll never do anything to hurt you, you know that, don't you?"

"Yes."

"You're perfect. And our life will be perfect. You'll see."

She smiled happily as he began kissing her again, but there was a little worry in the back of her mind. She had never told him she had epilepsy, and she didn't intend to until after they were married. It would be hard to keep her secret from him if they were living together, but maybe she would never have another seizure. She had to believe that in order to live like other, normal people. If it was so important to Richard that she was his Golden Girl, then she would be.

He was afraid of losing her, but she was just as afraid of losing him.

The Radcliffe graduation was held on a warm June day. Hundreds of seniors in caps and gowns and their parents filled the large Sanders Theater in Memorial Hall outside the Harvard Yard. The glee club sang. It was both as glorious and banal as any graduation; but even the most cynical graduates found themselves moved. Their diplomas were truly prizes for perseverance, hard work, and intelligence, and they felt proud and excited and special. Graduation was an era marked *ended,* a kind of pledge to go forth and be worthy. If real life was to surround them again in a few hours, at least right now they had this one moment to dream.

For Emily Applebaum, the first girl in her family to go to college, the Radcliffe-Harvard diploma was a treasure. She planned to have it framed and keep it in her house always, wherever she lived. It was the best souvenir of any she had ever collected. Her parents were in the audience. When her name was called she walked up to the stage, feeling like Eleanora Duse, her face serene, her head high, and received her diploma with whispered thanks. She had come to Radcliffe to win two prizes: one was in her hand, and the other was on her finger.

She was wearing Ken's engagement ring at last, but he was going on that ship to Europe. She would have to pretend to be brave, but she was filled with fear. A summer was long, and he would find someone else. It was only a diamond ring—he could ask her to give it back. You heard about those things all the time. In her mind the image arose of herself and Ken walking through the fallen autumn leaves, carefree, laughing, in a great phalanx of students going to a football game. There hadn't been a thing on their minds at that minute but fun. Now suddenly it was over: she was a college graduate, an adult. She should have been filled with hope, but she felt paralyzed; forced by someone else's selfishness to wait in limbo for her life to go on.

Annabel Jones glanced at the sea of little white faces and thought how glad she was to be getting out of this place. Good riddance to those holier-than-thou prigs in the dorm. She hoped they all ended up frigid with rotten marriages. She checked the tassel on her mortarboard to make sure it was hanging just right. When she received her diploma she would then move the tassel over to the other side, denoting that she was a gradaute. She watched the girls who were ahead of her go past the Dean to receive their diplomas and she noticed that some of them forgot to move the tassel. Those perfect girls forgetting one perfect little formality? She felt like giggling.

What surprised her was that she felt a little nostalgic and sorry that college was over. She'd loved her classes, even though she never took getting good marks very seriously. She remembered the sunlight striking the windows in Harvard Yard, and blue shadows on the snow. Cambridge was so pretty: all those little old houses, the cobblestone streets, the leaves blazing in the fall and the smell of people's gardens in the spring when she walked to class. Maybe she remembered those things so vividly because she almost always walked alone. But it was over now. She had Bill.

She took her diploma, murmured her thanks, and tossed her tassel to the other side. So nuts to you all, Annabel thought happily. I'm free.

Daphne Leeds heard her name and walked gravely to receive her diploma. When she touched it, it was almost as if she had received an electrical charge. She knew this was only a piece of paper. But not for her. This diploma meant she had won. She remembered that dreadful day when she'd had a seizure in the dorm dining room, and her decision that if anyone found out her secret she would leave. But they hadn't, and she was still here. Today was her triumph.

The most important rule in life was that if you wanted to be different, or couldn't help it, you must not be found out. The Eleventh Commandment: "Thou shalt not get caught." She hadn't. She had survived Radcliffe, she had found love with a wonderful man, and now the world was going to belong to her. She could hardly wait to go out and enjoy it.

Christine Spark was one of the small group of girls who had graduated summa cum laude. She wished she could be happier. Her parents had come to see her graduate, and her mother had so far remained sober for this event. For the first time in Chris's life her father had promised he would take some responsibility and see that her mother didn't take a drink all day. That was really something: for him to make her mother stay dry he first had to admit she was a lush. But beyond her misgivings about her mother's behavior, Chris had bigger worries. College was over for good, and Alexander hadn't said a word about the future.

She assumed they would continue to see each other in New York. She would get a job. She knew he

wouldn't have much money for a while, not enough
to make a commitment, even though she had never
minded not having money. If he asked her to live
with him she'd move right in, and if he proposed
she would die of happiness. She daydreamed that one
day he would just say casually, "Let's go get a marriage license," the way he'd invited her to his room
the first time. Alexander didn't make a big fuss about
the things other people found important. But where
it really counted, in feelings, she knew he had more
than anyone else.

She tried to look back over her college years to pick
out some important moment to keep as a souvenir
on this graduation day. But all she saw was Alexander.

It was over. They were all outside on the lawn
with their families, proud graduates. Annabel hugged
Chris. There were tears in her eyes. "We'll always be
friends, Chris. We'll see each other."

"You bet we will," Chris said. "Will you ever come
to New York?"

"Sure. And you'll come to visit Bill and me."

"It seems so far away," Chris said. She felt sad.

Chapter 16

Annabel was driving to the Atlanta airport to meet Bill's plane. She was in her graduation present from her parents: the new Thunderbird two-seater convertible. Hers was white. She had the top down and the radio on, and she was singing. It was a glorious June day, with a few puffs of white clouds high in the cobalt sky. Two young men in a truck whistled at her and honked their horn as she drove past them, and she laughed. She felt wonderful. Tonight there would be a quiet little dinner at home with just Bill, herself, and her parents, so he wouldn't be overwhelmed all at once by strangers. Tomorrow she would take him on a tour of her beautiful city. And then tomorrow evening her parents were giving an enormous cocktail party at their house to announce the engagement, followed by a small dinner for twelve of their closest friends and relatives at the country club.

She parked her car at the airport parking lot and went into the terminal. Bill's plane was on time. She was waiting for him at the gate, and gave him a big hug and kiss. She noticed that he seemed embarrassed, even though everybody else was kissing arriving passengers, and it occurred to her that there were still things she had to learn about him. College was so artificial. Once they were married and living together she would learn to anticiapte his moods. She hoped he didn't turn out to be stuffy . . . but no, he was probably just nervous at the thought of meeting her family for the first time.

"We'll go get your bags," she said, taking his hand to lead him to the baggage area.

"I don't have any," he said.

"What do you mean, you don't have any?"

"Where's the bar?"

She looked at him in dismay and led him to the bar. What a case of bridegroom's nerves this one had. A drink at eleven o'clock in the morning? They sat at a little table in the dark bar.

"Martini," Bill said to the waitress.

"A Coke, please," Annabel said.

"You'd better have a martini too."

"I have to drive."

"Two martinis," he said to the waitress.

Annabel was beginning to feel fear creeping all over her skin like some tiny crawling things. "What's the matter with you, Bill?" she said.

"I didn't bring any bags because I can't stay," he said.

She tried to light a cigarette but her hand was trembling. He lit it for her and she saw his hand was trembling too.

"Why not?" she asked, trying not to sound hysterical.

The waitress brought two martinis and Bill drank half of his in one big gulp. Annabel stared at him, and then took a sip of hers. She hated martinis, they tasted like medicine.

"I came because I wanted to tell you in person," he said. "I feel like a rat. I really do." He glanced at his watch. "I'm going home on the noon flight."

"Tell me *what*?" She heard her voice trail off into a little squeak.

Bill shook his head. "I don't want to marry you, Annabel. I can't go through with it."

The fear had now covered her skin entirely and crawled into her body. Her stomach contracted and she felt as if her heart was going to tear itself out of her body and lie right there on the table.

"Why not?" she said.

"I . . . I just don't love you enough. I thought I did, but I don't."

"Well," she said. Her voice was suddenly not the terrified squeak anymore but quite normal. She felt the wall rising; the one she had erected so long ago to protect her from all those people who tried to hurt her. "When did you find that out, Bill?"

"I don't know." He sounded frantic. He finished his martini and signaled the waitress for another. "Drink your drink," he said.

"I don't need my drink. I'd like to know when you decided you didn't love me anymore."

"I don't know," he said again, miserably. The waitress brought his martini and he took a sip.

"I'd also like to know *why*," Annabel said.

"I don't know."

"But you must have some idea. People don't just fall out of love for no reason. I still love you."

"You'll get over it," he mumbled.

She fixed him with a level gaze. He couldn't meet her eyes and he looked down at his watch again.

"I'm sorry," Bill said finally.

She wondered how many times she had heard that: *I'm sorry, I don't love you anymore.* Had he only told her he loved her so she would go to bed with him? But if so, why did he propose to her? Did he think he had to, to get her? Part of her wanted to run away from him and this humiliation, but another part of her wanted to stay until she could find out what was going on in his head, as if he contained the answer to all the mysteries that had made her miserable. She knew that under her calm exterior and the wall, inside was some horrible trembling thing that might come out at any moment and tear her to pieces. She had to feed it something to quiet it or else get out of here right now. At least Bill wasn't a complete coward; he'd come here to tell her instead of just phoning her, or even worse, writing her a letter. He had to love her a little to face coming here. She wondered if he'd heard about her reputation. That must have been it . . . Bill was always so conscious of the things a man had to do to become successful in his career. But she couldn't ask him what he'd heard, or who had told him. She would die before she asked him. And if he cared so much what people said about her, then she didn't want him.

But she knew she did want him. She had to get out of here this minute or she would start to cry and beg him to give her another chance. The hell with him.

Annabel smiled and stood up. She twisted the engagement ring she had been so proud of off her finger and dropped it daintily into Bill's drink.

"Good-bye, Bill," she said pleasantly. "Have a nice life."

She turned and walked out of the bar, and as she turned the corner to leave the terminal she caught a glimpse of him, still sitting there, with a stupid look on his face.

She didn't remember how she'd gotten home until she parked her new Thunderbird in her family's garage. She'd driven by rote. It was a lucky thing she hadn't been killed. Or maybe it was just too damn bad she hadn't been. She wished she were dead.

There was nothing left now, no future, no life, nothing to look forward to. She was all alone.

She went into the house. Her mother was in the living room arranging flowers. "Where's Bill?"

"We decided to call it off," Annabel said.

Her mother looked horrified. "Call it off? But why?"

"It's always better to find out before the wedding

than afterward, isn't it?" Annabel said. "I'm sorry."

"Well, Annabel, of course, you know what you're doing . . ." But her mother's tone said clearly that Annabel was demented.

Annabel went upstairs into her bathroom, locked the door, turned on both taps in the sink and in the tub so no one could hear her, and began to cry. She pounded her fists against the tile and sobbed until her knuckles and throat were raw. Bill doesn't love me. Nobody loves me. Nobody will ever love me. I'm doomed.

When she had finished crying she washed her face and turned off the taps. She wished that Max was there to cheer her up the way he always did. The thought of the stupid look on Bill's face when she had left comforted her a little. She smiled.

Whatever else I am, she thought, at least I have style.

Chapter 17

The great white ship the *Liberté* rocked gently at the pier like a dream of luxury and adventure, which it was to the people who were about to sail on it to France. Emily had come to see Ken off. Her parents had sent him a large basket of fruit, which sat in the middle of the small coffee table in his cabin, and his parents had sent flowers, which were on the dresser. His new luggage was neatly lined up against the wall. The cabin looked very festive, and Emily felt left out and wretched. Ken was so handsome, his face alight with anticipation. When she saw that look she started to cry.

"Don't cry," he said. "I want to show you the rest of the ship."

"Oh, I wish I was going with you," she sobbed.

"*Please* don't cry Emily. You'll make me miserable."

He had stopped looking so happy, and Emily tried not to cry, but it was impossible. She had a right to cry if she wanted to. He was going to go away and leave her and ruin her life. She sniffled into her lace-trimmed handkerchief.

"Let's go to the bar," Ken said. He took her hand and led her down the narrow corridor. The doors to the cabins on both sides were open all along the corridor, and inside the cabins Emily could see people drinking champagne and having parties. There was the sound of laughter and conversation. Emily followed Ken up the carpeted stairs to the next floor.

"This doesn't look like a ship," she said. "It looks like a hotel."

"It is," Ken said. "A floating resort hotel."

The walls were beautifully paneled, the brass railing to hold on to in rough weather was shining, the carpeting was soft and clean-looking. There were display windows showing all the things you could buy duty free once the ship sailed: perfume, watches, cameras, liquor, handbags. Ken led her into the bar. It was a huge, round room with windows looking out on the pier—later there would be an uninterrupted view of the ocean. People were already at the large bar in the middle of the room, and some were sitting on the small couches near the windows, but most were like her and Ken, taking the grand tour of the ship.

"Do you want some champagne?" he asked.

"No, thanks." She just couldn't stop crying.

He gave her an exasperated look. "Come on, Emily, let's go see the nightclub."

They saw the nightclub, the movie theater, the dining room, the upper deck with the deck chairs neatly set out around the swimming pool, and another deck where the deck chairs were lined up facing outward to the ocean. Everything was very glamorous and luxurious. The fact that it was so nice made Emily cry harder. He was never coming back to her, she just knew it. He would probably meet a girl right here on the ship. She looked around and saw lots of girls, but she couldn't tell if they were seeing people off or going on the ship themselves. It didn't matter; all it took was one.

"This ship is so big I think I'm going to get lost

the first day," Ken said. He was trying to cheer her
up. "Would you like to go to a party? We could just
crash. Nobody would notice."

"No."

They walked down the flights of stairs again toward
Ken's cabin. On the way Emily saw what was apparently a large suite. It was filled with people, all drinking champagne and having a good time. Flowers and
bon voyage baskets were everywhere. She had never
imagined there were cabins on a ship that looked
like actual apartments. This one even had a king-sized
bed instead of bunks, and there was a white telephone
beside the bed.

"Hey, let's go to that one!" Ken whispered.

"No. I want to be alone with you. There's so little
time."

He led her into his cabin. She knew she looked
terrible, all tear stained, her mascara running like a
clown's. This would be the last memory Ken would
have of her: ugly.

"Emily, *please* don't be so unhappy."

She didn't answer. What was there to say? They'd
had it out, and each of them thought the other was
being unreasonable.

"I'm going to miss you too, you know," Ken said.
He sounded sad.

She blew her nose.

Her handkerchief was so soaked it was useless, so
she took a wad of Kleenex out of the bathroom and
started in on that. She remembered the bandstand in
the nightclub and she wondered who Ken would be
dancing with tonight, cheek to cheek, flirting . . . his
own cabin, no more school rules . . .

"Emily, I'm going to have a rotten time if I have
to think of you suffering like this. I don't want to
make you miserable. I just want a harmless little last
fling."

"If it's harmless it's not a fling," she said. "I think

you should have a *big* fling. You should do everything."

"What are you going to do tonight?" he asked.

She looked at him. Tonight? Who thought about tonight? What did he think she was going to do?

"Look," he said, sounding desperate, "I'll write you every day when I'm in Europe."

"I don't want you to go," she sobbed.

He put his arms around her and held her close. She knew she was getting mascara and lipstick all over his clean shirt and she didn't care. He had plenty of other shirts in those suitcases. She didn't have any other man whose arms she wanted to have around her. Ken was patting her and kissing her hair. "Ah . . ." he said. "Ah . . . my little baby. I didn't know you'd feel so bad."

"Oh, Ken, don't go! Don't leave me, *please!*"

"Emily."

His voice sounded sad, heavy, and final. He held her away from him at arm's length and looked at her. Then he took his handkerchief out of his pocket —one of the dozen monogrammed handkerchiefs she'd given him on his last birthday—and he gently wiped her face. His eyes seemed very sad too. She looked into them and tried to read his mind, but she couldn't. All she could see in Ken's eyes was the tiny reflection of herself.

Ken let go of her and went to the telephone. "This is Mr. Buchman in C-21. Will you send someone to take my bags off the ship. I'm not sailing."

She stared at him. Now he smiled, and he put his arm around her. "Okay?" he said.

"Oh, Ken!" She flung her arms around his neck and covered his face with kisses. She began to laugh and gasp with joy.

"We'll get married right away," Ken said. "And we'll go to Europe on our honeymoon. Just the way you wanted it."

They walked out of the cabin hand in hand, up to the main deck, to the gangplank that led to the dock and home. The ship's horn sounded. People were crowding the deck now: visitors leaving, people who were sailing who wanted to stand at the rail to wave good-bye. People were tossing confetti and brightly colored streamers, and balloons floated in the warm June breeze. Emily bore Ken off triumphantly, entwining her fingers tightly in his, feeling as if all the confetti and streamers and balloons were for her. For her and Ken, forever together, from now on. It was the happiest moment of her life, one of those moments that remain in memory as a grand and romantic gesture, a heroic moment, a turning point.

It was one of those victories that would turn around in future years and become a regret, attaining its own ironic poignancy. If only we hadn't. . . .

The white bulk of the *Liberté* moved slowly out to sea, its sides touched with pink and gold from the sun. On deck the passengers cheered and threw confetti, waved, drank champagne. Max and Alexander stood side by side at the rail among the departing passengers, holding half-empty glasses of champagne. They looked at each other and touched their glasses in a toast of triumph and anticipation, and they both smiled happily. It was a smile such as no one had ever seen on Alexander's face, not even Chris. At this moment Max and Alexander were exactly what they wanted to be—two young men with their lives ahead of them.

Part 2

The Sixties:
Falling
Apart

Chapter 1

It was six years since they had all graduated from college. The young John Kennedy was president instead of daddy Eisenhower, and people were beginning to think anything was possible. Everybody loved James Bond, but his adventures in the movies seemed only a little more daring than what was happening in real life: civil rights uprisings in the South, a massive demonstration in Washington, D.C., in late summer. The silent generation had slipped gently into their preordained world of split levels and diapers, but some had joined the new, younger people and become vocal.

And then there were those who were neither conformists nor activists, but sleepwalkers existing in limbo, like Christine Spark.

She was living in New York, in a tiny rent-controlled apartment on the West Side, and she was a proofreader for *The Ladies' Home Journal*. Then she wrote to the *Radcliffe Quarterly* and called herself a Copy Editor. It sounded more important, although it was the same thing. She had bothered to write to the *Radcliffe Quarterly* only twice, once early on when she still saw news of people she knew, and a little later when Annabel got married. She knew Annabel would never write to those people to tell them anything, but she also knew that it would please Annabel to stick it to them with this news.

I had the pleasure of attending the wedding of Annabel Jones to Russell Buchanan, in what was Atlanta's major social event. They will live in Atlanta, where Rusty is an attorney. The wedding was beautiful, with 300 guests feasting and dancing afterward at the country club, and we all had a wonderful time.

The *Radcliffe Quarterly* always gave a lot of space to accounts of weddings and babies.

Except for Annabel's twice-yearly trips to New York, Chris didn't see any of the girls from Radcliffe. Their friendships, if they were even that, had been based on propinquity. She noticed from the *Radcliffe Quarterly* that the ones who lived in Cambridge still saw each other often, but she never saw Daphne, who was living in New York and working in an art gallery, apparently still single. Emily had been in Cambridge, taking a master's degree and married to Ken, and then after a while they disappeared from the pages of the *Radcliffe Quarterly* and from Chris's mind.

The person who stayed on her mind was Alexander. She went to her job every day, sat in her cubicle checking and correcting words and punctuation, precise and eagle-eyed, and it seemed as if she was an expert at discovering everyone's mistakes but her own. There was no way she could understand why Alexander had done such a heartless thing to her. Her mind told her he had simply considered her a college fling, but her heart kept thrashing around trying to find reasons.

When she first discovered he had gone to Paris with Max she had been miserable and shocked, but had told herself it was just another one of Alexander's impetuous summer vacations. Maybe he hadn't told her because he was afraid she would make a fuss. He should have known better than that. She always accepted everything he did. But when he didn't come back she ran out of excuses. At the end of a year Max came back to New York, as he had planned, bringing with him a play written by a new young playwright, and he produced it off Broadway. The play was such a hit that after three months Max moved it to Broadway, and suddenly he was the wunderkind producer. He was barely twenty-three years old.

Chris called him and they met for lunch. He took her to Sardi's, where all the theater people went, and there was a caricature of Max on the wall along with the caricatures of stars and other famous theater people. He looked exactly like a faun in the caricature, and much the same in real life as he had looked in college, except his hair was longer.

"What's happened to Alexander?" she asked him the minute they sat down.

"Same old Chris," Max said. He smiled at her. "I thought you wanted to see me."

"I did. I do." She felt like crying. "Why did he leave me?"

"Forget him," Max said, not unkindly, but not very kindly either. He unfolded his napkin, and when Chris sat there staring at him as if she could will him to tell her everything he reached over and unfolded her napkin and placed it gently on her lap. "Would you like a drink?"

She shook her head. He ordered a glass of white wine for himself and a Coke for her. He was smoking Gauloises now, and they smelled awful. He lit Chris's cigarette and smiled again. "I'm glad to see you, Chris. You look very well."

"I do not look well. I look like a crazy person and

I feel like one. Is he going to live in Paris forever?"

"He says so," Max said. He shrugged. "You know Alexander."

"I thought I did. Is he married?"

"No."

She sighed with relief. "A girl friend? Is he living with someone?"

"Forget him, Chris."

"Does he ever mention me?"

"It's *over*, Chris."

"I never knew you to be mean before, Max."

"Oh, God!" Max said. He started to laugh, but his eyes were sad. "Oh, Chris, you loon! You have your whole life in front of you. You are a treasure, do you know that? Any man would be lucky to have you. Forget Alexander. *Please*."

"I'm boring you," she said.

"Bore me? God, Chris, you never bore anybody. You have the most inappropriate response of any girl I know."

"Okay," she said. "Let's order." She forced herself to act cheerful, and Max told her funny stories about Paris and about the New York theater world. He seemed to go to every party and know everybody worth knowing, although Chris had never heard of most of them. He was having a wonderful time, he was kind and he was fun, and after a while she felt a little better. There *was* a world out there, and other people enjoyed themselves.

She kept up her brave front through the whole lunch, and then over dessert she said, "Max . . . please don't be mad at me. Just tell me why Alexander didn't want me anymore."

Max looked at her for a long time before answering, and she noticed for the first time that his eyes were golden. What extraordinary eyes he had.

"My darling Chris," he said finally, with a little smile, "do you think you're the only person in the world who ever got ditched?"

I'm nothing, she thought. I'm nobody. The whole world is full of failures like me. She forced herself then to change the subject, and the lunch ended with Max promising to invite her to a dinner party soon in his new apartment, and to leave two tickets to his new play at the box office for her.

He left the tickets, and she took her father. Max never got around to inviting her to any dinner party and he never called her. She supposed she had offended him by making it so obvious that her only interest in seeing him was to find out about Alexander. After she saw his play she wrote him a thank-you note. She wished she could think of some way to make it up to him for the way she'd acted, make him know that she really had been glad to see him, that she liked him, but he was a celebrity now and he awed her a little. He had so many chic and famous friends. What could she offer him? The only parties she got invited to were in dingy little apartments like her own, given by secretaries, attended by insecure young men on the make and on the way up. Max would hate them all. His social life was with older, more sophisticated people. She saw his picture in the papers occasionally, escorting debutantes. There would always be rich, young, beautiful girls. He was probably too busy to need a friend, and besides, he obviously had a million friends.

The years went by and she still thought about Alexander. At a party, in a better apartment now, given by an associate editor instead of a secretary, Chris met an advertising executive who was forty years old, handsome, and married. He invited her to dinner after the cocktail party—his wife was in the suburbs with their three children—and she accepted. He asked her to invite him up to her apartment when he took her home, and she did. He took her to bed, and she accepted that too. He began to stay in the city two evenings a week, although he always went home to Westchester to sleep, and he and Chris had an affair

that was different in only one way from the affairs
her friends were having with other married men. The
difference was that Chris never fell in love with him.

He filled the emptiness, he made the pain of loneliness go away for a while. He was a persistent and
skilled lover, very much more so than Alexander had
been, and she wished she could fall in love with him,
even though she knew that would be a mistake. But
at least when it was over she would have someone
else to grieve over, the way a new pain makes an old
pain seem less. But when finally, after nine months,
he told her he thought they should "cool it for a
while because my wife is getting suspicious," Chris
agreed pleasantly and pretended she didn't know it
was over. The only thing she regretted was that he
hadn't stayed around long enough for her to learn
to trust him so that she could finally have an orgasm.

She was twenty-seven years old now, on her way
to being an old maid. She was inadequately paid, she
had no decent clothes, she had no real friends, only
acquaintances. Annabel, for whom she always felt real
affection, had changed. She seemed brittle, as if she
had a secret. Chris wished they could be more honest
with each other when they met twice a year, but all
she knew was that Annabel's marriage wasn't going
well and Annabel was in pain. Annabel drank too
much, pretended to be happy, and Chris didn't pressure her to talk about it because she sensed that telling the truth would hurt Annabel more than pretending did right now. She deliberately refrained from
mentioning Alexander because she didn't want Annabel to think she was crazy. But she had been saving
what little money she could, and she had made a plan.

She was going to go to Paris in the fall for her
vacation, and she would look up Alexander. She telephoned Max. He had three solid hits behind him and
was such a big producer now that she was afraid he
wouldn't return her call, but he did, the next day.
Chris told him she was going to Paris and didn't

know anyone so she wanted Alexander's address. Alexander had an apartment on the Left Bank and was working as a banker, a job his father had gotten for him. She made sure to mention that she was getting names of friends of friends from everyone. Max was very nice and gave her not only Alexander's address and phone number but also a list of people including a couple who spoke English. She reminded him that she spoke fluent French, and asked him for a list of moderately priced hotels on the Left Bank. When she hung up she had all the information she needed.

On the first of November, as soon as the cheapest winter airline fares went into effect, Chris bought a round trip ticket to Paris. She left the return open.

Chapter 2

Annabel Jones had been married to Russell Buchanan for five years now; their daughter Emma was three. She adored Emma. Emma was her life. Emma and Annabel's twenty-pound Maine coon cat, Sweet William, were her family. Rusty was just the drunken but always courtly southern gentleman who happened to live in their house.

Annabel's perceptions had sharpened considerably since her days at Radcliffe, and she knew how and why all this had happened, and even when everything changed, but knowing it didn't help. She was aware that her mistake had been only the lesser of two evils. When Bill Wood had broken their engagement she was suddenly faced with the need to get a job, something she had scarcely thought about. A B.A. in English literature didn't qualify her for anything. Her social position in Atlanta made her overqualified for most of the jobs she could get. Dr. Jones's daughter standing on tired feet all day as a salesgirl? Besides, most jobs were boring. Her mother wanted her to do volunteer work with the Junior League. It would keep her busy and she would be with her old friends.

Annabel had nothing to say to her "old friends." Except for a few moments of giggling in the powder room at holiday dances she hadn't seen them for eight years. The girls who hadn't gone away to college were all married and had children now. The ones who had gone to college had managed to get engaged in their junior or senior years, and *not* get ditched. There was one girl Annabel knew from boarding school, but they had never liked each other much.

Her volunteer work consisted mainly of planning benefits. She had joined the social committee, but what she liked was going to dances, not planning them. Once a week she read fairy tales to little children at the public library. That was the only thing she enjoyed. That and riding—alone in the freedom of the countryside—something she did to escape.

She dated quite a few young men. Everybody was looking for a mate. Deadened and numb from her disaster with Bill, she thought she would never be attracted to a man again. She let them kiss her goodnight and pushed them firmly out of her family's front doorway. This coldness seemed to inflame them. She received two proposals before Christmas. She turned them down. She would never marry a man she didn't love.

Rusty Buchanan came from old money, a lot of it. He was a lawyer, but the opposite of Bill Wood in every way. Bill had been dedicated, but Rusty didn't seem to take anything very seriously. He liked to dance, play golf, drink, shoot skeet, and laugh. Sandy-haired, over six feet tall, built like an athlete, he was one of those people who would drink themselves to death without ever developing a roll of fat or bags under their eyes. One day the heart or the liver or the brain would go, but not the beauty. And now, five years after their wedding, Annabel thought that was the one thing she and Rusty had in common. She didn't look like a boozer either, and had never expected to become one, but neither had she expected to willingly marry a fool.

Loneliness . . . rebound . . . social pressures . . .

the narcotic of love. She supposed all those things had made her accept Rusty's proposal. His was the third. Her parents were well pleased with his family, and she thought they liked him too. She found out later they didn't *mind* him, but they thought Annabel loved him, and they wanted whatever she did. She had never really communicated with her parents.

Annabel married Rusty because he made her laugh. He was so handsome and kind that she thought she loved him. But six months after living with a fool she hated his laugh; it made her whole body tense up with annoyance. It was his family's' vast money that made it possible for him merely to play at law. More often he played at the country club. He woke up every morning with a hangover, started drinking at lunch, and was plastered by dinnertime. The things he'd said that made her laugh when they met were the same things he said for years and years, until they made her cringe as much as his laugh did. But she had Emma, a beautiful little girl who looked just like Annabel, and was lively and sweet and very bright.

Originally she had wanted to name the baby Daisy, so she could be Daisy Buchanan after F. Scott Fitzgerald's heroine, but then she settled on Emma. She wanted her daughter to grow up to be more than a selfish, beautiful, rich nonentity. And she hadn't named her after Emma Bovary. She didn't want her child to have a tragic life. It was just that Emma Buchanan seemed to be a name of strength. Annabel wanted this fragile child to grow up to be stronger than she had been. She would be Emma's friend and confidante and she would never let her marry a man she didn't love or respect just because she was scared.

Tonight was Friday, and they were going to have dinner at the club. Janine and Dickie Felton were giving a party for their seventh wedding anniversary. People gave a lot of parties, at their homes, at restaurants, at the club. Annabel and Rusty went to all of them. Sometimes they had a party, with caterers helping their regular help. Annabel liked to enjoy her own parties, and that meant not having to worry about anything. But parties weren't the same anymore, not like the ones at college. In those days that were so far away now, anything had seemed possible. Now everything seemed predictable.

Annabel had dressed early, and dressed up Emma, because tonight was Sweet William's first birthday and they were going to give him a birthday party before she had to go to the club. Emma was excited. They had gone shopping for all his presents, things a cat would like.

"Does he know it's his birthday, Mama?"

What did you tell a child? It was such a responsibility. Nearly every time Emma spoke it was to ask a question, pose a new challenge. Was she to lead Emma into the world of fantasy or reality? Which would make her happier, stronger, wiser?

"Of course. Look at his whiskers twitching."

"He smells the tuna fish."

So Emma, this time, had chosen reality. Good. Now a little fantasy was in order, to give balance to life. Annabel arranged all Sweet William's little presents and birthday cards on the floor where he could see them and brought out his birthday cake with the one candle lit in the center.

"Happy birthday to you, happy birthday to you, happy birthday Sweet William, happy birthday to you!"

Annabel and Emma sang lustily and then Annabel put the cake on the floor and let Emma blow out the candle before it burned the cat. Then she gave Sweet William his treat of tuna fish and she and Emma ate the cake. With it there was a bottle of champagne for Annabel, and a bottle of ginger ale for Emma. They both had champagne glasses.

"Daddy missed the whole party," Emma said.

"He had a business meeting, poor thing."

Emma hugged Sweet William. The cat was almost as big as the child. Annabel wondered if Emma was old enough to think that business meetings were what men did to make them come home walking funny and smelling bad. At least she had the decency to stay moderately sober until Emma was asleep.

Rusty showed up at ten minutes to eight, drunk as usual, and had to shower and change his clothes for the party, which was to be black tie and was called for eight. Emma was long since asleep. While she waited for him, Annabel polished off the rest of the bottle of champagne, sitting there in her beautiful living room filled with all the things taste and money could buy. There were always fresh flowers arranged in a bowl on the coffee table, and there were silver-framed family photographs on the piano. In cold weather a fire burned cheerily in the fireplace. She thought her home looked like a movie set. The only part of it that was really hers was the bedroom, which was always a mess despite the maid's constant care and Rusty's frequent complaints that it was his bedroom too. They had separate bathrooms and separate dressing rooms. Sweet William slept in hers, on a shelf of the closet, burrowed cozily in a tangle of cashmere sweaters and silk slips.

Rusty drove. He always drove. Annabel figured if one of them was going to plow drunkenly into a tree it might as well be Rusty so at least his southern gentleman's sense of masculine superiority wouldn't be offended. People were used to them being late to parties. Everyone said the Buchanans were worth waiting for because they were such fun. They didn't speak in the car because they had nothing to say to each other. But no one knew that. When they walked into a crowded room the two of them always lit up like light bulbs.

When they arrived at the club everyone was still having cocktails in the bar that overlooked the golf course. Waiters were passing around some uninteresting-looking little canapés. Annabel and Rusty headed directly to the bar where she ordered champagne and he ordered bourbon on the rocks.

"I declare, Annabel," Janine Felton said, sweeping toward them in candy-pink satin, "did somebody die?"

"What?"

"Well!" Janine fluttered feminine little hands at Annabel's black chiffon dress. "I mean, black is for mourning."

"I like black," Annabel said sweetly. She sipped at her champagne, taking in her hostess's structured little dress that could stand up by itself when she took it off, her blonde, teased, sprayed bubble hairdo that looked like a space helmet, her white lipstick, the black eyeliner that made a little check mark at the corners of her eyes. One of her pair of black false eyelashes was coming loose at the end. Annabel decided not to tell her. All the women in the room were dressed much like Janine, who was a leader of fashion. As for Janine, she was looking at Annabel's hair with distaste. Annabel still kept her hair long and free, but for parties like this one she put it up, casually, with tendrils around her face, and she never sprayed it.

"Black is very striking with red hair," Janine said.

"Thank you. And congratulations on your anniversary."

"Lucky seven," Rusty said. He raised his glass in a toast and drained it.

"Did you all see Dickie yet?"

"No," Rusty said. The bartender refilled his glass.

"Well, let me just go find him," Janine said. "Did you ever see such a mob? Everyone we invited came."

Where else would they have to go? Annabel thought. She finished off her glass of champagne and got a refill. Janine had vanished.

"Seven year itch," Rusty said, and laughed.

"Her or him?"

"Probably both."

"Oh, good," Annabel said. "Tell me the gossip."

"There isn't any gossip."

Of course not, Annabel thought. Men don't spread scandal, that's women's work. You're above all that. She wondered idly if Rusty had ever cheated on her. She very much doubted it. He wasn't the type. And she had never cheated on him. She knew which of her friends had already had lovers and she thought what hypocrites they were, making sure they were virgins when they got married and then considering their wedding the doorway to freedom at last. She had been the opposite. The last thing in the world she could ever be was a hypocrite, and if she ever took a lover she would have to leave Rusty. She hadn't been like those girls at college and she wasn't like these women now.

She glanced around the room. Everyone was in tight little groups, laughing, talking, looking glad to be together even though they saw each other all the time. Rusty was glued to the bar, but he already had three men around him, all talking about some football game they'd seen on television. She was aware that she was alone again. The men liked her, but they were afraid to spend too much time with her because their wives got jealous. The wives didn't like her at all. But whenever she took Rusty's arm and they became a couple, everyone adored them. Then they were The Buchanans Who Were So Much Fun. Then there was no more threat.

She went to Rusty and took hold of his arm firmly. "I don't know why you want to keep all these handsome men to yourself," she said sweetly. "It's such a waste."

The men were around her then, flirting and complimentary, telling Rusty how lucky he was to have a beautiful girl like her.

The dinner was buffet, but the dining tables all had placecards on them. There was a small band playing for dancing. The tablecloths were pink and the flowers were pink and white: roses and baby's breath. Pink was Janine's favorite color. Rusty had been placed at Janine's table, and Annabel at Dickie's, because the Buchanans were important, but Janine had carefully placed Dickie between her own two best friends. That was fine with Annabel. She thought Dickie was a jerk. Her private name for him was the Brylcreem *two*-dab man. *Brylcreem, a little dab'll do ya, Brylcreem, you'll look so debonair. Brylcreem, the gals'll all pursue ya . . .*

Annabel danced with Charlie on her left, whose wife was pregnant with their third child. They were hoping for a boy. Charlie slipped one of the waiters some money to get a bottle of champagne and leave it on their table for Annabel. Everyone knew Annabel hated hard liquor. If she finished it, it would be her second complete bottle of champagne for this evening, not counting the glasses she'd consumed at the bar. She wondered if any of them knew that.

"Rusty's a lucky man," Charlie said to Annabel on the dance floor. He put his nose into her hair and sniffed. "Mmm. What is that?"

"Perfume. Rusty and I are both so fond of you, Charlie." She drew back and gave him a big smile.

Then she danced with Cooper on her right, whose wife was the one Annabel had gone to boarding school with and didn't much like. They had two children. Their little girl was cross-eyed and had to have an operation. After that her only problem would be that she still looked like her father.

"You are a superb dancer," Cooper said.

"Only because you lead so well," Annabel said. She thought about all the songs the bands had played at college. Those lyrics had seemed magical, significant, as if they could zero in on a moment of her own real feelings and express them to the whole world. Now songs were just songs. Very few things were magical anymore.

"You must tell me if I step all over you with my big feet," Cooper said.

"You wouldn't do that."

"I've been meaning to ask you something, Annabel." His voice became conspiratorial. "What does a girl like you, so full of spirit and life, do with her free time?"

"I roll bandages for the Red Cross."

"You're kidding!"

"I don't have any free time, Cooper."

"I wish you did."

She drew back and looked at him. "And you don't either."

"I could make some."

"You must stop leaving your car in the Ramada Inn parking lot, Cooper. People will get the wrong idea, won't they?" He paled. She gave him a little kitty-cat smile and led him back to their table.

She had made quite an attack on her bottle of champagne, but she was not drunk, just high. She was at the point where she didn't want to dance anymore because she was afraid her coordination would show the effects of what she'd had to drink. She knew every step on her way to becoming plastered. Plastered was what she gave herself the luxury of becoming only after she was safe in her own house.

"My turn," said Dickie Felton, pulling her out of her chair and spinning her into his arms.

Try a little Brylcreem if you dare. "What a lovely anniversary party, Dickie. Janine is so creative." There had been pink salmon mousse, pink sliced ham and rare filet steak, pink iced petits fours, and a strawberry ice cream mold with little silver dots sprinkled all over it. Annabel was thankful they hadn't given her pink champagne.

"We always like to be a little different," he said.

"Oh, you succeeded."

"Are you having a good time?"

"Just delightful."

He drew her closer. "I like your black dress."

"Why, thank you, Dickie."

"I think black is a very seductive color."

"Thank you."

"I love a sexy black lace nightgown on a woman," he said. He winked. "And little black frilly under-things. I bet you have some of those, don't you?"

"Actually, I wear long johns in the winter," Annabel said.

He laughed, tentatively. "I've always thought you were very beautiful, Annabel. You always were just my type."

"What an awful thing to say on your anniversary," Annabel said sweetly.

"Oh, anniversary," he said. He drew her away to a corner of the dance floor where no one could over-hear them. "I love my wife, but seven years is a long time. And you know, we went together seven years before we got married. Janine was thirteen when we met. Her daddy used to sit in the living room and chaperone when I came to see her."

"A wise man."

Dickie tightened his arms around her. "You drink a lot. You're unhappy."

She didn't answer. She resolved to drink no more champagne until she got home.

"Well?" Dickie said. "Am I right? I'm right. I could make you happy, Annabel. Have lunch with me on Monday."

"No."

"Tuesday then? Wednesday I have a meeting. How about Thursday?"

"You know what, Dickie?"

"What?"

"You're the one who's drunk," she said coldly, and went back to their table.

I used to be so sweet, she thought sadly. I had flirtation up to a high art. For a moment there I almost told him he was an asshole. I'm getting to be like Christine.

And then a pang of such loneliness and longing hit her that she almost started to cry. She missed her friendship with Chris. Twice a year wasn't enough, and she had wasted all their lunches together by lying about her unhappiness. You had to confide in your friends. Your friends were so rare, and they were such a comfort. She couldn't tell any secrets to any of the women here; their world was too enclosed and she was afraid of gossip. If a husband made a pass at her there was no one to laugh with about it, and so all she had was rage. The next time she went to New York she would tell Chris everything, and they would make fun of all these people and Chris would make it be like the old days.

But the old days had stunk too. Why did she keep forgetting? What she had now was a hundred times better. But that wasn't nearly good enough. She would tell Chris everything, and maybe she would invite Chris to come home with her for the Christmas holidays. Then Chris could see everything firsthand. With Chris's clear-eyed honesty and wit all these people would become funny instead of annoying. Annabel smiled happily. She would go to New York right after Thanksgiving, and she would call Chris tomorrow to tell her she was coming.

It never occurred to her that Chris might not be there.

Chapter 3

For Daphne Leeds and Richard Caldwell, young and in love and not poor, New York was everything wonderful. After graduation they took a small rent-controlled apartment in Greenwich Village, a block from Washington Square Park. Each of them told their parents that they had taken the apartment alone, and each set of parents contributed to the rent, so Daphne and Richard had a lot of money. He was working in his father's real estate company. She was a receptionist at the Glass Gallery on the Upper East Side, where her finishing school looks and accent were as much of an asset as her knowledge of art.

They decorated their apartment together, with finds from little Village antique stores, a lot of plants, some nice lithographs, and a big bed that sat on the floor covered with a leather spread, a gift from Richard's father. Daphne's parents were not pleased that she had decided to live alone instead of waiting to get married, and they came to see the apartment only once. Before they came she removed the card downstairs beside the buzzer that said Leeds & Caldwell, and replaced it with one that said Leeds. Her parents sat gingerly on the edge of the bed, which doubled as a couch, their knees up to their chins, and sipped at their martinis.

"This is awfully bohemian, don't you think?" her mother said.

Daphne smiled.

"You could have put the bed in that alcove and bought a couch."

"I'm making the alcove into a dressing room."

Her mother dropped the subject. She was not the sort of woman who would dream of looking into her daughter's closets, or she would have found out why all that extra space was needed for clothes.

"Have you . . . been all right?"

"Yes, fine," Daphne said.

"You're still on the medication?"

"Dr. Michaelson says I'll be off again soon."

"I wish you had a roommate."

"Oh mother, how ghastly."

"Still . . . in case you . . . it would be good to have someone here." Her mother never said "seizure" if she could help it. Her father never mentioned her condition at all.

Her mother looked up at the ceiling fixture. "You remember about ladders, don't you?"

"I don't have to change the bulbs. I don't use the ugly thing."

"I'm not being overprotective, Daphne. I know you want to be independent. I just don't want you to be reckless."

"I'm not."

After her parents' one visit Daphne replaced the original name card. And her mother, as a combination house gift and rebuke for her wild life, sent her a set of hideous avocado-colored melamine dishes, as if to say that when Daphne regained her senses and either got married or returned home she could throw them away, along with everything in that apartment.

Daphne and Richard shrieked with laughter over the dishes. They found everything either funny or touching and beautiful. They ate dinner out often; Armenian food at dark, romantic Sayat Nova, or hamburgers and beer at noisy, cheerful Julius's, and every evening, even when they ate at home, they went for a walk to explore their new neighborhood. It seemed as if no matter how many different streets they found to wander along, there was always another new one. They walked with their arms around each other, free to be affectionate, like everyone else in that neighborhood. They were used to seeing black and white couples, or two men, or two women, and no one cared. The streets seemed full of teenagers, hugging and kissing. The Village was the place to live if you were in love. The night of their first snowfall they had a snowball fight in the park, and their first summer together they sat in the park at night and listened to kids playing guitars. They didn't even want to go away for vacations. Where would they go—to their parents, to pretend? Their new apartment, the Village itself, was their vacation.

Daphne had asked Dr. Michaelson to take her off the pills. He was letting her taper off. She knew she could keep on hiding them from Richard, but they were a daily reminder of her epilepsy and she wanted to forget it, to be the normal person Richard believed her to be. Besides, Richard was nosy. She took a lot of vitamins, and he would ask, "What's that?" She had the awful feeling that if he had seen the Dilantin and Tridione she would have given away the lie by a guilty look. There was something about living together and being very close that gave people a sort of sixth sense. She had to be careful. She filled her prescriptions at a drugstore near the gallery.

They opened a joint checking account where they both deposited their paychecks, and Daphne suggested Richard pay the bills. He liked being given this position of authority. The only problem with domesticity was that she discovered she didn't like cooking. Following recipes seemed so tedious and then you ate it up so quickly and were left with all those dirty pots and dishes. She was so bored with cooking that she burned things, and after a while Richard began to do some of the cooking himself, found he liked it, and eventually he was doing all of it. He became a gourmet cook, and Daphne happily bought him all the exotic ingredients he needed, and a set of expensive French cookware and a hibachi and a wok. Who would have dreamed that he would turn out to be such a sweetie? He was thoroughly domestic and very romantic—a lovely combination.

They were so happy and content together that she told herself she really didn't mind that they weren't married. The only thing that worried her was they wanted children, and she didn't want to be too old. She knew eventually Hope would have to give in. Richard told her he had stopped sending Hope money for anything except the boy. It would have to be obvious to anyone, even a dumb waitress, that she would be better off to take a divorce settlement.

"Richard, maybe she still loves you," Daphne said one day.

"She doesn't love me. She wants revenge."

"But you're so lovable, why wouldn't she love you?"

"Daphne . . . if I left you for ten years, would you still love me?"

"Of course I would."

"I mean if I told you it was all over and I was never coming back. After ten years you'd have to give up."

"Oh, if you left me that way"—she kissed him—"I'd get over you a lot sooner, so don't get any ideas."

Sometimes she wondered about his son. Richard never mentioned him and didn't want to talk about him. It seemed so unfair that The Waitress had Richard's child and she, who should be the mother of his still unborn and forbidden children, had nothing. All the girls she'd known since childhood were married and had children. The park was full of mothers and babies; so were the streets it seemed. In two and a half years she would be thirty. A woman was supposed to have her first baby when she was in her twenties, everyone said that. The older you were the harder it became. And she and Richard wanted three or four children. It wasn't fair.

And there was no use pretending that the things their friends and families said didn't hurt. "When are you two going to get married?" from married couples who invited them to parties as a couple and then whispered about them to anyone who didn't know already. "Do you still see that, what was his name, Richard Caldwell?" from her mother, and then her own casual lies. "Oh, sometimes. We're friends."

When Daphne looked around at the married couples she knew, only a few really seemed to think they had gotten everything they'd expected. It seemed so unfair that she and Richard, who had lived together for six years and learned to adjust so perfectly, had to be denied the right to marriage. It never occurred to either of them to find someone else. They felt they were already married . . . except about once every day, when the world interfered and made things complicated. The rest of society seemed to think there was some great mystique about marriage. Why else would Hope hang on to her marriage so desperately even though she had the name but not the man? Daphne wished her nothing but misery. The Waitress was the other woman, and she was Richard's wife. Why couldn't everybody understand that?

Chapter 4

Emily Applebaum Buchman sat in her bedroom in her house in Beverly Hills and looked through her old scrapbooks. She did this for some hours of every day, more and more lately. She had a lot of scrapbooks to go through by now. There was all of Radcliffe, and then there was her wedding album, and then the honeymoon trip through Europe she took with Ken that summer they were married. Then there were the scrapbooks she kept during the years Ken was at Harvard Medical School and she was at grad school getting her degree as a psychiatric social worker, and then working. She quit her job when she got pregnant with Kate. There was a Kate album, but Emily never looked at it. And there was a Peter album, started when he was born two years after Kate. She kept the albums up to date, but she didn't look at Peter's either. She knew what the kids looked like.

When Ken had graduated from med school he had spent a year interning at Massachusetts General. Emily had loved living in the Boston area; it was a city. Even after she had to quit her job because it would be unnatural and unmaternal for her to keep working when they didn't need the money, she still had her friends. She hoped that Ken would stay on at Mass General, or that he would take his three-year residency in dermatology at Bellevue and NYU because those hospitals were in New York and they were also the best. She wanted a city and all the things you could do there.

But Ken went to Cedars-Sinai so they could live in California. He said you couldn't bring up children in New York. California was warm and sunny, and California children were tall and tanned and healthy and athletic. Ken could play tennis all year round. And what could she do all year round? Why, take care of their home and children, of course.

So here they were, in a dream house built on the side of a mountain, with four bedrooms, one of which was a den, and glass walls that looked out on the palm trees and scrub of the mountainside on one side and the faraway lights of Los Angeles on the other. Their bedroom had a terrace that overlooked their swimming pool. Further down the mountain they had their own little piece of land where Ken was planning to build a tennis court. You could see the neighbors' houses perched along the mountain, but you couldn't walk to them. You went everywhere by car, down the twisted little mountain road, into what passed for a town. You could meet a friend for a drink and then you could get into your car and get killed, or you could stay sober and have some reckless driver plow into you. With all her heart Emily hated driving. She wouldn't drive when the children were in the car. She made the nurse, Miss Mary, drive. Emily didn't want to be responsible for anything happening to the children.

Tiny, vulnerable, shrieking children. Kate was a toddler, Peter an infant. Kate's voice was shrill and piercing, Peter's was a huge hoarse cry that shook his fat red cheeks. What had she done to make them so ill-tempered? She was always picking them up, fearful someone would hear them scream and think she was mistreating them. Miss Mary said some children were just more vocal than others. Ken rushed around with his Polaroid, giving Emily more snapshots to put in her albums. Of course you had to keep records of every important moment in your children's lives because they grew so fast. But somehow going through memories of all these recent things wasn't as rewarding as looking at and remembering the past.

How childish she had looked! Young and full of dreams. Was that little girl the one Ken wanted to marry? How brave of him to believe she could handle the responsibility of being his wife and the mother of his children. But she had handled grad school, and her job, and run their apartment too. Nothing had seemed too much then. She'd had energy for everything. Now she felt drained, and she was only twenty-seven years old.

All the happy times . . . It was different here where she didn't have any real friends. Ken was so busy. He had responsibilities too. He could accidentally scar someone. It seemed as though lately her life was filled with fears.

Ken had achieved everything he had ever wanted. Their parents wouldn't have to support them much longer. They were so proud of Ken. He had fulfilled all their dreams, too. He was a doctor. He would be successful and rich. He would have a luxurious lifestyle and he would have leisure. A dermatologist kept regular office hours and did not have to rush out of the house for emergencies. Beverly Hills was a perfect place for his future practice, in this city where everyone was either beautiful or intended to become so. He would be the magician who would get rid of unsightly blemishes, warts and moles, peel off wrinkles, shoot silicone into laugh lines, lift baggy eyelids, and transplant neck hair to bald spots. And she would have to worry about staying beautiful, because what kind of advertisement would it be for Ken to have an unlovely wife?

And she too had everything she had ever wanted. Didn't she? What was wrong with her not to feel happy and grateful? Why did she feel so trapped? She woke up every morning feeling depressed, dragged through the day in a fog of uneasiness, and felt such relief when she heard Ken's car finally coming into their driveway. She was so lonely, and she missed him so much all day when he was working. It made her feel guilty, because she had plenty of things to do.

It was time for the children's baths. Emily put her scrapbooks back carefully into her closet and went to get Kate. Miss Mary still bathed Peter, except on her day off. Bathing the baby terrified Emily. She imagined him slipping out of her soapy hands and dropping below the surface of the water, his hair fanning out like seaweed, his lung filling: drowning. She always washed him in so little water that sometimes she worried she was leaving some soap on. But it was better than being responsible for his accidental death. Drying and diapering him, especially when he started to scream because he was cold or annoyed, was an ordeal she dreaded. At least Kate could stand and sit alone, but then, she could slip and hit her head, so you had to be on guard all the time.

After the children were bathed and dried and put into their clean pajamas Miss Mary went downstairs to the kitchen to get their supper. Emily didn't know what she would do when the baby nurse left. She'd already given notice. She liked only tiny babies, not toddlers. Then Emily would have to do everything for the children herself. She would have to drive them to the pediatrician, and at home she would have to be sure they didn't fall into the pool or stick their fingers into light sockets or eat household cleansers. Ken wouldn't have minded if she'd hired a governess, but it would make her feel like an inadequate child. A mother was supposed to take care of her own children. Besides, she had nothing else to do. They had a maid who came in five days a week to clean and do laundry, and a Japanese gardener, and a young man who came by to clean the swimming pool. Emily did all the cooking. Miss Mary cooked for the children and Emily cooked for Miss Mary. That made her feel a little annoyed, as if it were she, Emily, who was the servant in this house, and the baby nurse who was the mother.

The children's rooms overlooked the driveway. Emily ran to the mirror when she heard Ken's car, to be sure she looked all right. He whistled a little tune as he bounded up the stairs. She loved him so much. She rushed to greet him.

"Hi, everybody!" He gave Emily a peck on the cheek and scooped up Kate. "How's my girl?"

I'm your girl, Emily thought. Kate was squealing with delight.

"How were the kids today?" Ken asked her. "Were they good?"

"They're always good."

He put down Kate and picked up Peter. Ken wasn't at all afraid of handling the children. It never seemed to occur to him that he might drop them, so sure were his hands. "Hey there, big boy."

"How was your day?" Emily asked.

"Good. Yours?"

"Fine."

"What's for dinner?"

"I thought we'd have chicken."

"Okay. When are we going to eat?"

That was her cue to go to the kitchen and start dinner. "Seven," she said. They always ate at seven, but Ken always asked. She went downstairs, leaving him to his happy parental scene, and took the salad things out of the refrigerator.

Chopping up the celery and green peppers she realized how dull the knife was, but she was afraid to keep sharp knives in the house. A person could cut himself, or a burglar could come and find a sharp knife and use it. She washed and dried the three kinds of lettuce and measured out the oil and vinegar for the dressing, keeping it separate from the salad until the chicken was done.

She wished Ken would come into the kitchen and have a drink while she was cooking, keep her company. When he'd been at med school they always sat in the kitchen together while she was preparing dinner, and they talked. After dinner they would study together. But now Ken played with the children, and then he watched the evening news on television while he had his drink.

They ate at seven promptly. There was cold white wine to go with the chicken, and fresh string beans.

"Look at those string beans!" Ken said proudly. "Look at those tomatoes! California."

"Don't you like the chicken?"

He tasted it. "It's great. Tell me what you did today, honey."

"Nothing. I played with the kids, I went to the supermarket."

"I thought you were going to start going to a gym."

She felt her face flush. "Do I look flabby?"

"No, honey, but you said you were going to start at a gym so I thought you did."

"I was too busy."

Ken looked at her. "You sound down."

"No, I'm fine."

"Why don't you take a day off and go shopping?" he said. "You haven't been out of the house during the day for weeks, except to go to the market. You have credit cards. Go buy yourself something nice. You deserve it."

She touched his hand. "Ken . . . you hate these pants, right? Tell me the truth."

His face was innocent, even bewildered. "I never said I don't like pants. I just thought you'd like to shop. All women like to shop, don't they?"

"Sure. What should I get?"

"Anything you want."

"I mean, a dress-up dress, or what?"

"Why don't you buy a nice dress and I'll take you out to a discotheque Saturday night."

"Oh, good," she said. "It'll be like a date." She felt better right away thinking about the weekend when she would have Ken all to herself—sort of—for two days.

The next morning Emily woke up feeling happy, as if she was going to have a little adventure. She would find a wonderful dress that Ken would love. They hadn't been out dancing in ages. There would probably be all kinds of new steps they hadn't learned. Who would have dreamed that the fox-trot would be replaced by people doing this new obscure choreography by themselves, ignoring their partner?

She went to four different stores before she found something that suited her. She wanted to be in fashion, but not look as if she were an old matron. She wanted to look young and sexy, but not as though she was trying to pretend to be a kid. She finally settled on a short black silk dress from Jax, strapless except for tiny strings. She liked a boutique like Jax better than a department store because the choices had been made for you. It occurred to her that her mother had gone along on all her clothes shopping expeditions until after she was married, and on her honeymoon Ken had helped her pick out her trousseau. Everything she'd bought alone since then had caused her an agony of indecision.

She stopped at a drive-in for some cottage cheese and iced tea, and then she drove home a different way. She didn't feel like going home just yet. The afternoon loomed long ahead of her. She was driving through the part of Beverly Hills the natives called "the flats." It reminded her of home in Scarsdale, with each nice house set on its small lawn, next to the next house, and real sidewalks. She wondered how expensive these homes were. Maybe she and Ken could move there instead of staying in their mountaintop retreat, and she could have some friends.

Emily drove slowly, looking at each house and playing her fantasy game. Would they like this Tudor house, or that Spanish one? How about Tara? The driveways were in the front, and some nice landscaping, and tall old trees arched above the roadway. She guessed that if these people had pools they were in the back where there was privacy. Oh, yes, these were expensive houses; look at the fancy cars. There was a little white Alfa Romeo, just like Ken's, and there was his license plate: DOCK, for Doctor Ken.

Ken's car! What was Ken's car doing at someone's house in the middle of the afternoon? Dermatologists didn't make house calls. Her heart stopped. She didn't dare go around the block to look again, Ken might catch her and get mad. She was shaking. For years she had heard stories that young doctors had affairs with shiksa nurses, but she knew if Ken fooled around it would be with someone chic and rich who lived in just that kind of house. Ken with some spoiled, blonde Beverly Hills housewife . . . She looked at the street sign. North Bedford Drive.

She turned into the traffic and drove blindly, hearing drivers honk angrily at her as she crossed lanes. Off the busy road now, up the winding series of turns that led to their own street. Her eyes were filled with tears. Husbands always told their wives to go out and buy things when they were cheating. That was guilt. What was his car doing in the driveway of that house?

She didn't even see the small stone wall until she had slammed into it. Her engine was still running. She was shaken up and had hit her lip and chin on the steering wheel, but she wasn't badly hurt. She backed the car into someone's driveway and headed to her own house. She was lucky she hadn't been killed! Her hands were slippery with sweat.

When she parked the car in her own driveway she was shaking all over. She let herself into the house quietly so the children and Miss Mary wouldn't see her, and sneaked up to her room. She shut the door and went to the mirror, and gasped. Her lip and chin were swollen and there was blood all over them.

Emily felt like throwing up. She washed the blood off gently, terrified of what she would find. It seemed to be only a small cut. She went down to the kitchen for some ice, wrapped it in a towel, and took it back upstairs again. Then she lay down on the bed, holding the ice to her injury to make the swelling go down.

She had left the dress in her car. Well, it didn't matter. Ken could get it later. She wasn't going to wear it to any discotheque on Saturday night anyway, not now with this ugly wound on her face. The pain was replaced by an unpleasant numbness. Ken would be so upset when he saw what had happened to her. She remembered something she had learned in Social Relations class about how people read some words differently than they really were because their minds wanted to make it so. It was called closure. That license plate probably hadn't said DOCK at all. It was just that she had been thinking about herself and Ken living in one of those houses, and then she had probably seen a license plate that was something like Ken's and had read it wrong. Closure. It was a way of making the unfamiliar familiar. Of course it hadn't been Ken's car. Ken couldn't get out of the hospital.

That evening when Ken came home and saw Emily's face he was concerned, but reassured her the cut would be all right and she didn't need stitches. She had smashed a headlight on her car. She told him to take the car to be repaired because she was too unnerved to drive for a few days anyway. She refused to go out on Saturday night, so they had a cookout by the pool, just the two of them. She never mentioned seeing his car in that North Bedford Drive driveway, because of course it hadn't been his car at all. She told him she didn't know why she had lost control of her car and had an accident. That was a bad and dangerous road.

But when her car came out of the body shop Emily couldn't bring herself to drive it. She couldn't even sit behind the wheel. The car was the vehicle that would take her into terrible danger. There was no way she could get her body to obey her command to start that car and drive away from her safe house. From the phone book she found a market that delivered groceries. There was a dairy that delivered milk, eggs, cheese, and bread. She could do her own hair. There was the pool, so who needed to go to a gym? Who needed a car?

When Emily felt her face was properly healed she let Ken take her to a dinner party given by another resident he knew from the hospital. Their host and hostess lived in an apartment. Their names were Fritz and Sandy. They had a baby, who was asleep in their bedroom, and they apparently had hardly any money. Emily felt sorry for them. It occurred to her then that she and Ken, who had lots of money, never gave parties, while this couple who were poor did, even though they had to serve potato chips and beer. She had always assumed she and Ken didn't give parties because they didn't know anyone. And they didn't, did they? She'd never even heard Ken mention these people before. Well, now they'd have to invite them back.

Sandy was plain and a little overweight, not at all like those sleek California girls, and Emily felt comfortable with her. "Tell me who everybody is," she said to Sandy.

"Well, they're mostly from the hospital. Ralph is a resident, and that's his wife Laurie. Ed is a bachelor, and he's going into medical research. That's Jody, who's a nurse, and her boyfriend Al. He's an actor. John is single and he lives with Marijane. She's divorced."

"People get divorced awfully young in California," Emily said.

"They do, don't they? I'm from St. Louis myself."

"Who's that?" Emily asked. There was a beautiful girl with a perfect figure, in a tight white dress, talking to Ken. He was smiling at her.

"Oh, that's Lani. She is *loaded* with money. She does some volunteer work at Cedars. Her husband is in real estate and he's older than she is. They just got divorced and she got this enormous house on North Bedford Drive, with a swimming pool and a tennis court, and a governess for their little girl, and she's only twenty-four."

"North Bedford Drive?" Emily said.

"Well, they were married seven years," Sandy said. "I hear he was just awful to her. I would never marry a man who's lots older."

Emily's hand went up to her face, covering her scar.

"Let me take you around and introduce you," Sandy said.

"I have to go to the ladies' room. Excuse me." She fled into the bathroom and inspected her lip and chin. Ken had lied. There was a scar. Why did he keep saying there was no scar when she could see it perfectly well, a thin pink line running down the side of her chin? And her chin seemed askew, too. How could he let her go out of the house looking so ugly, when all his friends could see her, and his girl friend could laugh at her? He obviously didn't think her pride was worth anything at all. Well, she did.

She put a layer of powder on the scar, trying to cover it up. Now the powder was all blotchy. She was hideous. She wanted to go home. She couldn't walk up to him while he was talking to his girl friend and have her see what a mess Ken was married to. She'd have to wait, and then she'd make him take her right home.

Emily stayed in the bathroom for ten minutes, and then she sneaked out and took hold of Ken's sleeve.

"Where were you, honey?" he asked. "I was getting worried."

"I feel sick. I have to go home."

"What is it, your stomach?"

"Yes," she lied.

"Do you want to lie down in the bedroom?"

"No. I want to go home."

Ken apologized to Fritz and Sandy while Emily stood in the darkened corner near the front door, her coat collar turned up to hide her chin. She couldn't look at anybody. She felt as if they were staring at her.

She and Ken drove home in silence. She could tell that he was annoyed at her, even though he kept casting concerned glances at her. When they got home she went directly to the bathroom, washed off her makeup, and looked at the scar in her magnifying mirror. Then she went to bed.

"I'm going to have to have plastic surgery," she said to Ken.

"For what?"

"For my scar."

"There *is* no scar," Ken said. "How's your stomach?"

"So-so. Why do you keep telling me there's no scar, Ken?"

He raised himself up and looked down at her. "Because the scar is all in your mind, Emily."

"I should have had stitches."

"It was a little cut. Stitches make worse scars."

"Ah, worse! You said worse! I do have a scar."

"Emily," Ken said, "sometimes I think you're crazy."

She dropped the matter. You could never win with a man. But after that night Emily refused to leave the house again. She would wait for the scar to go away. And if it didn't go away, then she would deal with that later.

She wasn't going to go out and let people laugh at her.

Chapter 5

By the time Chris had cleared customs and gotten to her hotel in Paris it was ten thirty in the morning, but four thirty A.M. in her head. She had been unable to sleep at all on the plane. Now she felt groggy and rather dirty, but still too excited to sleep. She was in Paris, and how could you not be excited about that? But the main thing was that Alexander was nearby, and tonight when he got home from work she would call him.

The Saint-Simon, the hotel Max had recommended, was an elegant *Directoire* mansion with a high street wall protecting it from the modern life outside. She had a room with private bath and two meals a day for only six dollars. She had chosen breakfast and dinner because that seemed most practical, although she hoped to be having her dinners with Alexander. Max had told her the rooms were furnished with antiques. Chris couldn't tell the difference between an antique and some beat-up furniture except that they were of different periods. Still, she could see that this was a very stylish place. You could always trust Max to have good taste.

She unpacked her suitcase, washed up, and went outside to look around. It was a gray, cold day, but very pretty. Wonderful old buildings with wrought-iron balconies, sidewalk cafés, little foreign cars driven recklessly, funny winding streets, cobblestones, kiosks with ads pasted on them—it was everything she had ever seen about Paris in the movies, but this was real. There actually was a man wearing a beret and riding on a bicycle, and a woman carrying a long loaf of hard bread in her hands without a wrapper.

Chris had provided herself with a street map and a guide book before she left, and she walked to the building where Alexander lived. There was a court-yard, and inside it were three little buildings which might have all been part of one. She looked up at the windows, wondering which one was his, and then she left quickly before anyone could notice her and ask her what she wanted. She walked for a while longer and stopped at a café for a sandwich and a cup of strong French coffee. It was so cold that the only people who had the courage to sit outside were the very young and the tourists. She was both. She didn't feel like the incipient old maid anymore; she felt as if everything might begin.

After her meal she walked across one of the bridges to the Right Bank, where Alexander worked. She stood for a moment looking at the Seine with the wind rippling its gray water, and wondered what it would be like to live here. Everything was beautiful and old and clean. She could understand why Alexander had chosen to stay. She walked to the American Bank and looked at it. She considered going inside to cash a traveler's check, but decided against it. Alexander wasn't a teller, but she didn't want him to come walking out of his office and see her this way for the first time. She wanted to meet him for a drink, looking her best, and play her game, according to the script she had worked out: be cool, pretend to be just friends, win him back.

She was suddenly exhausted, and she took a taxi

back to her hotel. She set the alarm and went to sleep.

When the alarm rang the room was dark, and for a moment Chris didn't know where she was. Then she remembered and sat up, her heart pounding. She put on the lights, drank some bottled water, and dialed Alexander's apartment.

The phone rang five times. She thought he wasn't there. Then she heard his voice, and it was so familiar and dear that her skin began to prickle all over and tears of relief came into her eyes.

"Alexander?" she said.

"Yes?"

She forced herself to sound calm and casual, just an old friend from the past. "This is Christine Spark."

"Chris!" He sounded pleased, and not surprised. "Max wrote me that you were coming. How are you?"

"I'm fine. How are you?"

"Just great." He sounded happy. It was strange to hear this new Alexander, who seemed more confident somehow. But of course they were both older now. "How long are you staying?"

"Two weeks. It's my vacation from my job." Now he knew she was temporary, not a nuisance, and that she deserved to be entertained.

"Well, we must have dinner," Alexander said. "How's your schedule?"

"Oh . . . I just got here and haven't made any plans yet. Whatever's good for you." Was that too pushy? Should she have lied?

"Well then, tomorrow?"

"That would be lovely. I'm looking forward to seeing you." Cool but warm, a friendly tone of voice, just right. She bit her lip.

"I'll pick you up at your hotel at seven. Where are you?"

"The Saint-Simon."

"I know where that is. It's near my house."

Chris smiled. She knew that. "See you tomorrow then."

The next day she went to the Louvre, but she was hardly aware of anything she saw. All she could see was Alexander. She wondered if he had changed much, and if he would think she had. She still wore her hair the same way, and had the same clothes, but what had looked drab in New York somehow seemed to fit in very well here. She looked like a little French schoolgirl. It was not exactly the image she would have chosen to seduce Alexander back, but at least it would be familiar.

Should she wait in the lobby or in her room? She sat on the edge of her bed wringing her hands. This wasn't Briggs Hall. She would wait in the lobby like a grown-up. She went downstairs, and just as she got there she saw Alexander coming in the door.

She couldn't catch her breath. He was more beautiful than ever; changed in these six lost years from a boy to a man. He was wearing an elegantly cut dark gray flannel suit, his dark hair curled over his ears, and she thought: Heathcliff. He could be a movie star, or even a young diplomat, or what he was, a rising young banker. She felt frumpy and inadequate.

"Chris!" He came striding toward her, smiling, and shook her hand. Then he realized what he was doing and he laughed. Maybe shaking hands with your former lover was hilarious. He kissed her lightly on each cheek. "There," he said. "That's French."

"You look very successful," Chris said lightly.

"Well, thank you. And you look very pretty."

He was another person entirely. And yet he was the same. Chris reminded herself to keep to her script. They walked down the street.

"We'll go to the Brasserie Lipp," Alexander said. "It's very famous. All the intellectuals sit around there and argue."

He pointed out places of interest while they walked, and Chris thought he hadn't spoken to her that much

in all the years she'd gone with him. He acted as
if she was a good, old friend from whom he'd parted
in the most amicable circumstances, instead of the
girl he'd loved and deserted, and she wondered what
in the world he was thinking. Maybe he saw it all
differently than she did. She would have to wait for
his signals.

He led her into a very crowded, unprepossessing-
looking restaurant with uncomfortable little tables
and chairs all jammed together. It had a turn of the
century look, but it certainly wasn't romantic or quiet
or dark, which she had hoped it would be.

"Do you still not drink?" he asked. They were facing each other and there were people screeching on
either side of them. The intellectuals arguing, no
doubt.

"Still," Chris said.

He ordered a carafe of red wine for himself and a
Coke for her. "How's old Max?" he asked. "Do you
see him much?"

"Not really. We had a nice talk on the phone be-
fore I left. He's a big success now; I'm sure you know.
I'm so pleased for him. I go to all his plays. He sees
Annabel. Do you remember her?"

"Sure," Alexander said.

"Well, she's married and living in Atlanta, and has
a daughter. She comes to New York twice a year and
we always have lunch. Max takes her to all the Broadway shows. They're still best friends. I wish she'd
married him instead of Rusty Buchanan, but life is
mysterious I guess."

"I guess so," Alexander said. "Do you see anybody
else from school?"

"Not really. Do you?"

"No. And you're not married?"

"Me?" Chris said. "No." She held out her ringless
hands. "Are you?"

"No."

"I have a very interesting job at *The Ladies' Home*

Journal. And I go to literary parties and screenings, that New York scene; there's always a lot to do. A few little romances, but nothing serious. I'm not ready to settle down."

"That's brave of you," Alexander said. "But you always were your own person."

"I guess you're happy in Paris," she said. "You stayed."

"It's a beautiful city. Do you know anybody else here?"

"Max gave me some names."

"Let me see them."

She took the list from her handbag and handed it to him. He nodded a few times. "Good. Yes. Nice people," he said. He gave the list back to her.

Chris sipped her Coke. "How is your mother?"

"She's fine. Pooch is going to graduate from Barnard next year. Amazing how time flies."

"Amazing," Chris said. "And Throckmorton?"

"He's practically senile. But he's hanging on."

"And your father?"

"He is unfortunately not senile. And hanging on too."

Chris laughed. It was the first time Alexander had ever shown the proper amount of disrespect toward his father. She supposed being safely across the ocean from each other did a lot of things to help family relationships.

"Let me order for us, all right?" he said. He did: *choucroute alsacienne;* some kind of boiled hot dogs with sauerkraut which he said was one of the house specialties. Chris pushed the food around on her plate and pretended to eat. She looked at his dark eyelashes, the planes of his face that were so familiar and yet so slightly different now, and all the love she had ever felt for him flooded her until she could hardly bear it. He was a thousand times better than he had ever been before! Maybe this time he could love her and it would work out. She knew she could never forget about him. Not now. The real Alexander she saw here was even better than the fantasy that had sustained her these past years. She would be careful this time, she would be clever, and she would somehow make him want her again.

"I'd love to see your apartment," Chris said casually. "I've never been in a French house."

"You could come for a drink on Wednesday," he said. "That's the day the maid comes, so it'll be presentable."

"I'd love to."

"And meanwhile, call those people on your list and arrange to meet them. French people make dates weeks in advance."

"All right," Chris said.

"I want you to enjoy Paris. It's more fun when you know people."

"Maybe you could introduce me to some people too," she said. The words nearly choked her. How perfectly casual I am, she thought, clenching her fists under the table.

"I'd be happy to," he said.

"You're being very nice and I appreciate it," Chris said.

"Nice?" Alexander said. "You're my friend and I'm glad to see you. Why shouldn't I be nice?"

"Why not indeed?" She lit a cigarette and gave him her best imitation of an insouciant smile. She remembered that carefree look Annabel always had and she plastered it on her face.

Alexander looked at his watch. "I'd better get you home. You still have jet lag."

"No, I don't."

"It'll catch up to you tomorrow. Listen to me." He paid the check and walked her home.

She felt sad when she saw the wall outside her hotel down the street. She didn't want Alexander to leave her. She wanted him to come upstairs with her, to make love to her, or just to sit and talk, but she knew she shouldn't even ask him to have a drink in the bar. She would not grovel.

At the outside door to her hotel he kissed her lightly on both cheeks. Stop being so phony French, she thought angrily. You bastard. I bet you've kissed a lot of girls since me.

"I'll see you Wednesday," she said sweetly. "What time?"

"Six thirty? And if you haven't made another date I'll take you to dinner."

"All right. Goodnight, and thanks for a lovely evening."

She went upstairs to bed. She was suddenly exhausted again. Maybe Alexander had been right and she did have jet lag. Or perhaps it was just that playing this game was very tiring for someone who was so madly in love and so alone. But she felt it was working. He had said: *I'm glad to see you.* He had also said he was her friend. Nothing had changed much. She would get him back. She knew it.

She didn't call anyone the next day because that would mean committing her time in case they asked her out. She would rather be alone than not be free for Alexander. Later, she would see. In the meantime she went to the Eiffel Tower, and the Rodin Sculpture Garden, and the Impressionists' exhibit at the Galerie du Jeu de Paume. She tried to keep her mind on what she was doing so she would have something to discuss with Alexander on Wednesday night.

She arrived at his apartment promptly at six thirty, looking her best. When Alexander opened the door she felt again that shock of love and awe that always hit her whenever she first saw him. He hung up her coat and then showed her around the apartment. The inside was a surprise after seeing the bourgeois outside. The living room was sleek and sexy and luxurious, with a dark leather couch, a lacquered screen, an oriental rug, and a glass-topped coffee table with small objects on it made of crystal. There was a portable bar with all kinds of bottles on it. Off the living room was a small dining room with a table and six chairs, and a crystal chandelier. Heavy silk curtains, tied back, hung from the ceiling to the floor over the tall French windows. The kitchen was large, with old-fashioned appliances, and the bathroom was huge, with a big marble tub.

"And this is the bedroom," Alexander said finally.

"Gee, I thought it was the kitchen."

He smiled. "People always say that, don't they. 'And this is the closet.'"

"'In my apartment you have to tell them which is the bedroom and which is the closet," Chris said.

Alexander's bedroom looked more like a study than a bedroom. Bookcases were built into two of the walls, and the third wall as well as the two built-in studio couches were covered in dark brown linen. There was a huge brown desk, and the room was dimly lit and very serious looking. The narrow little beds reminded her of the bed she and Alexander had used in his room at Harvard, and her eyes filled with tears.

"Well, that's it," Alexander said. He went into the hall again and she followed him.

"What's that room?" Chris asked. There was a closed door at the end of the hall.

"Oh," Alexander said mysteriously, "that's Alexander's Room."

She looked at him. He had a strange little smile on his face, almost a mean smile, that she had never seen before. "May I?" she asked, heading for the closed door.

"No."

"No?" Her tone was light but her heart was pounding. She put her hands into her pockets. One of those hands had already been outstretched to turn the knob. She felt pushy, ashamed, and left out.

"Nobody goes into Alexander's Room but Alexander," he said, his light tone matching hers. "You remember the story of Bluebeard. Anyone who ventures into the forbidden room gets his head cut off."

"I don't want you to cut my head off. Let's have a drink."

What the hell was in his secret room that was so private and special? The mystery seemed typical of Alexander, and of their long relationship. He had always shut off from her a little corner of himself, so she could never really get near him. He had been so elusive, at the same time warning her in little ways that if she tried to pry he would be gone.

They sat side by side on the couch in the living room. Alexander was drinking something called a kir, and Chris had her Coke. He had turned on the hi-fi and soft music was playing. She felt she could sit there forever.

"I love your apartment," she said.

"Thank you."

"It's sort of a surprise. I mean, it's not like you. I mean, it's like you now, so sophisticated and elegant, but I wouldn't have expected it."

"Why not? Were any of those places I lived in before like me? Was that ratty Harvard house me? Was my mother's apartment me? That old mausoleum where my father lives, was that *anybody*?"

"No, I guess not."

"Kids live where they're put. This apartment really is me."

"Yes," Chris said quietly, "full of secrets. What's in Alexander's Room?"

"Did you manage to get hold of any of the people on your list?"

All right, Alexander, she thought. "I called two and they were out," she lied. "And then I thought I'd just sightsee." Dutifully she told him everything she had seen. He seemed to approve.

"It's too bad you aren't going to London too," he

said. "Even just for the weekend. It's so near, and you should see it."

"I don't want to be one of those tourists who hops around," she said. "I'd rather see Paris really well. I want to do some shopping here too."

"I guess you're right."

"It's lucky we took that French class, isn't it?" she said.

"Do you remember your French?"

"Most of it."

"Well, tonight we'll just go to a little place in the neighborhood. I didn't know if you'd be free so I didn't make a reservation anywhere very chic or famous. At some of these restaurants you have to call a week in advance."

"Oh, I'm not dressed anyway," she said.

He looked at his watch. "You'll find the French eat late. Nine o'clock, even later. But I don't like to."

"I hate eating at ten o'clock."

"I remember," he said. "But most offices here don't close till seven. People have long lunches."

I could get used to that, she thought. I could get used to anything if I could be with him.

"Shall we?" he said, rising. He was holding her coat before she had a chance to ask if she could use the bathroom. Well, she'd go in the restaurant.

While Chris buttoned her coat Alexander went around carefully turning out all the lights. The moonlight shone in through the tall French windows, catching the crystal objects on the glass table and making them sparkle in the dim room.

As they headed for the front door Chris glanced back. There was Alexander's Room—closed, mysterious, forbidden—and there was a sliver of light under the door.

That night Alexander took her home with a promise to get two tickets for them to go to the Comédie-

Française on Friday night. The next morning Chris telephoned the Laurents, the couple Max said spoke fluent English. Agnes Laurent, who sounded young and cheerful, said Chris must come with her and her husband Jean-Paul for Sunday lunch at a country inn, old family tradition, and of course they would not bring the children because that would be too boring, and they would invite Alexander too because they hadn't seen him for a long time and they missed him. Chris adored Agnes immediately. She decided it would be good to have a woman friend here in Paris, and a couple was perfect because then they could double-date with her and Alexander.

She did not call any of the men on her list. She was seeing Alexander every other night since she'd arrived. This was definitely progress. The men could wait. It occurred to her that ever since she'd come to Paris she had been thinking in terms of the not-so-near future, as if her two week vacation was just another pretense. That afternoon, after a walk through the Bois de Boulogne, Chris went to the concierge of her hotel and asked if it would be possible to stay longer if she had to.

"Of course! We have long leases. Some of our guests stay for months, for years. Would you like your same room, or perhaps a small suite?"

"No, no," Chris said. "My room will be fine."

After the theater on Friday night Chris invited Alexander to have a drink with her in her hotel bar. He seemed pleased to accept, and as she sat there toying with her Coke she wondered if she should ask him to come upstairs. It was her hotel, so it was her move. But Alexander had always liked to make the first move. She wondered if he had changed.

"I love this hotel," she said. "My room is very nice."

"I'm glad."

He insisted on paying the check even though it was her hotel and she had invited him and had planned to charge it. She decided that was an omen to let Alexander decide when he wanted to resume their sex life.

At the elevator Alexander kissed her gently on the lips, for the first time. "Sleep well," he said. "See you Sunday."

The next morning she got up early and went to a boutique not far from her hotel where she had noticed a sign in the window advertising their need for a salesgirl. The sign was still there. They were pleased that Chris was bilingual, and offered her just enough to live on, plus a discount on their clothes. She accepted, and said she would start work on Monday. That way, she thought, if I hate it I can still go home.

Sunday lunch in the country was wonderful. Agnes seemed to be Chris's age, and incredibly chic, with long dark hair, a black cape, well-cut jeans, and cowboy boots. Her husband, Jean-Paul, was friendly and very handsome. They were both journalists.

"Only two weeks?" Agnes said. "What a shame. You should stay longer."

"I have to go back to work," Chris said. She smiled at Alexander and he gave her a sweet look.

"But Chris loves it here, don't you, Chris?" Alexander said.

"Oh, yes." He wants me to stay longer, she thought. He does!

The new job at the boutique was not very difficult, despite Chris's difficulty with changing American money into French money in her head. In the evenings she was tired, and she thought she could have a very normal life here with her work and Alexander and all the sights she had not yet seen. She wouldn't be bored. Home seemed less and less appealing. On Tuesday night she went to dinner with Alexander and Agnes and Jean-Paul, at a small café whose name she promptly forgot, where they sat in a booth and ate bouillabaisse. Chris insisted on speaking French all evening, and they agreed she spoke it very well. When they asked her what she had been doing during the day she lied and said she had been wandering around discovering new streets and had done some shopping.

At her elevator Alexander kissed her lightly goodnight and said, "Well, we both reek from garlic so it's all right. Sleep well, and I'll think of something special to do before you go."

She couldn't stand to go. There was no way she could leave him here; she felt paralyzed. She wrote a letter to her boss resigning her job, and then she wrote a more difficult one, to her father.

Dear Dad: Everything is wonderful here, and I hope you're okay too. You know I've never asked you for a big favor before, but this time I have to impose on you because there's no one else to ask. I've been offered a marvelous job here in Paris, as an editor on a magazine. You know I was bored being a proofreader and always wanted to do editorial work. I just couldn't turn it down. They want me to start right away. The problem is I have to get rid of my apartment. There are six months left on the lease, but I think the landlord will be glad to take it now because then he can raise the rent. If not, could you please manage to pay the rent as a loan to me and I'll pay you back? Right now I can't manage two rents. Prestige jobs pay very badly. About my stuff—it's mostly junk. Please take my books and records to your place, and give the furniture to the Salvation Army. That's where I bought it in the first place! And will you please send me my clothes? I will be eternally grateful to you for doing all this. My best love to you and to Mom. Chris.

When she mailed both letters she felt immensely relieved. She told the concierge she would be staying on indefinitely, and suddenly the Saint-Simon wasn't a hotel anymore—it was her home. On her way home from work she bought flowers and a glass vase to put them in.

For the first time in six years her life had some purpose again.

Alexander called on Thursday night. "I'm going to have a going-away party for you on Saturday evening," he said. "Cocktails at my place, and then you and I will go out, just the two of us, and have a late dinner at Maxim's. You'll have to wear something dressy."

"Oh . . ."

"When does your plane leave on Sunday?"

"I'm not going on Sunday."

"I thought you were. Is it Monday then?"

"I'm staying a little longer," Chris said.

She couldn't tell over the crackling old-fashioned phone line whether he was glad. "Don't they mind at the *Journal*?"

"No. You don't have to splurge on Maxim's now— we can go somewhere simple," she said.

There was a slight pause. "I'll be glad to take you to Maxim's, Chris. I'll come get you at nine."

She wore her only good black dress and hoped it was good enough. Alexander was wearing a very elegant black suit. Maxim's was all art nouveau and plants and glowing colors, reflected in mirrors. Chris felt shabby. The other customers looked as if they owned yachts and safes full of real jewels. Alexander ordered his kir and her Coke.

"This is beautiful, Alexander. Thank you."

"My pleasure. Now tell me, how long are you going to stay?"

What should she tell him? That she would stay forever? No, that might shock him. "Well," she said, trying to sound as if she had turned into the sort of person who lived for unexpected adventures, "I thought I'd hang around for a few months, until I got bored. I told you I don't want to settle down. My job at home was getting dull, and New York isn't as much fun as Paris."

"A few months? But how will you live?"

"I got a job."

"Where?"

"At a boutique."

"Good God," Alexander said.

She raised her glass. "Here's to . . . to what, Alexander?"

"To . . . you," he said.

At the end of the evening when he took her home he said he would call, and so she waited. Every evening when she returned from work she rushed to her mailbox to see if there was a message from him, and every night she waited in her room until the last possible moment before going down to eat her paid-for dinner at the hotel. He didn't call all week, and finally on Friday she called him. There was no answer. She called again on Saturday and Sunday, and finally on Sunday night he answered the phone.

"Hi, Alexander. It's Chris."

"How are you?" he asked.

"Just fine. And you?"

"A little tired. I went to the country this weekend."

"You're supposed to be relaxed from the country."

"My friends were afraid I'd be bored."

"And were you?"

"No."

"When can we see each other this week?" she asked.

"This is going to be a tough week," he said. "I'm very busy."

"I mean, we could have a drink one night after work," she said quickly. She shouldn't have made him think she wanted him to take her out. He must have spent a fortune entertaining her the past two weeks. "You could come here, or I'd come to your place."

"I have some people in from out of town," he said. "Dull German bankers. I'm sorry."

"That's all right. Maybe we could have lunch."

"I have a business lunch every day."

"Oh." He felt she lived here now, and he didn't have to give up his work to entertain the tourist. That was all right. As long as she could keep on seeing him. "You're my only real friend here," Chris said, trying to keep it light. "I need your advice."

"Sure. What do you want to know?"

What I want to know, she thought, is why you always shut a little corner of yourself off from me, like "Alexander's Room," so I can never really get near you. That's what I want to know. "Can't we have a drink when your German bankers leave?"

"Okay. I'll call you at the end of the week."

After they hung up Chris sat for a long time staring at the wall. She hadn't expected this, but she should have known that the pace of their relationship would change when he knew there was all the time in the world. She was willing to wait. It would be difficult, but nothing had ever been easy with Alexander.

She spent her free evenings during the week walking past his house, hoping to get a glimpse of him. She was partly afraid he would see her and be annoyed, and partly hoping he *would* see her and feel on the spur of the moment like inviting her in. But she didn't see him at all. He finally called ten days later.

"How's everything?" he asked pleasantly.

"Oh, fine. How are you?"

"Busy as hell."

"I've been busy too," she lied.

"I just wanted to see how you were," Alexander said.

"I'd love to see you. Why don't we meet for coffee?

We live practically around the corner from each other."

"Like the old days at the Bick," Alexander said. He didn't sound a bit nostalgic.

"It's a lot nicer here," Chris said, pretending to be cheerful.

"Have you met all the people on that list?"

"Yes," she lied.

"Good. Then I know you're in good hands."

"Why don't we go out one night with Agnes and Jean-Paul?" Chris said. "They'd love it."

"This week I have the *Japanese* bankers," Alexander said.

"My goodness."

"In fact, I'm late now. But I just wanted to check and make sure you're all right."

"Could we spend Thanksgiving together, Alexander?" There was such a pain in her throat she could hardly speak. "It's not a French holiday, but I'm going to be homesick."

"Poor little Chris," Alexander said. "Of course. We'll have Thanksgiving dinner. I'll call you before."

She looked at the appointment calendar next to her phone. Thanksgiving was in ten days. All the days between were empty spaces. "I'll be looking forward to it," she said.

The phone clicked as Alexander hung up. She replaced her receiver slowly. Everything at home was gone. But there really hadn't been anything at home. Her life was going to be in the future with Alexander. People who have nothing to lose are the ones who are able to take the greatest risks. She thought perhaps she might buy some wool and canvas and preserve that motto in needlepoint to make the time pass. But more to the point was to get out of this self-imposed isolation, which had been a period of craziness. It had been rude of her not to call Agnes Laurent, whom she liked so much. She would take Agnes to lunch. And she would definitely call all the people on Max's list. She would make friends, have a social life. If Alexander changed his mind and called her at the last minute she could always break any date she had made.

By Friday she was feeling pleased with herself. She had called Agnes, who had invited her to their apartment for dinner on Saturday night and seemed delighted that Chris was going to stay in Paris. And she had made two cocktail dates for the following week. She had managed to save enough money from her paycheck to buy a radio for her room, which made it seem much cozier. It was November twenty-second; Thanksgiving was less than a week away, and there was Thanksgiving with Alexander to look forward to. Her next purchase, when she had saved more money, would be a new dress with her boutique discount.

On her way home from work she stopped to buy a bottle of wine to bring to the Laurents the next day, and the man who waited on her recognized her accent.

"So they shot your President," he said.

"Don't be silly." Toothless old anti-American creep making jokes.

She went to her room and put on the radio. It was *true*. A man had shot President Kennedy in the head while he was riding in a motorcade in Texas, and nobody knew yet whether he was dead. Chris stood there stunned. How could anybody do such a thing? John Kennedy represented everything that was idealistic and young and honorable in their country; they were all going to do great things together. Everybody loved him and his young family. But evidently someone did not.

Then the radio announcer said that President Kennedy was dead.

If he had said that New York had been bombed she could not have been more horrified. What would happen to everyone now? The world that had seemed so full of promise suddenly seemed threatened by evil and hate. Why did they kill only the good people? Nobody had ever killed Hitler. Chris began to cry. She was a stranger in a strange country—and now these French people must think Americans were savages who killed their heroes. She felt ashamed, and the grief she felt for herself encompassed pain for everyone at home.

The new president, Lyndon Johnson, was being sworn in on board *Air Force One,* the same plane that was carrying the dead president. Chris couldn't stand to be alone in that room for another minute. The one person she needed to be with was Alexander. He would be going through exactly what she was, and they could comfort each other. She turned off her radio and ran blindly through the streets to Alexander's house.

Breathless, she rang the bell to his apartment, praying he would be home. Finally the door opened. A young blond boy stood there, about eighteen, wearing only jeans. He had a smooth, hairless chest and an arrogant, rather pretty face.

"Where's Alexander?" Chris said. "Is he here?"

"Who are you?" the boy asked in French.

"I'm Chris."

"You're Chris?"

"Why not?" she said in French, impatient with him.

He shrugged. "I thought Chris was a boy."

She pushed past him into the apartment. "Alexander!"

"Nobody's here but me."

"Who are you?" she said.

"I am a guest." He smiled. "This week."

The door to Alexander's Room down the hall was wide open, and the boy walked right in as though he belonged there. Chris followed him, numb. The room looked like someone's nightmare of a bordello. A huge bed with rumpled, dirty sheets stood under an enormous octagonal mirror that was attached to the ceiling. The heavy drapes were closed. Plates of partly eaten food were on the floor and the dresser, and male clothing was scattered around. There were empty champagne bottles and glasses. The walls were covered in dark red paisley material, and dim light came from hidden sources. The room smelled of incense and sex.

"Do you have an American cigarette?" the boy asked pleasantly.

Chris's hands were shaking. She gave him one and lit one for herself. The boy lay down on the bed lazily, lit his cigarette, and relaxed against the pillows. "I love American cigarettes," he said.

She couldn't think straight. That sliver of light under the closed door to Alexander's Room—someone had been in there. If not this boy, another one perhaps. She heard the front door close and her heart jumped with fear. What was she afraid of, that Alexander would catch her in his precious room? With this slob?

"Well, well," Alexander said behind her. She turned around and looked at him. He had that same mean little smile on his mouth as he had the first time she asked him what this room was.

"They killed Kennedy," she said.

"I know."

"I want a drink," Chris said.

Alexander turned and went into the living room where he poured two shots of vodka, one for her and one for himself. The boy followed them, curious.

"Go back in there," Alexander said to him in French.

"Why?"

"Because I say so." The boy gave him an annoyed look and left. Chris drank the vodka. It didn't have any taste at all, just a kind of sting, and then she felt very warm. "I still can't believe it," Alexander said. He turned on the television set. It was on the news.

They sat on the couch side by side like two zombies, watching TV.

"I'm sorry," Alexander said finally.

"*Sorry?*"

"About the boy in there. I'm sorry you know."

She realized then that she had known as soon as she saw the boy and the room, but that it had been impossible to take so many shocks at one time. She felt grief suddenly smashing through her.

"Is he your lover?" she said.

Alexander sighed. "One of many."

"Alexander, I don't understand."

"Yes you do," he said quietly.

"Is this what people do in Paris?" she asked stupidly, hoping he would say yes, it was the new chic fad.

"Chris, I'm gay. I've always been gay. Max and I were lovers in prep school and college. We came here because it's *shit* to be gay in America. People call you a pervert, a degenerate. Can you see me being a banker in New York and living my life?"

"Max . . . ?"

"It's easy for him in the theater," Alexander said. "We're just friends now. I play the field. This is my life. I prefer them young and beautiful and mindless. They're not important to me."

She understood it all now: his evasions, his misery at college, his secrecy. But what about her? He had loved her, she had to believe that. This man sitting here telling her the devastating truth was another facet of the happy man she had dated in Paris when she first got here and the shy, sad boy she had gone steady with at school. They were all Alexander. For the first time she had the whole person before her.

"Did you care about me at all?" she whispered.

"I loved you."

"You really did?"

"Yes."

"What should I do?" she asked.

"You don't have to do anything," Alexander said. "Just be my friend. I want you to be my friend. You don't stop loving someone just because the sex is over."

You don't stop loving somebody . . . She started to cry again. He put his arm around her and she put her head on his shoulder. He was patting her gently. Her whole life had blown up in one evening and she was bereaved. But Alexander was holding her, comforting her, and she loved him just as much as she always had. She looked up at him. He was watching the television newscast and his eyes were full of tears.

"Some maniac with a rifle just killed a dream," he said. "I'm scared."

Chris spent the next evenings with Alexander. He came with her to Agnes and Jean-Paul's, and they all watched television. None of them felt much like eating. The other evenings she went to Alexander's apartment to watch his TV set. They saw the funeral, and listened to the prognostications of what would happen. They saw Jack Ruby kill Lee Harvey Oswald. Chris postponed her two cocktail dates and Alexander left the blond boy alone in his room, at least until after she had gone back to her hotel. She and Alexander spent Thanksgiving quietly together, just the two of them at a neighborhood bistro.

Her pain was beginning to subside and she tried to think what she should do with her life. Alexander was kind and gentle with her, comfortable at last, relieved that she knew and accepted him. She didn't know what else to do. She loved him. He couldn't help being the way he was. She felt he didn't want to be that way. How could anyone want to be that way—frightened, a pariah? She tried to imagine what it was like for Alexander to feel physical attraction for a young man. She had felt it for him, still did, so it must be the same. It was easier for her to imagine a man wanting to go to bed with another man than it was for her to imagine a woman desiring another woman. She forbade herself to try to imagine what Alexander did in bed with his young men, but the thought of him kissing that blond boy broke her heart. Maybe they didn't kiss and it was all strictly business. She refused to think about it further, although it nudged the edge of her mind.

Alexander had said he still loved her. That was all that mattered. Homosexuals could go straight if they wanted to badly enough. She would change him. She had done it once before. She knew she could do it again if she was patient and kind.

She would stay in Paris. She would accept Alexander's life, and she would get him back.

Chapter 6

In New York, it was the year for big smash hit musicals on Broadway: *Hello, Dolly!, Funny Girl, Fiddler on the Roof, Golden Boy,* and the new Max Harding offering, *Penrod!,* based on the old Booth Tarkington novel. It was Max's first musical, and it was sold out for three solid months a week after the reviews came in.

Max was living on Fifth Avenue now, in a one bedroom apartment that overlooked Central Park. For the past four months he had shared his apartment with a beautiful blond nineteen-year-old boy named Phillip, an actor who had a small part in *Penrod!.* Max couldn't take their relationship too seriously. He felt the generation gap looming between them even though he was barely ten years older. One night he had overheard Phillip on the phone describing him to a friend—"He's twenty-nine, but he's still good-looking."

Max knew the value of youth and beauty in his world. He had chosen Phillip because of the smoothness of his almost hairless skin, his sensuous mouth and guileless eyes, his arrogant, hipless, sinuous body. Certainly not for his conversation or his education, which were limited to what was good for Phillip.

Phillip was as open and selfish as a child. He looked exactly like the young men Alexander always liked, and probably still did. It was strange, Max sometimes thought, how he and Alexander had avoided duplicating each other in their lovers, as if to keep their own love special.

The first time Max had ever seen Alexander they were both fourteen years old, their first year at prep school. He had fallen in love immediately: an electric shock of desire and the deeper emotional certainty that they were going to be lovers. Even then Alexander had been secretive and unhappy. At fourteen Alexander trought he was the only boy in the world who was queer, as they called them then, and Max already knew differently.

They became inseparable, best friends and lovers. They planned to go to Harvard together and room together, and they did. But at college Alexander's guilt began to tear at their relationship. He hated being gay. Max, who enjoyed the company of women and was in love with Alexander, liked being what he was, and had planned his future life. He would become a famous person and people would admire him for what he had accomplished. They would accept his private life, if they knew about it, because they would want him to be their friend. And for those who couldn't understand, he would remain discreet. He would grow old as one of those charming bachelors who are in constant demand as escorts, first for deb parties, later for single girls, and finally for divorced women and those whose husbands hated to go out. He assumed that well-planned life would also include Alexander.

At Harvard it was Max who encouraged Alexander to date girls, had told him to be nice to Chris. He never thought that Alexander would use Chris to try to go straight.

Max knew when Alexander began to have sex with Chris, and he had been pained and jealous, but he had also felt sorry for Chris because he was sure it wouldn't last and she would get hurt. He knew Alexander's own misery was the most important thing in Alexander's life, and whatever he gave of it to others was unimportant to him; he was simply unaware. Alexander was the Typhoid Mary of angst.

The trip to Paris for a year was to have been Max and Alexander's chance for freedom to live as they pleased. Then they would come back and resume their charade. But when they got to Paris where Alexander could for the first time be openly homosexual, Alexander refused to go home. For a while Max thought he would stay and try to become a producer in Paris, only for Alexander's sake, but then Alexander began cheating.

Max had tried to understand. Having sex with many young men was Alexander's way of fighting their relationship because it made him too guilty to be in love with a man. But what sense did that make? If he drove Max away it still wouldn't make either of them straight. Eventually Max began to cheat too. And then there were fights, the recriminations, the reconciliations. And finally, at the end of their year, Max had gone to New York alone, because he knew their nine-year love affair was over forever.

It was a year now since Chris had gone to Paris to find Alexander. Max didn't know what was going on between them. He knew what little he did know from Annabel. Chris and Annabel wrote to each other. Alexander never wrote to him, and Max wrote to Alexander only when friends were going to Paris. "Be nice to Chris . . ."

Max wasn't jealous this time. Those feelings were over. But he didn't want to fall in love again in the same way, ever again. The Phillips in his bed were sexy and cozy and fun for as long as it lasted, and kept away loneliness. Sometimes he wished his first real love had not been Alexander. Whoever loved Alexander was ruined. Or maybe he had been too vulnerable, too romantic, too eager to believe. . . .

There was no one moment when Annabel actually found out Max was gay; it was as if she had always somehow understood his love for her was different, and then when she first visited him in New York he let her see his life and she acted as if she had always known. Annabel was the only person Max could confide in. She accepted him totally. Her brief, semiannual visits always left him feeling refreshed and happy about himself. She was here now, just arrived for her week. It was the frenzied period before Christmas, and he had taken the afternoon off to meet her at the airport and take her to her hotel. He had sent champagne and flowers, and tonight he would take her to dinner.

She had looked tired at the airport, but he had thought it was from the trip. But when he picked her up at seven he could see the faintly violet shadows under her eyes, and her skin was pale. Still, he thought she had never looked more beautiful in all the years he'd known her.

"You get better every year," he said. "I wish I did."

"But you do," Annabel said. "Men always get better looking when they're older. Boys bore me."

"I thought we'd have a drink in the bar and then go to Pavillon."

"Oh, let's drink your champagne right here, Max. I want to share it with you."

He opened the chilled bottle and poured it into two glasses. "To your trip," he said.

"To your show."

"I've gotten you a ticket for tomorrow night," he said. "And afterward I'll get you and take you to supper. Do you mind going alone? If you want I'll get you a date. I'd go with you, but I'm sick of it."

"I should think so." She laughed. "I don't mind going alone. This is lovely champagne, Max. Thank you."

"You're welcome."

"I'm so glad to get away—you can't imagine." She held out her empty glass and he refilled it. "I shouldn't have married Rusty. It was stupid. And how is your private life?"

"At the moment it's a juvenile delinquent named Phillip. Nineteen."

"Oh, God. Are you happy?"

"My work makes me happy."

"Mine doesn't. I loathe being a housewife."

"You're not a housewife."

"Oh, yes I am. But I'm a mother too. I like that part of it."

"Are you going to have more children?"

"Not with him I'm not."

"The champagne is finished. I should have sent two bottles."

"Well, let's go to the bar," Annabel said gaily. "Is there time?"

They had more champagne at the bar and then went to Pavillon. They were seated at one of the red velvet banquettes opposite the door, reserved for patrons the restaurant considered important. The room was brightly lit, with murals on the walls, and the air was lightly scented from the fresh red roses on every table. People turned to look at Annabel when she came in. People always did.

They had more champagne with dinner. If Annabel was high, she didn't show it. She was smoking with a black onyx cigarette holder now that matched her black dress. "What do you hear from Chris?" Max asked.

"She seems to like her life in Paris," Annabel said. "She and Alexander are . . . best friends, she says. They're not lovers. She's crazy."

"Maybe they *are* best friends."

She looked at him. "Do you think so?"

"No. But I'm prejudiced."

Annabel smiled. "Against Chris or against Alexander?"

"Touché."

"He was a fool to give you up, Max."

"I don't care anymore. I really don't."

"That doesn't make him less of a fool."

He kissed her hand. "Let me tell you about my work. I'm going to become a director."

"You are?"

"At least I'm going to try. You know I always wanted to direct. I'm reading scripts all the time, but now I see myself doing something creative with them."

He told her about one of the scripts he had particularly liked, and swore her to secrecy. Her eyes were bright with excitement and she didn't look so pale anymore. Max thought again, as he often did, that Annabel had a quality of making the person who was talking to her feel that he was capable of doing great things. She just couldn't accept impossibility, except for her own wishes.

After dinner they went to the Peppermint Lounge, the funky, tacky discotheque that was popular at the moment. The noise from the band pounded at them, exhilarating yet tranquilizing. They danced the frug, the swim, and the watusi, and a new dance Max had seen for the first time a few nights before at one of the bars he went to with Phillip.

"I think I'd like to dance myself to death," Annabel said. "It would be a good way to go."

"Better than most," Max said.

"I hate it back home. You have no idea how much I hate it."

Why don't you leave your husband, Max thought, but he didn't say it. He had nothing to offer her—friendship and encouragement and laughter, yes, but not a life. They were both too honest. She would have to make her own life. He wished he knew how to help her. But Annabel would have to help herself.

"What are you so pensive about all of a sudden?" she asked.

"I just wanted to tell you," Max said, "that if you ever need me, I'm here."

"I know that, Max. And I'm always here for you."

"I really love you."

"I know," she said. "I love you too."

And they kept on dancing.

During the warm, sunny California winter days Emily sat by her swimming pool, reading books, her head and face shielded by a large-brimmed hat. Dark glasses protected her eyes, and a heavy layer of suntan oil covered her body. But it was important to keep her face out of the sun. Ken said too much sun was aging.

She spent a great deal of time inspecting her face and body. Besides the disfiguring scar on her chin there were the stretch marks on her stomach, the tiny varicosities on her legs, the faint beginning of cellulitis on her thighs. Sometimes it seemed so hopeless she wanted to kill herself. When she was alone she wore a bikini in the sun so her tan would cover these horrors. When Ken was around she wore things that covered her from shoulders to ankles. She knew that out there, in his world, he saw beautiful young women every day who were still perfect.

Ken was now a successful Beverly Hills dermatologist with his own office, shared with an older doctor, and his own practice. He worked long days and met interesting people. Emily was jealous of his contribution and his self-respect, and even more of his exciting life in the world. She was about as impor-

tant to him as the wallpaper: you hardly noticed it,
but if it peeled off it would be an annoyance. He no
longer even bothered to cover up his affairs. It was
over with Lani, the rich divorcée from North Bedford Drive; now it was Rebecca, the nurse in his office, with straight honey-colored hair and an English
accent. She wasn't Jewish. Ken pretended to have late
meetings and walked into the house at midnight with
wine on his breath. What kind of meetings did dermatologists have at night where they served liquor?
He didn't even care enough to make up a believable
excuse.

He no longer talked about building the tennis
court on their piece of land. Now he zipped away in
his car on Saturdays and Sundays with his tennis
racquet and a little bag beside him on the seat. Emily
knew where he was going—to Rebecca.

Her own car sat unused in their garage. Sometimes
Ken took it out for a drive so it wouldn't go dead.
They never invited anyone to visit them and he never
tried to make her come out with him anymore. He
told his friends: "Emily is busy with the children."

The children liked repetitive actions. Jumping off
the sofa, climbing back, jumping off. Throwing things.
Running in patterns, screaming nonsense words that
appealed to them. In the morning they liked to get
into bed between her and Ken. They would have
crept in there at night too, but Emily forbade it. Why
did you have to feel so guilty if you demanded a few
rights as a grown-up? Suddenly she had found herself
living in a children's world, where even Ken communicated with her through them. "How were the kids
today? What did they do?" Never "What did *you*
do?" He knew what she did.

Winter and summer were the same to her in this
place. The only difference was that summer days were
even longer and hotter. She sat outdoors under the
blue sky in the summer and tried to imagine where
Ken was. She went through his day in her mind, and

then her fearful fantasies took over as she pictured him in Rebecca's bed. That one hurt so much her heart nearly stopped, and she shut off the film behind her eyes. The books said you should talk about the problems in your marriage.

Saturday morning. Ken took the children swimming in the pool, their two sleek little wet heads bobbing safely above the surface of the water, their little bodies encased in bright orange life jackets. Ken was still so muscular and slim in his trunks, even more fit than he had been when they were first married. Maybe he did play tennis part of the time, the way he claimed. Maybe he played tennis with Rebecca. Emily covered her scar with makeup and put on a long white terry-cloth robe. She sat by the side of the pool and watched her husband playing with his two little toys, and then he handed them over to her to dry and dress.

"Ken, I want to talk to you."

"Let me take a shower first."

The children were screaming for food. She went to the kitchen to make their peanut-butter-and-jelly sandwiches, the only thing they would eat lately, her mind alert for the sound of Ken's footsteps on the stairs. He wouldn't sneak out on her this time!

"You may watch the cartoons," she told Kate and Peter, turning on the television set. They sat on the floor in front of it, making crumbs, smearing their clothes. Emily didn't care anymore. She went into her bedroom. Ken was dressed, snapping on his wristwatch.

"I have to talk to you," she said.

"Okay. Where are the kids?"

"Watching television."

He glanced at his watch. "I have a tennis date at ten thirty. What's on your mind?"

"You make me feel like I need an appointment to get a minute with you," Emily said.

"I'm here."

She lit a cigarette. "I . . ."

"Emily, I wish you wouldn't smoke."

"I don't smoke much."

"I'd like you not to smoke at all."

"And I'd like you not to cheat at all," she said. She saw him bite his lip. Her words poured out from between clenched teeth, angry and shrill. "Do you think I don't know about those other women? I knew about Lani. I know about Rebecca. You didn't marry a moron, you know. I was smart once. We talked once. We were in love once . . ." She started to cry.

"Oh, Emily," he said sadly. He put his arms around her. "You mustn't imagine things."

"Stop treating me like a moron," she sobbed. "Just tell me the truth, I don't care. Tell me why you want them and you don't want me."

"I don't want them."

"You do."

Ken sighed. "All right," he said. He stepped away from her as if afraid she would hit him. "You want the truth, I'll tell you the truth. I see other women, but they don't mean anything to me. I don't know why I do it. I've asked myself. I guess the real reason is we got married too soon. They're my fling, the trip to Europe I never had."

"Europe . . ." She had thought hearing him tell her it was true about the other women wouldn't hurt more than everything already did, but she had been wrong. His words were the worst thing that had ever happened to her.

He sounded very unhappy. "I never wanted to hurt you," he said. "I wish I'd never gotten off that boat."

"Why? Because then you wouldn't have had to marry me?"

"No, because maybe it would have been different."

"You just would have made up another excuse to cheat."

"I don't know. I wish I knew."

"Are you tired of me?" Emily asked. Say no, she thought. Please say no.

"No," Ken said. "I love you. But you're acting crazy lately. You won't go out, you won't do anything. You don't care about anything."

"I care about a lot of things," she said, angry again now. "You made me give up my job, you made me have kids, you made me stay home. What do you expect? I have responsibilities. I can't spend my days preparing to be interesting for you. It's me, *me* who makes your life bearable. I run your home. I make everything nice. I bring up your children. What more do you want?"

Ken shook his head. "I . . . think that's fine, Emily."

"Do you? Do I get an A-plus? Thank you."

"I'll stop seeing her," he said.

"Just like that?"

"If you want."

"And then you'll resent me and hate me."

"What do you *want*, Emily?" Now he sounded exasperated.

"I want it to be like it used to be!"

"Do you even remember how it used to be, Emily?"

"Of course I do."

"You *wanted* to give up your job. You *wanted* to have children. You *wanted* a home and a family. You *wanted* to be married. Emily, what the hell did you think it was going to be like?"

Emily stared at him. What did he mean?

"I'm going to be late for my tennis game," Ken said, and walked out of the bedroom.

She heard his car driving away, fast. She knew he was angry. Why was Ken angry? She hadn't done anything. He was the one who was acting crazy. What right did he have to insult her? She should never have stopped playing tennis. She could have been really good by now and they could play together. They used to do everything together before the children were born. She was sorry they'd had the children.

Absently, as she did so often, Emily rubbed her finger over her chin where she knew her scar was. Strange . . . she couldn't seem to feel it. She rushed to the mirror. The scar was gone! *Gone!*

She couldn't believe it. She scrubbed off the makeup she'd used to cover it and saw that the scar had really vanished. But how could that be? The sun? The air? It was a miracle.

Now she could go out and do all the normal things people did who weren't ugly and ashamed. She stood looking at herself in the mirror and smiling. Then she heard Kate and Peter screaming as they ran up the stairs and burst into the bedroom.

"Mommy, we want to go swimming!"

"Why don't you watch TV?" Emily asked absently.

"The cartoons are over."

"All right," she said. She felt very tired. Why hadn't Ken told her the scar was gone? He hadn't even really looked at her. Maybe he hadn't looked at her for a long time. She wasn't a woman to him anymore, she was just Mommy. And she was going to be thirty years old next year. She would be too old, and everything would be over. Those children were always in her life, coming between her and Ken. No wonder he ran off to play tennis and have his "meetings." Who would want to stay around here?

When Ken came home from his day of tennis Emily said, "Let's go out to dinner tomorrow night."

"Hey, great!" he said. He took that for her sign of reconciliation. "See if you can get a sitter."

The children. She'd never hired a baby-sitter before and didn't know where to begin. "I . . . maybe there's somebody at the hospital who would . . ."

"You don't need a nurse," Ken said. "You just need a sitter."

"I meant one of your friends might have a good one. I don't know anybody."

"It's kind of late," he said. "But I'll make a couple of calls."

He spent half an hour on the phone and came back with three names. Emily was beginning to have misgivings. She didn't want to leave the children with a stranger. They were so isolated here; what if something happened? How could she leave one teenager with two little children? Peter kept climbing out of his crib now. Suppose a burglar came, or a kidnapper, or a crazy murderer? But dutifully, because she had suggested it, she telephoned each of the three sitters on the list. They were all out. Of course, it was Saturday night, and they were working for other people.

"I won't know till tomorrow," she told Ken.

"That's all right. The good restaurants are closed Sunday night. Why don't we plan something for next Saturday?"

She felt disappointed. "A whole week away?"

"Sure. Maybe I'll get another couple and we'll double-date."

"Don't you want to be alone with me?"

"Whatever you want, Emily."

"I want a romantic evening. It's been so long."

"I know," Ken said. He put his arms around her. "I'm glad you want to go out and have fun again. It's been too long."

Emily leaned her head against his chest. She felt so safe in his arms. "Did you tell her it's all over?" she said.

She felt his body stiffen. "I didn't see her today."

"I thought you did."

He drew away from her again. "I played tennis today, Emily. I told you that."

"When are you going to see her?"

"I'll tell her Monday."

"Is that when you're going to see her?"

"Emily, leave the details to me, will you please?"

"Don't get mad."

"I'm not mad."

There was a wail from Kate's room, and angry sobbing. Ken rushed out of their bedroom to see what was going on. Emily followed him slowly, fingering her chin in the gesture that had become a habit, even though there was no scar there anymore.

Peter had grabbed one of Kate's toys and Kate had hit him. Ken was patiently trying to make peace and explain sharing. Didn't he know it was impossible? Little children wanted everything for themselves: their possessions, their parents . . . Ah, just wait until they grow up, Emily thought. Then they'll find out that they can't have *anything* in the world that they don't have to share. When you grow up people take everything away from you: your time, your life, your freedom, your husband. . . .

"Read to me, Daddy." Kate with a book, demanding, putting the book on Ken's lap, reaching up to sit there too. Peter was sucking his thumb, cradled in Ken's free arm. Ken was a good father and a nice person, Emily thought. She ought to be grateful.

"Why don't you read to them while I fix dinner?" she said, smiling at them. She felt exhausted.

In the kitchen there were lamb chops thawing on the drainboard. They would have lamb chops and spinach and baked potatoes, the same kind of dinner her mother used to fix when she was a little girl. It was a nice security meal. Emily wondered whether her mother had ever felt smothered and left out, the way she sometimes did. She doubted it. Her mother had been brought up to be exactly what she was, but she, Emily, had been promised a ride on the Ferris wheel, fireworks, an adventure.

She and Ken ate silently. Her mind seemed emptied out. She couldn't think of a thing to say to him. She couldn't even think of a question to ask him that didn't sound silly.

After dinner Emily scraped the dishes and put them into the machine and Ken went into the den to watch television. She thought she ought to feel glad and lucky that he was home. The children had been put to bed and the night belonged to the grown-ups now. She went into the den and sat on the arm of Ken's chair.

"Let's watch TV in bed," she said.

"All right."

Upstairs she brushed her teeth, washed her face, combed her hair, put away her clothes neatly, and put on a clean nightgown. When she went into the bedroom Ken was in bed reading, with the TV set on. She got into bed and picked up her book. Ken always made the first move.

"My scar is gone," she said.

"What?"

"My scar. It's gone."

"I'm glad you've finally decided to admit that there never was a scar."

What was the use of arguing with him? "Well, anyway, it's gone."

Ken snapped off the TV with his remote control, put his book on the bedside table, and kissed her lightly. "Goodnight, sweetheart."

"You're going to *sleep*?"

"I'm beat," he said. "I've been running around all day in this heat." He turned on his side, his back to her, and switched off his light.

She didn't dare ask him to make love to her. Pushy women made men insecure. Here they were, Saturday night, alone together in a big bed, just what they had always wanted when they were young, and it didn't matter at all.

The next morning when Emily looked into the mirror, she saw that the scar had come back. She was angry, swollen with rage, but oddly not surprised. There was something poisoning her body that made it heal and then sicken again. What could mysteriously self-regenerate could also relapse. She had read about these things in college. Freud's cases of hysterical paralysis, the stigmata of religious people, the mysteries of the body, all had to have reasonable explanations. She had had a moment of health and strength and then something had happened to destroy that progress. When she found out what that something was, the scar would go away for good.

She saw her empty Sunday looming before her. Her chores, the children, the paper to be read. Ken had a tennis game. She wanted to ask him to cancel it and stay with her, but she didn't want to make him angry. He was entitled to his relaxation. He worked so hard all week.

"When will you be home?" she asked him.

"As early as I can."

He kissed her and the children good-bye and went to his car whistling a little tune. He seemed relieved to get away. He never mentioned that the scar was back and neither did she. Her mind felt emptied again, except for that one question: what was poisoning her body?

"Can we swim, Mommy?"

She took the children's orange life jackets out of the closet and helped the children put them on. Then she relocked the closet because all their sports equipment was in there: the golf clubs they never used, her tennis racquet that she didn't use either, and the gardening equipment she had bought when they got the house, before she found out that she didn't like to garden. You never knew who could come by and steal things like that.

She lay by the pool, in the new chair with the sun umbrella attached to the back of it, wearing her big hat and sunglasses and sun protective oil, and she wondered why she bothered about future wrinkles. She never saw anybody anyway, except Ken, and he never looked at her. It's anger, she thought. It's hostility that's poisoning my body. It's some juice or enzyme that's being manufactured by my system in reaction to all that suppressed rage. Who knows what I'll try next? Any little bump or scratch, I could get another, bigger scar. I could develop keloids. It's all going to show. The inside is going to show on the outside. *What am I going to do?*

Two wet little forms hurled themselves on top of her. Emily screamed. Kate and Peter fell away from her, crying with surprise and fright.

"Go get dry," she snapped.

"I can't get the buckle open," Kate whined.

"Oh, for God's sake." They couldn't do anything for themselves. Emily took the life jackets off and dried the kids with a big towel. It occurred to her that she hadn't been in the pool herself for years. She didn't like to swim. She kept meaning to start and then she never got around to it. But how could she swim when she was all alone here? If she got a cramp and drowned, who would come to save her? It was so unfair.

Evening, finally. Ken came home. After the tennis game he had watched a tennis match on television with the boys. That was what he said. Boys play, Emily thought. Snips and snails and puppy-dog tails. Tonight he would have to make love to her. It had been weeks since he'd touched her. She hadn't kept track of exactly how long because it would be too humiliating. He had been wearing himself out with those other women, but he had promised her it was over. Now it was her turn again. He had to do something to prove he really wanted her.

She went to bed without her nightgown. That had to give him the message. He had the TV on, as usual, and he had his book. Emily reached over tentatively and touched Ken's thigh.

"Don't," he said.

"Why not?"

"Your hand is cold."

She put her hand on her breast. Her hand wasn't so cold. He had made it up to get rid of her.

"Why don't you want me anymore?" she said.

He put down his book and looked at her. "I do."

"No you don't. Not in bed, not for ages."

"Are you keeping track?" he asked in a mean voice.

"We used to do it all the time."

"I'm tired lately," Ken said.

"It isn't fair."

He picked up his book again and started to read. She reached over and grabbed it and slammed it to the floor. "Pay attention to me!" she screamed.

"You'll wake the kids."

She began to shudder with hate. The kids, the kids. What about her? She reached over to put her hand on Ken's penis and he shut his legs tightly so she couldn't find it. He acted as if she were trying to rape him. She had never reached out for him before unless she was sure it was time for him to want her to, and this rejection horrified her. He didn't want her to know that he couldn't get it up—there he was, hiding it as if he could fool her.

"I make you sick, don't I?" Emily said.

"No."

"What is it about me? My scar? My stretch marks? What makes you want to retch?"

"You said the scar was gone."

"Did I?" she said with sarcasm. "Well, if you ever looked at me you'd see that it's not. My body is being poisoned."

Ken sighed. "Emily, I want you to see a psychiatrist."

"What for?"

"To make you less unhappy."

"It's your job to make me happy," she said.

"I can't."

That meant he was impotent; she knew it. He was impotent with only her. He was the one who needed a psychiatrist, not her. It was typical of a man to try to blame the woman for something that was his fault. "Poor Ken," she said. She got out of bed and put on her nightgown. She wanted him to feel safe, unthreatened.

"There are some very good psychiatrists at Cedars," Ken said. "Everybody goes to a shrink today, it's no disgrace. When you admit you need help it's the first step toward getting well."

"Then you should definitely go," Emily said.

"Me?"

"It's all right. I understand." She closed her eyes and a sense of peace came over her. She didn't even realize she'd fallen asleep until she woke up and saw that it was morning and he was gone.

Emily lay by the pool under her umbrella, the hot blue sky arching overhead until it disappeared behind the mountains. It would be so nice if everything could be the way it was when she and Ken were first married. They could make it be that way again if they both tried. They would turn time back. She would be young and pretty and he would be sexy and virile, and they would fall in love all over again and be romantic. She would have many interests and they would share everything. Her book lay open in her lap as she daydreamed.

"Mommy, Mommy, we want to swim!" Kate and Peter were tugging at her.

"You may," Emily said kindly.

"Get our jackets," Kate demanded. The orange life jackets were locked up in the utility closet. Emily didn't move.

"You don't need them," she said, in that same kind, vague voice.

The children shrieked with joy and ran to the edge of the pool. It made them feel grown-up to swim without their life jackets. They didn't know that they couldn't swim. Emily lay in her chair, feeling the warmth of the sun comforting her sensuously. Her mind emptied out, as it did so often these days, and she felt peaceful. It would be so wonderful when everything went back to the way it used to be. What a soft day it was, with just that small breeze . . .

Dimly she heard the children screaming and splashing nearby, their sounds as inconsequential as the cries of gulls at the beach. There was a fog of peacefulness between her and their noises.

"Help! Help, Mommy!"

The first thing we'll do is get a little apartment, the same kind we had before, just the two of us, and I can walk everywhere . . .

Something whizzed by her and she heard a tremendous splash. There was cold water on her leg and she flicked it off. Then she heard a deeper, adult voice, and it was screaming at her too. Emily looked up and saw the Japanese gardener standing there, fully clothed and soaking wet, and he was holding a crying child under each arm. What was his name anyway? Oh, yes, Joe Morita. Nobody had given him permission to swim in their pool.

"Your children nearly drowned," Joe said. He sounded frightened.

Emily looked at him and the children calmly, and then she frowned. "I never let them go in the pool without their life jackets," she said.

Kate told Ken when he came home for dinner. She told him in her piercing little voice that Mommy had told her and Peter they could swim without their jackets, and then when Peter went under the water and didn't come up she had called and called and Mommy never came.

Ken got a baby-sitter and drove Emily to a mental hospital and made her sign herself in. He told her otherwise he would have to sign her in, and then she wouldn't get out. He told her she wasn't responsible enough to take care of the children anymore. Emily agreed. She didn't want Ken to know she had wanted to kill them. She was docile and sweet when she met the doctor and acted as if going into the mental hospital had been her own idea. She wasn't going to make any trouble: she didn't want them to drill holes in her head.

Chapter 8

One summer day when Richard Caldwell's son was twelve years old, Hope Loughlin Caldwell did an unthinkable thing: she got on a train to New York, went into Richard's father's office, and confronted him for the first time. The gap between this young woman —The Waitress—and her son's grandfather was so vast that her journey took as much courage and seemed to span as great a distance as the immigrants had setting out to cross the Atlantic Ocean at the turn of the century. But the purpose that Hope and those immigrants shared was the same. They wanted a better life for their children. There was only one way Hope could get it, and she finally understood the game. Richard's father told him what happened later at lunch at the New York Athletic Club.

"Hope is willing to give you a divorce."

Richard restrained himself from giving a yelp of joy. "How did you do it, Dad?"

His father smiled calmly and took a sip of his martini. He allowed himself only one gin martini before lunch every day, and two in the evening before dinner, now that he was growing old. "I simply let society help me."

"Society?"

"The world. The rules. Life has rules, Richard, even now in the Sixties when everyone seems to be going mad. She told me she wanted the boy to go to 'some kind of fancy foreign prep school,' she called it. She wants him out of the country. Apparently his classmates have been teasing him about the circumstances surrounding his birth. People are not as sophisticated in the backwoods as we try to be here. She doesn't feel he'd get a fair shake at . . . say, St. Martin's." He smiled again, this time with amusement. "Actually, I don't think it occurred to her that *we* wouldn't want the boy to go to St. Martin's any more than she did. For different reasons, of course. I think we'll send him to Le Rosay in Switzerland, what do you say?"

"It's fine with me," Richard said. "When do I get the divorce?"

"My lawyers are working on it now. Oh, and then she wants the boy to go to an Ivy League college. I agreed, provided of course it isn't Harvard."

"And what else does she want?"

"Not much," his father said. "Frankly, I'm surprised. She wants the boy's tuition and clothes and other needs to be paid for, but nothing at all for herself. At first I thought it was some sort of trick. After all, child support is a law. I told her we would arrange a proper amount to be sent to her monthly, for the boy."

"She could have had more," Richard said. "I wonder why she doesn't want more."

"Possibly she's stupid. Possibly she hates you and it's her primitive notion of pride. Or maybe she's a romantic and it's because she still loves you. You would know that better than I, Richard. You did marry the girl."

"But I never knew her," Richard said. He tried to picture Hope, but it all seemed so long ago. "To tell you the truth, I can hardly even remember her."

He excused himself then and rushed to the telephone to call Daphne at the gallery and tell her the good news. When he heard his cool, carefully sophisticated Daphne actually start to cry with happiness Richard felt filled to overflowing with love. He wished they could take the afternoon off from their jobs and go right to bed.

"I'll see you tonight, love," he said. "I adore you."

He went back to join his father at the table, hoping the old man couldn't read his mind.

"You and Daphne can have a big church wedding if you want it," his father said.

"Daphne would like that. I'd be glad to go to City Hall tomorrow."

"Still impetuous," his father said, and laughed. "This time you would please your mother and me very much if you would have a civilized wedding."

"Then we will," Richard said.

"There is one more thing Hope insisted on," his father said.

"What?"

"The boy is going to be in New York overnight in September, on his way to Switzerland. She wants you to meet him."

The boy. His father had never called him "Richard," nor had he. It was easier to keep him anonymous. Richard, Jr., was twelve years old, and he was his son. Richard didn't want to meet him. He felt afraid, and he didn't know of what.

"Well, he won't bite you," his father said. "Apparently she made sure he grew up thinking you were a fine fellow. I don't know how she managed that." He smiled, taking the edge off his words. "I took the liberty of saying you would."

In August the divorce from Hope became final. Right after the Labor Day weekend, when all their families' friends were back in the city, Richard and Daphne had the huge, formal church wedding, followed by the huge but tasteful reception Daphne had dreamed of years ago before she ever knew whom she was going to marry. When Richard watched her coming down the aisle toward him, radiant and ethereal in her white dress, all his cynicism about old-fashioned marriages evaporated. It didn't matter that they had lived together all these years and knew each other so well. This was that first moment he had ever seen and desired her, all over again. He supposed he would never get over that small lurch of the heart every time he saw her—his Golden Girl, the perfect, seemingly unapproachable, secretly passionate beauty who actually loved him.

They flew to London and Paris for their honeymoon, a week in each city, and then came back to their beloved little apartment in the Village. They had decided to buy a house in the country and start having children right away, so there was no point in taking a better apartment in New York for such a short time.

The first thing Richard had to do when they got back to New York was have his promised meeting with his son.

He had arranged that they would meet in the Biltmore, under the clock. It was the place where he had met so many girls during holiday vacations from school, a formal, dignified room that seemed festive at the same time. It would be crowded and impersonal, and he could sit at a little table and buy the boy a Coke. Hope was staying at the hotel overnight with the boy, but she would stay in her room during the meeting. Richard wondered what she hoped to accomplish. He was already married to Daphne. Hope must be trying to get some part of him back through his son. There was no way she could know how terrified he suddenly was of meeting this stranger who meant nothing to him. The boy was a living rebuke of lust and folly. Richard didn't know which would make him feel more uncomfortable—if the boy looked like Hope or like him. He just hoped he didn't look like a townie thug.

Richard was standing under the clock, smoking nervously, trying to look nonchalant. He wondered how the boy would recognize him. Hope had some snapshots they had taken during the summer they had lived together, but he looked different now. He had been a child himself in those days.

"Mr. Caldwell?"

A twelve-year-old boy with his own face, but everything slightly out of proportion in the way of awkward adolescents, stood in front of him, wearing a blazer and flannel pants.

"Yes."

"I'm Richard."

They looked at each other. He was a skinny kid, still growing, hard to tell if he would be tall. There was the faint trace of acne on his cheeks and chin, and above his lips a downy fuzz. He smiled and his mouth was full of metal braces. His hair was dishwater blond, Richard's own gold diluted by Hope's darkness. Richard gave the boy a charming smile and shook hands with him. "Shall we sit down?" he asked, already heading for a table in the corner.

Richard ordered a vodka martini, the boy a Coke. "Well," Richard said. "Off to school, eh?"

"Yes."

Poor naive Hope didn't realize that she was sending this unprepossessing specimen to a boarding school in a foreign country attended by the sons of millionaires and royalty.

"My mother sends regards," the boy said calmly.

Richard forced a pleasant expression. "I hope she's well."

"She's fine."

"Still working?"

"Yes."

"Good to keep busy."

"That's what she says," the boy said. He dipped his head to drink his Coke and the back of his neck looked very thin and white and vulnerable. Richard felt a sudden pang of guilt because he was unable to feel any affection or tenderness for him at all. The poor kid. This, then, was what had terrified him before their meeting: the fear that when at last he saw his son he would feel nothing. Or had he been afraid he would feel something? That might have been worse. He was getting a headache. He drank his martini.

"Do you like football?" Richard asked.

"Sure," the boy said, without interest.

"On the team?"

"I'm too light."

"Oh. I was a big jock at prep school, football and all that. Do you have a favorite sport?"

"Track."

"Yes, I liked track too."

They looked at each other. What did you say to a kid? "Do you have any hobbies?" Richard persisted, not because he cared but because he wanted the boy to go away thinking he was a nice person. Not that it mattered. But there was something about the boy's cool, level glance that seemed to be a kind of self-sufficient pride.

"I like to read biographies of famous people."

"And who's your favorite?"

"Abraham Lincoln."

Naturally. Corny. He wondered if the boy was smart. He couldn't be dumb or they wouldn't have accepted him at Le Rosay. On the other hand, his father had strings to pull everywhere. "How about John F. Kennedy?"

The boy gave him that same unsettling calm glance. "He was okay. Not my favorite though."

"Why not?"

"He was rich."

Richard felt a chill. He smiled his charming smile. "Are you a baby communist?"

"No. I like liberals. People are pretty conservative where I live. They think if you're against the war you're a commie freak."

"And what do you think about the war?"

"I think it's dishonest."

"You're twelve years old and you think the war is dishonest?"

"In six years I'll have to fight it if it's not over, and I don't believe in it."

"Well, don't worry," Richard said. "In six years it will be long over."

"Not if we don't pull out. We're not equipped to fight in a jungle. We didn't win in Korea either."

"Yes we did."

"Excuse me, a truce isn't a victory."

"Where did you learn all this stuff?"

"There's a guy I talk to. He's a veteran. He works at the gas station."

"I see," Richard said. He felt light-years away from this child and the strange man who had become his friend back in that town full of taciturn New Englanders. No wonder the boy didn't have any friends his own age. Nobody loves a smartass.

"Why don't we go across the street to Brooks Brothers," Richard said, "and I'll buy you some clothes."

They spent the rest of the afternoon in the store. He was glad not to have to make conversation. He made the boy try on a lot of things, trying to seem generous and fatherly, and he charged them. "I'd better not get too much," the boy said. "I don't have much room in my suitcase."

"Then I'll buy you a suitcase."

"Thank you, but don't bother. I'm growing, and they won't fit before I've had a chance to wear them all."

"You seem like a bright young man," Richard said, amused and at the same time feeling a little rejected.

"Thanks." The boy looked at his watch. It was

the kind of cheap watch you bought in a drugstore. "I have to get back now."

They walked back to the Biltmore, carrying packages. Richard stopped in the lobby in front of the bank of elevators. Hope was up there, and he could almost sniff her, the way an animal smells its foe.

"Do you have any message for my mother?" the boy asked calmly.

"Please give her my . . . best wishes."

"Okay. Good-bye. And thank you for all the clothes."

They shook hands, and when the elevator reached the lobby floor for the boy to get on, Richard turned and left the hotel quickly. He hoped the boy wouldn't decide to write to him. If he did, it would be a thank-you note, and would not require an answer. The visit was over and he was glad.

Before he went home Richard stopped at a bar where he had never been before and had another martini. He tried to sort out his feelings. He didn't even know if he had liked the boy or not. Was he intelligent, or just parroting the opinions of an older man he had a crush on? If that embittered veteran went around airing his opinion about Vietnam he would be an outcast, and that was probably why he wasted his time with an outcast twelve-year-old. He wondered if the guy was Hope's young lover. Maybe that was why she wanted to send the boy so far away, so she could be free to do whatever she wanted. Why should he feel guilty for not falling in love with his son at first sight, when the boy's own mother didn't want him around? The boy seemed like some distant relative, belonging to the family because everyone said he did, but a stranger.

When he and Daphne had their children he would be a good father. Richard was sure of it. They were in love, and they would have a warm, solid home life. He didn't want to think he was devoid of feelings. It occurred to him that instead of buying the boy a lot of clothes he didn't need, he should have bought him a decent watch. But a watch was too personal, somehow. It was better the way it had been. A clothes allowance was in the terms of the divorce.

Chapter **9**

Chris had been living in Paris for three years. She still had her room in the same hotel, she sold clothes at the same boutique, and she had many acquaintances, some close and others who drifted in and out of her life and were quickly forgotten. She felt she could honestly say to herself that she and Alexander were best friends, or at least that she was his. He still was, and always would be, the man she loved —passionately, obsessively, miserably, in the darkest secrecy and grief.

There were parts of his life that he kept away from her, out of decency and his sense of privacy, but they saw each other all the time. He had two sets of friends—gay and straight—but they all knew he was gay and accepted him completely. His straight friends, like Agnes and Jean-Paul, kept introducing Chris to eligible young men. His gay friends liked her and felt at ease with her. Alexander had a large extended family of people who made life bearable, and often even fun, and Chris had become a member of it.

She went to small dinners at people's homes where there were six men and she was the only woman. She went with Alexander and various friends to his fa-

vorite bar, Le Carrosse, which was on the Left Bank
near where they all lived. On the ground level there
was a room where men danced together, and upstairs
there were tables where all sorts of people—gay,
straight, regulars, tourists, clerks, writers, drag queens,
celebrities—drank and talked and met their friends.
The first time Chris went there with Alexander she
had been shocked to see two boys standing on the
stairs necking. Now she paid no attention to those
things, although a part of her still resented them because they represented Alexander's secret life.

Alexander felt free to be affectionate toward her
now. He held her hand when they crossed the street,
and he kissed her hello and good-bye. Sometimes,
when she had said something that particularly made
him laugh, he would hug her. He had no idea how
much he still aroused her by his slightest touch, and
she made sure he didn't know, because then he would
stop touching her. She kept waiting to feel dead inside, to give up. But her body kept its own vigil, beyond her control. He never made any secret of which
boy was his lover that week or that month, but instead of making her lose interest it made Chris vio-
lently jealous. It was not difficult to see what Alexander saw in those young men. They were all handsome, slim, and sensual, always nineteen. She thought
some of them pretended to be nineteen because Alexander found that flattering, but they were really
older. She and Alexander were thirty. Both of them
thought it was old.

Due to the influence of Agnes Laurent, and the
boutique, Chris had become quite chic. She let her
hair grow even longer—long straight hair was in fashion now with younger people—and she put together
a mélange of freaky clothes that made people pay attention to her when she walked into a party. She knew
Alexander liked it when his friends complimented
her. It was the only reason she bothered. She hardly
ever read anymore, except magazines, and she drank

red wine. She smoked incessantly, expensive American cigarettes, and a dozen thin gold bracelets jangled on her wrist. They were gifts from Alexander, six one birthday, the other six one Christmas. Now that they were best friends he felt free to give her jewelry, perfume, personal things. She felt in a way she had more of him now than she ever had before, but she would have been willing to give it all up if only he would go to bed with her.

Everybody else had someone to sleep with. She felt her own life was unnatural. Once, partly from desire and partly to show Alexander that she was a human being, she had gone home with a strikingly sexy-looking bisexual man she met at Le Carrosse. Alexander seemed a little worried when the two of them left the bar, but Chris wasn't sure if he was jealous or if he thought her pickup would murder her.

His name was David, and his body was like Michelangelo's David, white marble, a work of art. She responded to this stranger with all the pent-up need for love and purely physical contact she had been hiding from Alexander, and afterward she felt so depressed she couldn't get away from him fast enough. She had nothing to say to him.

The next day Alexander seemed pleased that she made a conquest, as he put it. Apparently David was one of the bar's best catches. If she belonged in a way to Alexander, then her night with David reflected on Alexander's taste in desirable women. David was at the same old stand the next time Chris went there with Alexander, and he wanted her to go home with him. When she refused he seemed disappointed and surprised. She didn't know why he was either one, since he had never bothered to try to find her.

"You don't need him," Alexander said then, looking approving.

"I know."

"He's not good enough for you. I'm glad you didn't take it for more than what it was."

"Did you think I would?" She was annoyed that he thought her so dumb.

"No, of course not."

She couldn't feel anything for the men she met through Agnes. They seemed so foreign. She was grateful to them for taking her out and making her look and feel popular, but physically they didn't attract her at all. She wished one of them would, but she felt nothing when they came near her, and she couldn't even let them kiss her. Nobody just kissed anymore. If a man took you to dinner and started to kiss you afterward it was understood you would go somewhere to consummate it. You could hardly even invite a man to your room anymore without him expecting to stay. A few of her dates lasted as platonic friends, but most of them didn't call again after the second time, or even the first. They read her signals as surely as a bird in mating time.

Frequently Chris and Alexander went to dinner alone, just the two of them. This happened whenever Alexander had broken up with one of his young men. Sometimes he got rid of them, sometimes they left. It was hard to tell if he was upset or felt nothing about these endings. Chris knew that he hated being gay too much to get emotionally involved with any of his lovers, but he couldn't stand to be alone either. Being with her didn't count. Alone, to Alexander, meant without one of his young men waiting patiently for him in Alexander's Room. Chris loved her dinners with Alexander. They ate greedily and laughed at everything. She wished at those times that this was her life, this closeness with Alexander, and that afterward they could go home together like a normal couple in love. But always, as the meal grew to an end, she felt his tension, and she knew he was going to drop her off at her hotel and go out to cruise. The young man he would pick up would never see this relaxed, happy Alexander. Or would he? What *did* they see when they were alone with him in Alexander's Room?

Sometimes, on a Sunday morning when she didn't have to work, and when she knew Alexander had someone with him for the weekend, Chris would find herself walking toward his house. She could no more stop this relentless passage than she could throw herself into the Seine. It was only, she told herself, a little walk for fresh air and exercise. She would stand outside Alexander's building, in the shadow of the gate that led to his courtyard, and look up at his draped windows. Were they asleep still, after staying up all night? What would they do when they woke up? Was Alexander happy or lonely? She was miserable.

After those weekends when Alexander stayed locked in his apartment with a lover he never asked Chris how she had spent her time. He didn't even say, "Did you have a nice weekend?" It was almost as if he was afraid she might ask him if he had. He only told her about parties, movies, or new restaurants, and whenever he had liked a new restaurant very much he took her there. Although they were old and good friends he still paid for everything when they went out, as if it were still the Fifties and he was still her date. She wondered if it was because she was poor and he was rich, or whether he would always think of her in some way as his girl.

She knew time was passing and she would be unmarried and alone until it was too late. Everyone else would be married and she would have no choice anymore. She knew she should leave, go home to America, or even travel, but she couldn't move. If more than two days went by without her seeing Alexander or speaking to him on the phone she was plunged into the deepest depression. She felt adrift, waiting for him to hold out his hand and save her again. She knew she was acting like a lunatic, fooling everyone because she knew what they would tell her if they knew how she really felt about Alexander.

She wrote to Annabel once in a while, and always pretended things were fine. She was ashamed to tell Annabel the truth because even though Annabel was unconventional she had never knowingly been self-destructive. She didn't think Annabel would really approve of her behavior. She didn't approve of it herself, but there was no choice.

And then Alexander's father died and everything changed.

Alexander went home for the funeral and stayed for a week. Chris thought about him the whole time he was away and wondered what it was like for him to be back with his family, back in New York, after all these years. He hadn't seemed upset when he got the news, but who knew what would happen? When Alexander came back to Paris he called her.

"Do you want to come over to my place tomorrow night about seven?" he said. "I'll just get some cold things and we'll eat in. I'm beat. But I want to see you."

"Of course."

She wondered if there would be other people there, but when she arrived she saw that they were alone. Alexander's apartment was very neat, and he had deliberately left the door to Alexander's Room ajar so she could see that the bed was made with the bedspread on it and no clothes were strewn around. Alexander kissed her hello and it was only an act of will that kept her from hugging him tightly. And then suddenly she couldn't stand this deception any more and she flung her arms around his neck. She could smell his skin and feel his heart beating. What the hell, his father had just died, and she was only showing a little sympathy.

Alexander was hugging her too. Then he let go and looked down at her. "I'm glad to be back," he said.

"Was it awful?"

"Moderately. My father remarried, you know, and divorced her too, and apparently I have a nitwit half-brother. Everybody's fighting over the will. It was nice to see my mother and sister, though."

He went into the kitchen and returned with a bottle of red wine, two glasses, and a platter of cheese and bread and *cornichons*. He set the food on the glass table in front of the sofa and poured the wine.

"Don't panic," he said. "There's more food than this."

"I'm not really hungry," Chris said. She looked at his dear, beautiful face and thought again that even the unfulfilling moments she had with Alexander would be far better than never seeing him at all. She had missed him so much this past week. Even if she had to die an old maid, she could never give him up.

"Did you see Max?" she asked.

"We had dinner. He's fine. He sends you his love."

"Did he say anything about Annabel?"

"Apparently she's taken up skydiving, and her husband is very pissed off about it. She's going to kill herself."

"Oh, no," Chris said. "The last time she wrote me it was jumping horses. Her hobbies don't last."

"I had an interesting job offer in New York," Alexander said.

"What?"

"Well, I can go to work in my father's bank if I want. It's a lot more money than here, and other things I like, such as prestige and power." He gave a mirthless smile. "I won't say it isn't tempting."

She felt a flutter of fear. Bad as things were, anything that threatened to disturb the status quo might be worse. "You'd have to live in New York," she said.

"True." He poured more wine for both of them. "I always knew there was a limit to how far I could advance here. After all, I'm a foreigner. And this would be in my father's bank, where the story is that

I'm here serving my apprenticeship for bigger and better things. I don't know, Chris. I feel like Peter Pan, just marking time here. Maybe I do want to go home and try to start a new life."

And me? she thought, panicked. *What about me?* She lit a cigarette, her hands shaking.

"We've always been honest with each other, Chris," he said. "Lately, I mean. Since you've lived here. You know me, and I think I know you. I love you, and I think you love me."

For an instant she wasn't sure he'd actually said it. His tone was so casual she was afraid he had meant "like," not "love."

"Yes, of course I do," she said.

"If I go back to New York and take that job I want to leave everything here behind me except you. Do you know what I mean?"

She could hardly breathe. "Tell me," she said.

"I want to get married and have children. There's only one person in the world I could marry and be faithful to, and that's you. I *would* be faithful—I mean that. It's what you deserve, and what I want. I've been doing a lot of thinking this past week. Especially coming back here on the plane. Sometimes when you get off the ground all the things that seemed important get into another perspective. I don't want to end my days as an old faggot."

"You never did," Chris said.

"I want to be fair," he said. "What I thought was, let's drive to Cannes and spend two weeks and see if we get along. We both have vacations coming. It's warm there now, and they'll have the little strawberries and the gray wine. We'll get a room in some romantic pension, and we'll see. What do you think? If it works out, would you marry me?"

"Oh, yes," Chris said. "Oh, yes." She took his hand and looked into his eyes, letting all the love she had for him come shining out at last. She smiled, and then she averted her glance so that he couldn't read her mind and see the terror that was mixed in with her joy. She could see the logic of his request, but the thought of being on trial this way was so frightening that she could hardly bear to think about it. She knew exactly what he meant. Could he have good sex with her, good enough to make him content to change his life? What would be good enough? Just being able to do it at all, or something that was better than whatever he had with all his young men? Would love make the difference? Was that what he meant?

"If we get along as well as I hope," Alexander said, "we'll go home and get married and live happily ever after."

To marry Alexander, to have him all to herself, to have his child . . . It had to work out. She would make it work out. "When do you want to leave?" she said.

They took turns driving Alexander's rented car, and stopped overnight at an inn where they took separate rooms. They were like a virgin couple waiting for their wedding night. They bought pâté and cheese and crusty bread and wine and had a picnic along the way. They remarked on the countryside, made conversation, and avoided any mention of what would happen when they got to their destination, although Chris thought of nothing else and was sure he was as nervous as she was.

Their college affair had happened to two other people. She tried to find courage in memories of the past, but she had lived for too long on memories and besides there were other, harsher memories that stood between now and then. She worried that he would find her diaphragm repulsive. She had thought of getting the pill, quickly, before this trip, but she was afraid of getting fat and bloated and nauseated, which would be more repugnant to him. Besides, once they were married—*if* they were married—they would want children right away, quickly, before she was too old, so why bother to fool around with her body chemistry? It was easier to be a man, she thought.

They reached Cannes in late afternoon. The sun shone brightly on the bright blue ocean, and palm trees lined the road. The pension Alexander had chosen for them was hidden from the main road by a narrow path with hairpin turns, and surrounded by a low yellow wall. It was called Le Cloître, and had been recommended as a romantic and secluded place for people who were in love. Their room had white painted walls and large, dark country furniture, with a double bed. There was a small balcony outside the room, overlooking a garden where lemon trees and bushes with red-and-pink flowers perfumed the air. It was very quiet, except for the chirp of birds.

"It's nice, isn't it?" Alexander said.

"Yes, lovely."

They unpacked meticulously, politely sharing hangers and bureau drawers. They washed and then went downstairs to the bar.

"We'll have dinner here tonight, all right?" Alexander said. "The food is supposed to be good."

"That's fine." She wished they could get it over with. The first time would be the most difficult. After all this time of longing for him she felt strangely shy. She didn't want to make any mistakes.

They drank a little wine, not too much, in order to feel festive and at ease but not get drunk. They picked at their dinner, unable to eat the roast pigeon with white grapes or the salad, and skipping dessert. They drank coffee. Chris smoked. Finally dinner was over, and they went casually up to the room they finally shared.

The maid had turned down the bed. Two little lights burned dimly, and the shutters had been closed. Chris and Alexander looked at each other and she began to shiver. It shouldn't be like this, she thought —with conditions. Let's do it tomorrow instead.

"I love you," Alexander said, and then he put his arms around her and kissed her.

The moment he kissed her she knew it would be all right. His touch, his body, the reality and fantasy of him, all aroused her in a rush of feeling: passion, love, sensuality, need. They were in the large bed making love, and now they were both the young lovers of their college days and the mature lovers they were now, and there was only a difference in the violence of her new desire. This was Alexander's skin over which her hands rushed insatiably, this was Alexander inside her, against whose body she thrust passionately while holding him to her with entwined legs so that he would never get away. When she heard him moan it was a triumph.

He was happy and affectionate afterward, and they fell asleep still locked in each other's arms. She woke up later with her arm and leg numb from his weight, but didn't dare move. Then she thought: this is going to be real this time, and we will be together forever. So she moved away from his sleeping weight and he turned over and sighed, dreaming. She looked down at him, asleep, and realized this was the first time they had ever spent an entire night together. She lay against his back, her lips against his skin, and inhaled the faint scent of him, listened to him breathe, and felt blessed.

They made love again in the morning, and Chris felt secure and happy. After breakfast they went to the beach, had lunch in a café, and in the afternoon came back to their room and made love again. She could tell that he was delighted things were working out so well. That evening they had dinner at their pension again and made plans for the other restaurants where they would eat, the places they wanted to see. They were completely at ease with each other now, their friendship sealed, nothing more to fear.

They continued to make love, to be affectionate, to be happy. But one afternoon on the beach Chris went to get drinks for them and when she came back Alexander was talking with a beautiful young man in a tiny bikini. It was nothing, a casual conversation between two strangers, but her heart turned over. This place was too full of beautiful young men, some of them hustlers, others just gay. She was afraid. Alexander smiled at her when she approached and turned away from the young man so casually she thought it was probably nothing. She couldn't panic every time he looked at or talked to a man. Still, the small fear stayed with her, and whenever they were near a particularly attractive young man, the kind she knew Alexander had liked, she felt on guard. She said nothing about this feeling, and neither did Alexander, if he even noticed she seemed tense. Part of "getting along together" had to do with trust as well as sex, didn't it?

They drove to the Colombe d'Or where they ate lunch outdoors with the white doves all around and the sea glistening below them. They explored the hills and small winding roads, drove to Nice to gamble, and had an aperitif at the old, elegant Negresco Hotel; and when Alexander won a hundred dollars at blackjack he took her to Hermès where he bought huge matching silk print scarves for both of them.

One afternoon they were having a nap in their room after making love and Chris woke to see Alexander standing on their little balcony, a towel wrapped around his waist, looking pensively out at the garden. Or was he looking at the other rooms that also faced the garden, wondering what was going on there that he would have to give up? She felt sadness wash over her. Would the time ever come when she would be completely sure of him?

"Alexander?"

He turned. "Are you up?"

"Yes. I was wondering—are you happy?"

"Of course I am. Aren't you?"

"Absolutely happy."

"So am I," Alexander said.
She saw no reason not to believe him.

Christine Spark and Alexander English were married in St. James' Church in New York City on an afternoon in early June. Annabel flew in from Atlanta to be the matron of honor. Max was a guest. The other guests were the bride's immediate family, and the family and family friends of the groom. Chris's mother got drunk at the reception, but Chris's father whisked her away before she made a scene. Alexander's younger sister Pooch, now called Elizabeth, was stoned on pot, but no one seemed to notice, except Max, with whom she shared a joint outside on the sidewalk. Chris's wedding picture was on the society page of *The New York Times*. It was Alexander's idea. After the wedding Chris and Alexander spent a long weekend in Maine and then came back to the Fifth Avenue apartment they had rented. Alexander had already started his new job at the bank.

Chapter 10

That June was the tenth reunion of their class's graduation from Radcliffe. Daphne, Annabel, Chris, and Emily didn't go. Richard, Ken, Max, and Alexander didn't go to their Harvard reunions either. They were all much too busy with their present lives. The four years that had shaped their destinies in so many ways seemed far in the past now, somewhat inconsequential. They were all attending to the serious business of being adults, each in his or her own way, whether it was pursuing a successful career, raising a family, or just trying to stay sane.

Daphne and Richard were living in Greenwich, Connecticut, in a Tudor house surrounded by lawn and huge old trees. Richard commuted to his real estate business in New York. Grand Central Station was only thirty-six minutes away on the express, an hour on the local. Their first child, Matthew, was a year old, and Daphne was happily pregnant with their second. She had everything she wanted now, except four children, and she was nearly halfway there.

When the questionnaire had arrived for the tenth reunion Daphne had tossed it into the wastebasket. She didn't have the time for things like that. But it set her thinking about her feelings at this point in her life. The Sixties had certainly turned out to be culture shock. She supposed it was the same for the rest of her classmates. On college campuses all over the country students were revolting against the war, and even rebelling against the curriculum offered them. Who could imagine students doing such a thing? It amused her to picture the girls back in her day in Briggs Hall revolting against curfew, or Social Pro, or washing dishes. And to say your studies were useless in preparing you for life—good grief, who ever thought about such things when she was at college? You believed what you were told. The drug scandal on the Harvard campus was the most incredible of all. Two professors actually giving LSD to their students, and taking it with them! Kids were taking drugs all over the place now. She was glad she and Richard had gotten out of the city. There was something small-town and old-fashioned and safe about Greenwich. As far as sex was concerned, it amused her to think that she and Richard had been so far ahead of their time, living together before they were married. Today, in one short decade, those college kids slept with just anybody and everybody from reports she'd heard. They didn't do it because they were in love; they did it for *fun*. The pill had changed everything. It was hard to understand how removing the fear of pregnancy could also remove the fear of being thought loose, but something had made this new generation of college students brave, all of them at the same time, and it had nothing to do with the way they had been brought up.

Daphne and Richard had a cleaning woman who came in three times a week because it was a large house, but she took care of Matthew herself. She loved playing with him and being with him. He was the most beautiful baby she had ever seen. People mistook him for a girl. That was because he had inherited her delicate features, her cornflower-blue eyes and long lashes, and all children wore their hair

long, even in Greenwich. It didn't bother her when
people stopped her in the supermarket to exclaim
over "the gorgeous little girl." She couldn't tell the
difference between the girls and the boys anymore at
any age, the way they all dressed alike and the boys
wore their long hair and the girls with no makeup.
It was getting so the only way you could tell a teenager was a girl was if she wore earrings, and that was
only in Greenwich. Back in the Village the men had
started wearing earrings too.

Of course she had worried that Matthew would in-
herit her epilepsy, and it was still too soon to know.
She had made her obstetrician, Dr. Gibbs, promise
not to tell Richard her secret. She had never gotten
up the courage to tell him herself, even now when
she was longing for his reassurance. If Matthew had
it, or if the unborn baby turned out to have it, she
knew it would be her fault. She would continue to
wait, hope, and pray.

Dr. Michaelson had told her it was very common
for a woman to have a seizure within hours after her
baby was born, and she was very worried about it.
When Matthew was born Dr. Gibbs got her a private
nurse who stayed at her bedside after she was back
in her room. Daphne got rid of Richard as quickly
as possible, saying she wanted to sleep. Later she
thought she'd been unconscious for a few moments,
but she wasn't sure—she was in bed and groggy anyway. But it hadn't been a convulsion; she was safe.
Imagine a real convulsion! What would she have told
Richard?

Dr. Michaelson put her back on her medication for
a while. Once again, she hid it. But now somehow
the medication made her feel more secure than insecure: it would keep her from having a seizure and
that was the important thing. She had to take care
of an infant now, and she didn't intend to drop him.

She really didn't miss the gallery at all. Now she
could do something much more important than sell

paintings to rich dumbbells who didn't know anything; she could mold a human life. She loved the changing seasons in the country, her little rock garden with carefully planted wild flowers growing in it. She used her talent for art with her garden, and filled the house in summer with tiny bunches of flowers in unusual vases.

She and Richard had joined the Yacht Club, only a ten-minute drive away. They both liked to water-ski. In warm weather Daphne and the other young mothers often went to the beach together, exchanging stories about their brilliant, marvelous children, while the children played in the sand. In the winter she had plenty of things to keep her busy. She loved to read. On weekends she and Richard entertained his clients or their friends, and were invited to parties and small dinners. Richard still enjoyed doing his gourmet cooking on weekends, and showing it off. Sometimes they hired a sitter and went into New York to see a hit show or just have dinner at a new restaurant. They also tried to see all the foreign films that didn't make it up to the local movie theaters.

The longer Daphne was married to Richard, the more she loved him. She didn't know many couples who were still romantic and in love. A lot of people were already having problems, but their children were still so young that they would put up with anything to stay together. Some of the husbands cheated. When Daphne found out that some of the wives did too, she had been shocked. They claimed that having an affair with another man was saving their marriages. Well, who was she to make judgments? She didn't know all their secrets. And they didn't know hers. People still put this burden of imagined perfection on her, the way they always had, and she thrived on their approval, afraid to spoil it, too insecure to destroy their illusions. If you thought you were worse than everybody else, then you had to be better than everybody else to make up for it. Her friends, and Richard's business associates, thought her home was so tasteful, her life so well-ordered, her disposition so serene, her mind so sharp and well-informed, and they admired her looks and her clothes.

She didn't know how long her popularity would last. When Matthew got older her friends would want her to join the car pool. She had always been afraid of driving a car with children in it, for good reason. It was one thing to drive around her own. But she would not take the responsibility of chauffeuring other people's children. She could black out—it was too risky. She would say she was too busy, invent ingenious lies. But she knew the other women in the group would think she was selfish and lazy; maybe they would stop being friendly altogether. Well, if it happened, so be it. There were worse things than that.

Sometimes she looked at herself from the vantage point of a mature married woman and mother and thought she should have done with this charade and risk telling Richard—but she just couldn't. It was such an appalling disease. He just wouldn't understand. He thought she was perfect, his Golden Girl: that was why he had fallen in love with her, why he had married her. He was proud of her. He *wanted* her to be perfect.

And she did too.

Chapter 11

Annabel and Rusty never had an actual fight; instead they had what she called "words." Tonight was typical. It was a beautiful June night, a little cool, with a fat moon sailing over the treetops and stars flung all over the sky, and it was the tenth anniversary of her graduation from Radcliffe, when she had thought the whole world was ahead of her. It had been a long time since she had thought about Bill Wood, but tonight she did, and she thought how different her life would have been if she had married him instead of Rusty. But there was no point in thinking about that, since it hadn't been her choice. Still, she felt sad.

"You go on alone to the club, honey," she said to Rusty. "I don't feel like going."

"Don't you feel well?"

"I'm fine."

"Then you have to come. It's Cooper's surprise birthday party."

"Cooper is a cretin."

"Why do you always put down your friends, Annabel?"

Rusty refilled his glass of bourbon. He was drunk already, as usual. When he was drunk he had a slow and precise quality, like a tightrope walker, very gently moving his large body to avoid disaster. In a smaller, lighter man it would have seemed effeminate. "What are you going to do here all alone?" he said. "Get plastered?"

"The company would be preferable," she said.

"You sit around and drink alone you'll become an alcoholic."

"As opposed to people like you who drink in bars and clubs."

"Are you trying to tell me I drink too much?" he said, sounding hurt.

"Nothing's too much for you, darling," she said sweetly.

Rusty looked annoyed. "You know, Annabel, every time you come back from those faggots you hang around with in New York you act like a bitch."

She was sorry she'd ever told him about Max. The only reason she had was that Rusty had started getting obstinately jealous about her trips to New York all alone. Now it seemed like a cheap shot. How much more dignified it would have been if Rusty could have trusted her, knowing that no man was a threat unless she wanted him to be. But Rusty had never had style.

"If it's true that I have so little personality of my own that I have to take on somebody else's," Annabel said with poisonous sweetness, "then I had surely better stay away from *your* friends."

"I'll see you later," Rusty said, and left the house. She heard him drive away, the tires squealing on the turn.

"Free at last," she said, raising her champagne glass. "Free at last. Thank God almighty, free at last." Why hadn't anybody ever told her that bad as it was to be alone it was worse to have to live with someone you couldn't stand? Didn't anybody else know that?

She left on all the downstairs lights so Rusty wouldn't break his neck coming home drunk in the dark, and took her champagne upstairs in the ice bucket she used for a cooler, swinging it by its handle. She stopped for a moment in Emma's room, leaving the cooler and bottle outside in the hall, and looked down at the sleeping child. Emma was seven now, the loveliest and nicest little girl in the world. Annabel loved her so much. Having Emma was worth all the rest of it. Annabel leaned down and kissed her gently, so as not to awaken her, marveling as she always did at the silkiness of Emma's skin. It must be scary to be only seven years old, so little and delicate. Emma's battered old toy bear slept on the pillow next to her, his black button eyes wide open even in his sleep, looking out for ghosts. Annabel walked softly to her own room, carrying her cooler and champagne. You have your growly bear and I have my joy juice, she thought.

She put on her nightgown and robe and settled on the white chaise that she had bought during her Syrie Maugham period, and turned on the radio to the all-night music station. "Eleanor Rigby," the Beatles sang, "picks up the rice in the church where a/wedding has been,/lives in a dream./Waits at the window, wearing a face that she keeps/in a jar by the door,/Who is it for?/All the lonely people, where do they all come from?"

Annabel liked the Beatles. They had a different kind of innocence from the Noel Coward songs she had loved in college, but there was something in most of their songs that seemed to speak to her. It was lucky they had come along. It had been a long time since she had felt music to be a part of her life. Now it was a part of her lonely drinking. But you couldn't very well read a book when you were drunk, and television was stupid. She lit a cigarette and sipped her champagne. Champagne was so delicious. She was glad they had invented it.

She felt herself drifting comfortably into phase one of her nightly drinking sessions: euphoria. She really ought to buy a nice little hi-fi set to keep in the bed-

room, and all the Beatles records. They had some of
them in their collection downstairs in the den, but
that was just as background for entertaining guests.
These would be her own. And she should get a small
refrigerator, the kind people kept in offices, to keep
in her dressing room, filled with champagne and ice,
and maybe some cheese. Then she'd never have to
go downstairs at all, once Emma was asleep.

Sweet William came out from wherever he had been
napping and jumped onto Annabel's lap. It was always a shock to have a twenty-pound cat jump on
you, he was so heavy. She stroked his soft, thick fur.
She would keep some little snacks for Sweet William
in her new refrigerator too.

The trouble was that after a while she always
slipped into phase two: anger and depression. The
bottle was empty and she had to go downstairs to
throw it away and open another. She hadn't had dinner, but she wasn't hungry. Sweet William padded
soundlessly along beside her as she went into the
kitchen, and meowed for his dinner. Annabel put it
into his bowl and opened her champagne. She wondered what Max was doing in New York, and what
Chris and Alexander were doing. Strange about life
. . . Alexander going straight for Chris, or maybe
Chris just being there at the right time. Annabel
didn't really understand how that had worked, but
Chris seemed to be very happy. It was a blessing to
have her home in America again. How ironic it was
that Chris was having a good sex life now, and she,
Annabel, the wife of that sexy Rusty Buchanan, hadn't
been to bed with her husband for two years, except
to sleep. There just wasn't any chemistry between
them anymore.

Annabel went back to the bedroom with her champagne. She lit a cigarette and poured a nice cold,
sparkling glassful of tranquility. When she was young
she had always thought that married people had to
have sex with each other. That was a rule and every-

body knew it. It was all right not to if you were middle-aged, but certainly people in their thirties . . . But Rusty just didn't seem to care anymore, and she was relieved. She'd been so disinterested the last year he'd made love to her that she wouldn't be a bit surprised if that had done it to him. On the other hand, he drank so much it was a wonder he had ever been able to do it at all. She wondered if he had someone else. Would anyone tell her? Supposedly the wife was the last to know, but a jerk like Cooper or Dickie, who was still after her, would be pleased to tell her, wouldn't he? Or did men stick together, even if they were trying to screw their friends' wives? She didn't care whether Rusty had anyone else or not. She didn't care what he did, as long as he continued to leave her alone.

She was wasting her life. The depression deepened. One part of her was aware that it was the champagne, but another part told her that the feeling had always been there waiting to be let out. If you were miserable with your life it had to come out in one way or another. Riding didn't help anymore, although she still rode every morning after she drove Emma to school. She had grown quickly bored with all her hobbies and she felt her education had been for nothing. You didn't need a college degree to love and raise a seven-year-old. As for pleasing Rusty, gracious living was a joke. Did anybody really take it seriously anymore? She had written poetry in college, but she knew she wasn't a poet, any more than Chris who had made all those funny caricatures in college was an artist. If a little knowledge was a dangerous thing, what was a lot of knowledge? Annabel was beginning to think it was even worse.

Suddenly Sweet William jumped off her lap and disappeared under the bed, and Annabel realized in disbelieving horror that the room was full of smoke. The fire seemed to start in a split second, crackling and wild: high orange flames devouring the bedroom drapes and the now huge billows of dirty-colored smoke making her cough and choke. She stood, looking around, dazed and drunk. It didn't seem real. Then she screamed and ran to Emma's room.

"Get up, get up, baby!" She pulled Emma out of bed, grabbed her bathrobe and toy bear, and pushed her to the top of the stairs. "Run out on the lawn, Emma, quick! The house is on fire."

"Where are you going, Mama?"

"To get Sweet William. Quick, run!"

Annabel could see flames creeping along the edge of the rug next to the window. Coughing, her eyes streaming tears, her nose running, she crawled under the bed and grabbed Sweet William by his thick tail, pulling it mercilessly, dragging him out. She could feel his body trembling with terror, his feet digging into the rug, but she was stronger than he was. He clawed her when she scooped him up in her arms, but she hardly felt it for the relief of having him safe. She ran down the stairs and joined Emma on the front lawn.

The house was silhouetted against the navy-blue sky, the fiery bedroom bright orange and red and yellow, the rest of the building mellowly lit by electric lights, shaded by silky drapes. Annabel let Sweet William drop to the ground and he flattened his body like a fat badger and scuttled away to the safety of the hedges. She put her arms around Emma and hugged her.

"We're safe now."

"Did you call the fire department, Mama?"

"I forgot."

"The house will burn down."

"I was more afraid of the smoke. Don't worry, someone will see the fire and call them."

"We could go next door and use their phone," Emma said, wide awake and logical in the face of her first disaster.

Annabel hugged her more tightly. She knew she was far too drunk to show herself, even though the shock had sobered her somewhat. How would it look to stagger to the Clarksons dead drunk, with her child trembling barefoot—the unfit mother who had accidentally set her own house on fire?

She watched the fire eating the top floor of her home, moving across it like some animal grazing. The bedroom wall looked like a blackened shell now, eerily lit from inside, a sizzling carapace. She felt nothing. This really wasn't her home. It was just the place where she managed to get through each day and night. It was expensive, but it was insured. Rusty would be furious. Maybe the firemen would come soon while there was something left.

They heard the sirens then. Emma hopped up and down with joy. "Somebody called, just like you said they would!"

The whole neighborhood must have called from the amount of noise those sirens were making. Two gigantic fire trucks, and an ambulance, and men jumping to the ground unfurling a long, heavy hose. Firemen in protective uniforms that made them look oddly like bulky Sherlock Holmeses, Annabel thought. One of them stopped in front of her.

"Is there anybody else in there?" he asked.

Annabel looked at him. He was so young, with a thin, handsome, high-cheekboned face, and longish dark hair curling out from under his hat. She'd never thought of firemen as being so young.

"No," she said.

He stared at her for an instant, and then he turned away and disappeared with the other men who were fighting the flames.

When the fire was out the ground floor and part of the top floor had been saved. The master bedroom and dressing rooms were gutted. Another young man, in a white intern's uniform, put something that stung like hell on Annabel's cat scratches.

"That was a very well-built house," one of the firemen said. "You're lucky."

"Thank you for saving it," Annabel said.

When all the vehicles drove away it seemed too quiet. Crickets and tree toads chirped. Sweet William came crawling out from under the hedge. He looked sorry that he had scratched her.

The family slept in the living room that night. An acrid smoke smell lingered in the air, and what hadn't been destroyed upstairs by the fire had been finished off by water. Rusty was furious because all his clothes were burned and he would have to spend the day buying more and attending to the insurance on the house. Annabel thought in disgust that he acted as if he had something better to do. She and Rusty pretended that he worked, but he really just went to his office to make phone calls. It was lucky he was so rich.

For herself, she had only the nightgown and robe she had been wearing when the fire started, and her riding clothes that she kept in the downstairs hall closet because Rusty complained they smelled. Emma was the only one who was well-off; there was a pile of her little jeans and shirts lying all clean and dry and folded in the laundry room. She went to school thrilled with the story she had for show and tell today. Annabel dropped her off and drove back to the house. She felt tired and depressed. She wondered if one of her cigarettes had caused the fire, or if it had been a defect in the electrical wiring. She didn't want to think about the guilt. Anyone could have an accident. But she'd been drunk as a goat, and that was her fault even if the fire wasn't. Suppose she'd been drunkenly asleep when it started, or passed out? They could have died.

She reheated the coffee that was on the stove and drank it down with two aspirin. She didn't think she would like to know what was going on inside her stomach with all the abuse she'd been giving it lately. I really must hate myself, she thought. I treat myself as if I do.

The doorbell rang. She went out to the vestibule and peered through the pane. A young man with long, dark curly hair and a thin, handsome face was standing there, wearing a red-plaid shirt and jeans. Annabel opened the door a crack, still on the chain. If he tried to sell her a magazine she'd slam it right in his face.

"Hi," he said shyly. "I came by to see if you were all right."

"Who are you?"

"I'm Paul Dumont. I was one of the firemen here last night. I guess you wouldn't remember me."

"Not hardly," Annabel said, and unexpectedly laughed. She remembered him now, mentally putting his uniform and hat on him. He was the boy who had asked her if anybody was still inside the house, and then had stared at her. She took the chain off the door and opened it. "Come on in."

He walked in and glanced around. "You have a real pretty house," he said. "I'm sorry we had to make such a mess."

"You saved it," Annabel said. "That's the important thing."

"Yeah." He was staring at her again, as if awed, and then he gave her a sweet smile. "Are you all right?"

"Yes, I'm fine."

"I was kind of worried about you. This is my day off, so I just thought I'd come and see how you were."

"That's very sweet," Annabel said. "I didn't know firemen made follow-up calls."

"Well, we don't," he said. He was actually blushing. She couldn't believe it. This adorable-looking boy had a crush on her!

"Would you like some coffee?" she said. She led the way to the kitchen. "I was just going to make some fresh."

They sat at the kitchen table while the coffee

perked. They both smoked. "Is your little girl okay?" he asked.

"Oh, she's fine. She's a very resilient little girl." Annabel looked into his eyes. They were green, with thick black lashes. "Tell me, Paul . . . what started that fire, do you think?"

"It could have been anything."

"This cigarette?"

She could see conflicting emotions in his face. He was as open and innocent as Emma. He didn't want to offend her, but at the same time he wanted to warn her. "It's dangerous to smoke when you're kind of . . ." he said finally.

"Kind of drunk?" Annabel said matter-of-factly. "I know."

"Last night," he said softly, "I thought you were the most beautiful and tragic woman I'd ever seen. I had to come back. I guess I fell in love with you."

"Me?"

"I never did this before," he said.

She smiled at him. "I think if you did I would have heard."

"I could get in trouble for this," he said. "The guys would really kid me. They'd think I was dumb. We're not supposed to get emotionally involved."

Annabel poured the fresh coffee into two cups. "Milk and sugar?"

"Thank you."

"What's it like in the firehouse?"

He stirred his coffee. "Like an army barracks. Everybody comes on very tough. Especially the older guys."

"You're very young," Annabel said.

"I'm twenty-three."

"You look younger."

"I know."

"Are you married?" she asked.

"Yeah."

"What's your wife like?"

"She spends all her time over at her mother's," he said. She could see from his expression that he was disillusioned and bewildered. She tried not to laugh. Poor kid. She could just picture his young wife, hair in pink rollers, married as quickly as possible because what else did a girl do?

"Do you have children?" Annabel asked.

"No."

"There's still plenty of time for that."

"Yeah."

Why am I coming on like his mother? she thought. I'm not so old. He shouldn't be the only one who worries about how this looks. I'm sitting here in my kitchen feeding coffee to a total stranger who says he's in love with me. Try explaining that to the neighbors! In spite of herself Annabel found herself smiling, flirting like the old Annabel of so many years ago whom she thought had vanished forever.

"You look real happy now," he said. "I wish you'd always look that way instead of how you looked last night."

"But you said you fell in love with the way I looked last night," she teased him.

"I did, but you look more beautiful today."

"Why, thank you, Paul."

"You and your husband don't get along," he said.

"What makes you think that?"

"You two had a fight and he went off and left you, and you got drunk."

"What makes you think he isn't dead?"

"Dead?" He looked appalled. "I'm sorry."

"He's just fine," Annabel said. She wanted to touch this boy's clean, long hair, to pat him like a puppy. He was so sweet it made her heart ache. Sweet and dumb and young. At eighteen she would have fallen in love with him at first sight and necked with him on the first date, but at eighteen she would never have met him because he was in the fifth grade.

"I guess I hoped you two didn't get along," he said.

"I made up a fantasy about you last night. It was kind of romantic."

"Tell me about it," she said.

"I never know if you're going to laugh at me or not."

"If you knew me better you'd know I wouldn't."

"I don't know how to talk to you," he said. "You scare me a little bit."

"Why?"

"Well . . . last night you looked like a ghost in the moonlight, so lost, and I thought, 'I wish I could take her wherever she wants to go.' I would if I could. I guess that sounds crazy."

Annabel looked at him—the lithe, lean young body, the emerald eyes and the young, sensual mouth—and she thought, where I want you to take me is to bed. The thought jumped into her mind so unexpectedly that she gasped. He was staring at her. She had the feeling he knew what she was thinking. He looked surprised and delighted. Well, she thought, it's a normal thought. I'm human and he's adorable and it's been two years. Even longer if you count how awful it used to be.

She stood up and took his hand gently. "Just hold me for a minute," she said softly.

He stood up then and put his arms around her, his cheek against her hair. She could tell he was aroused, but he didn't grab at her or try to maul her the way young men used to do; he was very tender with her, tentatively kissing her hair, then her forehead and cheek, then her mouth. Annabel put her arms around him and held him tightly. She knew she could still stop, make him stop, and he would believe whatever excuse she gave him.

"You're so beautiful," he whispered.

She led him into the living room and sat down on the couch. He sat beside her and kissed her for a while, and then she felt his fingers trying to undo the buttons of her blouse.

"Wait," she said. He stopped and looked at her, waiting. Annabel smiled at him, feeling herself bubbling over with tenderness and excitement and mirth. "It's just that first we both have to try to get my goddamn riding boots off," she said.

He was on the floor at her feet in an instant, pulling off her boots, while she wound his lovely hair around her fingers, the way she wanted to do, and she felt so young again, breathless with the anticipation of sex. Then she slipped down on the rug beside him and they undressed each other and kissed and made love.

Afterward they lay with their arms around each other, their heads cradled on each other's shoulders, their legs entwined. She thought she had never seen a more beautiful young man. She stroked his moist, silky skin, feeling the long lines of his muscles under it.

"That was just where I wanted to go," she said.

"Me too."

She sat up and put on her clothes. Who knew if the insurance adjuster, or even Rusty, might decide to make an appearance? She must have been crazy. Paul put on his clothes.

"Can I come by next week on my day off?" he asked.

"Well, I don't know . . ." She hadn't even planned to go to bed with him, and now he was planning an affair.

"I could call first," he said. "Tell me when to call."

"Well, I guess in the morning. Not too early." What the hell am I doing? she thought. She looked at her watch. "I think you'd better go now," she said. "My husband had to buy clothes and he'll be here to . . ."

"I love you," Paul said.

Her heart turned over. This was insane; he was a lay. "Oh, Paul, you're so dear, so sweet."

He kissed her good-bye. "I'll see you next week." Then he was gone.

Annabel went to the window and saw him backing
a battered old white car out from where he'd parked
it right in front of her house. If he came back he'd
certainly have to find a safer place to hide his car
than there in plain sight. *If he came back.* How could
she let him come back? All these years she'd been so
proud of herself because she wasn't like those other
wives who had lovers. No matter how rotten her marriage was she had been above it all. Now she was
just like them. She could see the years stretching ahead
of her—a few months with Paul the fireman, and
then what? The golf pro at the club, or the tennis
pro, or maybe one of Emma's teachers, or the delivery boy, and then, finally, God forbid, Dickie or
Cooper? She began to shiver. Somebody could just
ring her doorbell and she would invite him in and
. . . The young Annabel had believed in love at first
sight, and apparently so did the married Annabel,
but they had both always had pride.

She took a shower in the downstairs guest bathroom
and dressed again in the same riding clothes. She took
a suitcase out of the closet and packed all of Emma's
clothes that were left, and her bear. From the library
she took all her books that she had loved since childhood, the same ones she had brought with her to
college, and put them into the suitcase too. She added
her checkbook and household money from the desk.
She took Sweet William's dishes and litter box and
put them into a shopping bag. With the sense peculiar to cats he came walking into the kitchen, tail
held high, the minute she had her hand on his dish.

In the library again, Sweet William watching her
curiously, Annabel wrote a note for Rusty. "I am
leaving you before either of us does any more damage to the other—or to ourselves. Annabel." It seemed
pompous, but better than: Good-bye, I'm taking the
kid and the cat.

She propped the note on the bottles on the bar,
where Rusty always headed first when he came into

the house. Then she remembered her good-bye to Bill Wood so many years ago at the airport. She poured a glass full of bourbon and dropped her engagement and wedding rings into the drink. They fell with a fine plop.

The car pool dropped Emma off outside and she ran into the house. "Mama, I'm home!"

"Hello, darling. Get a snack and go to the bathroom because we're going for a long ride."

"Where?"

"New York City. We're going to stay with Uncle Max for a while and then we'll get our own apartment."

"Daddy too?"

"No. Just you and me and Sweet William. But Daddy will visit us."

Annabel went out and put the suitcase and shopping bag into the car.

Emma came out of the house with Sweet William in her arms. "Why are we going?" she said.

"I'll explain on the way."

"Will I go to school in New York?"

"Of course you will. We're going to live there."

Emma didn't look displeased. "Can Vicki come visit us too?" Vicki was her best friend.

"Sure," Annabel said.

"Can I go say good-bye to her?"

"We have to leave this minute," Annabel said gently. "It's really important."

They looked at each other for a long moment, and then Emma climbed into the car.

Driving down the highway, Emma and Sweet William beside her, the radio on, Annabel began to sing. She was both happy and frightened, but more than anything else she was excited. She had never dreamed she would have a chance for a new beginning, but here she was, breaking away. She knew that this time she would make something of her life.

Part 3

The Seventies: Together

Chapter 1

Six years had passed since the upheavals of the late Sixties. People felt older: disillusioned, more conservative, a bit cynical, but also stronger. The Watergate hearings went on and on as the mystery unraveled. The last American soldiers left Vietnam. The women's movement had become an established fact. People went less to discotheques and entertained more at home. There was a drawing-in. Seeing the world in disorder, they tried to set their own houses in order, as if that would help.

Emily Applebaum Buchman drove to her analyst every day in the little two-seater Mercedes Ken had bought her last year for their fifteenth anniversary. She also had a station wagon, in which she devotedly chauffeured the children to school, friends, the dentist, gymnastics lessons, Little League. It seemed a long time since those six months she had spent in the hospital, and yet she wondered if people still talked about it. The doctors had told her she was ready to come home at the end of two months, but she had been afraid. The mental hospital, where she had gone with such fears, had slowly become a place of security. She knew now it was one of her weaknesses to look for total security, but she was much better. She didn't think it was odd that after all those courses in psychology at college and grad school she had known nothing about herself. That often happened. Her analyst had told her: "The doctor who treats himself has a fool for a patient."

When Ken had put her away she had been angry at him, as if he were the father and she the punished child. She became less angry when her analyst in the hospital made her understand that the role of child was one she had always pushed herself into, thinking it would make her more lovable, more loved, more protected from hurt. But children, even when they are loved and cared for, are also small and vulnerable. Her feelings of smallness had made her angry, her self-erected fortress became a prison, her fears self-regenerating.

One of the things she had been told to do in the hospital was draw pictures. She remembered that test from college and felt smug. The house, the woman, the man were all clues to how you felt about yourself. Yet when she drew the house, carefully, with curtains at the windows and a curl of smoke coming out of the chimney, cleverly remembering to put a knob on the door, a welcoming light over it, she had thought the picture was perfect until the doctor told her kindly that she had drawn no path to the house. There was no way for anyone to get to her. She wouldn't let them.

In the hospital they made her take driving lessons. She was terrified. First she had only to sit in a parked car with a companion beside her; then she had to sit in it alone. When they drove it was in a dual-control car, but still Emily was perspiring and trembling. She could hardly believe she had once driven everywhere as if it were a normal part of her life. When finally she took the car out alone and drove around the block and parked it, she felt exhilarated. It was a triumph. Each small step toward her freedom made her feel stronger.

Ken was as proud of each advancement toward
strength as she was. He told her how much he missed
and valued her and she began to believe him. It must
have been hard on him too, after all. Emily and her
doctor examined at length the phenomenon of her
disappearing scar. He led her to understand how she
had hidden her rage from herself and thus turned it
from where it belonged—directed toward Ken—to
where it didn't belong: herself. She had been her own
victim. Her rage wouldn't kill her, nor would it kill
Ken. She was not a child and there was no bad magic.

"I was brought up to be a perfect lady," Emily told
the doctor.

"Perfect Lady is bullshit," he said. She was shocked.

"How can you say bullshit?"

"Does it offend you?"

"But you're a doctor."

"An authority?"

"Yes," she said.

"And so that makes me perfect?"

"Yes . . ."

"Emily, the first authority has to be yourself."

When she was released from the hospital Emily
started going to a woman analyst, Dr. Page: married,
middle-aged, with grown children. At first she didn't
want to go to a woman: women weren't as smart as
men. Then she realized that was only a part of her
upbringing. This woman had become a doctor in the
old days, something she, Emily, hadn't had the guts
to do, and so this woman was probably smarter than
many men. Every day Emily had new insights that
surprised and embarrassed her. Her life had been a
mass of preconceptions, platitudes, trivialities. She
had always been capable of more. Education for education's sake . . . she'd even gotten the meaning of
that wrong.

In the hospital they had started her on a new drug:
Valium. She was still taking it. Dr. Page wanted her
to stop. But it was so hard to give up the feeling of

security she had with the pills, even though a part
of her understood that she was stronger than she
thought. Besides, all her friends took something. Emily had a lot of friends now: mothers of other children
from Kate and Peter's school, other rich Beverly Hills
housewives like herself, wives of friends of Ken. She
was into self-improvement and keeping busy. There
wasn't an idle moment in her life anymore. She took
all sorts of lessons: gourmet cooking, flower arranging,
art appreciation (for enjoyment or purchasing), needlepoint, macramé, origami, yoga—not all at once,
of course, but ever since the driving lessons she had
always studied something. She went to her yoga classes
faithfully three times a week, to keep in shape. Now
she had started tennis lessons, and she was improving.
She had two tennis lessons a week, and then once
a week she met with a group of her women friends,
each week at someone else's house, and they played
doubles and had lunch.

Ken had finally built the tennis court he had
wanted. He was very successful now and his name was
instantly recognized in certain circles. He and Emily
had friends over during the weekend and they all
played. The children had tennis lessons too, and invited their friends or went to friends' houses to play
on their courts. Emily had become content with the
outdoor life. It was important to keep your body as
active as your mind. Ken was obviously delighted with
the change in her. He hadn't had another affair since
she got out of the hospital, and Emily felt with great
confidence that all that was over now. She and Ken
had a sex life again, and they shared more in every
way.

Why then was she still not happy? Each perfect
sunny day was like the one before, planned, full, cheerful. When she felt misused or angry she let it out.
There was no more rage held inside to poison her.
She felt free to yell at the children when they refused
to clean their rooms or whined at her for expensive

things they didn't need but wanted because their friends had them. They knew if she lost her temper it wasn't the end of their world. Why then did she feel like a tranquilized zombie?

She threw the rest of her Valium down the toilet. She was frightened when the magical little white pills swirled away with the water, and then she remembered that just as there was no bad magic there was no good magic either. Dr. Page was very pleased to hear that she was off the pills.

But somehow getting rid of the Valium didn't make the drugged feeling go away. "Is this what being normal feels like?" Emily asked Dr. Page.

"You use the word 'normal' as if there was a rule. There are all kinds of freedom within normal behavior. What we're trying to do here is show you how to be yourself."

"I feel like I'm drifting. I feel unimportant. Not unimportant like when I was crazy, I mean . . . I don't know."

"But you don't feel like a defenseless child anymore."

"No. I feel like a frivolous woman."

"In what way?"

Emily sighed. She had stopped smoking and right now she wanted a cigarette. She hardly ever felt that way anymore. "Okay. Yesterday the group played tennis at Alicia's house. Her husband is very rich. They have a live-in Chinese houseboy who made this incredible lunch. They have a tennis house that's separate from their pool house, and either one of them is a house I'd be happy to live in as my only home. Their tennis house has a *fireplace* in it, and their pool house has a sauna and you get Porthault towels to dry off with. After we finished playing tennis and were having lunch everybody started talking about clothes. It occurred to me that all they ever talk about is clothes. They sit and describe the dresses they just bought and the ones they saw and might go back to buy as if they were telling you the secrets of the essence of life. Well, suddenly they all got so excited talking about clothes that they jumped up and got into their cars in their sweaty tennis dresses and rushed downtown to go shopping. It was like they were a bunch of junkies looking for a fix. I went right along with them even though I didn't want anything, and then when I got to the stores I bought a handbag I didn't need. I don't want to be like them."

"You're not. They fill their time with shopping and you fill yours with other activities."

"Then why does it all seem the same?"

"Does it?"

"Yes," Emily said.

"What would give you satisfaction, Emily? What would make your life seem more meaningful?"

"I'd like to get a job," Emily said. "But if I left the children I'd feel too guilty, and people would say I was a bad mother."

"What 'people'?"

"Everybody. I'd have to hire someone to drive them around and that would look terrible. I can't have my children being taken around like two little rich kids . . . by a chauffeur."

"You could hire a college student."

"Your children are young for such a short time, and then they grow up and they're gone," Emily said. "It's better to enjoy them while you can."

"What about a part-time job, while the children are in school?"

"After all, if my parents hadn't wanted children, I wouldn't be here."

"You still resent them a little, don't you."

"Sometimes."

"You mustn't use the children as an excuse for your own fear of failure, Emily."

"I don't want some dumb job that doesn't mean anything. I want to do something important. I want to *be* important. The world is full of people who want to be somebody and they're never going to be anybody. The only difference between them and me is they can't afford an analyst to tell them how impossible it is."

"But I'm the one who's trying to encourage you."

"Don't push me. I'm not ready yet."

"*Now* we're making some progress," the doctor said.

Christine Spark and Alexander English had been married for six years. Their son, Nicholas, who had been born on Christmas day, was nearly five. They had decided to have only one child and take him everywhere they went. More than one would be too much trouble in the life they wanted to lead, and Alexander didn't want his son to have the lonely, neglected childhood he felt he'd had. He was a wonderful father and doted on Nicholas. The child was very bright and had a long attention span, and Alexander was endlessly patient with him, playing games, reading to him, showing him how to do new things. Whenever Alexander took a vacation the three of them went to some interesting place they'd never been. They went to Egypt to see the pyramids and the sphinx, to Rio for *carnaval,* to Africa to see the animals, and to London because Chris had never been there. She worried about such a young child having so many inoculations when they went to Africa, but Alexander wouldn't leave him home. She wasn't sure whether or not all this culture was sinking in, but at least Nicholas would know he was much loved.

She was blissfully happy being married to Alexander. They decorated their apartment together, with a mix of modern and antiques, much in the way he had done his Paris apartment. Chris deferred to his taste at all times since she had little idea of what she was doing and had never had so much money to spend before. At first the amount of money Alexander spent on everything from their furniture to their travels and their entertaining awed her, but eventually she got used to it, although she knew he would always do something new and outrageous to surprise her, like buying her a mink coat. She was aware that as the wife of Alexander English, who was now a very successful banker, she had to dress presentably, but she always felt a little uncomfortable in the mink and wore it only when they went someplace special. Under all the trappings of upper-class New York life she was still the Chris who felt her heart stop every time she looked at Alexander after he had been away from her, still astonished that anyone could be so beautiful, and that he could actually have chosen *her*.

Alexander continued to be tender and romantic with her. He made love to her once a week, and since Chris never compared these private things with anyone else she assumed that was about average for marriage. Considering Alexander's past, it seemed quite good. She knew that Annabel and Rusty hadn't had sex together for years before Annabel left him, and people had thought Rusty was such a horny stud. Alexander came directly home from the office in the evenings so that he could play with Nicholas before he went to bed, and then Alexander and Chris would have a drink together in the den and talk about what they had done all day, and make plans. They were always making plans, thinking of things that would be fun to do, weaving the enchanted fabric of their lives together—lovers, companions, and best friends.

When Nicholas was three he was admitted to a kindergarten for specially gifted children, run by Hunter College. On the IQ test his score went right off the top of the chart. Alexander told Chris he took after her, and she said it was a result of Alexander's patience with him. But they were both very proud. If only he looked like Alexander, she thought, then he would be perfect, but he looked like both of them.

When Nicholas started kindergarten Chris went back to work. She got a job as an assistant copy editor at Simon and Schuster. She was bored at home alone, and working made the time pass quickly until she could be with Alexander again in the evenings. They had a housekeeper, Mrs. Gormley, who picked Nicholas up at school and attended to his afternoon social life.

Chris was wholeheartedly in favor of women's lib. For a while she was a member of a discussion group that met for weekly lunches where they raised each other's consciousness and discussed better career opportunities for women. Most of the other women in the group were divorced, had children who were much older than Nicholas, and they all worked. They thought Chris was a fine example of a liberated woman. Secretly Chris knew she was deceiving them. Her whole life revolved around Alexander. Since she had been eighteen years old he had been her sole focus, and everything else had been done by rote. If he had told her not to work she would have stayed home. But he liked her to work, to be interested in outside things. It was by strict attention that she refrained from constantly mentioning his name at these meetings, pretending he was a part of her "other" life.

As he had in Paris, Alexander had a large group of casual friends, some from business but some from the arts too. But almost all these new friends were straight, and many were married couples. Max contributed a few people from the theater. Annabel always brought attractive younger men. Chris brought in some of the women from her discussion group, who brought their current lovers if they had any. It was

no longer necessary at dinner parties to pair everyone off, two by two, like Noah's Ark. Having a wife
and son seemed to give Alexander new confidence,
and when old friends who had known him in Paris
came to town he and Chris always entertained them,
although Alexander was careful to keep them away
from the people he knew from his work world. It was
the Seventies now, and the rock stars and Beautiful
People had made it suddenly chic to be bisexual:
outrageous but interesting. Unfortunately, Alexander
was a banker, and he could afford to be neither outrageous nor "interesting." But perhaps more impor-
tantly, he had been born in the wrong time. He
would always be ashamed of his past. He couldn't
help feeling ashamed. As he grew older and more
sophisticated he held on to his conservatism of
thought, as if he were trying to protect the happy
family life he had created from being touched by
any reminders. The gay men he included in some of
his dinner parties were eminently respectable, middle-
aged, successful, safe. They were not the sort of men
who would ever have the bad taste to bring an un-
suitable lover to someone's home. They arrived alone
or with a woman, and left the same way.

Annabel was still Chris's best woman friend. She
was divorced now, a buyer at Bloomingdale's, living
in her own apartment with Emma, who was thirteen,
and Sweet William, who was eleven, and usually a
young lover, who seemed about twenty. Annabel was
able to attract men as well today, at thirty-eight, as
she had in college. Chris thought she was even more
beautiful now than she had ever been. She was Chris's
link to gossip, delicious scandal, whatever was new.
Chris enjoyed hearing about these things as long as
it was secondhand. She relayed all the juicy stories
to Alexander and they laughed together. She felt very
safe now, looking forward to each day, and she thought
Annabel was brave to live the way she did. It must
be lonely.

Chapter 3

Annabel Jones felt that she had been given a chance
to live her life all over again, but this time knowing
all the things bad experience had taught her. When
she ran away from Rusty she and Emma and Sweet
William had lived with Max for a while, and she
had enrolled Emma in a private school while she
got herself a job as a salesgirl at Bloomingdale's. Max
had wanted to get Annabel a job in the theater, but
she had refused because she wanted to do everything
on her own from now on.

Bloomingdale's had a plan where every month the
employees had a talk with their supervisors about
their work and their career ambitions. Annabel said
immediately that she wanted to go as far as she
could. Her sales record was remarkable: she seemed
to have a knack for putting clothes together so that
the potential purchaser found them all irresistible.
Soon she was promoted to department manager, and
she found the apartment she and Emma and Sweet
William were still living in—a half-floor-through in
a brownstone where she could walk to work. She
divorced Rusty and took back her maiden name. Her
desire to do everything on her own did not go so
far as to make her refuse alimony and child support.

Money meant nothing to Rusty, but without it she would either have to live in a dangerous neighborhood and send Emma to a public school where she might be knifed, or else take money from her father. Annabel felt her father had done enough already.

In a few years Annabel worked her way up to buyer. She was happy with her work, and very busy. She was a little surprised when Rusty remarried. She hadn't thought he was interested in sex. But when Emma, who had to visit Rusty for her summer vacations, said she didn't like to go there because both of them were always drunk, Annabel realized he had married for his idea of companionship.

Her own idea of companionship these days was sleeping with attractive younger men. She seemed to meet them everywhere: at parties, on dates with other men, even in the park and on the street. She had met her latest lover, Steve, on line waiting to get in to see a movie. He was twenty-one, gentle and beautiful, and a painter of sorts. She couldn't understand any of his pictures so she supposed he was either very good or very bad. It didn't matter. She no longer fell in love with her lovers. She found them sexy, cuddly, affectionate, and fun, but that was all.

During the week whoever was Annabel's current lover was sent home to his own apartment because she had to concentrate on her work and Emma, and get up early. Sweet William slept on Annabel's bed during the week, and whoever slept in her lover's bed she couldn't care less. Then on Friday and Saturday nights her lover stayed over at her apartment. Sweet William, with that curious psychic sense cats have, always bedded down in the closet on Friday evenings, even before her lover came to the door.

Emma seemed to be handling all of this very well. At thirteen she had lost her southern accent completely and become very New York. She had many friends and a vast social life. She spent hours on the telephone giggling with her girl friends about boys,

boy crazy but still too shy to date. But she had boys
her own age for friends. It was lucky, Annabel thought,
that Emma wasn't as precocious about sex as most
kids seemed to be today, because she was growing up
to be a beauty. When she got the iron off her teeth,
watch out. Meanwhile she was getting good marks in
school, and last year Annabel had gotten her into
Dalton. It was odd how hard it was to get your child
into a good private school here in New York. It
was supposed to be a cultural center and there weren't
enough good schools. Emma was interested in writing
and photography, and was the star of her gymnastics
class. She adored Max.

On this particular Friday, a crisp fall evening, Annabel walked home from work with a bag full of food
from the store's gourmet department: cheeses and
salade niçoise for tonight, brioches and croissants and
honey for breakfast, and a pound of freshly ground
coffee. She was looking forward to a relaxing weekend with Steve, away from all crises and problems.
She really liked him, perhaps more than was wise, but
she would be careful about that. She didn't intend
to support a twenty-one-year-old boy when she already
had a thirteen-year-old daughter to worry about. She
tried to remember whether there was enough wine.
Her champagne guzzling days were long over, except
for celebrations. Now it was a discreet glass or two of
white wine. She didn't smoke anymore either, not
even grass, although those young boys seemed to love
it. She stopped at the local liquor store for a jug
of white wine, just in case, and then struggled up the
three flights of stairs to her apartment.

When she opened the door Sweet William came
running out to greet her. "Emma?" she called. No
answer.

She put the food away in her small kitchen. From
the closed door of her bedroom she could hear rock
music coming from her hi-fi, which meant that Steve

was already there. Emma must have let him in. None of her lovers ever got his own key.

"Emma?"

Maybe she was in the bedroom with Steve, being deafened by that music, or maybe she had gone out. Annabel looked around the kitchen for the note Emma always left when she went out, but there was none. She wasn't really concerned. She had always trusted Emma. As she walked through the apartment to her bedroom Annabel thought again, as she always did, how much she loved this place. It reflected her own taste, not that of the decorator who had done her home when she lived with Rusty. There were big cushions on the floor in front of the fireplace, a fat, soft sofa, lots of books, and tall palms in baskets in front of the windows. Everything was inviting and nothing was hard to take care of. No matter how many times she came home here she always had this sense of privacy and peace.

She was aware of the familiar sickly sweet smell the moment she opened her bedroom door. Steve was lying on the bed, the hi-fi blasting. Annabel smiled when she saw him. He was sweet even though he did stink up her bedroom because he always forgot to open the window. She had forbidden him ever to smoke pot in any other part of the house because she didn't want Emma to know about it.

Then she saw Emma lying on the floor on the other side of the bed, stoned out of her mind. Emma stubbed the joint out quickly in an ashtray, but not before Annabel saw that too.

"Oh, hi, Mama."

"What do you think you're doing?" Annabel said. She wondered if every mother in the world came out with this same dumb remark when everyone knew perfectly well what everyone was doing.

"It won't hurt her," Steve said. "It's first-class grass."

"She's thirteen years old," Annabel snapped. "If she isn't old enough to know better, you are."

Emma sat up. "Oh, Mama."

"Don't 'Oh Mama' me. I don't want you poisoning your body with drugs. It's the only body you have and you're going to need it for a long time."

"Pot is perfectly harmless," Emma said.

"That's what you think."

"Didn't you read the La Guardia Report?"

"I don't want you stoned in a bedroom with an older man." She turned to Steve. "And you—you're a guest in this house. You're not to give drugs to my daughter. I could have you arrested."

Steve laughed happily. "Me? You'd arrest me?"

Annabel looked at him lying there, relaxed and at home. She had brought him here herself, made love to him, fed him, complimented him, petted him, made him almost a member of the family, at least on weekends. Her anger at him dissipated into annoyance at herself. She was the only grown-up in this room and she was therefore the one most responsible. She had warned him not to let Emma know about his pot, but she should have forbidden him to bring any here at all. She had been too indulgent with him because she didn't want him to think she was old and square. This was what she deserved for being weak.

Annabel picked up the ashtray, carried it into the bathroom, and flushed the contents down the toilet. She heard Steve squeal indignantly when he saw what she had done.

"Hey man, that stuff's expensive," he said.

Annabel opened the bedroom window, ignoring him. "Do you smoke this stuff at school?" she asked Emma.

"No."

"Is that the truth?"

"Yes."

"Have you ever smoked it before?"

Emma looked uncomfortable. Then she shrugged. "No. I just wanted to try it."

"Well, now you have."

"I don't think it's any wore than certain grown-ups being drunk," Emma said.

"We'll discuss them later," Annabel said.

"Listen, it wasn't her idea," Steve said. "She walked in while I was turning on so I offered her some."

"That was very gracious of you. I hope she never walks in while you're playing Russian roulette."

Emma giggled.

"Emma," Annabel said, "please go to your room. I want to talk privately with Steve."

"Don't be mean to him," Emma said. She got up and slunk out, looking back once. Annabel wondered if Emma had a crush on him.

Annabel sighed. She had a headache, she was tired, her evening had been ruined. But most of all she felt like a fool. It was a feeling she seldom had and that she detested. All the warm and loving feelings she'd had for Steve evaporated, as if she had never met him before. That was her fault too. She had kept him a stranger and so she had ended up with a stranger.

"I think you'd better go home now," she said gently.

Steve got up and came over to her. He put his arms around her and his head on her shoulder like a cute child. "Why?"

"Because I want you to."

"Are you mad at me?"

"No, not anymore."

He nibbled her ear. She drew away. "Don't you want me to stay tonight?"

She shook her head. "I want to be alone. I'll call you. Go now. Please."

"Okay."

He picked up his jacket and walked quickly through the apartment and out the front door. When it closed she felt a sharp pain as if a hand had seized her heart, and then she felt calm again. She would be lonely as hell for a few days, but she would find someone else. She would not see Steve again. The next young man she brought into her home would have no bad habits.

She went into Emma's room. Emma was lying on the bed watching television, but she had the sound so low that Annabel was sure she had been trying to hear what was going on. "May I come in?"

"Sure."

"Steve left."

"I'm sorry," Emma said. "You liked him."

"No, I told him to go."

"On account of me?"

"Partly. Can we have a serious discussion?"

"Sure."

Annabel sat on the edge of Emma's bed. "Do you think maybe I shouldn't have my dates stay here?"

"I don't mind," Emma said. "I like some of them."

"Are you sure you don't mind?"

"If you sneaked around I'd know anyway," Emma said. "And then I'd know you didn't trust me."

"You know how I feel about all kinds of drugs, including pot. It was wrong of me to have a double standard. I should never have let him bring it into the house."

"But lots of people do."

"Lots of people's kids turn on, but I don't want you to. You're too young to handle these things. When you're eighteen you're legally free, you can do as you please. By then I hope you won't want to. I don't think you wanted to today. I think you wanted to seem grown-up because Steve's so young. He's more your contemporary than mine."

"He's too old for me," Emma said quickly.

"I don't want to be a bad example for you," Annabel said.

"But Mama," Emma said, "that's so old-fashioned.

I'm not a little kid. I *like* that you have a normal life. Most parents try to hide what they do, and that's worse. You're still young and I don't expect you to give up men."

"Why, thank you."

"Well, you asked me what I thought."

Annabel hugged her and Emma hugged her back. She was so lucky she had Emma for a daughter. Whatever problems they had, she was sure they would be able to talk them out.

"I bet you're starving," Annabel said. "Let's go into the kitchen and I'll show you what I brought for supper."

Chapter 4

Daphne and Richard Caldwell had four children now, all boys: Matthew, seven; Samuel, six; Jonathan, five; and Theodore, three. They all looked like her, with her straight blonde hair, slanted cornflower-blue eyes, and delicate bones. If it were not for Richard's smile that flashed on the faces of her two oldest she would have thought she had created four clones. She watched them carefully for signs of blackouts, minor seizures, and worried about the older ones, away at school all day where anything could happen—a major convulsion, perhaps, and serious injury. But so far they all seemed fine. They were athletic, well coordinated, and full of healthy energy. She blessed her luck and prayed for the future.

Richard wanted a daughter. He kept saying: "Wouldn't it be wonderful to have a little Daphne?"

A little Daphne . . . yes, the curiosity, the desire to create herself again, and the wish to make Richard totally happy were strong pulls. But what if the "little Daphne" had her epilepsy? It was too much of a chance to try for a fifth child.

"I *like* being the only female in a house of five men," she would tease him. "Little boys are such flirts. And I have you all to myself."

"But imagine a little Daphne. Your looks are wasted on those boys."

"Suppose she looks like you?"

"Then she'll have to resign herself to being ugly." They both smiled at that because Richard was so handsome. A daughter of theirs couldn't lose either way. She could only lose if . . .

"Seriously," Daphne said, "I'm thirty-eight, and these four little monsters all nearly the same age are exhausting."

"I'll hire more help. Anything you want."

"But what if it turns out to be another boy?"

"Either way, after this one we'll stop," Richard said. "But I have the feeling the law of averages is on our side."

The law of averages was what she was afraid of. But Richard wanted a daughter so badly. Her pregnancies had all been easy, her complaints seemed minor to his sweet cajoling. A girl would grow up to be her friend. Boys grew up and you lost them. Maybe it would be all right.

"Okay, let's," Daphne said.

After she became pregnant she was glad. Richard was so excited and pleased. His attitude was infectious, and while she bought new white ruffles for the antique cradle that had held all their infants, she imagined a baby girl in it, wearing a little pink jumpsuit. This little girl would have too many clothes, too many toys, and four big brothers to protect her. She would have a perfect life, the youngest and most adored, the unique one. Daphne and Richard decided to call her Elizabeth. If it was a boy it would be Luke, but Daphne saw a girl in that cradle at last.

As her time grew near Daphne became calm and turned inward, waiting for it to be over with, to be rid of this grotesque hugeness and get on with the business of life. She and Richard were having dinner at the nearby home of friends when her water broke.

"I think I'll have another cup of coffee," Richard said, not knowing.

"I think I'll go to the hospital," Daphne said. "And have the baby." Richard rushed her to the hospital.

The Lamaze method of natural childbirth was the new in-thing and everybody was doing it, but it meant the father had to stay in the delivery room by his wife's side the whole time and Daphne would never allow Richard to see her like that. She thought she looked too disgusting. She had her baby the way she'd had all the others: she went to sleep and woke up when it was over.

"It's a girl!" Richard was holding her hand and she was back in her bed. She remembered waking up several times in a drowsy state of pain and finally hearing a baby's cry. "A girl, sweetheart! Congratulations!"

"You did half," Daphne said.

They didn't bring her the baby that evening and she was worried. "Is she all right?" she asked her doctor.

"She's healthy," he said.

"I want to see her."

"Tomorrow. You sleep now." The nurse gave her a pill.

The next morning Daphne woke up at six, furious at being treated like a child. "I want to see my baby," she demanded. They didn't bring her the baby until half past nine, after she'd had breakfast and washed, and by then she was in her robe, on her way down the hall to the nursery to look for herself.

Dr. Gibbs himself came in carrying the baby, wrapped in her little pink blanket. Daphne sat in the armchair beside the window and he put baby Elizabeth into her arms. Daphne smiled at her.

"Well, I thought I'd never see you," she said.

Then she felt icy cold, as if someone had thrown freezing water on her. There was something wrong with this baby. The slanted eyes had an oriental cast, and the hair was rough. The little face didn't look like either hers or Richard's, or like any baby's she had ever seen. And from the mouth protruded an enormous pointed tongue.

"What's the matter with her?" Daphne screamed.

"I'm sorry, Daphne," Dr. Gibbs said. "She's a mongoloid."

Mongoloid? A mongolian idiot? A freak?

"This isn't my baby," Daphne said. She held the thing out for him to take. "Where's my baby? I want my own baby!"

"Do you want a tranquilizer?"

"I want my baby."

"This is your baby. I'm sorry."

He had left the baby lying there in her lap. Daphne looked down at it, touched the tiny hand with her finger and then ran her finger gently over the funny little face. The huge tongue drew back into the mouth for a moment and she looked better.

"Is she going to be retarded?" Daphne whispered.

"I'm afraid so."

"How could this happen?" Then she knew and she started to cry. It was her bad genes, at last. She had been reckless and impertinent to tempt the gods. "It's me, it's my lousy epilepsy. I did it to her—didn't I?"

"Epilepsy has nothing to do with mongolism, Daphne. It's not your fault. Mongoloids are born when there's an extra chromosome. We don't know why it happens. It could happen to anybody."

"Why me?"

"The chances go up in women over thirty-five. Even higher in women over forty. We know that, but we don't know why. You have four lovely children. I don't think you should have any more."

"I have five," Daphne said. She blew her nose and wiped her eyes. Elizabeth seemed so tiny and vulnerable in her lap. She had a right to live and be loved.

"Yes," Dr. Gibbs said. He sounded nervous and uncomfortable.

"How retarded will she be?"

"I don't know yet. It ranges from functional to . . ."

"To what?"

"Let's not worry about that now."

"Does Richard know?"

"Yes. I told him."

"Well, where is he?" For a moment she was afraid he had run away, not wanting to face her, because she had failed him.

"He's waiting outside. I'll get him."

"Wait a minute," Daphne said. "I'm thirty-eight. Was I too old?"

"Let's just say thirty-eight isn't as optimum a time for childbearing as twenty-five."

"Or twenty-eight?"

"Yes."

"It wasn't my fault I was so old," Daphne said.

"Of course it wasn't. Nature is capricious sometimes. It's nobody's fault."

Oh, yes it is, Daphne thought. It's Hope's fault. It had been a long time since she had thought about The Waitress, but now she remembered her with a blast of hate that made her shudder. If Hope had let Richard get a divorce all their children could have been born ten years ago, and Elizabeth would have been perfect. I'd like to kill her, Daphne thought. If she walked into this room this minute I'd break her neck with my bare hands.

But instead, Richard walked in, and his eyes were full of pain. He never once looked down at the baby.

"I love you, Daphne," he said quietly. "Just remember I love you."

The doctor took Elizabeth back to the nursery and Richard helped Daphne into bed. He sat in a chair beside the bed and they held hands for a long time without speaking. Finally he said, "This is all going to be over soon."

"What do you mean?" Daphne asked.

"There's a wonderful private place, sort of a home, where they'll take very good care of her. We'll have the papers before you leave."

Daphne sat up in horror. "What do you mean? Put her away? She's just an *infant*!"

"She's going to stay that way," Richard said.

"We don't know that. Dr. Gibbs said she could be functional."

"Functional? Does that mean she'll be toilet trained at eight? We have other children to think about."

"I'm taking her home," Daphne said. "Babies die if they're not loved."

"I wish she had died."

"Richard . . . you're just upset."

He looked at her blindly. "Daphne, I went past the nursery where they have all the babies lined up in little cribs with their family names on them, and it said 'Caldwell' on that *thing*. I didn't want anybody to see our name attached to the crib. I was embarrassed."

"Embarrassed?"

"Ashamed."

"Nobody said it was your fault."

"I can't help it; I don't love her at all."

Daphne stroked his golden hair. "I know," she murmured. "I know. But you will. When I first saw her I was disgusted and horrified, but then she was so little and helpless and she needed me so much that I knew I had to take care of her. I won't let you put her away. I'm taking her home."

"I would never do anything without your consent, Daphne."

"Just give her a chance," Daphne said.

"But if you grow to love her and then we have to send her away it'll be worse."

"Let's wait and see," Daphne said. "Maybe she'll be all right."

"She'll never be all right."

"Just wait."

He humored her because she was still weak, and she lay back on the pillows and relaxed, thinking she had won.

That summer the boys played at the beach and became tan, and Richard and Daphne water-skied at the club and went to dinner with friends and pretended everything was fine. Elizabeth stayed in the house with the housekeeper. Hot sun was not good for young babies. When she was at home Daphne played with her endlessly, trying to coax some reaction from her, some sign that she knew attention was being paid. Elizabeth was so slow. She didn't watch the mobiles that swung above her crib, or try to lift her head. The boys didn't seem to notice. They treated her like a not very interesting new pet. Richard refused to go near her. Daphne thought she saw him actually cringe. It's that huge lolling tongue, Daphne thought. She'll outgrow it.

She was very careful to give the boys as much attention as she gave Elizabeth so they wouldn't be jealous of the new baby. The summer passed without friction. In the fall the older boys went back to school and Theodore started a half-day play group. In the mornings when Richard had gone to work and the house was empty, Daphne took Elizabeth into her bed. She cuddled her there and talked to her, or sang softly. Elizabeth cried when she was unhappy and smiled when she was happy, and Daphne considered this a triumph. Her little heart beat so strongly, and her fingers gripped Daphne's as if she knew something. But as she got bigger she grew to look more and more mongoloid every day. It didn't matter anymore; she was her own person and she could love. Daphne was sure of it.

Dr. Gibbs sent Elizabeth for tests. They were not hopeful. Now Richard began to pressure Daphne to get rid of Elizabeth—in the same sweet, insistent way he had talked her into having the baby in the first place. There were moments when Daphne actually thought she didn't love him anymore. She fantasized he might kidnap Elizabeth and put her away in that home while she wasn't watching. She remembered Richard's son by Hope, whom he had deserted, and she worried so much she couldn't sleep. She chain-smoked. Her face looked drawn, her skin dry. The boys picked up on the tension in the house and Theodore started wetting the bed. Daphne kept pretending they were a normal family, and on the evenings when she and Richard and the boys all ate dinner together she insisted on carrying Elizabeth down and putting her in her little carrier so she could see what was going on.

It was winter now, cold. After the children were in bed Richard lit a fire in the living room fireplace. Daphne sat in front of it, wrapped in a blanket, gazing into the flames, smoking, dreading the sleepless night to come. Richard brought her a glass of warm milk with sugar and brandy in it. He put his arm around her.

"I want you to drink that."

She sipped it. "That's good," she said.

"I have to take care of you, sweetheart. You're very important to me. You don't seem to know how to take care of yourself."

She sighed. What could she say to make him stop his campaign?

"I only want what's best for you," Richard said. "I love you very, very much."

"I love you too, sweetheart."

Richard took a piece of paper out of his pocket and handed it to her with a pen. "Just sign this and don't read it and don't ask any questions."

"The hell I will!" She knew what it was.

"Look, Daphne, you've got to give her up. She's tearing our family apart. You have four little boys who love you and need their mother. The longer you wait the harder it will be."

"No. Please, Richard, don't."

"Daphne, I'm begging you."

"You hate her that much?"

"I don't hate her at all. I just want to put her where she belongs and will be happy. They'll be good to her. She won't know the difference. She doesn't belong here with us."

"No."

He never gave up. Every day she refused. She began to lose weight and her hands trembled. She was afraid the strain would give her a seizure. When she remembered how anxious Richard had been for a "little Daphne," a perfect replica of her perfect mother, she would find tears pouring down her face. He had been given something flawed; now he wanted to get rid of it. Just as he had gotten rid of his first child. Just as he could do to her if she disappointed him. She had been right all these years not telling him about her epilepsy. He would have left her long ago. She began to be afraid for her marriage. There was no other conversation between her and Richard anymore, except about putting Elizabeth away. The boys had started misbehaving at school, their teachers reported, and it was all too obvious how difficult and cranky they were at home. Daphne found herself yelling at them. She didn't know what to do.

She made Richard drive her out to see the place where he wanted to put Elizabeth. It was a series of very pleasant dormitories, more like large cottages, where groups of retarded children of all kinds lived with house parents. It was extremely expensive. There were people to feed and bathe and dress the helpless children, and others to supervise play for the ones who were functional. None of the children seemed unhappy. The place was clean and nicely furnished. She saw a whole group of mongoloid children and they all looked alike. They all looked like older versions of Elizabeth.

"When we're old and we die she'll be taken care of," Richard said.

"Mongoloid children don't live very long," Daphne said. "A nurse told me that in the hospital. I can't stand to think of her alone and dying away from us."

"These will be her family and friends," Richard said. "She doesn't know us."

He seemed so rational, so sure of himself. She was so tired, and so afraid. It seemed like a nice compassionate place. Elizabeth would have friends. Who would play with her out in the real world?

When they came home Daphne signed the papers.

Richard and Daphne took Elizabeth to her new home. Daphne brought all her toys, even though she never played with them. A nurse took her at the door.

"Please, will you hug and kiss her sometimes?" Daphne said. "She likes that."

"I promise," the nurse said.

Elizabeth let the strange woman carry her away, as calmly as if her parents had never existed.

Afterward Daphne and Richard and the boys settled into their normal lives. A pall of doom seemed to have been lifted from their house. The boys were happier and Richard was his old self. He told the boys that the baby had been sent to a special school because she had been born with a kind of sickness. They were too young to ask what, and Daphne suspected they were rather glad to be rid of her. For herself, she felt a permanent ache, even though she pretended everything was exactly as before.

On Valentine's Day Richard brought home a special present for Daphne. It was a purebred pedigree

golden retriever puppy: bright-eyed, tail wagging, affectionate, and merry. It was an absolutely perfect dog.

Of course it was. Richard **always gave away any-**
thing that wasn't perfect.

Chapter 5

Max Harding, nearing forty, was content with his bachelor life. He was much in demand at parties as a single man, and he had a lot of friends, gay and straight, men and women, mainly in the theater and other arts, but in business and the professions too. Occupations overlapped in New York social life; it was the mix that made it so interesting. He was directing and producing now, with a few failures as well as many successes. His most notable successes were musicals and plays based on nostalgic old themes, like his old *Penrod!*, and his failures came when he tried to be avant-garde. Just last winter he had directed a play using no props, against a wall that had a series of photographs projected on it instead of scenery. It ran one night. The critics hated it, and to tell the truth Max himself had not been especially enamored of it, but it was what the playwright had envisioned. For himself he felt that no matter how hip he became in his everyday life, following fads and fashions, his heart would always remain in the Twenties, a period he had never seen but where he knew he really belonged. More than anything else he was sentimental and romantic, even though the partners

in his many brief love affairs would have been surprised to know it.

His close friends knew it. Annabel, his best friend,
knew it, and so did Emma. Max's work was his life,
and Annabel and Emma were his family. Emma, who
was fourteen and a half now, was like his little niece.
The braces were off her teeth, she was even taller
than Annabel, and at moments looked so much like
Annabel had at eighteen that it stunned him. She
had the same thick copper hair, the innocent green
eyes, the same exquisite face, although a little softer
and unformed yet because she was so young. And she
had Annabel's same disdain for subterfuge.

He had wanted Emma to become an actress because
he thought she could become a movie star.

"Yuck!" Emma said. "I want to be on the other
side of the camera. I'm going to make my own movies."

Sometimes she changed her mind and thought she
would like to be a photojournalist, travel around the
world, interview interesting people, expose corrup-
tion. She saw herself as Lois Lane *and* Superman.
She had very little interest in the theater, but she
saw every movie ever made, and particularly liked to
go to the New Yorker with her boyfriends to see
movies made before she had been born. She also
haunted the Museum of Modern Art's little movie
theater where she saw films made before her parents
were born. It was a wonder she managed to keep up
with her schoolwork.

She knew Max was gay. She accepted it even more
calmly than she did her mother's love life. Now that
Emma was older she felt a certain amount of competition with Annabel, but none whatsoever with Max.
He was like her favorite uncle. If Emma and Annabel
hadn't heard from him for a while, sometimes it was
Emma who called him.

"Hi, Uncle Max. How are you?"

"Okay." Lie.

"Are you depressed again? Come on over and see us and we'll cheer you up."

There were times in his life when Max was very depressed. If he was in between plays with nothing to do, except to read scripts and search for something he liked, or if he was in between flings or quasi-romances, he would envision himself old and alone, lonely, unloved. Annabel had chosen to be alone, but she had Emma. He was totally alone with no commitments. Sometimes he thought he should try to trust someone, to make a life with another person, a man his own age. He knew several very happy couples: men who were loyal to each other, supportive, never destructive, never deserted. Some of them had been together for many years, as he would have been with Alexander if it had all been different. And now Alexander had Chris, and their son, and he, Max, was still alone and afraid to love.

But he was also set in his ways. He liked being solitary, having everything neat and in its place, doing whatever he wanted to do when he wanted to do it, not having to be nice to someone when he felt grouchy. His periods of depression always passed eventually, and he went on: productive, busy, popular, sexually fulfilled. And when he saw Alexander with Chris, both of them so happy, he wasn't the least bit jealous.

Once a month Max took Emma to lunch. He had taken her to every fashionable restaurant where she had ever been, and now he let her pick the place. She always liked to try new ones.

"You're my only rich friend, Uncle Max."

"That's because I'm your only middle-aged friend."

"Oh, you're not middle-aged."

"I'm glad you said that or you would have gone to the Automat."

On this spring day Emma decided she wanted to go to Chinatown. She had her midterm vacation so they were having lunch in the middle of the week instead of on a Saturday as they usually did. She wanted to walk around and see the souvenir shops first. They took a taxi and Max asked the driver to let them out on a main street, hardly knowing Chinatown at all himself.

Emma was enchanted with the phone booths that looked like Chinese pagodas, painted red, and her favorite shop was one that sold strange herbs to be used as medicines.

"Do you think they have an aphrodisiac?" she said.

"What would you need with an aphrodisiac?"

"I'm just asking."

"Oh, yes, very good," the proprietor said, smiling, pointing at a glass-fronted drawer full of dried leaves. "Good for gentleman."

Emma shrieked with laughter. "Wow, he thinks you're my boyfriend!"

"Good for tourist," Max said drily. "This is my daughter."

"Of course," the proprietor said unconvincingly. "I see family resemblance right away."

Max and Emma ran out on the street and fell into each other's arms laughing. "No, we all look alike," Max gasped.

"Incest," Emma said. "Oh, don't make me laugh anymore, my stomach hurts."

"I'm hungry. Let's go eat."

They walked down the street looking at the selection of restaurants, totally unsure of which one was the best. "Let's get a cab and go to Bo Bo's," Max said. "At least I've heard of that."

"No, let's live dangerously. I pick this one."

"Okay."

Max led the way in. The restaurant was nearly empty—not a promising sign, he thought. It seemed clean, although it was too dim to tell for sure, but the tablecloths gleamed white in the ocher light. The house cat, a lean gray-and-white tabby, strolled by them and rubbed against Emma's leg. Her eyes gleamed; she loved cats. She bent down, rubbing the cat's neck affectionately.

It was then that Max saw Alexander, sitting at a secluded table in the back, having lunch with a young number Max recognized from the gay bars. Alexander was wearing his conservative, dark, well-cut suit and tie, on his two-hour lunch break from the bank, and the boy was in ratty jeans and a leather jacket. He had long blond hair and a sexy street-wise face. He was gobbling down his lunch with a fork, while Alexander, elegantly using chopsticks, looked at him as if he'd prefer to have him for the main course. When you're forty and you want to fuck a nineteen-year-old you have to feed him first, Max thought. He was saddened to have caught Alexander cheating, but not really surprised.

The waiter came over to them. "Two?"

"No . . . I just thought of something," Max said. He propelled Emma out the door before she could see Alexander. "Come on, Emma, I just remembered that a friend of mine told me the restaurant we passed down the street is fantastic."

He took her into a restaurant he'd never even heard of, choosing a table in the back so that if Alexander and the number passed the window on their way to bed Emma wouldn't notice them. Poor Chris, Max thought. Poor, poor Chris.

"There isn't a word of English on this menu," Emma said. "Do you think they have bass with black-bean sauce?"

"I'm sure. I'll ask." He would never tell Chris, nor even Annabel, because to tell Annabel would be to tell Chris.

"With a lot of garlic in it, I hope," Emma said. "I love garlic."

"I should have taken you to an Italian restaurant." He supposed it had been going on for a long time. He wondered how long. Alexander seemed destined to live a double life.

"And can we split an order of fried rice? It's not so fattening if we share."

"It's less fattening if I order it and you eat it." He felt sorry for Alexander too. He felt sorry for all of them.

"This is so much fun," Emma said. "Thank you."

"It's my pleasure." Max smiled at her affectionately, wondering why he always had to worry about the lives of people who didn't care about him, when he had his real family right here.

Chapter 6

That summer Chris and Alexander rented a house in Connecticut, where they went every weekend. It was an hour and a half from New York, but it was a totally different, pastoral world. The house had once been a farmhouse, and what had been the stables was now a pool house with a Ping-Pong table and soda fountain in it. The pool was heated, and they had six acres of wooded land. Nicholas always brought at least one friend, and they took Mrs. Gormley along to take care of everyone. Chris and Alexander decided to try to grow vegetables. They were delighted by their success, even though they had planted so that everything ripened at the same time and they were always trying to give away lettuce and tomatoes to their friends.

Sometimes they invited weekend guests, but often it was just the family, with friends driving up to spend Saturday, arriving in late morning to swim and lie in the sun, have lunch, jog, drive to the nearby stables to rent horses, play badminton, swim some more, and generally do their best to get a charley horse or a heart attack by dinnertime. The athletic activities of their Saturday visitors amused Chris and

Alexander, neither of whom cared for any sports at all. Chris liked to cook Saturday dinner herself, although she didn't cook during the week. In the large, old-fashioned kitchen, with plenty of time, she would prepare a large but fairly simple feast, using as much of their home-grown produce as possible. They even grew their own herbs.

This particular Saturday was typical: a couple from New York up for the day, a doctor and his wife, bringing their six-year-old to play with Nicholas and his own weekend guest. Wine and cheese on the screened porch before dinner, watching the sunset, smelling the grass and flowers and the scent of the stew bubbling in the kitchen; the children playing tag on the lawn, Chris talking about the new books for the fall, Alexander looking at her proudly, surveying everything that he had—all this tranquility. Then the children were allowed to eat their dinner in front of the television to get them away from the adults, and the adults sat down to dinner by candlelight, with more wine, funny stories, gossip, some financial observations by Alexander, but mostly nothing very serious because they were all dazed by too much sun and activity. Good-byes by eleven, the guests' child already asleep, carried to the car in his father's arms.

Alexander locked the front door and turned out the lights, and they went upstairs. He had his arm around Chris as they walked up the stairs.

"You know what I was thinking?" he said as they undressed. "We might go to Switzerland for Christmas vacation. It's supposed to be beautiful there, and Nicholas could learn to ski."

"But what would *we* do?" Chris said. "You're not getting me up on those two little sticks."

"We'll feast, and drive around and look at the scenery, and go shopping, and breathe all that clean air."

"That sounds good."

"Or else we could go someplace tropical and lie in the sun."

"I've always wanted to go to Hawaii," Chris said.

"It's turned into a tourist trap now," Alexander said. "Too many people, too much civilization."

"What a shame."

"How about a South Sea island? Fiji?"

"Where's that place Marlon Brando lives?"

"I forget, but I'll think of it. Do you want to go there?"

"It sounded like paradise in an interview I read," Chris said.

"Well, you find out the name," Alexander said. "And I'll see if they have any hotels and if they do I'll get the tickets."

"Would you rather do that than Switzerland?"

"Sure. Whatever you'd like."

They got into bed. Alexander put his arms around her. "Of course, there's always Turkey," he said. "It's supposed to be gorgeous."

"Is it cold at Christmas?"

"We could ask."

Chris laughed. "If we don't sound nouveau riche!"

"They never taught vacations at Harvard and Radcliffe," Alexander said. "We learned manners so we could look like we were very rich, but they didn't tell us how to spend the money."

"Nobody has to teach you," Chris said. She stroked his hair, looking at the breathtaking beauty of his face, even more beautiful now that he was mature, and she thought again what a miracle it was that Alexander had fallen in love with her. She had never been able to tell him that, and she supposed she never would. You had to pretend you thought you had some worth, after all, or he might begin to wonder why he did love you in the first place.

"I want our lives to be fun," Alexander said. He put his head on her breasts and tightened his arms around her.

"It's perfect," Chris said. "I love you so much. More than anybody in the whole world." She held him close to her, waiting to see if he would become aroused, hoping he would.

Then he lay back, his head on his pillow, waiting for her to stroke him. She lay on top of him, her body pressed against his, her fingers, practiced now, running skillfully over his body, her hand stopping finally at his cock, encircling it, moving up and down until she felt some slight swelling . . . hoping, worried as always that he was tired of her at last, his wife of seven years, the old shoe . . . feeling his cock grow large and pulse, knowing it was all right . . . he didn't want a man, he still wanted her, it was all right . . .

Alexander made love to her then and she thought of nothing but her passion. It got better for her all the time with him. His lovemaking was more affectionate than ardent, but once he had entered her she took over. She went crazy when they were making love, and he always seemed pleased that he had caused such a reaction. Afterward he always had that same smile, as if he had had a triumph.

Sunday morning they read *The New York Times* together on the screened porch, with orange juice and blueberry muffins and coffee on a tray in the sunshine, reading aloud to each other when they found funny items. After breakfast Alexander taught Nicholas and his friend how to play baseball, which was sweet, Chris thought, since he didn't know how to play baseball himself. But he was good enough for two six-year-olds. They all had a picnic lunch on the grass, and in the afternoon they swam and lay in the sun. She hated seeing the afternoon end because they would have to go back to the city. It had been a perfect weekend. Their weekends together always were.

The summer went on peacefully. Alexander still hadn't decided where they should go for their Christmas holidays, but that was part of the game. The planning and daydreaming were as much fun as the trip itself. To know that the possibilities were endless and that they could have them all was what he wanted life to be. And part of their plan was what sort of birthday party they would have for Nicholas on their trip. They were the Three Musketeers. Nicholas flourished and became more interesting all the time. Chris thought the idea that unhappy families were self-perpetuating was just a myth: she and Alexander had both had rotten childhoods and they had turned out to be superparents. Insecure as she was about most things, she was confident of that.

One hot, muggy August Friday Alexander was detained in town for a business meeting, but insisted she go on to the country anyway and he would be there late that night. Nicholas had invited a friend, Chris had bought groceries, they had already made plans.

"I hate to leave you," Chris said.

"Don't be silly. I'll call you if I miss the last train."

He was right, so she left, feeling sorry for him. At least he would be in an air-conditioned office.

When they got to the country house the air was still and the sky crackled with ominous flashes of lightning. Thunder rumbled far away over the hills. The birds flew straight up and away over the thick leafy trees.

"We'll have a storm tonight," Mrs. Gormley said. She helped Chris unload the car and rummaged through the kitchen closet to set out candles, matches, and flashlights in case the power failed. Nicholas, who had ridden a camel, been forbidden to drink the water in six countries, and slept in a tent on the African plain, was clearly looking forward to all this as another adventure, but his friend, a little girl from his class named Jane, was nervous.

"If there's no water you won't have to take a bath tomorrow," Nicholas told her. She seemed a little reassured.

"The storm should cool things off," Chris said, thinking about Alexander in the hot city. She wondered if it would rain there too.

Instead of grilling hamburgers outside Chris cooked them in the living room fireplace to pacify the children, and then they toasted marshmallows on wire coat hangers over the flames. The storm began, colorful and wild, and yet it was somehow peaceful to be snug and dry here in the old house. Chris gave the children flashlights to take to bed and told them they probably wouldn't need them—it was just a summer storm and would be over in the morning. When they had gone upstairs she filled several pots and bottles with water for cooking and drinking, just in case, and filled her bathtub too.

At eleven o'clock she was reading in bed when the phone rang. It was Alexander.

"I missed the train and I'm beat. It's raining like hell here. I'm at the apartment and I'll just go to sleep and come up first thing in the morning."

"All right, love. We have a storm here too. Call me and I'll meet your train."

"Are the kids all right?"

"They're fine. I love you."

"I love you, too. Goodnight."

Chris hung up, feeling depressed. She would have liked to have Alexander here beside her, to hold her tightly when the thunder crashed, and she missed him. They hardly ever spent a night apart; she couldn't think of more than three times in their entire marriage, when he'd had to go on overnight business trips. Well, the sooner she went to sleep the sooner it would be morning and they'd be together again and have a wonderful weekend.

She was sleeping fitfully when the phone rang again. She looked at the clock beside her bed. It was half past one. It was her mother, voice slurred with liquor but urgent too.

"Dad's had a heart attack."

"Oh, no!"

"He's in Mount Sinai Hospital. You better come in. He's in intensive care."

"I'll be there as quick as I can," Chris said.

Her heart was pounding with fear and she was wide-awake. Her skin was burning. Her father! He'd never had heart trouble before. But this happened to old people all the time. Thank God he was still alive. Maybe he'd pull through. She thought of calling Alexander but she didn't want to wake him. There was nothing he could do now.

Dressed, she went quietly into Mrs. Gormley's room to wake her and tell her, and then she went outside to the car and set off into the storm. The roads were empty at this hour, rain pelting down on her windshield, water spraying out from beneath her wheels. She was afraid to drive any faster. She remembered all the things her father had done for her: the time he had taken care of everything in her New York apartment when she wanted to stay in Paris, the lie about her good job that he had always believed so proudly, the times he had been her friend and confidant. He had been such a kind father, making up for her lack of a real mother. All these years she had thought he'd stayed with her alcoholic mother out of weakness, but perhaps it had been strength. Who knew about love? It was different for each couple. Certainly her father had put up with a lot, patiently and cheerfully. God couldn't let him die, not yet . . . She loved her father so much, even though she didn't see him as often as she might have. Now she felt like a little girl again, remembering the sound of his key in the lock when he came home, that sound seeming so loud in their apartment, filling her with reassurance and joy.

When she finally reached the hospital they wouldn't let her see him because it was the middle of the night. She sat with her mother in the waiting lounge, drinking vile coffee from a Styrofoam cup, noticing how old and wrinkled her mother looked in the harsh light.

"He's conscious," her mother said. "They don't think there was any brain damage. He might be all right."

"Why is he in intensive care?"

"Always, for heart attacks." Her mother was sitting there wringing her hands. Chris supposed she wanted a drink desperately.

"I'll get you some coffee," Chris said.

"No. I don't need coffee."

"I didn't think you *needed* it, I just thought you might like it."

"You always hated me," her mother said. She started to cry. Chris felt her stomach turn over.

"No, I never did."

"You resented that I drank."

"That's over now," Chris said. She put her arm around her mother. The older woman's body seemed smaller than she remembered.

"One Christmas I tried to give you a piece of fruitcake and you screamed and ran out of the room because there was whiskey in it."

"I was seven years old," Chris said. "I'm almost forty now. I drink wine every night. Forget it."

"I drink to relax. You'll never understand."

"I understand," Chris said. "I really do." She wanted to tell her mother that she loved her, but the words stuck in her throat. Why couldn't she say them, particularly now when they were so needed? She did love her mother—everybody loved their mother. But it seemed so phony to say so now. She felt sorry for her mother, but she didn't like her.

"You and I ought to try to be better friends," her mother said.

"Yes," Chris said, and then she began to cry because she was so tired and so worried about her father. Her mother took her tears for a sign of reconciliation and squeezed her hand and smiled.

Finally, at six A.M., the nurse took pity on them and said they could tiptoe in to see Mr. Spark if they stayed only five minutes. He was awake and asking for them. Chris's mother glanced in her compact and quickly put on a slash of lipstick, and Chris thought again of the mysteries and complexities of love.

Her father's face looked gray against the white pillowcase. There were all sorts of mechanical attachments linking his body to machines. Chris watched the television screen that recorded his heartbeat as a pattern of leaping lighted lines and wondered what was normal. What did his mean? He smiled when he saw her.

"Oh, you came in from the country."

"How do you feel?"

"Okay."

Chris kissed his cheek. "Dad, I love you."

"Good." He was holding her mother's hand. "They gave me some pills that make me feel stupid. They keep you doped up in this place so you don't bother them."

"He's going to be all right," Chris said happily.

"Don't you give the nurses trouble," her mother said to him.

"Me, trouble?"

"Do you want me to bring you anything?" Chris asked.

"No thanks." A young nurse came into the cubicle. "Isn't she pretty?" The nurse smiled. "Look how pretty she is," he said.

"He's getting along fine," the nurse said. "You'll have to go now so he can rest."

They went out into the hall. "Why don't you go home too and get some sleep?" the nurse said. "The doctor will be in later and then you can talk to him."

"I think I will," Chris said. Fatigue hit her and she almost staggered. She wanted to go to her apartment and crawl into bed beside Alexander, have him hold her and tell her everything would be all right.

Her mother insisted on sleeping on the couch in the lounge until the doctor came, and Chris wondered if this was her way of staying away from the liquor that was waiting seductively for her in her apartment. Extreme stress seemed to bring out the best in her mother; it was only the daily aggravations that seemed to make her want to drink. I ought to be more sympathetic, Chris thought. I have my own family now and my own life, and whatever my mother does can't possibly hurt me anymore.

"Goodnight, Mom. I love you."

The words were out and she felt better. Her mother's eyes lit up. Chris got into her car and went home. The storm was over and the sun was shining. The city streets looked freshly washed. She let herself into the apartment quietly so she wouldn't startle Alexander, and hung her raincoat in the hall closet. She felt the familiar warmth and anticipation fill her as she walked to their bedroom, imagining him asleep and vulnerable, waking with surprise and pleasure to see her.

She opened the bedroom door. Alexander was asleep in their large bed, holding in his arms a very young man, the boy's head on Alexander's shoulder, Alexander's face buried in his blond curls.

At first it seemed totally unreal, like a hallucination. Then Chris felt the hideous tingling start at the roots of her hair and continue down the skin of her entire body, while the emptiness inside her screamed.

She yanked the cord of the venetian blinds viciously so the dim room was flooded with light. The two bodies on the bed moved, startled, sleepy, annoyed. Then Alexander looked at her and his face froze in an expression of disbelief.

"This isn't Alexander's Room," Chris said coldly. "Get him out."

The boy, released from Alexander's embrace, looked at her with embarrassment and pulled the sheet up over his nakedness. Chris realized then, with hatred, that he wasn't embarrassed because she was Alexander's wife, but because he didn't want a woman to see him undressed.

"You better go," Alexander said to him.

"Make her turn her back," the boy whispered. Chris wanted to strangle him.

"I'm not turning anything," she snapped. "Take the sheet and dress in the hall, you . . ."

The boy wrapped the sheet around him and scurried into the bathroom, picking up his scattered clothes as he went. Alexander got out of bed and put on his bathrobe, ashamed.

"Chris . . ."

She didn't want to say a word to him until the boy was gone. The room seemed polluted. She could never sleep on that mattress again. Her life was over, destroyed. How could he do this to her, in her own house? How long had he been doing it, lying to her? Did he ever really love her at all, or was it a lie and she a convenience, his gesture toward propriety? She fought back the tears and glared at him.

"What are you doing here?" Alexander asked gently. "Did something happen?"

"My father had a heart attack," she said. "He's all right. I didn't come in to spy on you, if that's what you think."

"I never thought that." His face was full of pain.

The boy came out of the bathroom wearing jeans and a T-shirt. He had a young, slim, hipless body and a stupidly handsome face. "I can't find my socks," he whined.

"For God's sake!" Alexander said, annoyed. He pulled a pair of bright green socks out from under the bed and threw them at him. Then he pushed him down the hall, the boy still holding his socks and sneakers in his hand. Chris heard the front door slam. She sat on the chair and began to shake. Alexander came back and sat on the edge of the bed, facing her.

"You don't know how sorry I am," he said.

She didn't say anything. There were too many questions. She couldn't stop shaking.

"Oh, Chris, don't." He started to get up to come over to her and then sat down again, watching her face to see if she would allow him to approach her. "Do you want a blanket?"

"No."

"Can I touch you? Please?"

"No."

"I never meant this to happen," he said. "I did work late last night, and I did come home alone, and I was alone when I called you. But after I hung up I felt lonely and nervous and . . . I hate to be alone . . . I thought I'd just go out and take a walk."

"In the rain?"

"I went to a bar for a drink."

"A gay bar?" She could hear the implacable hate in her voice, as if she were a stranger.

"No. You don't have to go to a gay bar to pick up a man."

"*You* don't."

"I never saw him before. He doesn't mean anything to me. I even forgot his name."

"Why did you bring him *here*?"

"He said he lives with some old guy who's supporting him. His idea of an old geezer is probably somebody my age. Anyway, that's why I had to take him here."

"Why didn't you just blow him in the men's room?"

"Okay," Alexander said quietly. "I deserve that."

"How long have you been doing this?"

He clenched his hands into fists. "I . . . about three years. Not very often. Maybe once a month."

"That's your idea of not very often?"

"I can't help it. Chris, I *love* you. You're the only person I do love, except for Nicholas. I can't help the way I am. It builds up, and then one day I see some number and think: who will it hurt if no one knows? These guys mean nothing to me. They're just sex. Afterward I feel guilty and terrible. I swear I would do anything to stop, but I can't."

"You can," Chris said. "I don't cheat on you. I control myself."

"We're different."

"Did you ever bring anyone here before?"

"No, never," Alexander said. "I swear it."

"Where did you do it?"

"Why do you want to know all this?"

"Because I do," she snapped.

"All right, I went to their apartments."

"When did you find time?"

"At lunch."

"Oh, yes," Chris said, "I forgot about long executive lunch hours. That's when the married men screw their secretaries." She had stopped shaking. "How could you bring him *here*?" she said again.

"I don't know. I'd say a part of me wanted you to find out so I could get it out in the open and have you understand and forgive me, but there was no way I could have known your father would have a heart attack and you'd come in. It was just a dumb thing for me to do and I have no excuse."

"You *wanted* me to know?"

Alexander's eyes filled with tears. "I don't know."

"You told me, before we got married, that after we were married you'd stop. You said you didn't want anyone but me."

"I don't." He got up then and came over to her. "Chris?"

She looked at him. She was melting at the sight of him, that beautiful face, tormented again as it hadn't been for so many years. She had caused him that suffering. He deserved all of it, and more, because she was suffering too, but still she couldn't stand to hurt him. Alexander took her hands gently and pulled her to her feet, and put his arms around her. She could feel his heart pounding against hers.

"Don't leave me, Chris. Please. Since we've been married is the only time in my whole life that I've ever been completely happy."

"Better than Paris, when you could do what you wanted?"

"Our marriage is what I want. You and Nicholas are what I want. I love you, Chris, and I don't want to lose you."

"I was happy too," she said softly. "I was so happy." She started to cry.

He stroked her and kissed her hair. "We'll be happy again. I'll make it up to you. Think of me as a . . . sort of epileptic, who blacks out and has attacks."

"But you're not! They can't help it and you can."

"I know," he said, so quietly she could hardly hear him.

She drew away from him. Without his arms around her she felt cold. "I'm going back to the country," she said.

"Wait and have breakfast first," Alexander said. "You're exhausted. Then I'll drive."

"You're not coming."

"Please let me come."

She felt drained, almost unable to think. "The kids will be scared if I don't go back."

"I'm afraid to let you drive the way you are. You look ready to collapse."

"I think I'm going to throw up." She ran into the bathroom and retched, but there was nothing to come out. She was empty of everything, a shell. But under the numbness she knew the pain was still waiting to overcome her as soon as her body adjusted to the shock.

When she came out of the bathroom she could smell fresh coffee and burned toast. She went into the kitchen. Alexander had set the kitchen table and was trying to make breakfast.

"I'm not hungry," Chris said.

"Just have some orange juice."

She let him hand her the glass of juice and drank it, trying not to look at him. If she looked at him she would weaken, if she weakened he would destroy her. How could she ever let him make love to her again, knowing that in between he was making love to men? How could they have a real marriage anymore? But how could she leave him? She would rather kill herself than have to live without him.

Alexander handed her a piece of buttered toast. "Look," he said, "this one isn't burned."

She took a bite and gagged. She put the toast on her plate and sipped her hot black coffee. "Some fine father you are," she said. "For a son."

"That's beneath you, Chris," Alexander said quietly. "I've always been a good father."

"Yes, you have. I'm sorry."

"I feel old today," Alexander said. He sounded very tired. "I feel like a failure."

"Me too."

"*You're* not a failure. This had nothing to do with you."

"I know. But it doesn't help how I feel." She looked at her watch. "I have to go now."

"Will you be back tomorrow evening?" He sounded scared.

"I don't know," Chris said. "I have to be alone to think. I'll tell Nicholas you had to work. Please call him, he'll like that."

"Of course I will. Do you want me to visit your father?"

"That would be nice. Let me know when you plan to go so we don't both go at the same time. He can only have two visitors, and there's my mother."

"Maybe I'll take your mother to dinner tonight," Alexander said.

"You're free," Chris said. "You can take anyone to dinner you please." She hadn't meant that to sound so bitchy. She didn't want to hammer at him anymore. He was sorry. But everything was so out of place. "I . . ."

"What?"

She had almost been ready to say "I apologize." Chris the doormat. She got up and went quickly to the closet, took her raincoat, and went to the front door. Alexander followed her.

"What were you going to say, Chris? Chris?"

I love you, she thought. "I forgot," she said.

And then she ran away.

Chapter 7

There was a drought in Los Angeles that fall. Day after day of relentless sunshine replaced what was normally California's rainy season. Fires burned in the hills. Ken sprayed the roof of their house with water at Emily's insistence, even though they were far away from the site of the fires. She didn't consider it neurotic to worry; they were surrounded by dry brush here on their mountain, and just the other day a friend of theirs had lost his entire house when he lit a fire in his fireplace and a spark ignited his roof. She took the firewood out of their fireplace, which they seldom used anyway because ashes were so messy, and replaced it with a brass bowl full of fresh cut flowers.

She was still going to Dr. Page, but only three times a week now. Emily knew she would never be well until she had the courage to change her life or else accepted the dead dream. She could adjust to being a housewife, realize it had honor, and respect herself for what she was. Peter was ten now, Kate twelve. They were tall, slim, athletic, healthy California children. But they looked like her and Ken, with the lean curious faces of people who were meant to

..tellectuals. Kate liked to read, Peter did not.
. mily hoped they would make something of themselves, but she knew that ultimately it would be up
to them. She and Ken would supply the schooling and
the love, try not to bring them up in a sexist or too
materialistic way, and then hope.

That afternoon she came back from her biweekly
trip to the supermarket, unloaded the car and put
everything away, went out again to pick up Peter
from his Hebrew lesson, got him home, called Kate
at her friend Amy's house to see if she had to come
get her, was glad when Kate said Amy's mother would
drop her off later if she could stay at Amy's for dinner, pried Peter away from the television set and
made him start his homework, decided to make a
Chinese dinner to show off the result of her latest
ethnic cooking lessons, and went upstairs to take a
quick shower and put on something pretty for Ken.
She was in the kitchen chopping vegetables when
Ken came in.

"Guess who I ran into at the Polo Lounge," he said,
sounding excited. He was wearing his company face.

"Who?"

A tall, lean, sandy-haired man walked in behind
him, smiling. Something about him was both alien and
familiar.

"Do you remember Max Harding from college?"
Ken said.

Max . . . after all these years . . . But she did
remember him now, which was why he had seemed
familiar. What had appeared alien was that mixture
of New York breeding and what she had thought of
in the old days as slick, Gentile, society upbringing.
He wore it in with him like clothes, before he even
said a word. It was the way he would walk into her
kitchen without a flicker of insecurity, not caring
whether she remembered him or not, since that was
not necessary for a successful social encounter. She

wondered if he remembered her and if he thought she looked old.

"Max, of course, how nice to see you!" she said, noticing that unconsciously she had slipped into her old proper Radcliffe tones.

"Emily . . ." He strode over to her and shook her hand, then covered it with his other hand and looked into her face, nodding approvingly. "You haven't changed at all."

"That's what you think." She laughed lightly. "But it's sweet of you to say."

"Max is here on business," Ken said.

"Yes, you're a big Broadway producer now," Emily said. "We read about you in the papers all the time."

"I'm here making a movie deal for *The Magic Forest*," Max said.

"I told him we saw it when it played here," Ken said. "I'm going to make us a drink. What will you have, Max, the same?"

Emily joined them in the living room. Max walked around the room, admiring the view and the way she'd decorated, complimenting everything. They were all drinking white wine.

"How is New York?" Emily said. "I miss it."

"It's still wonderful," Max said. "A little dirtier, more crowded, bankrupt, crime-ridden—but I wouldn't live anywhere else. It's the most exciting city in the world."

"Maybe I'll take Emily and the kids for Christmas," Ken said. "We've planned to go several times, but something always came up. The kids have a big social life. We can't pry them away from it."

"How many kids do you have?"

"Two," Emily said. "Kate and Peter. She's at a friend's house but he's here, studying. I'll bring him out in a minute to meet you. First let's just relax for a minute. You two have both been working hard all day." God, she was handling this well, so charming and at ease . . . he didn't know that her hands were getting cold with fear. Seeing Max Harding brought back all her old insecurities from college. "Do you have children, Max?"

"No. I'm not married."

"Never got married?" Ken said. "A wise man."

"Thanks a lot," Emily said.

"Oh, I was just kidding," Ken said. He put his arm around her and smiled. Emily remembered then that she'd heard some rumor that Max was gay. She decided to change the subject quickly.

"You're lucky to be here during the drought," she said. "It's not so good for us, but you're missing the dreary rain. I guess you're glad to be away from the cold."

"It's not cold yet in New York," Max said. "I should have come here in January, but unfortunately I can't pick the time to do business."

She felt like a hick. Why was she talking about the weather the way everybody did here when they met someone from New York?

"How do you like L.A.?" Ken said.

"It's great," Max said.

"You should come out again when you can stay longer. It's really a relaxed way of life."

"I'm glad you didn't say you hate it," Emily said. "People from New York come out here to live and all they do is complain."

"But people from the Coast complain about New York," Max said.

Ken refilled their wine glasses. Emily wondered what they would talk about now. She felt she had covered every cliché in the book, and she was beginning to feel very ill at ease. What would Dr. Page tell her to do? A year ago she might have made some excuse and gone to phone her analyst, but now she could handle it on her own, even if badly. She decided to shut up and let the men carry the conversation.

"I want you both to have dinner with me," Max

said. "I'm having dinner at La Scala with a terrific woman—a good friend—named Charlie Lord. She's an executive at Paramount. I've booked a table at eight. Can you join us?"

"Sure," Ken said. "Is that all right, honey?"

"Wonderful," Emily said. She wondered why Max wanted to spend the rest of the evening with them when they'd been so boring already.

"May I use your phone?" Max asked. "I'll change it to a table for four."

He must have a lot of pull, Emily thought, to be able to change his table at La Scala at the last minute. We always have to call a day in advance and then they put us in the back.

"I'll just change my clothes," she said, and fled to their bedroom.

Things to say . . . things to say . . . what had she said to men on dates back in the dark ages when she was at Radcliffe? Mostly nothing. She couldn't remember one intelligent thing she had ever said to a man until she met Ken and they felt as if they had known each other forever. What could she say to Max now? He didn't want her opinion of road company versions of Broadway shows, or the latest movies, and what did he care about the P.T.A.? If he was gay maybe he liked to cook. They could talk about that.

When she got back to the living room Ken had introduced Max to Peter, who was being polite and making a good impression. "You'll have to make your own dinner," Emily said to Peter. "I chopped up some Chinese vegetables. You can eat them raw. Peter's a health-food freak," she said to Max. "And there's some cold chicken in the refrigerator."

"Okay," Peter said. "May I be excused?"

"Of course."

"Nice kid," Max said when Peter had left.

"Yes, we're proud of both our kids," Ken said.

"I was going to make a Chinese dinner when you

rescued us," Emily said. "I'm quite a gourmet cook, if I say so myself. I've now mastered seven countries. Someday my poor family is going to get stewed yak."

Max laughed. "I envy you. All I can do is boil water."

"Oh," Emily said.

"You'll like Charlie," Max said. "She's an amazing woman. She was the former Miss North Carolina, when she graduated from high school. But she worked her way up to becoming a movie executive. She's bright and interesting and a lot of fun."

"How old is she?" Emily asked.

"I guess thirty-five."

"And an executive . . . My!"

"Oh, they're all young," Max said. "But they age fast in this business."

"I bet they do," Ken said cheerfully.

Ken is so confident, Emily thought with pride and a little envy. *Max Harding doesn't faze him a bit. None of those friends of his did, ever, even back in college. He was Buchman who gave the wild parties. I was just Emily Applebaum who had more cashmere sweaters than anybody else. I guess in a way I still am, except instead of my father paying for them Ken does.*

"You didn't know," Emily said quickly, "but I worked as a psychiatric social worker for a while back in Boston after we all graduated. I got my master's degree while Ken went to med school. We have a lot of catching up to do."

"We will," Max said warmly.

Oh, my God, Emily thought, *how can he stand us? Ken at least is fun, everybody likes Ken, and even theater people think doctors are important. But what can Max see in me? How can he put up with this charade with a straight face?*

"I remember you had that yellow Stutz Bearcat," Ken said, as they went outside and got into Ken's car.

At La Scala they were seated at a banquette in the front room. Emily was impressed and felt even more inadequate than ever. Max's date was late. Then she came rushing over to the table: tall, blonde, beautiful, slim, looking younger than thirty-five.

"Charlie Lord, Ken and Emily Buchman," Max said, rising and letting her sit in his place.

"I'm sorry I'm late," she said. "I was in a meeting and it lasted longer than I expected it to."

They ordered a bottle of wine. Emily was beginning to get high. She didn't care. Maybe it would help the shyness. Max had launched into a funny story about a meeting he had been at during this trip, with a director who had wanted to make all sorts of ridiculous changes in his play when he brought it to the screen. He had not been chosen. Max and Charlie knew who everybody was, and had so much in common, while Ken clearly enjoyed all this show-business talk. He even seemed to know who those people were too, and if he didn't he wasn't afraid to ask.

"How did you get your job?" Emily asked Charlie.

"I just worked my way up," she said calmly. "The secret is never to stay in the same job for more than three years. I was in New York for a while, and then when they offered me this job if I would relocate I grabbed it. You have to be flexible."

"And good at what you do," Max said. "She modestly omitted that."

"I guess you're not married," Emily said. "Or you wouldn't be able to pick up and move."

"I'm divorced," she said.

"Children?"

"No."

"Ah."

"You have children," Charlie said.

"Yes," Emily said. "Two. You make choices in life, I guess."

"Not anymore," Charlie said. "People can do both.

We just didn't want to have children at first, and then the marriage broke up anyway, so that was fine. I might get married again someday."

"He'd have to be very independent."

"If he wasn't I wouldn't want him," Charlie said. "If he wants a maid he can hire one."

"Yes, of course," Emily murmured. She drank her wine. Their food came and she only picked at it, moving it around her plate so they would think she was eating. She wasn't hungry. "I envy you."

"By Friday night you wouldn't envy me," Charlie said. "It's a hard job. But I love it."

She looked so relaxed and happy, not hard or tough, nothing like what Emily had thought a woman executive would be. She had started out by winning a beauty contest, and probably marrying some football player when she was nineteen, and she hadn't stayed in that stereotype either. Emily was only five years older than this woman, but now she felt sure that life had passed her by. Would it have been any different if Ken hadn't gotten off that ship?

"I envy you," Emily said again, drunk. She wondered if they noticed she was drunk. She hoped not. She moved very carefully so she wouldn't upset a water glass or drop a piece of silverware on the floor and make a fool of herself.

"You could get a job, Emily," Max said.

"In the movies?" She giggled.

"No. In the field you specialized in. Do you realize you could be a psychiatrist with your credentials?"

"Just a master's degree?"

"Sure. Everybody I meet here seems to be going to some shrink. They're all into self-help, or you-help-me, or screaming sessions, or group therapy, or some kind of esoteric new technique. It's a seller's market."

"Oh, Max." She giggled again. "Do you think I want a bunch of loonies in my house?"

"She thinks I'm funny," Max said. "Okay, what

about getting the same kind of job you had before?"

"I'm much too busy," Emily said.

"Oh," Max said pleasantly. "All right."

"I mean, I have these extremely important decisions to make," Emily pressed on, her laughter bubbling up in her like hysteria, closer to tears than mirth. "You have to make creative decisions in the theater every day, and you, Charlie, you're an executive, you make them too, but so do I. Like only this morning I had to help my daughter decide what color bow she wanted on her costume for the school play, green or yellow, or if she even wanted a bow at all. You're in the creative arts, you understand how important all these little details are. I'm very busy. Very, very busy."

"You're very, very drunk," Ken said, but he didn't sound angry.

"Just like the old days back at Harvard," Max said. "We always tried to get the girls plastered. We've done it again." He smiled at Ken and then they both laughed.

"Charlie isn't drunk," Emily said. "She's like those dates you always had at Harvard. Cool and blonde and never got drunk. Annabel . . . what ever happened to Annabel?"

"She lives in New York now," Max said. "She's a buyer at Bloomingdale's and she has a lovely daughter named Emma."

"Where's her husband?"

"They're divorced."

"You see?" Emily said. "You can't do both."

"Do you want to trade me in?" Ken asked.

"No." She took his hand and squeezed it. "No, never."

"I'm relieved to hear it," Ken said, and squeezed her hand in return.

He was being so nice. She wondered why he wasn't annoyed that she was making a fool of herself. Maybe he really didn't mind because he knew how she felt, how scared these people made her feel. She looked at Ken and felt her love for him rise up soothingly, calming her laughter before it became tears. He was still holding her hand. Ken would hate to be married to someone like Charlie, Emily thought. He likes *me,* the way I am. Ken dated girls like Charlie too, at college, before he met me. But I'm the one he married. And look at her, so pretty and self-sufficient and successful and smart, and who can she find to go out with? Just somebody like Max, who'll never be more than a friend. I'm lucky.

But she felt herself sinking into depression. She blamed it on the wine.

Chapter 8

Emma was seventeen, worrying about college already, planning to apply to Radcliffe. Annabel couldn't decide whether to treat her like a teenaged girl or a grown-up. One minute Emma was sophisticated, intellectual, cool, and the next she was clowning. Boys hung around the house all the time. That summer Max had gotten Emma a job as a gofer on a film being made in Italy. Besides being a good extracurricular activity to list on her résumé for college, it was the most exciting thing that had ever happened to her.

Annabel spent a peaceful summer with the apartment to herself without Emma and her noisy entourage of admirers and friends, but she was glad when Emma came back in the fall. She had missed her. Now this was Emma's last year at Dalton, then off to college, and then she would probably never come back. Annabel was glad she had an interesting job and friends and a life of her own. It must be awful to live through your child the way so many women did.

As for herself, she was in between boyfriends. She didn't know what else to call them. "Beaux" or "lovers" was too archaic, too romantic. "Friends" implied a closeness that wasn't there. It seemed that the quality of men was getting poorer, or perhaps she was getting bored. The men she met lately seemed to lack imagination, the talent to make something of nothing, an adventure out of an ordinary evening. Most of them were just dull. She didn't mind being alone for a while. Se knew that when she got restless she would find someone new, invest him with a little glamor he didn't possess, and have a pleasant romance.

She was making Saturday morning breakfast when their downstairs buzzer rang. Emma, who was usually still asleep at this hour on a weekend, rushed out of her room fully dressed with freshly washed and dried hair and answered the intercom.

"Who is it?"

"Me."

"Come on up."

Emma opened the door to a boy of about nineteen, who looked like a very young Bobby Kennedy. He was carrying two large suitcases.

"Mom, this is Jake O'Hara. This is my mom. He's going to stay for the weekend."

Jake shook Annabel's hand politely. "I'm glad to meet you, Ms. Jones." Oh, my God, Annabel thought, it's the first time anybody called me *that*.

"Well, I'm glad to meet you too, Jake. Have you had breakfast?"

"Yes, but I'd love some coffee." He smiled winningly at her, and Emma whisked him and his suitcases off to her room.

He is not sleeping in her room, Annabel thought. She went to the linen closet and took out two sheets, a pillowcase, their spare pillow and comforter, and pointedly dropped them on the living room couch.

"What's that for?" Emma said, standing at the entrance to the living room.

"For your guest."

"Don't be silly," Emma said calmly. "He's staying with me."

"Who *is* he anyway?"

"Shh . . . he'll hear you."

"And why has he got all those suitcases?"

"He's on his way to college," Emma said. "He goes to Yale. I told him to come by on his way and visit us. I met him this summer in Italy."

"Ah. On the film?"

"Yes. He was another slave, like me. We're both interested in making movies. You'll like him, he's very smart."

"He's also very polite, but he's not sleeping in your room," Annabel said.

"Why not? We slept together all summer."

So Emma's sex life was out in the open at last. Annabel had wondered about it, but she had never had the nerve to pry. In her heart she had pretended Emma was still a virgin, and if she didn't ask she wouldn't ever have to cope with the alternative. Emma's words were casual, but Annabel knew her well enough to hear the undercurrent of defiance. Emma was saying: Accept it or else.

"I didn't know that," Annabel said.

"Well, wouldn't *you*?" Emma whispered. "Look at him—he's *gorgeous*!"

"I don't suppose I dare ask if he was the first."

"You dare ask, but I don't dare tell," Emma said, smiling.

He came out of the bedroom, Jake the threat, the defiler of her daughter, and Annabel had to force herself to look pleasant. "I hope you found everything you needed," she said.

"Yes, thank you." He looked at the linens on the couch and then he looked at Emma.

"It's all right," Emma said. "My mother thought you were a stranger."

He, at least, had the good grace to show a flicker

of embarrassment, but only for a moment. Then he smiled warmly at Annabel. "Emma said you were great, and you are."

They went into the kitchen where Annabel poured coffee. She decided to be modern and not make a fuss, but there were all kinds of worries going through her mind. Did Emma love this boy? Did he love her? Would he ditch her, hurt her? He was off to Yale, so there was no future. Sweet William jumped into Jake's lap.

"Emma didn't tell me much about *you*," Annabel said lightly. "Why don't you tell me something."

"What would you like to know?"

I want to know how you feel about my daughter, she thought. "Oh, uh . . ." I want to know if you sleep with everybody you can get or if it has to be someone special to you. I want to know if you're the same kind of wretch I kept falling in love with when I was her age. "Just anything you want to tell me."

"I would like to write and direct films," he said.

"That seems to be the thing today, doesn't it," Annabel said.

"Sure. We were all brought up on them. That's all we know. I certainly wouldn't want to go into TV."

"Of course not," Annabel said.

"I love movies," he said.

"What's the difference between movies and films?" Annabel asked.

He looked at her oddly, as if she were trying to trick him. "I don't know. Is there one?"

"I asked you."

"There's no difference."

"That's a relief," Annabel said. "I never thought there was one myself."

"Movies are yummier than films," Emma said.

He laughed, sounding relieved. "Yeah."

"*Nashville* is a movie," Emma said. "*Buffalo Bill and the Indians* is a film."

"No," he said, "*Buffalo Bill* wasn't a film; it was just boring."

"Okay. *Gone With the Wind* was a movie. *Viridiana* was a film."

"Right," he said.

"What was *Psycho*?" Annabel asked.

Jake and Emma looked at each other. "Both," Emma said.

"Why?"

"Because it was yummy and also a classic."

"Then why isn't *Gone With the Wind* both?" Annabel asked.

"Because it was dippy," Emma said.

"It was *not* dippy!" Annabel said, insulted. "It's a classic!"

"There are no set rules," Jake said. "It's what you think."

"I'm glad to hear that," Annabel said tartly.

"Hey, do you want to go to the museum?" Emma said to Jake.

"Sure."

"Okay, Mom, we'll be back later."

"Will you be here for dinner?"

They looked at each other. "I wouldn't count on it," Emma said.

"I'll leave some food in case I go out," Annabel said.

When they left she telephoned Max. "Are you free tonight, Max?"

"I could be."

"It's not that important, but . . ."

"I'm free," Max said.

He took her to La Goulue, a sort of *grande époque* bistro on the East Side that was supposed to remind her of Toulouse-Lautrec and did. Max had reserved a booth in the back where it was less noisy. He ordered champagne.

"What are we celebrating?" Annabel asked.

"Being together. We haven't had a night on the town in a long time."

"I know. You were on the Coast, and before that I had what's-his-name."

"What was his name?" Max asked.

"I wish to forget."

They looked at each other lovingly and raised their glasses in a toast. "To friendship."

"Emma has a lover," Annabel said.

"Well then, we are celebrating something after all."

"Why do I feel like a mother lion that wants to swat him away?"

"You?"

"I hate to admit it," Annabel said, "but I'm scared to death. I don't want her to sleep with boys and get hurt."

"Getting hurt is part of life," Max said gently.

"But you remember college. I was always getting my heart broken. I don't want that to happen to her."

"It won't."

"She's my daughter. She's a romantic, like me."

"She lives in the Seventies. It's a different century."

"Oh, I know they won't think she's a whore . . . Will they?"

"Why should they, when she won't be?"

"I wasn't," Annabel said.

"But the guys you slept with were," Max said. "They just didn't know it. They gave their bodies and never their hearts. If that isn't a whore then what is?"

"Emma's going to get hurt. If she falls in love she'll get hurt, and if she gets tough she'll be hurt by that."

"Friendship is a giving of the heart," Max said.

"The best . . ."

"And I'll bet anything, knowing Emma, that this boy is her good friend."

"Well, anyway, he seems like a friend. I don't know how good."

"Tell me about him."

"He's a mystery to me. He talks about movies."

"How old is he?"

"Nineteen."

"The same age as what's-his-name."

"He wasn't a mystery, he was just limited," Annabel said. "He was a kid."

"So's Emma's friend. Where did she find him?"

"Working on that movie set where you sent her." Annabel realized how accusing her tone sounded and began to laugh. "Oh, Max, am I turning out to be an uptight, prudish mother after all these years?"

"Tell me more about him."

"He goes to Yale. He wants to make movies. He's beautiful."

"So he and Emma have a lot in common."

"More than I ever had with those fools I fell in love with at college."

"Does she want to marry him?"

"Marry him? Good God, no! She wants to go to Radcliffe and then become the greatest filmmaker who ever lived and get three Academy Awards."

"Then why are you worried?"

"She's so young," Annabel said.

"She'll be okay," Max said. "I trust Emma. Don't you?"

"Yes. Yes, I do."

"Then don't be the mother lion. I know you want to, but you mustn't. It would be wrong. Emma will do what she wants to no matter what you say. It's better for her to know you love her and trust her."

"She never liked her father very much," Annabel said. "I hope that doesn't matter."

"It doesn't matter."

"I wonder why she never confided in me about sex before."

"You mean about her boyfriends?"

"Yes."

"Because some things should be private."

"You're right," Annabel said. "You know, you're right." She laughed with relief. "Why don't the grown-ups have a little more champagne?"

Chapter 9

The Christmas and New Year's holidays were finally over, and people settled down to reading thin newspapers, battling the end of winter sales, paying their bills, and waiting for spring. The letters that had been coming to tantalize everyone about the Radcliffe Twentieth Class Reunion took on a more urgent tone. "Plans are being finalized, make your reservations now before it's too late, send us money, photos of your husband and children for our bulletin board, information for our class album, deadline . . . hurry, hurry . . ."

A few of the people who had tossed the previous leters into their wastebaskets, lacking class spirit after all these years, took another look at the new correspondence and filed it with their unpaid bills. For them the class reunion took on a certain possibility, for various reasons. For Chris, living with Alexander in an armed camp, college was where their relationship had started. In the back of her mind the idea began that to return for the reunion would be a sort of quest to find out how it had happened. Perhaps if she could get to the source of the pain, and the enchantment, she could rid herself of the obsession once and for all.

Some days she thought she should leave Alexander, and some days she knew she never could. It was he who had deserted her, even though he was trying to keep her. She had finally come back from the country to live in their apartment with him and Nicholas, but she slept in the den. Alexander remained in what had been their bedroom, sleeping in the contaminated bed. She told him he could do as he pleased, have sex with whomever he wanted, as long as he never brought any of them to the apartment, ever again. She had told him to be free because she knew now he was going to cheat anyway, and she used her honesty as a shield against pain. Forewarned is forearmed. For herself, she desired Alexander more than ever, but she pretended she did not. She told him they would continue to be friends, and the parents of Nicholas—two things that could not be changed.

She and Alexander were both very careful to be kind to each other. They were polite and considerate, but they didn't laugh together anymore. How could they, when she didn't know if she could even stay? If she was going away then she had to start now to be strong and independent, because then she would be alone. When she thought about being without him, sometimes she wanted to run to him and put her arms around him, burst into tears, tell him she adored him and nothing else mattered. But she knew if she did she wouldn't be able to take it back. She was an adult trying to make a life decision, not a torturer.

He had his own ways of torturing her, though. When the phone rang for him he didn't always tell her who had called. He had told her to trust him and she couldn't, so now he behaved the way he had before she caught him, and expected it to be the same. Before, he obviously hadn't told her every moment of his working day, and he still didn't. Too detailed explanations reveal guilt, he had said. He wanted a normal life. How could he expect their life to be normal?

Nicholas was edgy since Chris and Alexander had started sleeping in separate rooms. He picked up their tension, and being eight years and bright, he used it.

"Why aren't you doing your homework?" Chris would demand, finding Nicholas watching forbidden television in his room.

"I have an unhappy home life."

She didn't know whether to laugh or yell at him.

"Can I have an advance on my allowance?" he asked one day.

"Not again. How else are you going to learn to handle money?"

"Things are different now. Life is difficult," he said.

"We all have to learn to cope with inflation," Chris said.

"It's not that." The downcast look, the long hair falling forward over his eyes, the pathetically hunched posture. "I have an unhappy home life."

That time she laughed. But afterward she hurt for him. He was only a child, and using their armed camp as a way to get little favors was the only way he could cope with the fear that had to be surrounding him.

Nicholas was a safe subject for her and Alexander to discuss. "Maybe you could come back," Alexander said, trying to sound casual. "I won't touch you if you don't want me to."

Why not be honest? There was so little left. "Because I would want you to," Chris said. "I love you. You couldn't hurt me so much if I didn't love you so much."

"What can I do then? Tell me what to do."

Give them up, she thought. Never look at another young man again. But she knew it was impossible. Maybe someday he would be too old to care anymore, but what about now? "I don't know," she said.

She and Alexander stopped going to parties. They couldn't bear to fake it for a roomful of strangers. The only invitations they accepted were with close friends, who understood they were having some kind of trouble but were too tactful to ask questions. People assumed whatever was most commonplace: the marriage was floundering, one of them was bored, one of them had met someone else. Chris confided in Annabel, who told her to take Alexander back anyway. No one else knew the truth, although Chris suspected that Max did. She couldn't bring herself to discuss her marriage with Max. What would he tell her—I told you so? Years ago, in New York, at that Sardi's lunch, he had told her to forget Alexander. "My dear Chris, do you think you're the only person who ever got ditched?"

She and Alexander would be married ten years this June. Ten years ago, in Paris, waiting for spring, she had been alone and in love with Alexander, thinking nothing would ever change, willing to stay anyway. Then he had told her they could try. And they *had* tried. God, how hard they had tried, until it was no longer trying but real love and a way of life. Had all that been a fake? How would she ever know?

If she kept staying away from Alexander, hardening her spirit against him, would she ever become strong enough, independent enough, to leave? She took off her wedding ring, and it seemed as if she had cut off her only support to life. She felt cast out, cold, miserable. She wore it again.

Her father was well now, completely recovered from his heart attack, and he and her mother had gone to Florida for three months. On weekend afternoons if Nicholas didn't have a date with one of his friends, either Chris or Alexander took him to a matinee, or to an art gallery or a museum. It was as if they were tentatively trying out the life they would have if they were divorced, sharing Nicholas separately.

That Christmas they had not gone to Switzerland after all, or anywhere. They were both in mourning for their marriage. They told Nicholas it would be fun for him to have his first New York Christmas, and Chris arranged for him to have ice-skating lessons every day at Rockefeller Center. He hated it; it was full of tourists, the ice was crowded and mushy. Chris knew he wouldn't like anything. It was her fault, but she couldn't help it.

No, it wasn't her fault, it was Alexander's fault. She hadn't driven him away. At meals they made bright small talk for Nicholas's sake, and after dinner they watched television together in the living room on the new set they had bought because the living room was now the family den. Alexander read the evening newspaper and things he had brought from the office, Chris read manuscripts she had brought home. It was all work they could have done during the day, but they used it as a shield against silence. Their marriage had turned into anybody's marriage; they were like miserable people all over the world. The only difference was they had not faked anything. They were waiting for something, afraid to face it, pretending they were waiting together—both of them knowing they were really waiting alone.

Chapter 10

That spring Daphne and Richard decided they would go to her twentieth college reunion. He had been so much a part of her Radcliffe years that they felt the reunion belonged to both of them. Husbands were welcome. Richard sent in the check for reunion expenses and reserved a suite at the Ritz-Carlton Hotel in Boston. Daphne sent in the family photo: Matthew, eleven; Samuel, ten; Jonathan, nine; and Theodore, seven—standing in front of a smiling Daphne and Richard, the boys each holding a piece of athletic equipment of their choice, dressed in the uniform of the sport. It was sort of a campy picture, but it amused her. She had always been the center of attention at college, and this picture would be certain to be noticed among all the others on the reunion bulletin board.

There was, of course, neither a picture nor a mention of Elizabeth. Daphne seemed to be the only person who ever thought about her anymore. Richard just sent in the monthly checks for her keep, as casually as he paid their household bills.

She would be four years old soon. Sometimes there were days when Daphne didn't think about her at all, and that made her sadder than the days when she thought about her all the time. The snow melted and grass began to grow on the dark hills. Flowers bloomed, the trees were bright with new green leaves. Their ducks came quacking back to the artificial pond Richard had had made, and walked in single file to the back door for bread. Daphne thought how they would have amused Elizabeth. She didn't want the little girl to be alone on her birthday. This year she would go to visit her.

She didn't tell Richard her intention. He had made it clear how he felt about visits to Elizabeth. Things that made you uncomfortable were to be avoided. It was easy enough to go without telling him. She had her own car, Richard was at his office in the city, and the boys were in school. She called the home for directions because she had forgotten, and bought a large, soft doll that opened and closed its eyes, and smiled and squeaked when you squeezed it. The doll had on a blue dress, and she bought a similar dress for Elizabeth. Then she went.

When she drove up the place seemed smaller than she had remembered it. Elizabeth would be brought to her in the reception room, by her cottage mother, and after they got acquainted Daphne would be able to watch Elizabeth's birthday party with the other children. It reassured Daphne to know that they hadn't forgotten Elizabeth's birthday at the home. She waited nervously, smoking.

A small, smiling, dark-haired woman came through a door, holding the hand of a little girl. As they came closer Daphne had the same feeling she'd had in the hospital when she first saw Elizabeth: *Take her away, she isn't mine!* No matter how many times she had visualized her daughter in her imagination it hadn't been like the real thing. Elizabeth was the size of a normal four-year-old, and her rough hair was sandy-colored instead of black, but otherwise there was no family resemblance at all. When she saw Daphne, she smiled happily, with only the tip of her pointed tongue protruding, her slanted eyes amused. Daphne smiled back, and went to greet her.

"Hello, darling," she said softly.

Elizabeth smiled.

"She doesn't talk," the woman said. "My name is Jane Baldwin." She put Elizabeth's small hand into Daphne's. "This is your mother, Elizabeth. Say hello."

"Should you . . ." Daphne began.

"She doesn't understand. But she does know you care about her. Even infants know that."

"Will it scare her if I hug her?"

"Go right ahead."

Daphne kneeled down and put her arms around the child . . . her child, her daughter Elizabeth. The child's body was little and firm. Elizabeth gave a gurgly sound of pleasure but did not hug her back. It occurred to Daphne that this child would willingly accept any stranger, that she was totally without suspicion or defenses. "I brought you a doll," Daphne said. She stood up and brought Elizabeth to the doll, which she had propped on the chair. "Look. This is for you."

Elizabeth's hand opened and she touched the doll's dress with her finger. Daphne unwrapped the box that held the blue dress and held the dress up. "This is for you too, sweetheart. It's a dress."

Elizabeth touched the blue dress, and then she touched Daphne's skirt. "She knows!" Daphne said.

Jane Baldwin smiled and shook her head. "She's just getting to know you. She's a very sweet, good-natured child. She's happy all the time, except when she's hungry or wet, and we don't let that go on long."

"Wet?" Her finger came out instinctively and felt the plastic pants under Elizabeth's skirt. "She's not trained yet?"

"She's only four," Jane Baldwin said calmly. "It takes a little longer with some children. Why don't we go to Elizabeth's room?"

They went to the cottage where Elizabeth lived and Daphne put the doll on Elizabeth's bed. "Could she wear her new dress for her party?"

"Of course. Would you like to wear your new dress, Elizabeth? Let me help you put it on."

Daphne watched while this woman took off her daughter's dress and put the new one on her, the child standing passively, watching her with interest, smiling that eternal smile. The dress fit perfectly. If Elizabeth had been home, she thought sadly, she would have a different one every day. Would she care?

Over Elizabeth's bed there were two large pieces of paper with paint smeared on them in bright colors, hung up the way she would have hung her own child's art work at home. "Did she do those paintings?"

"Yes. They're her finger paintings. She ate more paint than she put on the paper, but we're all proud of them and she is too. Your mother likes your pictures, Elizabeth, see?"

Elizabeth smiled. Daphne wondered what she was thinking.

"Has she . . . had any seizures?" she asked.

"No. She's fine so far."

"Thank God for that at least, poor baby."

Jane Baldwin looked at her watch. "It's almost time for the party. Why don't we go to the rec room now?"

The rec room was large and sunny, like a kindergarten. Children of various ages were at tables, finger painting, trying to learn to string beads with teachers beside them. Some of the children were on the floor playing with toys, but many of them were just sitting and rocking dully back and forth or not doing anything at all. The thing that was most appalling was that not one of them was pretty or even attractive. In her mind Daphne had always seen them as perfect but just retarded, the way she had seen autistic children look in photographs; but autistic children *were* perfect children who lived in a different world, and these were flawed in every way. She looked around in fear, wanting to believe in her old dream instead of this bedlam. In the corner she saw, finally, a beautiful girl of about sixteen.

"What's wrong with that one?" she asked.

"Brain-damaged."

"She looks normal."

"They're all normal here because here we have no norm. Nobody has to measure up to things they can't handle. We want them to learn as much as they can, no matter how little that is, and to be happy."

As they walked past the tables some of the children looked up at Daphne, recognized her as a newcomer, and tried to get her attention. Hands reached out to touch her, to tug at her skirt, to inspect her. She tried not to flinch. Elizabeth walked along with her hand in Daphne's, still smiling, looking proud because this big visitor was hers. Except for that girl in the corner, Daphne thought, my child is the prettiest.

A long table had been decorated with a bright paper cloth, balloons hanging over it, and now a woman came out bearing a big white iced birthday cake. "Party time!" she sang out. Some of the children rushed over to the table.

"Happy birthday to you," the woman and Jane Baldwin and Daphne were singing. Some of the children joined in. "Happy birthday to you. Happy birthday dear Elizabeth! Happy birthday to you!"

Elizabeth smiled and gurgled.

The teachers got most of the children over to the table, and they sat in chairs and were served pieces of cake on paper plates and paper cups of milk. Elizabeth played with her cake, flattened it with her hand, smacked it, and laughed. She put some of the mess she had made into her mouth and looked happily at Daphne. Daphne felt her throat close with the beginning of tears. She was just like a dear infant, a promise for the future, waiting to be taught and molded, but . . . there was no future. She would only grow bigger.

"Will she ever talk?" Daphne whispered.

"I hope so," Jane Baldwin said cheerfully. "She already points at things she wants. Everything takes time. But we have lots of time."

"Yes," Daphne said.

"Would you like to feed her?"

"Oh, of course." She drew up a chair beside Elizabeth's and began to spoon cake into her daughter's mouth. Then a sip of milk. "Isn't that good?" Daphne said. "Cake. Mmm."

"Ga," Elizabeth said.

"She talked! Did you hear her? She tried to say cake!"

"'Ga' is her favorite word," Jane Baldwin said. "She has two words. The other one is 'Ah.' I'm hoping that in time she'll be able to understand that those sounds mean something so she can use them to ask for things she wants."

"Well, it sounded like cake to me," Daphne said.

When Elizabeth had finished her cake and milk and been wiped off Daphne gave her a balloon, folding her small fingers around the string. Elizabeth looked at the balloon and then let it float away. Daphne looked at her watch. It was a long drive home and she had to be back before the boys wondered what had happened to her and made her have to lie. "Walk me to the door, sweetheart. I have to go home now."

The three of them went back to the reception room. Daphne kneeled down again and gathered Elizabeth into her arms. She kissed her cheek. "I love you," she said to the blank little happy face. "I love you with all my heart."

Elizabeth put the edge of Daphne's scarf into her mouth and chewed it.

"Thank you, Jane," Daphne said. "Thank you for
being good to her."

"It's easy. This little person hasn't a mean bone
in her body."

And she needs to be watched every minute, Daphne
thought. She's so helpless . . . Just like Richard said
she would be. She stood up and lit a cigarette, draw-
ing the welcome smoke deep into her lungs.

"You really shouldn't smoke," Jane Baldwin said.

"I know."

"I shouldn't bug you about it now. I know today
wasn't easy."

"It was different than I thought," Daphne said.

"You feel a bit relieved?"

"Sort of."

"What you did was for the best. She's happy."

"I know."

She drove home, thinking about the day. These
people were so patient, as she would have been, but
they had her compassion without her pain. They
could be infinitely patient, letting each day be its
own reward. Richard had been right. He hadn't been
a heartless monster. Elizabeth was content and
healthy, the boys were secure and well-adjusted, they
had a normal family. She had really been unfair to
Richard, resenting him so much when he put Elizabeth in this pleasant, compassionate environment. It
wasn't just a place to hide away your mistakes. How
could she have thought such angry things about Richard when she knew he loved her and all their children?

She stubbed out the cigarette butt and almost immediately wanted another. If I could only stop . . .
I'm going to kill myself with these things and then
my kids will have no mother, and Richard will be
alone. What's the matter with me?

It was then she realized she wanted to tell Richard
about her epilepsy. Now, at last, get it out into the
open. She had been stupid to pretend she was perfect

all these years, afraid he would reject her. They had built a life together. She would tell him, and he would accept it, and then they could go on harmoniously, with him really loving her for herself for the first time, flaws and all.

She would tell him at the class reunion. Back at college, over twenty years ago, was where the deception had started. Back at the source was the proper place to set things right. Daphne smiled. She would tell him in the living room of Briggs Hall, where he had come to get her for their first date.

Now that she had made up her mind she could hardly wait.

That spring Max was forty-one. He had steeled himself for turning forty because everyone said it was a depressing milestone—the admission of middle age—and so he had gotten through his fortieth birthday with no trouble at all. No one had told him that forty-one would be much worse because it was the one that sneaked up on you. When he mentioned this to Annabel she immediately decided to have a wonderful birthday party for him at her apartment.

They made the guest list together. Annabel, Emma, and Emma's latest boyfriend, Gary, a musician. Annabel and Max were not in love with anyone that spring, so they would be each other's date. Chris and Alexander, still having trouble and trying to hide it. Four old and dear friends of Max's, who had worked with him through the years: theater friends or personal friends? Who could know the difference? Your work friends became your personal friends too when your work was your life. Three of them had a lover or a date to bring. It would put the total at thirteen, but Annabel said Sweet William would be the fourteenth and keep the table from being unlucky.

There would be Dom Perignon and Iranian malassol caviar, which cost a fortune this year, and everyone would have to come in formal clothes. All the music played would be from the Twenties, with the exception of hits from Max's past shows, and Emma and Gary would be the disc jockeys. Max sent masses of white flowers. He thought how lucky he was to have such good friends, and pictured himself and them all growing old together; and then the thought depressed him again and he determined to think only of the moment. Perhaps that was the way to get through life. After all, in ten years he would look back on this birthday and think he had been young.

The days were longer now and it was still light when the first guests arrived, but Annabel had drawn the drapes and lit the apartment in the most romantic way imaginable. She floated toward Max in the dimness, wearing black chiffon, her red hair up, and he thought she looked almost as young as Emma. She kissed him.

"Happy birthday, Max."

"Happy birthday, Uncle Max." There was Emma, the devotee of L. L. Bean camping clothes, wearing a real dress in his honor, tiny gold-hoop earrings in her pierced ears. Her boyfriend Gary was wearing a suit. He was very attractive, as all Emma's boyfriends were, and the only thing bad about him was that he had shaggy bleached-blond hair that belonged more appropriately on a chicken. But Annabel had explained it was for his professional image. Max hoped he would take his professional image on the road soon. A failed rock musician was wrong for Emma, but a successful one would be worse.

"Don't you think Gary looks like Rod Stewart?" Emma whispered.

"Yep."

"Oh . . . you don't like him."

"Do you care?"

"Nope," she said, grinning.

Noel Coward was singing softly through the hi-fi speakers, a ghost from the past. The other guests started to arrive, and everyone drank champagne. Annabel had had all the food catered, and a young man in uniform slipped quietly through the crowd, passing the caviar in its bowl of ice, and then disappearing into the small kitchen to attend to their dinner.

Max's presents, festively wrapped, were piled up on the coffee table. Chris and Alexander were the last to arrive, carrying more, smiling party smiles. Max looked into Alexander's eyes for an instant and he could see fear. It made him sad. Alexander seemed to have a talent for wrecking other people's lives, but now he had finally wrecked his own. Annabel had told Max that Chris had caught Alexander, but nobody had to tell him that. He had always known it would happen someday.

"First let's open the presents before we get smashed," Annabel said gaily. She held out a long flat box wrapped in silver paper. "This is mine. Happy birthday, dear Max, and many more, with us."

He kissed her and opened the box. Inside was a very long white cashmere scarf with fringe at either end. He had seen it at Bendel's and had coveted it, but would never have spent a hundred and twenty-five dollars for a scarf for himself. Only Annabel would pick something so extravagant, so silly, and so absolutely right.

"Like your long scarf at college," Annabel said, "but this one wasn't knitted by Emily Applebaum with dropped stitches."

Max laughed. "I love it. Thank you."

"Now mine," Emma said, holding out a package wrapped in the funny papers and tied with red yarn.

Inside was a photograph of Annabel and Emma, in a silver frame. It was a professional-quality photo, and the only one he'd ever had of the two of them. "This is great," Max said. "It goes right on my piano. Who took it?"

"Me," Emma said. "I set the timer and leaped in front of Mom. How do you like it?"

"I think if you become a moviemaker the world will lose a talented photographer," Max said.

"Oh, how he lies," Emma said, pleased and embarrassed. "Tell me more."

There were books and records from Chris and Alexander; a Gucci wallet from Sylvia, the actress he'd discovered fifteen years ago, who was now a star; a Krön's chocolate birthday card from her latest lover; ties; more books; another wallet, this time from Mark Cross, and one from Hunting World. "People must think you have a lot of money," Chris said.

"Or a tacky wallet," someone said. They all laughed.

"Are you going to the Harvard Reunion?" Chris asked Max.

"In Emma's immortal words," Max said, "yuck."

"I'm going," Chris said. "To my Radcliffe reunion."

"Alexander?" Max said, surprised.

"Not me," Alexander said. "I hated it then and I won't like it anymore now."

"Did you hate college, really?" Emma asked.

"Nobody's perfect," Alexander said lightly.

"Well, if you go, Chris, then I'll go," Annabel said. "It might be fun. Although I hated college too."

"You too, Mom? Look how smart you all turned out anyway."

"I loved college," Max said.

"I'm glad somebody did," Emma said, "since I'm going to go to Radcliffe."

"Oh, it's different now," Annabel said. "You'll like it."

"I think I liked it," Chris said.

"Dinner is served," the young man in uniform announced.

The dinner was buffet: a whole cold poached bass with sauce, a huge salad, crusty French peasant bread, cheeses, and more champagne. For dessert there was

a big birthday cake and ice cream forms in the shape
of little animals, the kind Max hadn't seen since he
was a child.

"I want you to know we had to go to Brooklyn to
get these," Annabel said. "They're to remind you that
good things go on forever, like us, and also that they're
hard to find, like us. And that's my final toast."

Everyone applauded. The young man brought out
hot, fragrant coffee, and brandy. Gary the chicken
deftly put a pile of new records on the turntable.
Max fed Sweet William a piece of birthday cake and
a bit of ice cream. He was an old cat now, fourteen,
with a large Cheshire-cat face, and he had grown
calm and lazy. If only I could become calm and lazy,
Max thought, and accept my life. It's not so bad to
be alone. Here are all my loving friends, and the ones
who are with someone aren't sure if it will last.

He glanced at the young caterer's assistant with dis-
interest. He would never cruise at a friend's house,
and besides, the boy looked straight. It would have
been nice to have a date for this party, someone to
go home with, particularly because no one should
have to be alone on his birthday. Maybe he should
have invited someone, but there was no one he cared
about enough to share an intimate personal evening
like this. Forty-one was an undistinguished year. He
was beginning to get depressed.

"Matinee tomorrow," Sylvia said. She kissed Max
goodnight. "Next year your birthday will be on a
Saturday, and I hope Annabel has another party so
I can stay until four in the morning."

"I will," Annabel said.

For the rest of them, who did not have to work
the next day, the serious drinking began, and the
reminiscences. Birthdays seemed to remind everyone
of the past, and each of them had a funny story to
tell. The champagne was long gone and now it was
brandy. The young caterer's assistant slipped away,
leaving a spotless kitchen, the remaining coffee heat-

ing on the stove. At two o'clock Chris and Alexander left, Chris looking pale, with dark circles under her eyes. Gary had become bored with Annabel's collection of Twenties records and had put on her collection of Beatles records, figuring anything that was old was all right. Max's depression deepened, mixed with a restlessness that was almost claustrophobic. The more they talked about the past, the older he felt.

Finally, at three, the party drifted apart, people yawning, the room emptying out, suddenly too fast. Max wanted to leave, to breathe the fresh air, and at the same time he didn't want to go. Where could he go? His lonely apartment or a gay bar. The bar, at least, would be swinging if he hurried. It seemed almost ungrateful to run off to a bar to bring home a number, but it would be his birthday present from himself to himself. The party had been wonderful, perfect, except for him feeling his age, and he couldn't help that. He was careful to keep Annabel from picking up on his sad mood. It wasn't her problem.

When everyone was gone but Max, Annabel, Emma, and Gary, Annabel packed Max's present in two large shopping bags.

"I can't tell you how much this party meant to me," Max said.

"I'm glad," Annabel said. She kissed him lightly. "When I'm forty-one you can give me one."

"When will that be?"

"Not for years, I'll tell you that." She laughed. "Next year let's both be thirty-six. I think we can get away with it."

"You can. I can't."

"Of course you can. If you care to. Personally, I think you're perfect just as you are."

"Goodnight all," Max said. "Thank you again, Annabel . . . Emma."

"Happy birthday, Uncle Max," Emma said. She kissed him goodnight.

Annabel put her arm around Max and walked him to the door. "Happy birthday, my best friend," Annabel said. "Happy dreams."

He took a taxi to his apartment and unpacked his presents neatly, putting the picture of Annabel and Emma on his piano, the books on the coffee table, the records on top of his turntable to be played during the weekend at leisure, and the three wallets on his dresser. He would exchange them next week. The claustrophobia closed in on him, stifling. He would not bother to change his clothes. He could take a cab to Harry's Back East. There wouldn't be much left this late, closer to four than three; just diehards who didn't want to go to the baths or risk the streets, but maybe there would be someone young and attractive, and if there was the formal clothes would make an impression. He would look like someone who had just come from a chic party, which was true, an older man who lived a glamorous life, a successful figure, a little mysterious perhaps. No, strike "older man." He wasn't forty-one, he was ageless. He rushed out again into the clear night air.

Harry's Back East had a long bar in front, a jukebox, pinball machines, a pool table, and shuffleboard in the back. Over the bar hung an overhead canopy made of the naked coils of bedsprings, tied up with Christmas lights all year round. Crazy things hung from the ceiling: a real baby carriage, plastic plucked chickens, lace panties, dildos. Whatever decorations had been put up once were never taken down, remnants of Halloweens past, Thanksgivings, St. Patrick's Days. The decor was what Max and his friends called the epitome of gross-tacky, but they went there, they always had. There was action, and it was familiar. But most of all, to Max at least, the tackiness gave it a certain unreality which he liked.

Dancing was forbidden, although sometimes a few people broke the rules. The primary action was cruising the long line of numbers who were waiting to get into the men's room. But tonight it was so late that there was no line at all, and the few men left at the bar looked desperate and sad. Max sat down at the bar and ordered a Coke. He looked around. There was a boy standing by the jukebox, with long black hair, tight jeans, a black leather jacket. He looked like a Fifties greaser, but he seemed only nineteen. He saw Max cruising him and smiled.

Max smiled back. The boy came ambling over to him then, with a walk he had obviously copied from the Fonz on TV. So this is to be my birthday present, Max thought. Do I want it, or should I return it?

"Got a cigarette?" the boy asked. He even had the Fonz's accent. Max suspected it was real. He seemed harmless enough, and there was an air of desperate sexuality about him that was intriguing.

"I don't smoke, but I can buy you a drink," Max said.

"Yeah? Okay."

The boy sat on the stool next to Max's. "Frankie Scandoli," he said.

"I'm Max."

"Max what?"

"Harding."

No sign of recognition. "I'll have a seven and seven," Frankie said.

Of course, Max thought. He nodded at the bartender.

They were out on the street in five minutes. The longer you lingered over a drink the more you had to talk, and the more you had to talk the worse these numbers got to look. Better to keep the excitement of the mysterious stranger and fill in with whatever you wanted him to be. They took a cab to Max's apartment. The night doorman was used to seeing Max bring unlikely-looking people to his apartment at late hours and nodded a tactfully sleepy greeting. Glancing at Frankie in the lobby lights Max noticed with gratitude that his long hair wasn't greasy. It was shiny with health, blue-black, thick. His wrists were hairless. Max was glad. He didn't like hairy boys. Ordinarily he would have preferred a blond, but what could you expect at four in the morning? And there was that coiled energy in the kid which had first attracted him, a restlessness that matched his own at this moment.

They went upstairs and Max unlocked his front door. "Make yourself at home," he said, nodding toward the bedroom.

Frankie was looking around the living room approvingly. Then he walked into the bedroom and Max followed him, feeling the familiar anticipation, the growing excitement.

"Hey, hey," Frankie said. "You have a fur bedspread. I knew you'd have a fur bedspread." He pranced around the bedroom like a large monkey. Max took off his jacket and hung it up, took off his tie. He glanced meaningfully at Frankie to hurry up. The boy was still fully dressed, leather jacket and all, in front of the dresser now, fingering things. He opened the dresser drawer.

"Hey!" Max said.

"Hey what? Hay is for horses, ha ha." The boy had Max's jewel box in his hand and flipped it open, smiling a mean smile. Then he scooped up all Max's cuff links and watches and stuffed them into his jacket pocket.

Max started for him and the boy whirled around, taking a switchblade knife from the pocket of his jeans, snapping it open. Max stopped.

"You still think I'm cute, huh?" Frankie said. He waved the knife in tiny circles, the point out toward Max, who stood there, his heart pounding with fear.

It had finally happened. All those nights in gay bars, all those numbers, he'd thought he was streetwise by now. It had been too late, and he had been too desperate.

"You didn't know I had this in my jeans, huh?"

Frankie said. "Too busy thinking about what else was in there. Where's the money?"

Max took his money out of his pants pocket and held it out.

"Put it on the dresser, dummy."

He dropped the bills and coins on the dresser and Frankie scooped them up.

"Where's the rest?"

"There's no more."

"Shit there ain't. You got a safe?"

"No."

Frankie was rummaging through the drawers now, tossing things on the floor, finally pulling the drawers out and dropping them on the floor too. He found a cashmere sweater he liked and draped it over his shoulders. From time to time his wary eyes flickered toward Max to make sure he hadn't moved. This, then, was what Max had mistaken for sexual tension in the bar; this pent-up violence waiting to spring, the desperation of the robber.

"Bring me a suitcase," Frankie commanded. He gestured toward the closet with his head, the blue-black hair sliding forward and back. Greaser, Max thought. He didn't move. Frankie came toward him, circling the knife in those tiny arcs. "I told you, a suitcase."

Max went into the closet and took his Vuitton bag down from the shelf, thankful the closet had no key in the lock so Frankie couldn't lock him in. He brought the suitcase out and put it on the floor. Frankie put the cashmere sweater into it and then began to stuff it with everything he could get his hands on: the table radio, the clock, various objects Max had collected, clothes. All the things that had meant something to Max were just junk this boy could pawn or sell for a few dollars. It seemed so unreal, something that happened to other people but never to him. What a fool he'd been. If only this boy would take what he wanted and go away. Max stood

very still, hardly breathing, terrified but angry too.
He thought of jumping the boy and overpowering
him, but realized it was a stupid idea. There was the
knife, and he wasn't in any kind of condition for a
fight.

"Give me another suitcase."

"You going to walk out of here with two suitcases?
You won't get away with it."

"The hell I won't. I'm leaving you, baby. Lover's
quarrel." The boy laughed mirthlessly. "You're too
old for me."

Max brought him the other suitcase. The kid
wouldn't get far. Unless . . . the kid was going to
do something to him so he couldn't call the doorman.
He felt a chill in the pit of his stomach.

Frankie pulled the fur bedspread off the bed and
stuffed it into the second Vuitton bag. "I've got a
girl friend who'd just *love* this," he said, in that
same taunting voice. He snapped the suitcase shut.
"You faggots are all alike. Disgusting, you know what
I mean?"

He's crazy, Max thought.

"You make me sick," Frankie said. "Somebody
ought to cut your throat. You think you can just
buy me a drink and I'll come home with you because
I *liked* you? You think you're so sexy? You know
what's sexy? Cunt is sexy. Not some old faggot like
you who wants to do disgusting things to me."

The boy's voice raised to a squeal of rage on "disgusting." Max felt his own rage rising inside him
like nausea, bitter as hate. What right did this lunatic have to come into *his* bar to prey on him, into
his home to rob and threaten him, to revile him?
Who had he bothered or hurt?

There was no way that boy could pick up two suitcases and still have his knife in position to threaten
anyone. If he picked them up Max could jump him.
Otherwise . . .

The boy pulled two of Max's ties off the back of

the closet door. He walked toward Max then, the ties in one hand, the knife in the other. Max picked up the bedside lamp and smashed the kid over the head with it.

The blow didn't even stun him. The china lamp shattered. There was a small cut over the boy's eyebrow that seemed to infuriate him. He lunged at Max. Max turned and ran.

They ran through the bedroom into the living room, circling, knocking over furniture. All Max could think of was that he would get out of the apartment, race down the fire stairs, get away. He felt light on his feet, not out of breath at all, numb. For some reason it seemed as though if he slammed the apartment door with the kid inside and himself outside the kid would stay there and he would be free.

He got to the door, opened it, and felt the stinging pain in his back. It was nothing, just a gnat's bite, but there were more, a swarm of gnats, and suddenly he felt heavy and weak. His legs wouldn't do what he wanted them to. He couldn't run anymore. He forgot why this had happened.

It just didn't make any sense at all. . . .

Max Harding's murder was in the newspapers because he was a famous Broadway producer and director, and because it had occurred in an expensive Fifth Avenue apartment. The coroner said there were thirty-two stab wounds. It was the first of a series of gruesome murders that swept the homosexual community that spring and almost emptied the gay bars. The subsequent murders did not receive as much publicity because the victims were not as well-known as Max, and there were some people who said he had not even been the first at all.

Annabel, stunned and grieving, felt as if the anchor pin had fallen out of her world. She knew that she would never again go through a day without missing Max, no matter how long she lived. She remembered the last thing she had said to him when he left her party, and it seemed ironic that it was nothing special. Life did not warn people of approaching endings so they could deliver appropriate exit lines. She wished she had told him how much she loved him—but he knew. It was she who needed the reassurance that she had told him. She told him now, in her mind, wondering if people did go on as atoms, surrounding the people who loved and remembered them. There had to be more than just *over*.

For Emma, Max was the first person who was close to her who had ever died. She was so young. His death frightened her. He had been more of a father to her than her own father, and she loved him. She felt half orphaned, and she knew for the first time that you could never take anyone for granted, or anything, because it could all be over in an instant. She would never look at life in exactly the same way again.

Epilogue:

The Reunion

Chapter 1

A class reunion is more than a sentimental journey. It is also a way of answering the question that lies at the back of nearly all our minds: *Did they do it better than I did?* There were always other choices, other ways to go, even for those whose lives were laid out in advance by the rules of our time. Each one wonders how the others will look after so many years, fearing that if they look old it will be the inescapable sign that all this time has really passed. It passed so quickly. And we are strangers to who we were then, those frightened and reckless children who made the decisions by which we live now.

For Daphne, driving up with Richard, the class reunion would be her chance to give up her secret at last. She felt she had been a victim of the Fifties myth of perfection, and yet a part of her knew that she had always enjoyed being the Golden Girl. Why else had she bought the gold dress that was now in her suitcase, the dress that would show off her still slim body and flawlessly dyed golden hair, and remind the others of her old nickname? She had lived with the fear of being shunned for her illness, and the need for adulation. She had been their movie star. Now, twenty years later, she was a successful housewife and mother, star qualities that were now passé, for which some women even apologized. It didn't bother her. She hoped most of the others were like her, and that there wouldn't be a lot of dreary women's lib speeches to listen to. If there were, she would avoid them.

For Chris, traveling alone on the train the way she had first come to Radcliffe, and staying in the dorm, this reunion had an almost mystical significance. She was sorry she couldn't stay in Briggs Hall, her old dorm, but they were being put in Currier House because it was newer, bigger, and had more amenities. It didn't matter. She would see the old places, be awash with the old feelings, and perhaps make up her mind what to do about her life. Nicholas was staying in New York with Alexander. She could pretend he was not born yet, and she had not yet met Alexander. The ghost of her mother waved good-bye at the station, not the old woman with whom she had made peace, but a youngish woman, a drunk, just a little older than Chris was now, filled with her own pain and secrets, loathed by a young Chris who had pain and secrets of her own.

For Annabel, mourning Max, the reunion was important because it was a link to Emma. It was not just her look at the past but her view into the future, and so it was part of an unending chain. She knew Max would be waiting behind every corner, and she didn't know whether this would make her sad or bring her happy memories to cover her present emptiness, but she also knew life was fun, and that she would probably enjoy herself. She hoped that all the girls who had made her college years so miserable were dried up old bats now, and dissatisfied with their prim little lives. She felt more a part of Emma and the strength of the future than she did of them and the past. Still, she felt a little nervous. She took the air shuttle, and checked into a suite at the Ritz, and ordered up champagne.

For Emily, this trip all alone from California without Ken or the kids was her first, the first time she had ever done anything alone except go crazy. She was proud of herself. Ken had declined to go with her, saying he would be bored out of his mind, but he had been pleased she wanted to go. He told her to stop in New York for a few days on the way back to do some shopping, see some plays, go to museums and galleries. If she decided to stop in New York, and if she got lonely, she was to call him and he would join her. He wasn't forcing her to be on her own, but he was leaving the way open, encouraging her with things that were fun to do. He said he would leave the kids in California. They were old enough to take care of themselves for a few days since the housekeeper was sleeping over. School was out and they could survive without being driven around, or they could use the telephone and find some other mother to serve as chauffeur. Emily felt very free, without any guilt at all.

She was staying at the Ritz. She couldn't imagine why anyone would want to stay in a dorm unless they had to save money. Her room was large and airy, with windows that looked down on Boston Common, the trees covered with leaves, children playing by the lake, and lots of young couples walking together or sitting on the grass. The first event of the reunion would be the joint Harvard-Radcliffe Commencement tomorrow morning, with all the alumnae marching in together, then a picnic lunch in Harvard Yard, then speeches, then an afternoon reception in the Radcliffe Yard, and then an outdoor buffet dinner. Emily decided to order room service, take a bath, and go to sleep early. The long plane trip had been tiring and she didn't want to get jet lag and look awful all day tomorrow.

She looked at the schedule again. The day after tomorrow there would be panel discussions, speeches, another outdoor buffet lunch, a symposium, and a

formal dinner. Every moment would be full. Despite
her excitement Emily was nervous. Would anyone
remember her? Would they think she had changed a
lot? Would the girls who had scared her so much still
scare her now? She was just dying to get a look at
Daphne Leeds and Richard Caldwell. A bitchy little
part of her hoped he had lost his hair.

She inspected her makeup in the artificial light of
the bathroom before she creamed it off. Tomorrow
she would make up by the window in the sunlight
so she would look all right outdoors. The light here
in the East was so much kinder than that Southern
California glare. All her little lines had almost disappeared. She smiled as if greeting a friend. They'd
have to remember her. She wasn't the young Emily,
but she hadn't changed so much as to be unrecog-
nizable. She still had the same lively look about her.
She fingered her wedding ring and the large diamond
beside it. She had been chosen by a real catch, she
was somebody. No one would look down on her now,
they wouldn't dare. Being here was sending her right
down the time tunnel! She hadn't once thought of
herself as "just a rich housewife" since she got here.
Besides, how many of those girls had made any more
of themselves than she had? Not so many.

She wondered if those society girls were still anti-
Semitic. If they were it was their fault, not hers. Life
was different now. Hadn't Maxwell Harding III taken
Ken and her out to dinner when he came to Los
Angeles, after all those years? She had been shocked
and sorry to read in *The New York Times* about his
death. It seemed everybody had a secret, even the
people you thought were so lucky.

Chapter 2

Chris walked to Harvard Yard, glad the sky still stayed light so late this time of year. She walked through the gate and was immediately disappointed: workmen were obstructing her view of the past, parking their truck right in front of the statue of John Harvard, putting up a huge tent, making everything look wrong. She turned and walked quickly through the Yard to the Widener Library where she and Alexander had spent so many evenings studying together.

Once inside, the musty library smell filled her with nostalgia. She could see Alexander's dear head bent over his work, and herself beside him, sneaking glances when he didn't notice. She had been so starstruck, so in love, that the magic of her book had been only words to be memorized while her heart pounded and she wondered if perhaps tonight would be the night he would do more than just kiss her.

Now when she remembered the unhappiness on his face, it was different somehow, because she could see into his mind. How naive they had all been then! He had been a complete mystery, and yet she had considered him her dearest friend. She sat down at the long table where they used to sit together and closed her eyes. It was hard to remember exactly the way Alexander had looked at eighteen, as it was to remember herself, because the reality of the way they looked now interfered. It was even harder to believe that she had spent so many years of devotion chasing a stranger, but she had, as if the single-minded chase was more important than the participants. That had been love, then.

She opened her eyes and looked down the rows and rows of tables, in this huge, high-vaulted place that had once reminded her of Grand Central Station, now nearly empty, and she remembered with what awe she had come here, chosen to be Alexander's companion, to share his time, his life. What had he really thought of her? They had never had a real conversation, never admitted they thought about anything but their school work and their social life. She had made jokes. It had been so important to everyone in those days to seem to be in control of life, well-adjusted, amenable, that small talk kept them safe. They had both been frightened and faking, and from that they had pretended a relationship. She wondered who she had loved after all.

Alexander had been like a shadow. It had taken these past ten years to find the human being.

She left the library and walked to his old house, remembering with what anticipation those walks had filled her on their Saturday nights. She stood trembling in front of the door and then rang the bell.

After what seemed endless time a man opened the door. He looked a little disconcerted.

"I'm here to see one of the rooms," Chris said. "Old time's sake, you know?"

"All the rooms are being used," he said. "You could knock on the door, maybe someone's in there and would let you look around."

She walked up the stairs and down the hall to Alexander's old suite. Nobody answered her knock. They were probably out to dinner. She felt suddenly very depressed, as if Alexander himself was in there, still keeping her away. Then she realized it was just an old room. How many people must have stayed there since Alexander had. He himself had said the room at Harvard had nothing to do with the real him. He had hated it. She went back down the stairs.

The man who had let her in was still in the downstairs hall. "Did you come here alone?" he asked.

"Why?"

"Because it's dangerous out there at night. Things are different from when you were here. You'd better grab a cab in Harvard Square. Don't walk around alone. I'm not kidding."

"You mean Jack the Ripper's in the Common?"

"Don't joke about it," he said. "Take a cab."

"Thank you."

She sat in the taxi, watching familiar places flashing by before she could get a good look, feeling frustrated. But she had three more days. She would find the ghost of Chris and the ghost of Alexander and try to see them as they had really been. Those people they had been were gone, replaced by two who had been through so much, finally knew each other very well, and loved each other more because of it. They had trapped each other with their kindness. She felt sorry for both of them.

Annabel was restless. She didn't feel like having dinner all alone at the Ritz. The champagne had picked up her spirits, so she took a cab into Cambridge and went to Currier House looking for Chris, but Chris was gone. She supposed Chris was wandering around on her pilgrimage and she hoped whatever she found would make her want to stay with Alexander. If you loved somebody that much you had to accept him, faults and all. Lots of men cheated on their wives with women, and their wives accepted it. She wouldn't have, but then she had never loved anyone as much as Chris loved Alexander.

What a gigantic, impersonal building this new dorm was! There was a secretary desk in front with a guard at it, and a long table had been set up along one wall of the large entrance hall for people to register for the reunion. She could tell that the women here were from all different classes, and many of them had brought their husbands with them. It must seem rather titillating to them to be screwing legally in the dorms at last. She supposed the kids did it now whenever they wanted to since there were no more rules and it was coed in the bargain. She saw a few women she thought she'd known and they smiled at

her and said hello. None of them were particularly
warm and friendly, but she hadn't expected them to
be. Some of them glanced at her almost timidly, as
though wondering if she'd gotten the exciting life
she'd wanted or the bad life she deserved. It amused
her. God, how she wished Max was here so she could
share this with him.

She had been secretly afraid that when she got
back to Radcliffe the old misery would come over
her, that feeling of being the outcast, but so far so
good. It was as if it had all happened to other people. She felt sorry for the girl she had been then, so
long ago, but she couldn't take it personally anymore.
The few women from her class she'd seen so far did
indeed look as old as she'd hoped they would, but
she didn't even feel any satisfaction in that. She
would see what happened tomorrow at the commencement, when her old enemies from Briggs Hall would
be out in full force.

Annabel walked over to Briggs Hall and went in
to look at her old room. It was empty. They had
painted the public hall and stairwell a ghastly shade
of green and her room was even worse than she remembered. What wouldn't they put up with to get
an education! She'd heard the newer dorms were better and she certainly hoped so. No wonder a college
education was reserved for the young; who else could
stand it?

Oh, I am truly spoiled, Annabel thought. Emma
thought this looked like paradise, even after those
nice homes she's lived in.

She walked in the romantic twilight in the direction of Harvard Yard. It was a long walk from the
dorms to the classes. Hard to believe she'd done it
through snow and cold all winter. She took a detour
to find her favorite street, where flowers bloomed in
private gardens in front of old houses, but either it
was gone or she'd gotten lost. She remembered that
street so well, and the smell of the flowers in early

spring. Maybe she'd passed right through it and the memory was more real than the reality. The Window Shop had a new name, and her other favorite places had vanished. Harvard Square wasn't one bit the same except for the Coop where they used to buy their textbooks, and the subway entrance and newspaper kiosk on its island surrounded by traffic, and the movie theater. All those new stores, and restaurants, and all those people . . .

"Hi." A cute young man with curly reddish hair and glasses and a mustache smiled at her. He looked like a cuddly ginger bear.

"Hi," Annabel said.

He walked right along with her. "Are you here for the reunion?"

"Yes."

"What year?"

"Twentieth."

He looked surprised. "I can't believe it."

"Believe it. My daughter is coming here in the fall. She'll be a freshman."

"Really?" His eyes twinkled at her and he adjusted his step to match hers. She realized he was trying to pick her up and she laughed out loud. Oh no, not here!

"What's so funny?" he asked pleasantly.

"It's just nice to be back," Annabel said.

"What do you think of the old place?"

"It's different. And the same. Are you here for a reunion, or graduating?"

"I'm a grad student at the business school," he said. "My name is Jonathan Engel."

"I'm Annabel Jones. I'm a buyer at Bloomingdale's in New York."

"I'd like to work in New York," he said. "For a while anyway. I thought I'd go into public relations because I'm very good at bullshit."

"That's a good start."

"Would you like to get some coffee with me?" he asked.

They walked down a side street. Everything looked different here too. "Where's Cronin's?" she said.

"What's Cronin's?"

"It used to be the place everyone went to drink beer and make a fool of themselves. Don't tell me it's gone!"

"I think I heard of it," he said. "I guess it's gone."

"Oh, dear."

They went into a souvlaki joint and sat at a small Formica-topped table. A young waiter brought them coffee in thick cups. "What was it like when you were here?" Jonathan asked.

She told him about the rules, Social Pro, the sign-out book, the kangaroo court. He thought it was hilarious.

"I can't believe it," he kept saying, laughing. "You let them do that?"

"It never occurred to us not to."

"But that's crazy!"

"I know."

She told him about men calling girls a week in advance for Saturday night dates, about dancing at the Fife and Drum Room, about rules for not kissing on the first date. She wondered if he thought she was the ancient storyteller by the fire or if he was attracted to her. She decided he was attracted to her. It was too bad they hadn't met in New York where she had some free time.

"Where do you go on dates?" she asked.

"I usually go to the movies or a Chinese restaurant, or both."

"You like Chinese food?"

"It's cheap."

"Aha," Annabel said. "And where does one go dancing?"

"We really don't," he said.

"You never heard of the Fife and Drum Room."

"No, but there's a discotheque in Boston."

"Oh, my. And do you live with a girl?"

"No. Are you . . . attached to anybody?"

"No," Annabel said.

They looked at each other. She'd never had a cuddly bear. He smiled at her. "How would you like to try a Harvard date now?" he said. "Do you like Chinese food?"

"It's cheap," Annabel said, and they both grinned.

So she had a dinner date after all. They went to Boston on the subway, to a little place called the Lotus Garden where there were holes in the tablecloth but the food was surprisingly good. They drank wine, but not much; he because he didn't drink much and she because it was uninteresting wine, and after dinner they split the check. She eyed his clothes, the sports jacket, shirt, jeans, Frye boots, and decided he didn't look too disreputable to invite back to the Ritz.

"I'm staying at the Ritz," Annabel said. "Would you like to come back and have a drink with me?"

"I thought you'd never ask."

Later, in bed with him, she thought how nice it was to be back at Radcliffe and not have to make love in one of those terrible little single beds or the back of a car.

Chapter 4

The sun was shining brightly, the early morning had not yet turned hot, and in Harvard Yard a mass of people stretched from the wide stone steps of the Widener Library across to the Chapel and pressed out to the black wrought-iron gates that bordered the Yard. Radcliffe alumnae from every five years were there, from the Fifth Reunion Class to one woman from the Seventy-fifth. There were also husbands, some grown children, the parents of the graduating class, and the graduating class itself, in cap and gown. The alumnae were to line up at the Johnson Gate, at the edge of this chaos, find their own class, and then the classes would march in separately, announced by the Harvard Marshal. Women were milling around, recognizing and greeting old friends, or looking for people they knew.

Chris found Annabel standing under a tree. "Where were you?" Chris said. "I called you last night and early this morning."

"I'd hate to tell you," Annabel said.

"You can tell me anything."

"I was at the Ritz but I didn't answer the phone."

Chris laughed. "Oh, Annabel. Only you. Did you bring him?"

"I should say not. *They* would have enjoyed it too much."

"Did you see your old room?" Chris asked.

"Yes. Aren't they awful?"

"Awful."

"We are supposed to find this event very moving," Annabel said, glancing around. "I don't find it very moving. Do you think we're going to have to stand up and sing 'Radcliffe Now We Rise to Greet Thee'? If we do, I think I shall puke. In a ladylike way, of course."

"I don't even remember the words," Chris said. She smiled at people she had known slightly at college and now didn't know at all. They looked so old. Annabel didn't look old, but maybe that was because she was used to her. It had never occurred to Chris before that she might look old herself, and now that it did she didn't care.

"Look," Annabel said, "there's Emily."

Emily Applebaum . . . Chris knew her right away. Her face had thinned down, the cheekbones were more prominent, and she looked even prettier than Chris remembered. She smiled when she saw Chris and Annabel and rushed over to them.

"You're Chris! And you're Annabel! I'm Emily!"

They shook hands, feeling silly, and then they all hugged, even though they hadn't really been such great friends, and that made Chris feel even sillier. Still, it was nice.

"Annabel, you're just as gorgeous as ever," Emily said. "And Chris, you're so glamorous I didn't even recognize you at first."

"I was a frump, wasn't I?" Chris said.

"Oh, no. But don't you remember how we were always trying to fix you up so you could get Alexander English?"

"She got him," Annabel said.

Emily's eyes opened wide. "You married him? Is he still so handsome and sexy?"

"More," Chris said. She felt as if she were choking. She was sorry she'd come to the commencement, and the picnic would probably be worse. She was going to have to do chitchat all day with these well-meaning people who only opened old cuts.

"I married Ken," Emily said. "Do you remember Ken?"

"Sure," Annabel said.

"We have two children and live in Los Angeles. Ken's a dermatologist. I heard you have a daughter, Annabel."

"Yes. She's coming to Radcliffe in the fall."

"Isn't that wonderful. Oh, Chris, do you remember all those cartoons you used to draw? I still have them in my scrapbook. I kept every one you ever gave me."

"Good grief," Chris said, surprised and a little embarrassed. She'd forgotten about the cartoons.

"They were *prized*," Emily said. "You had the fastest tongue and the fastest pen in the East. You could knock somebody off in one second with your wit. I'll never forget how you made us all laugh."

"Thank you," Chris said. She didn't know what else to say.

"Is Alexander here?"

"No."

"Ken isn't either. He's not a reunion type." Emily lowered her voice to a cozy tone. "I heard you got divorced, Annabel. A lot of our class did. They got married too young, that's what happened."

"I'm surprised you managed to stay married," Annabel said.

"It wasn't easy. Ken had to put up with a lot." Emily smiled, but Chris could see from her eyes that she meant it.

"You shouldn't think that," Chris said.

"Oh, that's easy for you to say," Emily said. "You were always interesting."

What is she talking about? Chris thought. I hardly knew her after freshman year.

"You and Annabel are among the few people I remember," Emily said. She didn't elaborate, and Chris glanced at Annabel and saw her stifling a giggle. They both knew what everybody remembered Annabel for.

"My God, that must be Bunny Glickstein," Emily said. "Excuse me. See you later."

"What did you think of her?" Annabel asked when Emily had pushed her way through the crowd and disappeared.

"I don't know. What do you say to somebody you haven't seen in twenty years?"

"I like her," Annabel said thoughtfully. "She was one of the people I would have sworn would end up smug, and she didn't at all."

"No. She was gushing all over me."

"That wasn't gushing, you nit. It was all true."

There was Daphne Leeds, with a strange look on her face. Chris squeezed Annabel's arm. "Daphne," she whispered. "Still beautiful."

"Did she bring that wretch Richard Caldwell, do you think?"

"Let's find out," Chris said.

"I just hope he's fat and old," Annabel said. "He deserves it more than anybody."

They strolled over to Daphne, smiling. "You must be Daphne," Annabel said.

"Annabel? Chris?"

They all shook hands. "You haven't changed at all, Annabel," Daphne said. "And Chris, you look smashing."

"If one more person tells me how awful I used to look . . ." Chris said.

"But it's so much better to have improved, isn't it?" Daphne glanced around and began to whisper. "Half the people here look so old it scares me to death. I wonder what kind of lives they had to make them look that way."

"Nothing a little makeup wouldn't fix," Annabel said.

"Richard is going to join us here later," Daphne said. "He went off on a little sentimental journey of his own. You know, Chris, I never forgot how you used to get all A's, but you still had time to help me cram for exams."

"Me?"

"Don't you remember how scared everybody was except you, and how you kept encouraging everybody? I never did tell you how grateful I was."

"Why is everybody telling me how terrific I used to be?" Chris said. "You're talking as if I'm dead."

"You were just complaining that people said you were a frump," Annabel said.

"I guess it's just that you remember one special thing about each person," Daphne said. "I remember Chris as being terrifyingly smart and very kind."

"How about me?" Annabel said.

Oh, that was mean, Chris thought. Now we'll see what Daphne is made of.

Daphne looked into Annabel's eyes for a long moment. Their glances locked, their minds back in time, and then Daphne's face took on the brittle mask of the good hostess. "I remember you were very popular," she said lightly. "And you had the messiest room. And you dated Richard for a while before I met him."

"Yes," Annabel said. "That's just about the way it was. Do you know what I remember about you?"

"No," Daphne said. "What?"

"Smoke rings. You blew the most perfect smoke rings I ever saw."

They all laughed. Daphne lit a cigarette and blew a perfect smoke ring. "I still do," she said.

Through the noise of the crowd, far at the other end of the Harvard Yard, they could hear the band beginning to play. Daphne waved at a woman in a gray gauzy dress. "I'll swear that's Helen Peabody," she said. "I'll see you two later. Richard will be dying to say hello." She moved away.

Chris and Annabel looked after her. "I bet he is," Annabel said.

"It all seems kind of funny now," Chris said. "The things that were so important, that made us cry. We're different people."

"You're not that different, Chris. Neither am I."

"Sure I am. I don't know what Alexander ever saw in me."

"Chris," Annabel said, "you're not a lucky horse."

"A what?"

"You took Shakespeare. Remember in *Antony and Cleopatra* when Cleopatra says: 'O lucky horse, to bear the weight of Antony!' You always thought Alexander was Antony, and you were the lucky horse. But you weren't. You were Cleopatra."

"Oh, sure I was," Chris said, annoyed.

"Alexander really needs you. He needs you more than you need him. He always did."

"You're so romantic, Annabel."

"I'm also right."

Everyone was lined up neatly now. The Harvard Marshal announced each class, from the oldest down to the youngest, as they marched into the Yard and sat down on folding chairs. Then the joint Harvard-Radcliffe graduating class stood up. It's enormous, Chris thought. She saw black and brown and oriental faces, and boys with beards and mustaches and long hair. A lot of the girls looked like she had so long ago: hair pulled back, no makeup, glasses, no attempt to be glamorous. No one looked like Alexander, but she was sure that there were homosexuals, just as there had always been, but now they were living openly and unafraid. The graduating class was so big that the Harvard Marshal announced them in groups for their degrees, instead of individually as her class had gotten them so long ago. A boy stood up, one of the graduating seniors, and began to give a speech in Latin.

"I'm going to sleep," Annabel whispered.

"I thought you understood Latin."

"That's why."

Then another graduating senior, a girl, got up and gave a speech in English. How bright she is, Chris thought. How mature . . . Were we like that? I wasn't, but maybe some of us were, weren't we? All she could remember about her own graduation was worrying about her future with Alexander. She supposed if Armageddon had struck she would have thought: Oh, dear, Armageddon—it's going to make me late for my date with Alexander.

And where was Alexander now? Out with Nicholas, or cruising? She would never know anything anymore. Each thing would have to be tested. She didn't think she could stand to live that way, but she couldn't live without him either.

She glanced at Annabel beside her. She wondered if Annabel was thinking about Max right now. Today must be painful for her too.

Then the commencement exercises were over. People got up and started milling around, some of them leaving, others heading for the tents that had been set up in the front part of the Yard where a picnic lunch was to be served. Beer and chicken salad were available for two dollars. A hospitality room had been set up in Greys Hall, where Radcliffe alumnae could have a glass of wine and find their friends if they couldn't find them here. Wives and husbands, who had been seated separately, were now walking around looking for each other. It was a little less crowded, but still too mobbed for Chris's taste. She could see the top of the John Harvard statue poking over the crowd.

"What do you feel like doing?" Annabel asked.

"I guess we could get on line to eat."

People were sitting at tables and on the ground, holding paper plates of chicken salad and paper cups of beer. "You must be joking," Annabel said. "I'm too old for this."

"You have no school spirit."

"I never did."

They walked through the crowd to leave. "Look there!" Annabel said. "That's Wink or Bink, I never could tell the two of them apart."

"I think there was only one," Chris said.

"No, there were two. There's that same little stupid face, with gray hair on top of it. He must have married a Radcliffe girl." She smiled wryly. "My old flame. A few more of those will put the past away for good."

"I wish it were so simple," Chris said.

"It is."

They approached the gate, still smiling at anyone who looked vaguely familiar. "Where shall we eat?" Chris asked.

"I vote for the Ritz. My treat."

"Okay."

A gray-haired, thin woman with a tense mouth came up to them and put her hand on Annabel's arm, peering into her face. "You're Annabel Jones," she said.

Annabel smiled at her politely with no sign of recognition.

"Annabel Jones," the woman said. "I'd know you anywhere."

"And you're . . . ?"

"You remember me."

Annabel kept looking at her, her face frozen in politeness and embarrassment, trying to recall and obviously hoping the woman would get them both out of it by introducing herself.

"Maybe you don't remember me," the woman said. "I've changed. But I bet you remember Skip."

"No," Annabel said, looking honestly confused.

Chris didn't know who they were talking about.

"You went out with Skip," the woman said. Her voice was tight, held in. "The night he came to see me and I wasn't there. You went out with him. Don't tell me you don't remember."

"I don't remember anybody named Skip," Annabel said. "I'm sorry."

"Then he never came to see me again," the woman said. "You bitch! You ruined my life. My husband left me, I had a hysterectomy, I went on welfare . . ."

Annabel's face was pale. Chris tugged at her arm to get away. The woman tossed the contents of her paper cup of beer into Annabel's face and sprang on her, clawing for her hair. Annabel screamed.

People came rushing over to them, a man tearing the crazy woman away from Annabel, everyone babbling concernedly. Chris was stunned. Some people, who apparently knew her, took the woman away; she was crying.

"Are you all right?" people were asking Annabel, touching her, patting her. Helen Peabody, who had ostracized her at college, was tenderly wiping the beer off her face and dress.

"Oh, how awful," Helen Peabody kept murmuring. "What a mess, you poor thing."

"Who the hell was *she*?" Annabel said. Her face was dead white, a line of blue around her lipstick.

"Barbara Forrester," someone said.

"I remember her now," Annabel said. "But I didn't know any Skip."

"He was lucky he didn't marry her," Chris said. "Do you want a beer?"

"No, vodka."

"There's only beer," someone said, handing her a cupful. Annabel sipped at it and smiled at the people standing around her. "Hey," she said pleasantly, "forget it."

"What was that all about?" a man asked.

"She apparently blamed her whole life on me,"

Annabel said. "Some people definitely need psychiatric help."

They all chuckled merrily because they couldn't think of anything else to do. Annabel set out for the street and Chris followed her. Massachusetts Avenue was filled with people and cars.

"Don't they have any cabs in this town?" Annabel said, annoyed.

"She was trapped in the Fifties," Chris said.

"If we ever find a cab we'll have a decent, quiet lunch."

"It's amazing . . ."

"What's so amazing?" Annabel said. "Lots of people are trapped in the Fifties. You are, in some ways. Lucky horse."

She would have to think about that.

The night before, Richard had seen the item in the Boston newspaper: Richard Caldwell, who was running for city councilman, and his opponent, Michael Curry, would be having a debate at noon in the Boston Common. In the grainy photograph he recognized his own features at twenty-four and knew this was his son. The brief biography confirmed the facts he knew about Richard's schooling, and facts he didn't know about his work and public service. Of course the boy didn't call himself Richard Caldwell, Jr.—never had. He was curious to see how he'd turned out. Daphne hadn't bothered to read the paper this morning, and when Richard told her he wanted to be alone for a while to go over old times she kissed him and said she'd wait for him at the Radcliffe picnic.

It seemed suitable to be able to look at his son after all these years, even though he had no feelings about this stranger. But the boy's existence had been so important during Richard's Harvard years, and even afterward, that his appearance in Boston at this

moment was irresistible. It was almost as if Richard
Caldwell's presence was the deity's planned entertainment for Richard Senior's own reunion. He wondered
if Hope would be there, and if he would be able
to recognize her. He would stand anonymously in
the crowd, look and listen, and go away unobserved.

The debate had a sort of carnival atmosphere. A
cheap wooden platform had been erected, covered
with bunting, and a speaker system had been set
up. A truck stood at the curb outside the Common,
with bunting on it, and a large poster of Richard
Caldwell. It looked almost like Richard's own Harvard yearbook picture, but surer, and with much
longer hair, discreetly curling over his ears. The smile
was the same dazzling Caldwell smile that Richard
himself had used in the old days to seduce Radcliffe
girls. It was eerie to see this face that was so much
like his own, to realize that this adult person he did
not know had come from his own genes. This was
the only one of his sons who looked like him. Too
bad in a way; it would have been nice if one of the
others had too, just as a kind of ego trip. He remembered the awkward young boy who had gone off
to Le Rosay, and wondered if his manner had improved as much as his appearance. He stood at the
back of the crowd and waited.

Michael Curry, the opponent, was a pink-faced,
earnest Irish boy. The crowd applauded as he climbed
up to the platform, and he nodded and waved at
them. Then Richard Caldwell appeared, tall, blond,
wearing a suit and tie, smiling the family smile. The
braces had certainly worked. The crowd applauded
again. A row of folding chairs had been set up on
the platform, and a balding man and a woman with
dyed dark hair came up, followed by two young
women and a teenaged boy. Curry introduced them
as his parents, two sisters, and brother. They were
pulling out all the political stops today, Richard
thought, amused. Parents and siblings. Next year it

would be wives, and the year after that a baby. A stocky gray-haired woman climbed the steps to the platform as Richard Caldwell (why couldn't he think of the boy by anything but that whole name, as if he were truly a stranger, some unknown politician?) held out his hand to help her.

"I'd like to introduce my mother."

Applause. Hope sat down. God, she was old! Why couldn't she at least put a rinse on her hair the way Daphne did? She was only forty or forty-one—he couldn't remember exactly—but she looked fifty. Her dress was embarrassing, a cheap polyester print that made her look even dumpier, and she was wearing a corsage. She didn't have on any makeup at all. It was as if she had deliberately tried to make herself look worn out.

"I'm very proud of my mother," Richard Caldwell said. "She worked very hard as a waitress to put me through school." Hope smiled.

Richard cringed. He looked around at the audience of badly dressed working-class people and saw the approval on their faces. What did the boy mean, "put me through school"? What a crock! It was his grandfather who had put him through school. It was a matter of public record that his grandfather was a very rich man. What was that working-class bull-shit? Maybe he meant it, maybe it was a political ploy.

The two young men launched into their debate. Richard had no interest whatever in local political issues, but the boy's charisma caught him almost immediately. Richard Caldwell was much too far to the left for the two of them ever to agree, as he might have expected, but the way he spoke made his ideas seem actually attractive, even logical. Curry was smart and armed with what seemed like endless facts, but everywhere he turned Richard Caldwell was right on top of him, obviously winning. The mood of the crowd went over to him; there were bursts of applause, laughter. He was making them happy. It was as if this young, blond man with the confident gaze and tall rangy build was some kind of knight, not leading them into battle but doing their battle for them. Richard looked around the crowd. Their ages were mixed, and now he was not sure if the younger people were working class or not. The kids today dressed like soldiers or campers or communist workers regardless of their family background. He saw the light on the faces of the kids, the eagerness, and he realized then that the younger ones at least would be willing to go into battle right alongside Richard Caldwell. If he could do this much with some dopey little political position that hardly anybody cared about, what couldn't he do if he ran for the Senate, for President?

President . . . his son. Why not? He was brilliant, articulate, caring, and handsome as a god. If the mood of the country stayed as liberal as it was . . .

He thought how nice it would be to go up to the boy after the speech and congratulate him, introduce himself, take him off for lunch perhaps, or make a date for later. But it was impossible. If he went up to this young stranger he would receive the same warm but impersonal handshake the other anonymous people in the crowd would get, and if he introduced himself Richard Caldwell would have to reject him. Why would the boy want him now? He had never been a father or even an acquaintance. Now he would appear to be the villain in this piece, the long-lost profligate father reappearing at last to swarm around the celebrity. The thought was appalling.

Richard Caldwell, Jr., had turned into the son Richard would have loved to have, but now it was too late. He felt the pain of loss for both of them.

And then, because Richard's life had always been *Rashomon,* he told himself that finally, at this moment when he so much wanted to get to know him, it was his son who had rejected him. The debate was over. The crowd was surging up to the platform. He turned and walked away.

Daphne was glad when Richard came to the picnic earlier than she had expected, because she wanted to show him off. She could tell from the admiring looks on their old friends' faces that they still made a beautiful couple. They strolled along holding hands and she felt proud. But after they'd seen everyone and been seen, and eaten lunch, she was anxious to take Richard to Briggs Hall alone and tell him what she'd planned. If she didn't hurry the speeches would start, and then they'd be trapped. The afternoon had turned hot, and at the side of the crowd someone's child was throwing up. Richard laughed.

"Same old college food," he said.

"How silly to bring a young child," Daphne said. "He must be bored to death. I don't want to hear the speeches. Let's go to Briggs, okay?"

They walked through the Common, under the leafy trees, and stopped to look at the statue and the cannon, filled with nostalgia for the few things that hadn't changed through the years. The Common was full of people, lying on the grass, eating and drinking, or just walking. Finally they reached the Radcliffe Quad, and there was Briggs Hall, just the same. They climbed the steps, crossed the stone patio, and entered the red brick building.

"I'm going to show you my old room, which you were never allowed to see," Daphne said, and took him upstairs.

Everything seemed smaller, shabbier. There were locks on all the doors. "This?" Richard said in disbelief.

"This."

"I used to imagine you like a princess in a tower," he said. "But this is the maid's room."

"It was a little nicer when I fixed it up," she said.

"I'm sure of that."

Richard's presence seemed to fill the little room and it suddenly looked less alien. The past was over, and what lingered would soon be put to rest. Daphne took Richard's hand and they went downstairs. They both appeared to have the same thought as they headed toward the alcove beside the living room fireplace, without saying a word. They sat down.

"Do you remember the first time you said you'd go out with me?" Richard said.

"We sat right here. I was so nasty to you!"

"You certainly were." He smiled. "But you made it up to me later."

"I hope so," Daphne said. "We've had a happy life together, haven't we?"

They were still holding hands. Richard kissed her hand. "I didn't believe then that I could ever love you more than I did, but I do."

"I love you more too."

"We're lucky."

"People had so many secrets then," Daphne said. "We all wanted so much to conform, to be perfect. There were rules for everything. It was a sin to be different."

"You were different," he said. "You were better than they were. You still are."

"I thought I was worse."

He looked surprised. "You?"

"I couldn't tell you on our first date—I was afraid you wouldn't want me anymore. By the time we knew each other well and loved each other I was too afraid of losing you. Then, after a while, I didn't know how to tell you—it had been too long. It's not a terrible thing. I just thought it was . . ."

"What was?"

Her heart was pounding. "Richard . . . I have epilepsy."

"You have *what*?"

"I've always had it. My family doesn't know how

I got it. It could have been a brain injury at birth, or heredity. But our boys don't have it, they're fine, you know they are."

He was staring at her. "But you never had a fit."

"Seizure," she corrected him automatically. "I did when I was a child. Lots of them. Then there were less and less, and then it became dormant. I don't fall on the floor and froth at the mouth and thrash around the way you see in the movies. I just black out for a few seconds. But I haven't for years."

"I can't believe it," Richard said. "Why would you be afraid to tell *me*?"

"Because I was stupid and it was the Fifties."

"But we got married in the Sixties."

"I was afraid you would think I wasn't good enough . . ."

"Jesus!" he said. He dropped her hand.

Daphne felt her skin begin to crawl with fear. "What is it?"

He didn't answer. She could see his face change. There was not the look of revulsion for which she had steeled herself, but something worse: the look of betrayal. Finally, when he spoke, his voice was somehow different.

"What else haven't you told me?" Richard said.

"Nothing."

He was shaking his head, looking at her as if suddenly she had become another person disguised as Daphne. "How could you live with me for twenty years and not tell me?"

"I'm neurotic, all right?"

"I thought I knew you. I thought we trusted each other. I love you so much, but you never trusted me."

"It's not your fault."

"I know it isn't," he said. "That's what's killing me. All that time . . . when the kids were born, you must have worried they'd get it. You worried all alone. You never confided in me."

"I'm sorry."

"I thought I understood you, Daphne. You were not only my wife and my love and the mother of our children, but you were my confidant and best friend. I thought what we had was perfect."

"I hate that word perfect!" she said.

"You drove a car . . . you must have taken medicine for it; they . . . epileptics take medication, don't they?"

"Sometimes I didn't have to."

"And sometimes you did. What else haven't you told me, Daphne? Any other little secrets in your life that you thought I was too selfish to understand?"

"No," she said. "You know everything about me, I swear it."

"I'm going to try very hard to believe that," he said. He stood up. "Let's go. I know you don't want to miss the President's reception."

"Damn the President's reception! Richard, wait . . ." She had to walk fast to keep up with him. She tugged at his arm until he slowed down. "Richard, please don't be angry."

"I'm not angry," he said.

She knew he wasn't. He was hurt, and that was worse. She had spent years of effort to deceive him, and now he knew it. She had made a tear in the fabric of their marriage and it would take a long time for it to mend.

She was dying for a cigarette but she knew Richard didn't like women to smoke in the street. She would try to make it up to him for the unhappiness she had caused him, but she was afraid. Through all these years she had behaved as if he were still the arrogant boy she had met at college, as if he had never changed at all. She had the feeling their marriage would never be quite the same again, and it was all her fault.

Chapter 5

Friday morning Emily was up early so she could rush to see her old room at Briggs Hall before the panel discussions started at Harvard. Now she stood there, staring at that dingy little cell, wondering how she could ever have lived there. There was the old buzzer that used to summon her to phone calls and dates, but now there was a lock on every door. It was like a fleabag hotel. Did she actually use that little bathroom down the hall? How had everyone managed to take a shower? She'd heard Briggs Hall was coed now. Did the boys and girls use the same toilets? Well, they had to.

The dining room was gone, and in its place was a huge room where meals were served buffet from a giant kitchen. The living room looked so big and dark and scary. No wonder she had always been frightened. The bell-desk was still there, but the sign-out book was long gone and the bell-desk looked unused. People had their own phones if they wanted them. Next to the front door there was a large bulletin board with ads and messages tacked to it, left over from the school term.

Attention: The police have asked us to make the following announcement. Due to the recent rapes and muggings in Cambridge, do not go out alone. If you go to the corner, go with another person or in a group.

Attention: Lock your room. Due to the recent robberies, everyone is warned to lock their room whenever leaving it, even for a minute. People from the neighborhood have been getting into the dorm.

Robbery . . . she remembered that time at college when everyone thought Annabel Jones had been stealing money. They never found out if she did it, or who did. Now it was outsiders. Imagine! If a stranger had come into Briggs Hall in the old days everyone would have been alerted in one second. And who ever thought about rape? There were flashers in the Common in the spring, but the only man who might molest you was your date. All that sexual freedom now and girls still couldn't go out alone at night.

She didn't like anything that had happened to the Radcliffe Yard, or Harvard Square, or any of this. The one thing Emily remembered clearly from her Radcliffe days was being able to walk down the street and feel the sense of space, of small-town safety, but now this was a city and everyone seemed anonymous. If she had been terrified as a freshman years ago, imagine how terrified these poor kids must be today. She was glad she didn't have to be a student here now. She consulted her map and found Currier House, where someone had told her the photos of everyone's families had been posted. She wanted to be sure the picture she had sent of herself, Ken, Kate, and Peter had been prominently displayed. There were lots of women she didn't know at all from their pictures, and who she hadn't known yesterday either. It had never before occurred to her how few people in her class she had actually known. There was her family. They seemed so familiar and lovable that for an instant Emily felt a pang of homesickness.

She had been feeling like a young girl again, lost in this huge unfamiliar place, but these people in the photograph were *hers*. She loved them. Kate was beginning to look just like she had when she was a teenager: delicate, starry-eyed, vulnerable, pretty. But Kate was strong. If Kate decided to go to Radcliffe, and if she had the marks to get in, she would be lonely and frightened too, but not nearly as much as Emily had been. And there wouldn't be the anti-Semitism to deal with. All that was over now. Kate could even be president of her class.

There was Ken, so warm and reassuring. She missed him. Tonight she would call him. The reason I know hardly anybody, Emily thought suddenly, is because I spent all my time with Ken. Is that possible?

She hurried to the Harvard Yard, glad that she'd played tennis so much lately that she was still in shape for the hike. The panel discussions were being held at the Science Center, another new building she'd never seen before, all full of computers and other impressive things. The first discussion was "Women in Government." Emily took notes. She looked around and didn't see anyone she knew. It no longer surprised her.

The next panel discussion was "The Function of the Museum in a University Setting." She took more notes, although to tell the truth she was beginning to find this last panel discussion very boring. She hadn't expected to see Annabel here, nor Daphne. Neither of them was an intellectual. But she would have thought Chris would come. She stifled a yawn. She was looking forward to the speech on "Women and Success." Dr. Sarah Margolis, M.D., one of the alumnae from her own class. It was hard to believe that a girl who had gone to college with her had managed to fulfill her secret dream. Emily wondered what that woman's life was like, whether she had married, and had children, and stayed married.

At last the panel discussions were over and it was time for the speech. Dr. Sarah Margolis was a pediatrician, a soft-spoken, attractive, self-possessed woman. A pediatrician, Emily thought . . . what I wanted to be. And you can tell she was pretty too. She introduced her husband, Dr. Alan Pressman, and her two children, a girl and a boy, who seemed the same age as Emily's children. When she started to speak Emily began to take notes, and then she stopped. The words were too important to write down; she would remember them without aid because it seemed as if this woman was speaking just to her, to her thoughts, her fears, her questions, her perplexity.

"I always wanted to be a doctor," Sarah Margolis said. "When I was six years old and played doctor with my friends, *I* meant it."

Everyone laughed.

"At that time," she went on, "as you'll remember, it was more appropriate for a woman, if she wanted to go into the medical field at all, to be a nurse. Or, to grow up to be the wife of a doctor and live in reflected glory."

Emily cringed, remembering the words of her career advisor.

"Most of my high school teachers were unmarried," Dr. Margolis went on, "and they thought my goals were too high—that I was 'too aggressive' because I wanted to be a successful doctor *and* a married person. But it was important to me to have my work and I was prepared to make sacrifices to do what I wanted. I was lucky because my father paid for my college and medical school, and because my mother baby-sat my two children every afternoon until they were old enough to go to school. I also had a live-in housekeeper, which is hard to find these days. My husband, who is a research chemist, understood the sort of person I was from the beginning because we met in medical school. We both shared the same sense of purpose although our careers went in slightly different directions.

"It was difficult for women then, but it is just as difficult for women now if they do not have the temperament for achievement. To reach your goal must be a passion. Your goal must be part of your life, one of the things that makes you happy, that makes you the person you are. It is too easy to blame the secondary role of women, or our former brainwashing, for lack of success. I believe a woman must be lucky enough to have help in the form of money or supportive family, but so must men. Men who want to be doctors have wives to help them along and to bring up their children. In fields other than medicine it is somewhat easier, but the *need* to succeed must be as strong in any field.

"I have had to give up certain things to become a success in my chosen work. There were many times when I would rather have been with my family, or with friends, or just have time to read. I was always a well-organized person and I realized you must have priorities. This involved sacrifice. But in the end, I must admit it was never as much of a sacrifice as it seemed because my work gave me the utmost pleasure and sense of fulfillment, and that is why I do it."

The audience applauded. Some of them got up and went to the stage to compliment Sarah Margolis and to renew their old acquaintance. Emily stayed in her seat, waiting. This soft-spoken woman had talked like a dragon, but what she'd said was true. Successful people were different from people who just talked about it. They had to be different from the very beginning. Emily doubted if she could ever have had the guts to go through all of it. Wanting to be a doctor had been like wanting to be a ballerina or a movie star, but the dream had never included the discipline and hard work. Ken had been working thirty-six hour shifts, watching an autopsy and throwing up, cutting up a cadaver. She had been daydreaming of an office filled with cute children with runny noses. It was the dream of the ballerina's airy leap without the reality of the bruised and swollen toes.

The room was empty now, Sarah Margolis trying to get away from the last well-wishers, her family waiting. Emily got up and went over to her.

"I'm Emily Applebaum Buchman. We never met at Radcliffe. May I ask you a question?"

"Yes." A sweet smile. They were sisters, after all, fellow classmates.

"What dorm were you in?" Emily asked.

"Whitman."

The greasy grind dorm. Emily had never known anyone from there. "Did you like Radcliffe?"

"I adored it."

"What did you like best?"

"Learning so many things."

Of course . . . Sarah Margolis had been studying while she, Emily, had been out with Ken. "I hope you don't think this is rude, but . . . did you go to football games?"

Sarah Margolis laughed. "Sure I did."

"I guess your father was a doctor."

"Why?"

"A role model . . . I don't know."

"He was a furrier," Sarah Margolis said.

"Thank you for your speech," Emily said. "I wish I had known you at school."

"Thank you for saying so."

Emily went out and walked through the Harvard Yard. Workmen were finishing taking down the tents and stacking the folding chairs in a truck. She sat down on the wide stone steps in front of Widener Library, the place where she had studied so many evenings with Ken. For a long time she gazed into space, thinking, forgetting all about lunch and the

afternoon's events. For years she had resented Ken
and the kids and herself because she hadn't the faintest idea of who she was. But they still loved and
needed her, and were glad to have her with them.
They had always accepted her for herself, while she
had hated herself. But what was so terrible about
being ordinary? To many people she must have seemed
special. Ordinary was relative. Just being here at all
was out of the ordinary.

When she got back to L.A. there was no reason
why she couldn't get a job. She could take brushup
courses in psychology if she felt too insecure. And if
there was no job to be found, or if she had been
out of her field for too long to qualify in the minds
of the people who hired psychiatric social workers,
then she would do volunteer work. Not the sort of
volunteer work her mother would have recommended,
that endless trekking to charity luncheons with ladies
in hats. She would work with troubled kids. There
was always an opening for that. She didn't need to
work for money, and they needed her experience. She
would ask Ken who to talk to, where to apply. That
wasn't childish dependency, it was good sense. He
knew so many people. Hadn't Dr. Margolis said that
everyone needed help from their family? Maybe she
would teach crafts in a hospital. All those years of
meaningless lessons would be good for something
after all.

Emily's eyes filled with tears, but they were tears
of joy. She felt as if she could fly. She *would* have
it all, in her own way. And that was good enough,
that was just fine.

Chapter 6

The formal dinner for the twentieth reunion class was held at the Graduate Center, another building they had to use their maps to find. It was to be a Chinese banquet. Each class decided what sort of entertainment they would have: one class had a night-club entertainer, and another invited a professor to make a speech. It was perhaps typical of the diversified nature of their class that they had chosen to have no entertainment at all. Long tables had been set up, with tablecloths on them, and flower arrangements. The husbands weren't in black tie, but the wives had gotten as dressed up as possible.

Wine was served beforehand, in the front room. Chris had somehow expected sherry, because sherry always reminded her of Radcliffe as she had known it: that genteel drink served in tiny stemmed glasses, its taste bringing back a way of life that had already become old-fashioned when they were freshmen so many years ago. Sherry was "gracious living," and Boston Brahmins she had never really known or understood.

She sat next to Annabel at the dinner. Annabel looked marvelous. For two days people had been telling the two of them how wonderful they looked. They

told Chris that she must be happy, that her life must
be agreeing with her. That just went to show you
nothing was ever the way it appeared on the outside.
Yet her life *had* been happy, and it could be again;
it was up to her. Ever since she first met Alexander
she had waited for him to make decisions that would
concern her, until they got married, and then they
made all their plans and decisions together. This was
the first time that it was she, and she alone, who held
their future in her hands. It was strange to think she
had so much power. She had never thought of it in
exactly that way before.

She had called him when she went to her room to
get dressed for the dinner, to see if everything was
all right at home. His voice sounded so lonely. She
wondered if he would go out and cruise tonight, or
stay home after Nicholas was asleep. Sex took such
a short time compared to the rest of life, especially
furtive sex. If she left Alexander she would leave him
with nothing but those tiny moments of loveless sex.
He needed their life together as much as she did.
They were equal now, and had been equal for a long
time. The old Chris was gone. Perhaps now she was
even the stronger one.

Annabel tapped her on the arm and handed her
a flat book. "Would you look at what Joanne Hollis
brought? An old yearbook! Look at yourself and pass
it on."

Chris flipped through the pages. The people who
had already seen it were talking and laughing about
their old photographs. There she was, young and unformed and vulnerable, trying to look dignified, the
suggested white blouse with face-framing collar, the
mandatory stare. She didn't know that person. That
person had nothing to do with her anymore. She
closed the yearbook and passed it to someone's husband.

Across the table were Daphne and Richard. Daphne
was wearing a shiny gold dress, and when she dipped

her head to light her cigarette with the flame from the gold lighter Richard held out to her, Chris thought they still looked like the golden couple from their college years.

Chris glanced at Emily, a few seats down on her left, chattering, looking happy. "I'm going back to work, and . . ." Emily's eyes were bright with anticipation of her future. It came to Chris then what she'd heard about Emily a long time ago; she'd had a nervous breakdown. That was obviously far in the past.

Fragments of her classmates' lives drifted past her in briefly overheard conversation. "So when the children get a little older, we'll make it official," a woman was saying quietly to the friend next to her. "We have such different lives anyway."

"I don't think children care that much about divorce today, do you?"

"It's not for *them. I'm* not ready."

"Who would believe I'd end up owning my own business?" someone else was saying, her bright voice overriding the muted confession. "I'm very good at it too."

". . . so glad I came back! Not just to see my friends, but . . ."

What was it the Alumnae Association called it? The Continuing Tie. Chris supposed that meant a tie to the college. But for the first time she saw herself and all of the others as links in a chain of generations: Annabel, next to her, with her daughter going to Radcliffe in the fall, and herself going off to Radcliffe the first time, ashamed because Emily Applebaum had seen her mother drunk at the station. She remembered again what she had thought about her father on the way to the hospital after he'd had his heart attack: her father had stayed with her mother all those years through strength, not weakness. He had simply loved her, faults and all. If she went back to Alexander in a loving marriage like the one they'd had before, she would be going back not because she was still his self-deprecating love slave but because she was strong enough to accept his problem. His weakness had nothing to do with their life together. They had a wonderful marriage, and he loved and needed her more than anyone in the world.

She missed him terribly. She couldn't sit there another moment. She only wanted to be home with Alexander, to tell him everything would be the same again. She touched Annabel's shoulder.

"I'm going now. Good-bye."

Annabel's green eyes looked into hers. "You're going home."

"Yes. It will be all right."

"I'm so glad!" Annabel said, her face glowing with pleasure. Chris leaned over and kissed her.

She ran out then and rushed to her room in the dorm to pack. She didn't bother to change her clothes. She called a taxi and went to the airport, caught the shuttle, and soon saw the lights of New York glittering below her. There was always the chance that Alexander wouldn't be home, but if so she would wait for him. It was something she would have to take in stride. He would always come back.

When her taxi stopped in front of their apartment building she forced herself to be calm. Remember, she told herself, if he isn't there it doesn't matter. She rode up in the elevator and opened the door with her key.

The apartment was dark, Nicholas's night-light casting a small warm glow in the hall outside his room. He liked it there, more grown-up than in his room, where it had been last year. Eventually he wouldn't need one. But if he did, so what? Most people disliked the dark but were just ashamed to admit it.

She walked into Alexander's bedroom, their bedroom again, carrying her suitcase. Alexander was asleep in their bed, alone. Chris watched the gentle movement of his breathing, saw him turn and sigh, and then she took off her clothes and got into bed beside him. He woke up immediately.

"I'm back," she said.

He put his arms around her and held her so tightly he could hardly breathe. She could feel the loneliness pouring out of him, and the love, and the good, warm feelings pouring in, as if their closeness were bringing him back to life.

Chapter 7

In September Emma Buchanan, who had just turned
eighteen, was packing to go to Radcliffe for her freshman year. She took all the new clothes her mother
had half-forced her to buy, her favorite books and
records, her stereo, and her camera equipment. She
was a little scared, a little wary, and very excited. She
needed college because she would learn things that
would help her in her career, but more than that she
needed the time to grow that college would provide.
She knew she could have chosen to go right to work
but she would have missed something she wanted very
much. It was more than the degree, which was becoming a necessity in the world today. It was . . .
she wasn't sure what. Certainly college would be different for her than it had been for her mother. But
in some ways it was the same. She thought it would
change her life. She intended to make demands on
Radcliffe to extend her imagination and fill her mind,
and she knew Radcliffe would make demands on her.
She was afraid the work would be very hard, and the
classes so big that she wouldn't be able to ask questions. It was a struggle to be one person in a huge
university. But that was preparation for the competition in the outside world.

Emma wasn't sure how much of her education would be of practical use in her future work, but she would wait and see. A good education was never wasted. *Educo,* from the Latin: *to lead out.* Her mother had told her that. When her mother was in prep school they had made her take Latin. When she was in prep school she had taken film. You had to prepare for the future.

When it came, she planned to be ready.

THE PASSING BELLS

by

PHILLIP ROCK

A story you'll wish would go on forever.

Here is the vivid story of the Grevilles, a titled British family, and their servants—men and women who knew their place, upstairs and down, until England went to war and the whole fabric of British society began to unravel and change.

"Well-written, exciting. Echoes of Hemingway, Graves and *Upstairs, Downstairs.*"—*Library Journal*

"Every twenty-five years or so, we are blessed with a war novel, outstanding in that it depicts not only the history of a time but also its soul."—*West Coast Review of Books.*

"Vivid and enthralling."—*The Philadelphia Inquirer*

A Dell Book $2.75   (16837-6)

At your local bookstore or use this handy coupon for ordering:

Dell Bestsellers

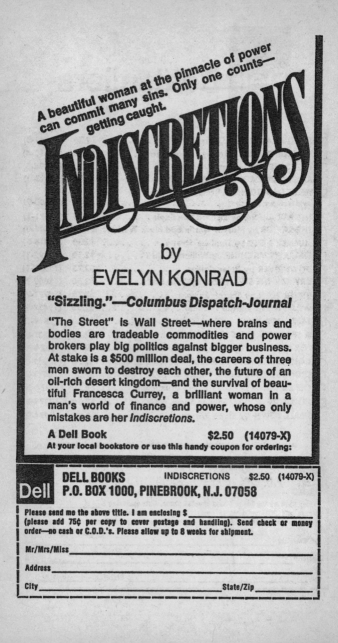